Deep Space
Ocean

Kate Sparrows

Cover Design: M.Y. Cover Design
Printed by KDP Print, An Amazon.com Company

Deep Space Ocean/ Kate Sparrows. -- 1st ed.
ISBN 978-1-943797-18-9

"At the end of the day, how you are imprinted on someone's life and heart is the only true mark any of us leave on this earth."

CHAPTER ONE

Another year of recruits; another year of disappointment.

It was painful to watch this year's bunch saunter in. They casually dumped their packs on the floor without order and grouped up to gossip. They did not report in, line up in formation, and stand at ease with their pack on the floor to their left. Clearly the school wasn't vetting hard enough. Perhaps it was time to go back, if only to be the force to properly mold the next generation of space cadets.

"Where is Commander Tanaka?"

What? She glanced left at her fellow commander. Was she daft? Commander Tanaka was right… not here.

What the hell?

All commanders were supposed to report to the docking bay to greet the new cadets and dictate assignments. Tanaka was laidback, but this was even too far for him. Commander Heather McGrey warned the other commander not to start without them, and she left the docking bay in search of the delinquent.

In all the years they had worked together on the Force, it was never like this. Tanaka did his duty. Heather was always the stricter one, with every rule needing to be followed. That meant reporting for duty and being ready for detail on time.

She heard giggling as she surveyed the halls. Two female base workers were outside the commanders' breakroom. It wouldn't have been suspicious if a certain name wasn't being tossed around.

"Charlotte, you gotta go now. They're going off-planet today and who knows when he'll be back," one lamented. "Besides, if you won't go in there and do it then I call dibs on Alex Tanaka."

The two were oblivious, chatting to each other while peeking in through the thin vertical window of the door. They didn't hear Commander McGrey come up behind them until she stood there, arms crossed, and purposely cleared her throat.

The one called Charlotte had let out a squeak at getting caught. She stammered, "C-Com-mander McGr-rey."

"Don't you two have work to be done? The commanders' breakroom is not a place to be loitering." The message was received loud and clear. The two practically ran down the hall after mumbling apologizes.

"Lighten up, Heather." His feet were kicked up on the table and crossed at the ankle. Tanaka was leaned back in his chair, relaxing, and blowing up a ring of smoke when she walked into the breakroom. "They're harmless."

Yes, office personnel were not trained in combat but they were dangerous other ways. "Those Rocket Bunnies are far from harmless, Tanaka. Or have you forgotten Maggie? Unless you're planning to sleep with them instead of reporting to the docking bay for orders, like you were to have been five minutes ago."

Maggie Elis had been Tanaka's longstanding girlfriend the last three years. Her heart was nearly broken for good when Tanaka had taken home a blonde cadet, fresh off the spaceship. Why she bothered to put up with Tanaka's laidback personality, promiscuity, and smoking habit were beyond her. Then again, she had been romantic with Tanaka once. Well, as romantic as she could get. One night on the bridge of the SS Hydrosis would forever be etched in her memory. But that was three years ago, on their last mission together. Before Maggie.

He sighed and sat up, feet dropping to the floor. "Heather, they're nothing." Tanaka stood and walked over to the sink to extinguish the cigarette. "Besides, the one with glasses has fucked around the Force more than I have. And Maggie's really not part of this."

"Oh, not part of this? I'm sure she'd be thrilled to know that you no longer take her into consideration when you're screwing around behind her back." Heather crossed her arms over her chest.

"We broke up."

"Wait, what?" There went Heather's main argument. It was an argument based only in principle, not the fact that she wanted him in a relationship. In that way, she was no better than the Rocket Bunnies that just screwed anything that had to do with space.

He shrugged and walked back towards the table where a manila folder was resting. "Maggie couldn't handle me being off-planet so much. She gave me an ultimatum – space or her." He tucked the folder under his arm so that both hands were free to dig out another cigarette from his pack. "I'm almost as bad as you."

Tanaka was chuckling as he headed towards the door, so she knew not to take it personally. Not that she truly would. Heather took mission after mission. Being on Earth was mundane and, honestly, it was hard to fit back into society here. There was no purpose for her. At least in space, she had her whole ship to run and missions to see from plan to completion. Heather had even forged her identification paperwork to enlist two years younger than the age restriction. It had been almost a year before anyone realized and, by then, she was too valuable and too experienced to discharge from service based solely on her age.

"Smoking's still prohibited in the building." She walked passed him, snatching the unlit cigarette from his mouth. Instead of snapping it in half and tossing it out, she tucked it in her back pocket for later. Either he'd get it back or she'd barter it to some desperate cadet.

"It's going to be a long three months, Heather." Tanaka fell in step with her as they headed towards the docking bay and the mass of recruits.

She spared a quick glance his way. "What do you mean?"

"I mean, we're assigned to the SS Alphecca. First time together in years and they give us their brand new ship to celebrate."

That last part was a tease. It was luck of the draw. The Starship Alphecca was the newest in the fleet and the most technically advanced. Whatever their mission was, it must be something good. Heather would have expected the starship to head into hostile territory with its accron-plated armor and molitechnic – molecular-tech – weaponry.

"You're blowing smoke up my ass, Tanaka. You don't know that we got the Alphecca or that we're even working together."

He paused, slipping another cigarette between his lips. "Do too." He nodded towards the manila folder. "They gave me the assignments to announce at the meeting."

"A meeting you're late for. I doubt General Ruthesford actually gave you the assignments."

Tanaka chuckled. "You can bet your fine ass on it, Heather."

There was just something about the way he said it. Yes, it was a flirty comment, but something didn't sit right. Heather reached behind her and felt that the pocket of her uniform was empty. The ass! He had stolen back his cigarette without her knowing.

"Alright, everyone gather round!" He was already inside the docking bay, gathering up the cadets. Heather stood there for a moment, dumbfounded.

CHAPTER TWO

Looked like father finally got his wish – and the old fucker couldn't even show up to send him off. It was a shit thing to do to a shit son, but Malcolm Harrison already knew his father didn't care. His father never listened to a word he said nor took anything from him into consideration. One too many fucking awesome keggers and a couple counts of peddling drugs had landed him in this hellhole. Of course it was all to clean up his image. Couldn't have the son of a successful businessman looking worthless and squandering all the cash. That was the only good part of this fucking deal. His father deported him to the Force's training school, but he doled out enough money to buy some guy into making Malcolm a commander after his first mission was over. Some bullshit about valor or something. That was the story his father wanted out there.

Mal dumped his bag on the floor and surveyed the scene. A bunch of uptight goody-goodies that would make this mission unbearable. Guess it was a good thing he packed ahead, just in case, and had something to get through it. But there was only so much some pills could do.

He glanced around, getting more disappointed by the lack of options. Few girls here fit his criteria; but then again, after a couple months in space, one couldn't be too picky. He didn't swing for the dudes. No dicks unless it was an orgy with some kickass drugs and then that prick was bottoming. Mal could only hope that the veteran crew on the ship had something better to offer.

"Mia! Over here!"

He glanced over to see a hot Asian chick come in the docking bay doors. Must be this Mia. She looked banging. Sure there were a couple tattoos peeking out of her jumpsuit sleeve, but that ass made up for it. Girl actually had some curves. It just put her at the top of his Bang List.

She was walking over this way, and he knew it was because she wanted him to fuck her. It was written on her face. She knew what he was packing. Mia glanced up at him, smiled… then walked around him.

"Hey, Tabitha. Sorry I'm late. My dad wanted to run some safety checks on my equipment. He honestly thinks something's going to happen to me. It's like he doesn't believe that they send first year cadets on only agricultural and study missions."

Tck… Mia was fucking wrong. There was no way he was going to be plowing a field. Naw, he'd be plowing something else.

"It's only been a year since you lost your mom. I'm sure he's just thinking about that," Tabitha noted. "And he's got like nothing to worry about. You're going to go to space, come back, and he'll feel stupid for worrying. There's… wow, fuck me."

The fucking gnat finally stopped talking! Mal was seriously considering not fucking her if it meant protecting his ears, and sanity, from that annoying chick. She was flaky and he… he glanced over at the two – more to check out Mia's ass again – and noticed their attention was up at the front. He followed their gaze to find an Asian dude up there trying to command attention – a fucking joke – but what walked in behind him was more interesting.

Long legs. Slim build with soft curves. Auburn hair that he could wrap around his fist while he fucked her ass. Yea, he was going to fuck that commander. She was going to beg for his dick by the end of the mission.

"Alright, everyone gather round!" The dick commander repeated, holding up some folder. "I'm Commander Tanaka. I have everyone's assignments right here. After your name's been called, grab your packs and head to your loading dock for further instruction from the starship crew. Failure to report and depart for duty will result in disciplinary action... and we'll still put your ass on the ship."

Disciplinary action. Mal hoped Commander Fuckable was the one dishing it out.

"Reporting to SS Alphecca under the command of Commanders Heather McGrey and Alexander Tanaka are as follows," he rambled off the list. Mal was pretty sure everyone had just tuned him out at this point. But the idea of this McGrey punishing him really got the fantasy going, and he almost missed his name being called.

"Malcolm Harrison."

He grabbed his pack and was going to head up front to pass McGrey to get a preview of the ass he'd be destroying tonight when another name caught his attention.

"Mia Ha."

So there were two chicks to bang on this starship. Maybe... oh, a fucking threesome! He was sporting a partial as he walked up along the front. Of course the few buddies he made in school were calling out and bullshit teasing him. Something about getting stuck with Hard Ass McGrey. It just made him want a look that much more.

Just a look.

He walked by and glanced back over his shoulder. It looked fine. McGrey must have had ten years on him but that ass was ageless. He told himself just a look but... Mal reached back to cop a feel. He was sure that the uptight commander wouldn't care; didn't sound like she got much action. She'd probably love it.

Mal felt a hand on the back of his neck then cold, hard concrete. Commander McGrey had grabbed him by the back of the neck and flipped him over and to the ground so fast that he had no idea what hit him.

"Sexual harassment will not be tolerated as per code 2.34a. Disrespecting a higher ranking offer will also not be tolerated,

Cadet Harrison. You are to report to the kitchen on-board to assist with food preparations and then you'll report on janitorial duty for the week."

She glared down at him as she talked, but he heard none of it. Mal just saw the fire and thought about how fucking awesome it would be to have that riding his dick. For once, he might make the exception to have someone top him.

McGrey backed off to let him up. She was completely unfazed as she took her spot next to the dick reading his list, trying to seem important. He'd get her later…

The cadets selected for the agricultural mission to explore Zenox-5 made their way to the SS Alphecca. Just on-board, a veteran crew member gathered them to give everyone a brief tour of the ship and a rundown of the protocols and ship rules.

"Men's dormitories are on the left and the women's are on the right. Two cadets to a room, and fornication is frowned upon." The tour guide basically meant don't get caught. "Ship assignments are on your bunks. Your duties have been assigned based on placement during training and preferences you selected upon enlisting. Breakfast is always served at oh-six hundred hours. Lunch is open between ten hundred and fourteen hundred hours. Dinner will be hot and ready, usually, for a few hours after eighteen hundred hours. Drinking is prohibited, in case anyone was wondering, and only for off-duty officers… so try to befriend some if you want to survive this."

The guide walked off, probably going back to whatever their normally scheduled activity was. This all just seemed so rigid and planned out. Where was there going to be enough time to fuck? At least pussy was close by. Mal hung back a moment and made sure he saw which room Mia took. She'd be getting a call later.

He walked into his room, noting that his roommate already took the bed on the left side. That left he bed on the right for him. With a small trunk under the mattress, there wasn't much room for anything else in this prison cell. Just one desk in the middle of the far wall to share, a chair, and a mirror on the back of the door.

"Fan-fucking-tastic." Mal plastered on a fake smile as he kicked his duffel bag under the bed. Screw securing his petty belongings in the trunk. Mal grabbed the sheet of paper on his bed before plopping down on the stiff, uncomfortable mattress. His assignment was protective detail for exploratory needs and tactical gear maintenance. At least he was getting to do the one thing he liked about training – playing with guns.

"Name's Brandon Myers. I got linguistic translator. What 'bout you?"

He glanced over at his roommate. Guess it would be an easier life not to piss him off in the first five minutes. "Malcolm Harrison, but you're calling me Mal." Not the fucking name his father gave him. "Protective detail."

"Cool. So you'll, like, get to shoot up some aliens and stuff." Brandon nodded his head as he talked. "At least your ass won't be bored – you'd get all three chicks that came with us. Chicks like guns. Ain't nothing going to be around for me to fuck."

A smile tugged at Mal's face. Yea, chicks like guns. "You don't fuck with me and I'll make sure your dick is wet."

Brandon smirked and nodded his head. Fornication was frowned upon, but they wouldn't be catching blue balls.

Mia sat down, cross-legged, on her bunk. Her things were neatly tucked away in her trunk. The photo of her mother was taped up on the wall next to her pillow. Another hung below it of the whole family – all three of them and their small maltase Matcha. It was bittersweet to see her mother's smiling face. It had been a long year, but it never got any easier. The therapist, and her father, said that she was passed the stages of grieving and needed to accept her death to move on. It was just so hard when all Mia's dreams died along with her. Her father just didn't understand her artistic side.

All the downtime on this ship was only going to give her chances to think about her mother. Space was something that she had loved, but only for the twinkling stars at night which Mia had learned by heart to impress her. All Mia was going to have was time. And now she just sat here buying time until she needed to report to the bridge.

Her assignment was navigation. It didn't make any sense to call it a fancier name than what it was – pilot. She'd get to inject the engine codes and run the system checks on the starship. Ask any kid and they'd tell you that it's the best job ever. It was just that it was less luxurious than what it was. Tons of activation codes to memorize, and even then some were only known by the commanders. Then there was autopilot, which the ship would run on most of the time. It sounded like an impressive job, but it wasn't until there was trouble.

Mia was excited to be working with Commander McGrey. She was an excellent pitot, and had the track record to prove it. She had flown ships through basically minefields of black holes and alien territory. Commander McGrey knew every starship like the back of her hand, and she was the most badass female Mia had ever heard of. It was intimidating, and reassuring, that between the two commanders that there was not one failed mission. This one was going to be easy and she was going to learn tons.

CHAPTER THREE

Alex walked beside Heather on the way to their ship. He wanted to ask if what that cadet had done had shaken her and if there was anything he could do. Sure, she already gave out the punishment but he was thinking more about for her, personally. Alex never heard of a cadet laying hands on a commander, much less if Heather ever encountered it before for being a woman. That much he hadn't heard about her, and she wasn't going to tell him. They were friends, at best, but he couldn't even get her to call him by his first name.

She was always so formal, even in boot camp. He remembered seeing another cadet challenging his test scores and was surprised to find out it was Heather. Unbeknownst to her, there had been a firm rivalry. She was determined to graduate top of her class; he was expected by the family to be valedictorian. In the end, it didn't really matter. They both had ranked up to commander and there was already talks of promotion. Alex knew that it was just another mission or two before he made captain. Captain Tanaka had a nice ring to it.

Maybe he could dress up as a pirate for Halloween and the pun would make Heather laugh... or at least crack a smile.

"So who's the commander for this mission?"

"Um, we both are," he replied. It was an odd question to ask.

Heather shook her head. "No, I mean who's commanding this mission? Who's the commander-in-charge?"

Whom had the power, that's what she meant. Alex had a feeling that she wasn't used to sharing control. Then again, neither was he. This was an odd situation that they found themselves in, especially for an agricultural mission. These cadets wouldn't need that much supervision and guidance.

"We'll take shifts."

"What?" She questioned. "That doesn't solve the issue. The point is who is the crew going to report concerns and problems to during the mission. We have new cadets, so this must be kept simple. They hardly seem capable of the smallest task. Just look at the poor display of their packs and standing at the ready during the meeting."

"Heather, whoever is on the bridge at the time that something arises is the one that it will be reported to and who has to deal with it. Besides, they could tell either one of us and it'll get taken care of. I know you're not going to let something slip if you happen to be off-duty at the time."

He had forgotten how stubborn she could be sometimes. Alex had proposed a viable solution, addressed her concerns multiple times, and it still looked like she wasn't ready to let this go. He needed a smoke. She was sure to get on his case about that, quoting every protocol that he was breaking.

"Would it make you feel better to take the first shift and fly us out of here?" Alex could be reasonable. He'd let her take control and then nab a cigarette in his room. She'd never know the difference.

She paused in the hallway, causing him to stop as well. "Tanaka, I don't want to seem difficult. I just..." Heather paused for a moment, trying to figure out what she needed to say. "Protocol calls for only one commanding officer and I've really been pushing to make captain. I need to prove it more than anyone that I'm capable of it. If I can't do it soon, then I might as well be teaching at the school."

What?

Alex knew he was staring at her with his mouth open. That was something Heather would never say. She loved space more than anyone he knew. She hardly stayed on-planet more than a minute. While he jumped back into space to avoid commitment and running into old fuck buddies, she did it to make a difference. For her to say she'd give it up to teach was insane.

"Heather, you don't mean that. You and space are like… you just can't not be together." He struggled to get a thought out. This was just insane.

She sighed, shaking her head slightly. "You don't understand." There was something else.

"Then tell me. Help me understand, Heather, because this is crazy talk. There's no way they're going to let you resign."

Heather didn't say anything else. She just walked away, either heading to her room or the bridge. He wasn't sure there was a difference to her.

Tanaka could never understand because he could never know. Heather unlocked the door to her room and stepped inside. The familiar stiff bed and stark room furnishings were comforting to her. The uncomfortableness of the bed reminded her – with minor aches – that she was still alive and that she had lived with much worse.

At the desk, she opened the top drawer and tucked in her journal before securing the lock. The therapist had said she should keep a daily record of thoughts and happenings so that she could reflect and improve. It barely came to that. The attacks weren't happening as frequently now, but it still was a good reminder to carry around. It reminded her never to get close to anyone because no one cares about anyone other than themselves. Except maybe her grandma, but that was it. The woman was a saint. Then again, she also had no idea what kept Heather up at night.

She took out a pencil box sized case and set it atop the desk. It was almost time for another injection. This mission had to go smoothly and she had to be in charge, just to make sure they met and exceeded their schedule. The doses were already running low and she couldn't be caught in space without anything. Heather already felt that familiar itch scratching.

It was something that needed to be taught patience. Heather forced herself to neatly stow her uniform and belongings in the trunk under her bed. It found her staring at the case, sitting on the edge of her bed, after the fact.

She didn't want it, but knew that she had to take it. She didn't want to have to do it.

A pain stabbed her lower abdomen. *So it starts...*

Heather folded over in half, trying to ride out the wave of pain. It wasn't that bad. There were worse. She tried to sit back up, and almost managed to get upright. Heather fell off the bed as she tried to reach for her trash bin as the nausea started. That was worse than the stabbing pain. At least the pain she could take and try to ignore. The vomit lingered in her mouth and would make her throat ache for hours.

"Fuck," she groaned.

Heather leaned her back against the desk, trying to catch her breath for a moment. She wasn't strong enough to beat this. She didn't know why she had tried. She reached up for the case and popped it open on the floor next to her. She took one of the syringes and a vial of the neon liquid. Three milliliters. That's all she needed to take. That's what she could get by on.

The syringe was going to hurt, but it would hurt less than this pain. Heather lifted her shirt and pushed down the top of her pants. Her hand hesitated every time.

She cried out as another pain stabbed her in the stomach. She knew that she couldn't wait forever to do this. It was only going to get worse.

Heather closed her eyes and jabbed it into her hip. It burned as the liquid entered her bloodstream. Everything hurt. Why did everything always have to hurt all the time?

"Attention! Attention! All personnel, please report to your stations for departure in five minutes."

She felt her eyes getting heavy. Between the medication and the strain, she wasn't going to last long but Heather had the first shift and she needed to get them off the ground. It was too late to see if Tanaka would cover for her. Besides, he might report back that she was unfit for duty. Then she'd never make captain; never prove *him* wrong. She wasn't worthless, and the one that needed to know that the most was herself.

Alex waited on the bridge. The announcement had come on throughout the ship's communication system and already the crew was starting to show up to their stations. He recognized Mia Ha – a recruit that he had nominated for this mission – take her seat at the controls. Her test scores proved her to be an eager, smart one. He had selected her because she had reminded him, in some ways, of Heather – and he hadn't imagined that Heather would be assigned this mission with him. Meanwhile, Malcolm Harrison had strolled in and now stood talking by the navigation station. After what he did to Heather, the cadet wasn't on his good side. Knowing that Harrison wasn't assigned here, he knew that he could get his own little payback by cock blocking. It was so obvious what the cadet was trying to do.

"Cadet Harrison." That got the boy's attention. "Your assigned station is not on the bridge. You need to leave, especially as how you're distracting our pilot. It would unfortunate if it had to be announced that you were the reason we couldn't get off-planet and failed our mission before it even started. This mission is important to so many people." It clearly pissed the boy off to be interrupted.

"Cadet Ha, how familiar are you with the starship specification of the Alphecca?" He asked, making conversation. She seemed to be unsure of the situation after what happened with Harrison.

"I'm confident that I can handle her, sir. I've done the simulations in training. Departing procedures are fairly standard amongst the Force's fleet. I'm hoping that, once we're off-planet, I'll be able to get into the system and see everything in the ship's operational system." Mia fidgeted with her bracelet for a moment. "I'm hoping that Commander McGrey may have time later to review the system with me and mentor me on any specific issues that are common with this starship model."

It wasn't too surprising of an admission. Oddly enough, it would give Heather the chance to play teacher like she had threatened to do earlier. It probably meant that she'd have to be buttered up to do it though. Alex couldn't have it coming from him because it would see like the request to sit with the cadet was a favor.

"I'm sure Commander McGrey would feel honored that you want to learn from her. She's taking the first shift on the bridge, so she may be more preoccupied. Once I relieve her, though, I'm sure it wouldn't be a problem. I can ring you on the intercom system, seeing as you'd most likely be off duty by then."

The cadet had a nice smile. "I'd appreciate that, sir."

He wanted to tell her to call him Alex, but held his tongue. She was his cadet – basically his mentee, his grasshopper. Besides, it was too soon to hook up with someone. They weren't even off-planet yet.

"Commander Tanaka, is everything ready?"

He turned to see Heather walking in. She didn't look that great and something seemed off about her. When Alex nodded, she tried to put on a smile but it faltered. Instead of standing at the bridge, like she had done last time, Heather sat in the captain's chair and asked for a system's scan. How could things have changed so fast? He knew one thing that was sure to pick her up. Alex called in the request with his com device before walking over to Heather.

"Got some eager cadets this year. Good to see some of the veterans have returned." Small talk to buy him time – and to figure out what was going on with Heather. Because, right now, all he got was a non-committal head nod. "You miss being in the driver's seat?"

Her eyes were closed when he glanced back to her from his peruse of the bridge. Was she asleep this whole time? Without opening her eyes, she said, "Sometimes. Coding is such an exact art. It's reassuring when nothing changes."

Okay... he was getting nothing out of her today. It must be because.... Prefect timing!

"Commander Tanaka, here is your order. I made sure to follow your instructions precisely."

The aroma of coffee seemed to have stirred Heather's attention. "Did that cadet just bring you coffee?"

Alex chuckled, a smile remaining on his face. "Yes. Yes, she just did."

"Why?" Heather asked slowly.

"Because she's my coffee cadet." It was hard not to take the opportunity to mess around with her a little.

"You have a cadet just for coffee?" Heather couldn't believe it.

Alex just shrugged. "Doesn't everyone?"

What made it worse was knowing how addicted Heather was to coffee and playing it off like no big deal. If anyone needed a coffee cadet, it was her. The one that had delivered these two steaming cups of goodness was someone he found a couple missions ago. He just kept finding excuses to assign her to tag along on his missions. The fact that she kept it interesting in bed wasn't lost on him. Alex rarely swung at it twice, unless he was in a relationship. Coffee cadet knew the arrangement and her place, and that's why it worked out so well for the both of them. There was no lies and that's what they both wanted.

"You're horrible."

Heather made grabby hands for one of the cups but he held it back, just out of her reach. "Na-uh-uh... not until you ask politely."

She groaned and leaned over the side of the captain's chair to grab it. Alex let her have it, just chuckling to himself as she practically downed it. He took a couple sips of his own, not really feeling any effect from it. What he really needed was that cigarette.

He waited until she had a good bit of her coffee gone. "Feeling better?" God, he hoped she was. It was going to do nothing but worry him if Heather wasn't running at her normal 110%.

"Yea, thanks," she said quietly. Heather set the cup of coffee in the chair's cup holder and stood to acknowledge the crew. The system scan had come back fully functional. It was time to get off this planet.

"Initiate launch sequence."

Mia started to frantically enter code after code before giving word that engines were online and thrusters were initiating.

"Carter, set coordinates to Zenox 5 galaxy quadrant. I want notification once we've left Earth's shield."

A man down front started to pull up holograms and set points of entry and departure in mid-space that appeared on the digital blue colored schematic in the bottom corner of the starship's view screen.

Alex could feel the ship turning alive under Heather's command.

"Cadet Ha, release docking locks and open vertical thrusters two percent." There was an unsure glance to the captain's chair from the cadet.

"Start a programing loop to open thrusters by 0.1% and then begin disabling the locks. Once you've gotten all eight locks disengaged, the ship will momentarily sigh and then hold attitude. It's a mere foot until we've cleared the docking bay. You'll initiate the rear thrusters then to get us out the door."

That seemed to ease Mia's nervousness. After all, first time flying and it was a new ship. Everyone would notice those dings and scratches. But the cadet followed Heather's orders as the commander got the rest of the crew running through protocols. When the starship eased out of the docking bay doors, there was a momentary blinding glare on the view screen as the Alphecca stepped out into the sunlight for the first time.

Alex noticed that it was that moment when Heather's balance faltered. She had to reach back to the chair for support. Everyone else had been busy enjoying that moment of triumph and getting high off the excitement of starting the mission. He had been keeping an eye on what mattered to him. Just as quickly as Heather had shown a moment of weakness, it passed.

CHAPTER FOUR

Mal couldn't believe the prick of a commander he was stuck with. He had the gull to come and interrupt the conversation he was having with Mia, just to have a pissing match. Yea, he got it. He was the commander and he owned all the pussy.

It just made him want to fuck Mia more. Fuck her and then let Commander Dick have his leftovers.

He left the bridge agitated. The hallways were a maze, seeing as he hadn't bothered to pay attention on the tour. He was too busy calculating. The supply closets and empty rooms were all mapped out in his head for later. It just wasn't helping him find the way back to his room.

Mal paused in the hallway and threw his fist at the nearest wall. It didn't rupture or dent the metal, but the pain in his hand felt good.

He needed to fuck.

It was the only way to get his frustrations out. He needed to find someone – almost anyone would do when all he wanted was to hurt someone – and just go at it. There was Brandon, his roommate, but that guy was more straight-laced and too soft to handle everything Mal was down for.

He grabbed the first chick he came across, holding her by the wrist. "Fuck me."

There was no asking. She either fucked him or she didn't. It would prove if she was some uptight bitch if she left. With both commanders on the bridge, this was the perfect time to screw the rules.

She nodded slowly at first and then gave a couple fast, confident ones. Instead of leading the way, Mal felt her tug on his arm. He followed, trusting her to have someplace nearby. His dick needed to get fucking wet – mouth or pussy. She opened the door to small room with just a cot.

"Quarantine," she explained. There was no way someone would be there when they hadn't even made it off the ground.

She stood back and started to undress. But it was Mal that hesitated for a moment. How did he want her? On the floor? Against the wall? On the bed?

How could he make her hurt?

One thing he'd give her credit for – she was a quick one. This blonde stripped down in under ten seconds and actually had the foresight to shave the bush. That almost deserved a reward. Almost. He'd see how well she'd scream for him before he'd decide.

Mia could feel her hands shaking as she typed in the launch codes. She knew that she knew them all. She knew that she had passed simulation after simulation. She knew that she was capable of doing this and accomplishing it without problem. She knew it, but she didn't quite believe in herself. The fact that Commander McGrey was on the bridge with her should have been reassuring, but it was more intimidating. She wanted to prove that she could fly just as well as anyone else and didn't want to end up humiliating herself.

She took it a few deep breaths and followed the commander's instructions. If anything, part of her mind could see how the blame would be off her if something went wrong and it helped calm Mia's nerves a bit. She felt the ship sway a little, and tried not to let it cause a panic inside her. She eased them forward and got caught up in the moment of light breaking through the view screen.

She was doing it! She actually did it!

Mia punched in the travel authorization codes after the other cadet inputted the destination. Her fingers flew over the hundred of input keys on the navigation station. The starship cleared the approach runway and turned slowly towards the west as the ship's algorithm navigated the best angle for departure. All Mia had to do was wait until the algorithm finished and for a green light to illuminate, then it was a simple press of a button to get them on their way to space.

The starship slowed to a stop. "Brace yourself," the commander warned.

The light came on and Mia pressed the button. The ship jerked forward, streaking along the ground. After a few hundred yards, it turned sharply upwards towards the skies. Unlike the simulations, the ship didn't shake and rock, but everyone could feel it hum and vibrate their seats. When the Alphecca broke the atmosphere, it really felt alive.

"Cadet Ha, status report." Commander McGrey looked expectantly her way.

"Status report?" Mia stammered. What could the pilot give for a status report? We're flying?

It seemed to annoy the commander, at least a slight annoyance was visible on her face. "Yes, status report. What's the state of the engines and thrusters? Is the ship ready to enter hyperspace?"

Oh.

Mia mumbled an apology and rapidly typed in codes as everyone waited and watched her. She managed to bring up the system status. "Engines running on 10% power at 100% efficiency. Thrusters are two seconds from complete cooldown and can be initiated for hyperspace. System is good, commander."

Commander McGrey gave a curt nod. "Initiate thrusters and enter hyperdrive. Carter, estimated time until arrival?"

"Fourteen hours, commander."

Mia could just make out a sigh from McGrey. She was in agreement. Fourteen hours – in hyperdrive – was too long. That meant that there was going to be nothing for her to do, seeing as the ship would be set to autopilot. It was common procedure and, seeing as Commander McGrey was strict on procedure, it was what would happen.

"Cadet Ha, initiate hyperdrive and set the ship to autopilot."

The view screen blurred as the ship jumped forward. Everything blended into everything else to the point where there was no reason to keep the view screen active, but the commander didn't give the command to turn it off. The ship was zooming through space, and Mia put everyone's lives in the digital hands of the Alphecca.

Mia slid out of the seat and headed towards the bridge door. She paused, though, and looked back over everything. This was her life now. The huge view screen. The chrome and sensor lights. Even the frantic part where the only sounds are hundreds of buttons and switches being used. Everyone was so confident and sure of the mission and what they were doing. She was determined to learn everything there was and to be the best possible.

She headed off the bridge. The ship was abuzz, but it didn't seem to reach her the same way. Mia could feel the distance between life and her in that moment. It was quiet enough that her mind had started to drift back to her mother.

A blonde came around the corner and ran into her. So incredibly rude. The last place Mia expected it was on the Commander McGrey's ship after what happened at the docking bay. She was about to open her mouth to point out that she existed in this hall and deserved an apology, but then she saw the bruise around the blonde cadet's neck. Where did that come from? The cadet moved around her and hurried down the hall without a word.

"Mia!" She turned to see Mal jogging up to meet her. "Aren't you supposed to be on the bridge or did Commander Dick kick you out too?"

"Commander Dick?" It was hard not to laugh a little at that. Commander Tanaka didn't really seem to come off as a dick. He was following protocol and trying to get the mission off the ground, literally. She chose to brush it off. Mal was the only one on this ship that tried talking to her. Tabitha was off on another starship doing medical outreach on a territory planet. So, for now, she was going to have to make an effort with Mal. "No, we entered hyperspace and the ship's on autopilot until we get there."

Mal leaned up against the wall. "So you got nothing to do?" There was a huge grin on his face. "Come with me. I'll show you something."

It was a tempting offer. She was off on the bridge and that feeling just wouldn't shake off, and now her mother was in her thoughts. Maybe she was a little spacesick. But then there was the idea that all she had to look forward to was silence in her room. Her stomach grumbled and offered a compromise.

"Maybe you can show it some other time. How about we just grab something from the cafeteria?"

Mal shrugged. It was probably the best offer that he was going to get. "Guess that would work. Had me worried that you were trying to ditch me already."

She laughed. "No, not trying to ditch you."

They stared at each other for a long moment. Mia searched his face, trying to figure out what he was waiting for. Then she got it – he had no idea where it was. The problem was neither did she. Mia had tried to pay attention during the tour, but it had been too soon after meeting Commander McGrey and then they had walked out of the bridge with all the fancy gadgetry and shiny things. They had walked out and taken a left…

"I think I have an idea of where to go." Mia clasped her hands behind her back, taking a step away from him. She nodded her head to the side. "Come on."

Mal pushed off the wall and started after her, once she turned around to walk. "So, you got us off the ground. That is kind of impressive. Means you should be celebrating now, Mia."

She shook her head. "It's not really something to celebrate. I just did my job."

"Naw, it's more than that. Let me celebrate it with you."

He was really pushing it. It was simply her job. It didn't make sense to her at first, because she didn't want to stick with stereotypes of being tech savvy. She wasn't oblivious to her Asian privilege, but like she couldn't completely ignore Mal's of being the privilege jock. The air about him and how he acts above the law was what made her realize that he thought he was entitled. The muscles on his arm proved that he was probably a jock, or at least a gym rat that thought highly of himself. The fact that he targeted her out of the recruitment class was proof that he was running stereotypes. Mal probably expected her to be smart, but rebelling to the point where she'd be down for anything from tattoos to tentacle porn and needing to date a white man to put the nail in her father's coffin. The tattoos, she had. The porn, not really.

"Alright, but if the food sucks then you got to sneak out a bottle of something from the commanders' stash." It was a condition that Mia hoped it wouldn't come to. She just wanted to eat and get back to her room.

"Deal."

Mal definitely was the cocky one. They walked into the cafeteria together and headed up towards the buffet style layout. There were hot dishes of shredded beef in gravy for sandwiches, mashed potatoes and yams, three different kinds of vegetables, a salad bar portion, and then the desserts. Mia could already see the selection of sugary goodness. Her eye was on a slice of cheesecake with cherry topping.

"Guess this doesn't suck." Mal almost sounded disappointed. "Definitely better than what they served up back in school."

"Totally." That much Mia could agree on.

It had been boring thawed meat sandwiches, overly processed vegetable mush, and most of the time unidentifiable goo. The vending machines out by the Force's track field had been her best friend, even if it was just chips and a soda. With classes and

31

training so close together, it was nearly impossible to venture off-campus to a restaurant or food truck nearby.

So Mia – and it appeared Mal too – filled up their plates with real food. While Mia took her single dessert, Mal grabbed a whole second plate to load up. They picked a table off to the side and sat alone. For the first ten minutes, there was silence. The food was too good to break from eating to talk. But after their stomachs started to get full – and Mia was onto dessert – they started to talk a little.

"So tell me about yourself. You got some tats, so I'm guessing either gang member or rebelling against the 'rents."

Mia shook her head. "Neither actually."

"So tell me about them then." Mal wasn't just going to let her get off the hook that easily; although, she wasn't sure why he cared. Maybe it was all about the stereotypes.

"I got this one when I first started dancing." Mia moved her watch up her arm so that he could see the little ballet shoes on her wrist. "My mom wanted me to get into dancing, like she had. Ballet wasn't for me, but the more street kind of dance was. That's why there's a boombox next to it. It's kind of a tattoo about where I've been and where I'm going." Well, to put it mildly.

"So your mom's okay with you out on the street and not in some tutu?" He took a huge bite of a cookie as he waited for her answer.

"No, actually, she never saw me dance. She passed away last year before I could tell her what I was doing." And it was so hard to dance since. "I was putting together a routine to show her how hard I was working. I was going to mesh in the ballet with the hiphop. I wanted to make her proud of me, ya know?"

Mal nodded, even though he didn't know or understand. He could care less what his father thought of him, and his mother never stood up for him so she was barely a thought as well.

"So how'd ya end up here then? You a shit dancer?" Although, Mal was hoping she was a different kind of dancer than what they had been talking about.

32

"No." She tried not to take offense to it. It was just a question, but the way he asked irked her. "I'm a good dancer, but I've been doing it in secret and I just want to make my own way. To dance full time, I need to have money saved up for rent and food and studio rentals. Joining the Force gives me that money to save up and I can practice on my own when I'm off-duty. When I get back on-planet, I can hit up my crew and go out for gigs."

Mia poked around her dessert. It was hard to know how much to admit. What she said really wasn't answering his question. Not completely anyways. That had been the idea that got her into the recruiter's office. It wasn't the whole reason.

"Also, my dad's good with computers and stuff." Usually saying "cyber security" scared people, so she kept that fact to herself. Knowing her dad, he was probably hacking into the starship's surveillance system right now, just to keep an eye on her and make sure nothing was happening. "He pulled some strings to make sure I was tested for coding and navigation. Obviously, I was good at that or else I wouldn't be assigned that now. I think it's that and just needing space to myself to grieve. Back home, I'm too worried about my dad all the time."

Although, now she was worried about him because she was gone. Had he fixed something for lunch? She didn't know if he used the stove and if it was turned off or left to burn the house down. Being gone for possibly months, would he know enough to go out and buy groceries? Mia could only hope that their neighbors would keep an eye on him if something really bad happened. But she didn't want to think about that right now. It was going to make her too emotional.

"So how'd you end up on the ship?" Mia asked, diverting the attention. It seemed like Mal was the type to crave attention, but he wasn't exactly jumping at the chance to dominate the conversation.

He shrugged a shoulder and tossed the half-eaten cookie back on the plate. "My dad's an asshole." That was all he offered until the silence between them grew awkward enough for him to say more.

"You probably can guess who he is with Harrison as a last name, and you can probably guess that some fucking uptight politician wants his family to fall in perfect fucking line behind him." Mal paused. It looked like he was debating leaving this conversation or not. "You can probably tell that didn't fly with me. I love drinking and fucking too much to keep up his appearance. Life ain't fun if you're living it for someone else, and he didn't like that. He threw money around, got me enlisted, and paid for me to get through the school. Only good thing about this whole shitstorm is that I get to shoot all the fucking guns I want... and I'm damn good at it."

Usually when someone said they liked playing with guns, it was a bad thing. Mia was sure that at some point on this mission, knowing that would be reassuring. Even if there never was an issue, it seemed like Mal found something that he liked and could do well. It might have been the first time in his life that he felt that way.

"I'm gonna head back to my room. Jerk around or something. Catch ya later."

Mia watched him get up. His tone and body language had changed so much since this conversation started. He almost seemed defeated, to her, and maybe that's exactly what it was. Seemed like his father got exactly what he wanted and now Mal had to suffer through it. Maybe when they got home, he could transfer to the base police force and stick it to his dad. He's still get to play with guns, but all the nonsense of space would be avoided for him. He could still live the life he used to, whether his father approved or not.

CHAPTER FIVE

Something was wrong with Heather. He knew that much. She wasn't acting like she had on the last mission they ran together. Hell, she wasn't even that excited over the coffee – and she was practically an addict! Alex couldn't put his finger on it. She had been fine when they boarded. There wasn't much time between then and now. What could have happened?

"You got this?" He asked.

Heather had sat back down in the captain's chair and was staring straight ahead at the blurred streaks of color on the view screen. He knew that she wasn't looking at anything; she was zoned out in her own little world.

She nodded slowly.

Guess it wasn't a world he was going to be allowed in. Not that Alex expected her to just open up. She always did err on the side of more reserved. He had no idea how he was supposed to break through that wall she had up, or even how to put a crack into it.

The thing was, Alex knew that he had to get through to her. He was forty-four; she was just a couple years younger. That rivalry in school only blossomed into more of a longing as the years went by. He even dated women with similar features, just to pacify that childish crush. No one could replace Heather McGrey. And then they had worked together a while back and the mission was the best he'd ever been assigned. They had laughed and gotten close. Alex had thought there might have been something there but the next time he ran into Heather, on base, she seemed different. Distant.

Maybe she had never felt anything towards him. Maybe she did. It was just that he was getting older and time was running out. He wanted a family like his siblings had. A house, and maybe even the white picket fence. A couple kids would be perfect and a cuddly dog would complete the image.

It took years to run into Heather again; he couldn't wait years until the next time. When he made captain, there were only so many missions that he could assign her to be with him until people started asking questions or until Heather began to hate him over it.

For now, he'd let her have her space. Eventually, she'd come around. Until then, he really needed to grab a smoke and now was the time to steal one. Alex could feel the ache in his lungs. He was craving a cigarette almost as bad as he was craving the woman next to him.

"I'll just head back to the room then," he casually informed her. She didn't make a move or sound to acknowledge that. "Call me on the com if you need me; otherwise, I'll see you in about twelve hours when I relieve you."

Even to that, Heather said nothing. For being so concerned before over whom the commanding officer was, she was really letting go the chance to push it and completely take it from him. She was logged into the starship's system, so could easily dictate the Alphecca to respond only to her and put it in the log that she was taking full command for the duration of the mission. But she hadn't. She probably wouldn't.

Alex turned slowly and started to head towards the door. This mission definitely was off to an odd start. He was at the bridge bay doors and almost out when the coffee cadet stopped him.

"Commander Tanaka, are you relieved?" He nodded and she continued. "I was wondering if I could be of any assistance to you, sir."

He had an idea of how she could be of assistance. She was a pretty young recruit. Her auburn hair did remind him of Heather's, but the cadet's was short and curly where the commander's was long and straighter. All Alex had been thinking about was a cigarette. Sex hadn't been on his radar... yet.

He glanced back at the captain's chair, not seeing even a flinch of movement. Taking the cadet up on the offer of anything could hurt his chances later with Heather.

"Not at the moment. I'm about to retire to my room for the night; however, you could bring me a coffee in a couple hours. The two you provided were perfectly done." He smiled at her and watched the rosy blush tint her cheeks. "You can leave it black. I'll need something to keep me up all night."

With that, he stepped around her and off the bridge. Rationally, he knew that his voice was quiet enough that Heather wouldn't have heard. He also knew that the word "sex" wasn't said. He knew that he was a grown unattached man that could do what he wanted. That's why he needed to leave and get that cigarette. He'd determine his future later – if it was just coffee filled or not.

It was a relief that the Alphecca's floor plan was similar to the Uriath's, which he commanded on his last mission. Sure, he had been briefed on the layout when the starship joined the fleet, just like every other commander required to know all in-service deployable ships. Alex made it back to his room without incident, but not without stirring up whispers. It seemed like he was the most eligible bachelor on this ship as well. If only Heather wasn't on the ship, he'd be free to have his fun.

Alex locked his room door, in the off chance Heather wandered back this way. Honestly, she was the only one with the rank to do something about him. He pulled out the pack of cigarettes from his trunk and tapped a single one out. He slipped it between his lips and just let it rest there as he savored the feel and smell and taste of it. Even unlit, it could calm the urges and his soul.

He sat down on the stiff bunk mattress and pulled out a small notepad from his pant pocket. It was just his own little way of keep track of missions and making sure the ship logs were kept up-to-date. With Heather at the helm, he probably wouldn't have to worry at all, unlike he had with the junior commanders on missions past. Alex scribbled down the time they departed, when command fell to Heather, and estimated time of arrival.

After stowing away the notepad, he finally lit the cigarette. The first inhale was bliss. It was everything he had been craving and it made every possible problem and thought disappear. The familiar burn in his lungs just made him feel whole. He laid back on the bed and stared up at the stark white ceiling. If he was going to be smoking in his room, he was going to have to eventually figure out a way to cover up the evidence. But again, that was a problem for another time.

Maggie somehow crept into his thoughts. She had decided to leave him for good, and he couldn't blame her. Things hadn't been going great for a long time. He had started to avoid her when she started talking commitment. Ironically, so. A wife and kids was what he wanted, yet he ran from it. All the weeks and months in space, they were just to give distance to Maggie until she could realize he wasn't worth it and move on. But that was the thing – she wanted to wait for him. After a while, she tried convincing him to take an on-planet position and even said that they'd try for kids, and having a dad around was a must. Maggie didn't feel like home anymore. If anything, she was great sex and knew what he liked – both inside the bedroom and inside his life. It was bringing home cadet after bar chick after rocket bunny that did it. She had forgiven him the first time, and even tried the second time she walked in on him balls deep in another woman. Alex knew that he broke her heart but, at that point, he wasn't capable of caring.

Even now, he couldn't care about how she felt or was feeling. That was if he was being honest with himself. Alex was over her, even though she had been one of his longest relationships. Now, he was more focused on the smoke rings drifted up towards the ceiling. That was another great thing about smoking – he could do whatever he wanted with the smoke. Just puff it out fast or slow, a long stream, or rings. Hold it in or take them quick. Each breath could be different, and that was more fascinating that his ex-lover.

All too soon, the cigarette was gone. Alex checked his watch. It was too soon for the cadet to show up, too late to really take a nap. There wasn't much to do in his off time. Usually, he wasn't confident in the other officer to warrant time away from the bridge. In reality, neither of them needed to be holed up on the bridge – especially while they were in hyperdrive. Maybe he could call Heather on the com and convince her to come spend time with him. Then again, she might catch the scent of smoke on his uniform and berate him. Second thought, as hot as the fantasy was, he wasn't up for that.

Should he sleep with the coffee cadet?

It was obvious that she wanted him now, and they had been together in the past during missions. This time she was here for a different reason though. He was going to give her to Heather. Not sexually; more as a slave to fetch coffee. The cadet was a quick learner, and Heather had such specific tastes depending on when she had a cup and how many cups she already had. Sometimes cream, others just sugar, and occasionally strong and black. But now Alex was wondering if that was a good idea. There was a remote chance that they'd find out about each other. Maybe it was best to just casually have the cadet lingering nearby with a steaming cup 'o joe. No, that would be more awkward. Regardless, it was too soon to really be concerned about it. They just left home and there was plenty of time to weight it all out later. Maybe a couple good lays would help him figure it all out.

So it was settled then – sex with the cadet was on the table. Things with Heather would go along as normal until she took a chance on him or nipped it in the bud. He was no saint to wait.

Alex decided that he needed another cigarette, but first he needed to grab something to eat. He was definitely going to need energy for later, and then something to curb his hunger when he took over command. At least for the first couple hours, he wanted to stay on the bridge and enjoy the brief amount of silence before the bustle of the mission truly began.

He made a beeline for the buffet, picking up a cold pasta dish from the salad bar and a couple of the shredded meat sandwiches. Desserts and sweets were his weakness. Other than cigarettes, Alex would say sweets were his addiction. He wrapped up a handful of cookies in a napkin before hiding the treasure in his pant pocket, safely hidden next to his notepad.

When he turned to leave, he caught sight of two cadets off at one of the tables. Cadet Harrison had his back to him, which was a relief. That was one more interaction that Alex would be able to avoid. He knew the kid had some authoritative issues. He was with Cadet Ha, who didn't seem to notice him at all. She was talking about something, which had Harrison's undivided attention. For the sake of the crew, he hoped Ha had the smarts not to get caught up in whatever it was the politician's son was playing at. They needed a pilot. While Heather was more than capable to fly, she was a commanding officer and she might outright refuse to pilot. Instead, she could always opt to keep the display of her rank and take the weakness of Ha as a learning experience – forcing her to work through whatever heartache was bound to come from the company she was keeping.

Alex tried not to let it dominate this thoughts. It was best if he left before either cadet had time to register his presence. Besides, the aroma of a hot meal was going to make his stomach growl like a beast and he was hungry enough now to devour the plate of food as such. He made his way back to his room to enjoy the meal. No sooner had he stowed the cookies in his desk after finishing his meal did a knock come at his door. He brushed off the stray cookie crumb and went to answer.

"Commander."

He stepped aside and let the coffee cadet enter his room. Sans coffee.

The pain was subsiding. It was nothing more than a dull ache now. Heather had thought that it was going to be painful all night, but the fortunate turn of events was not something she was going to complain about. Maybe it was the coffee that helped. She had missed out on cups number four and seven today, between the meeting and the commanding the bridge. Overall, she was lacking caffeine – and that coffee cadet was nowhere in sight.

Sighing, she eased herself up and out of the captain's chair. Not another soul was on the bridge. The peace and quiet was definitely welcomed, but there were just more pressing matters at hand. It was about that time to get something to eat. She remembered Tanaka and thought he might like to join her. If nothing else, she could apologize, in her own way, for earlier and they could catch up. It had been a long time since they were both in the same room together, and now they had a whole ship together. She wandered the halls, briefly observing the crew going about their duties but never staying too long. It wasn't like she could wait forever to eat.

Heather made her way towards the commander rooms. Tanaka's shared a wall with hers, so it was hard to get lost in between. She walked up to his door and paused mid-knock.

"Yes! Yes! Yes!"

She could make out the muffled moans through the door. She could also hear a soft knocking, which she assumed was the bed ramming into the wall and was only reduced to the small noise by the thick door. It seemed like Tanaka was... occupied. She thought it best not to interrupt him, especially for something as meaningless as eating. She didn't want to spoil their working relationship on this mission over interrupting his "fun". Heather knew, firsthand, how annoying it was and could only imagine how long Tanaka would be pissed off.

She walked away, unsure of how she was feeling at that moment. Her mind was in a million different places and, being distracted, she almost ran into a couple cadets leaving the cafeteria. One tall guy, she almost completely ran into. Only at the last moment did Heather snap out of it and step aside. To her slight horror, she recognized him as Cadet Harrison – the cocky one.

"Evening, commander." He smirked and gave a slight nod of his head as he passed her.

The second cadet was the navigator, Cadet Ha. She was mildly confused when that smart girl went to catch up to the cadet. Heather watched as they didn't say a word, and then part ways at the end of the hall. She was sure that they had just been together, or maybe her mind was just making scenarios up.

Malcolm Harrison was an attractive young guy. He had seemed to appreciate her body earlier. At some point during this mission, and most likely soon, she was going to need someone. She was willing to bet that Harrison wouldn't object. The only thing working against him was the fact that he probably couldn't keep his mouth shut, and she didn't need rumors spreading amongst the crew about her. Heather had always tried to keep things discrete, especially when the urges struck and she didn't have a syringe handy.

She headed into the cafeteria, deciding to wait until things got dire before figuring out someone to scratch that itch. She picked at the buffet, not really adding much to her plate. The cafeteria was basically empty, not that it mattered. She would have still ended up sitting alone. The crew rarely wanted to be around their boss more than was necessary.

Heather took a seat and pulled out her com device. She could run basic system scans on it, and plugged in codes to do a simple check on the engines and their progress. Seemed like everything was running on-track. She debated if she even needed to be on the bridge. Usually that was a thought that she had on the way home after a successful mission. It felt like she was almost not needed, especially if Tanaka was on-board. There was no need for two commanders, and this was a trip that any novice could command. Not that she was calling Tanaka a novice. He had, at least, as much experience as she did.

Normally, when things were running smoothly, she'd retire to her room and keep the com nearby in case something came up. With Tanaka keeping company, she really didn't want to return only to listen to wall knocking. It would only make her imagination kick into hyperdrive and run away with the idea of him naked and how everything would feel to be physical with him. His kiss had been one of the best Heather had, so she could only imagine what sex with him would be like.

Her food had turned cold before her mind returned to reality. Cold shredded beef wasn't as good as hot sandwiches. It felt like a waste of food, but her appetite was no longer on things to be eaten. Heather cleared her spot and went to grab a cup of coffee to-go. She wasn't sure the exact plan, but she knew that her room would be safe to return to eventually. Heather grabbed the mixed coffee and a pastry before making her way back "home".

Just as she was opening the door, so did her neighbor's and out walked the all-too-needed cadet. Her face faltered when the cadet spotted her, and Heather could guess that her presence really was a huge surprise.

"Commander," she quickly tried to cover up her presence here with the polite show of rank.

"I told you that you to stop. Just call me Alex when we're alone."

Heather stared at the door, having heard the voice from within getting closer. Alex walked out, shirtless, with eyes set only on his coffee cadet. He quickly realized by her diverted gaze that it wasn't him whom she was addressing. Alex slowly glanced over and saw her a moment away from being in her room. He stared at her, looking more surprised than the cadet had been. Heather knew that she could make this run-in awkward or save his skin and break the tension.

"It's hot beef sandwich night. Not entirely bad if you're hungry and haven't ate yet." She watched as the spell broke on the cadet and she hurried away. "I tried stopping by to see if you wanted to grab a bite together, but I heard you were busy so I didn't bother to interrupt."

God, he looked good shirtless. That, alone, was the only thing distracting Heather from seeing the embarrassed blush tint his face.

"Heather…" This was happening all wrong.

She shook her head. She didn't need to hear anything. "Tanaka, we're both grown adults. You're off-duty and there's nothing I can say. I'm just going to take some time to relax, enjoy my coffee in the room, and then I'll get back to the ship. Just don't… don't worry - I won't be bothering you."

Heather didn't give him a chance to defend anything. He was free to do as he pleased. He owed her nothing, and she knew he just got out of a long-term relationship. It was too be expected. Part of her just wished she had been considered, and that part was now suffering from a bruised ego. The logical part was relieved that they could just be colleagues. It would make this mission run a lot more smoothly.

Alex stared at the closed door for what felt like an eternity. He had fucked up. Not only had Heather come wanting to spend time with him, but she ended up hearing him fucking someone else. And if that wasn't as damaging to his chances, she then saw the cadet leaving his room and he made a fool out of himself in the process. Even if he had caught on that the cadet was addressing his co-commander, it would have been too late to completely save his ass. He could have at least put a shirt on and thrown out some story, not that he wanted to start lying.

He stared at her door, wondering what she was doing. Leaning his ear against it, he almost wished he heard her crying – just to prove she had feelings for him. At least then he could go in and talk to her and do whatever she said to make things right. Alex would beg, if he had to, for her to forgive this and just be with him.

But he heard nothing through the door. If Alex hadn't just seen her with his own eyes, there was no sign telling that she was even there. For once, Alex was in a real pickle and he had no idea what to do.

Heather sat at her desk. She could make out the slight shadow underneath the door. Tanaka was still out there. She had no idea what he was waiting for out there, shirtless. Maybe there was a second round in the schedule for him and he was making sure that the crew member found him.

The bitter thoughts bombarded her while she tried to drown them in coffee. The cup was empty before she even take a bite of the pastry she had nabbed to pair with it for dessert. And the last thing Heather wanted to do right now was step outside where he was waiting just to be able to get more coffee so that she could enjoy her time alone. Even if she slipped out, he could follow her around the ship or even to the bridge. Her room was the only safe haven. Realistically, she couldn't hide forever.

It took a while, but the shadow eventually disappeared. Through the wall or the door, Heather couldn't hear anything. She left the pastry, but grabbed her cup. Cracking open the door just a few inches, she didn't see anyone lingering outside. As commander of this starship, she decided that a refill was in order and then she'd resume her duties on the bridge until she was relieved. During her time hiding, Heather had already pulled out her casual clothes which consisted of pajama shorts, a white tank top, and a pair of fuzzy socks. There was just something about fuzzy socks that fixed everything. Plus, they had been a gift from her grandma.

The cafeteria was bustling when she slipped inside for a refill. There were bodies in every seat and a few of the crew standing as they ate and chatted. Heather tried not to disturb them as she made her way up to the front and mixed up the proportions for this cup of coffee – she wanted it a little stronger to get her through the night on the bridge.

A couple crew members came and went – checking their own stations. There was no sight of Tanaka, making her fear irrational.

Maybe it had sunk in and became awkward for him as well. But when the twelve hour shift was up, there he was. He reported for duty, verbally signed into the starship's system as commanding officer, updated the ship log, and handed her a cup of coffee like nothing happened.

"Anything interesting happen last night?" Tanaka asked, sipping his own cup of coffee.

She shook her head. "Nothing worth saying." Other than the incident outside her bedroom door. "I ran some diagnostic scans last night and everything came back as running optimal."

That seemed to puzzle him. "Why'd you run those?"

"I'm just not used to a fancy, new ship. Usually, by now, there's some minor repair that needs to be fixed or a line of coding left incomplete." Heather paused to sip and evaluate the brew. It must have just dripped through the filter – it was that good. "We got a great crew apparently. Nothing's lacking."

Tanaka chuckled. "And that's just as rare."

They fell into silence. For a while, it felt fine.

"Heather, I..." The sound of the bridge bay doors swooshing open stopped him. The crew was filtering back in and greeting the commanders, preventing him from completing that thought.

"I'm going to go catch a couple hours of sleep before we arrive. I'm going to assume it'll be a long day of making camp once we land, and I know with these new recruits that it'll be like herding cats – complete chaos."

She relinquished the captain's chair and disappeared out the bridge doors with a shoosh. Again, she had avoided the awkward conversation that he seemed set to have. Heather made it back to her room, barely noticing anyone that she passed. No sooner had her head touched the pillow, she was out.

Chapter Six

Mia certainly had a different life than he did. Parents that cared and didn't bribe them into slavery. He wished that he had her problem. Then again, he probably wouldn't be himself and that was a fucking shame and a half. There'd be too many disappointed chicks out there.

Even though he got laid once already, he was considering another hunt for a new prize. The trouble was if that blonde chick talked. She had left pretty fast after he came. He didn't even have time to tell her to cover up the finger-shaped bruises on her neck. Although, if word did get out that he was rough, maybe it wouldn't be such a bad thing. He'd land with chicks that wanted the bad boy; chicks he didn't have to concern himself over being careful with.

Instead, he decided to find this gym that was promised. Mal changed into a pair of basketball shorts and a white wife beater to work out in. His water bottle hung at his side as he roamed the halls in search of dumbbells and treadmills. When he finally found it, the gym was empty. What irked him was the note on the window of the door going inside. A long list of rules and procedures.

The whole bullshit thing brought up this morning and those damn commanders. Why couldn't he get assigned reasonable ones that weren't so fucking anal and knew people were going to act like humans? Fuck! They were all hot-blooded animals.

Mal got on the treadmill, ignoring all the bullshit rules about using it. He kicked it up in high gear, going straight into a fast jog. It felt good to use the ol' muscles, and it helped him think clearer. He had been too rash in wanting revenge – that much he decided. The beef wasn't really with the piece of ass McGrey. It was that fucking prick Tanaka.

McGrey probably wanted a ride on his cock and just didn't know how to handle herself. If not, she'd definitely want a go when every other chick was fucked passed being satisfied. But that prick Tanaka – fucking cock-blocker! He'd give Tanaka one last chance to do right by him, then it was war. Didn't that prick know who he was? He was Mal-fucking-Harrison. And he didn't have to take shit from nobody.

"Essential bridge personnel report for arrival."

The com next to her bed started to go off. It didn't feel like she had slept at all. The bed was incredible uncomfortable and her mind had been all over the place once she got back to her room. Her roommate had been out and was still gone, so it was like Mia had it all to herself. It should have been easy to get some rest, but it was not. And now, any hopes of getting more shut-eye were gone. She was "essential bridge personnel" and she needed to report again for duty.

Mia sat up and reached under the bed for her trunk. Pulling out her uniform, she got dressed in the flight pants – which looked like Army combat pants – and the black polo that matched her black boots. She ran the brush through her hair to tame the strands that got away while she was tossing and turning in the bunk. She also wiped on some more deodorant. Being on the starship with no real window to the outside – hell, even just being in space – it was hard to determine if it was day or night now. She was going to have to find some way to measure time so that she could keep her hygiene up.

Once she thought her appearance was acceptable, she made her way back to the bridge. There was a fine line between being late and trying to look decent. All Mia could hope for was that she was not the last one to report for duty. When she did get to the bridge, she made it to her seat at the exact moment another member of the crew did. Together, they were the last ones. When she looked to the captain's chair, expecting to be reprimanded for the tardiness, she noticed Commander Tanaka was at the helm.

He didn't seem in much of a rush. He was leaning back in the chair, hands behind his head. On the giant view screen in the front, there was a countdown clock running. By the look of it, they still had thirty minutes until arrival. Maybe that's why he was so calm.

Mia watched as another cadet casually walked up to him and passed over a cup of – what she could guess was – coffee. Tea wasn't something she really saw at the ready when she had been in the cafeteria. The commander took a sip before leaning close and saying something that got the cadet to laugh.

She didn't get it. Why wasn't he taking this seriously right now? Mia felt conflicted. She knew that there was nothing anyone could do until the ship came out of hyperdrive. Even then, by the simulations they ran, the ship would coast and give them ample time to plug in the navigation codes. Maybe it was just that the commander seemed to be more willing to flirt than do his job, and that rubbed her the wrong way. She tried to put it out of her thoughts though. She didn't want any kind of tension or trouble during her first mission. Mia knew that she had a job and – even if Commander Tanaka was goofing off – she had a lot to prove to herself. She was sure that Commander McGrey would notice her effort too. Really, that was whom she was going to learn from the most and who could help her career advance the fastest. It just was a shame that Commander Tanaka had nominated her for this mission and then wasn't even giving her the chance to prove he was right in his choice. Maybe if she wore her pants down low and opened up her polo just a little... No, that wasn't what she was about. Mia wouldn't use sex to buy her way, which she assumed the coffee girl was trying to do. And honestly, didn't she know that Commander McGrey was the one that coffee would work on the most? Maybe she did and realized Commander McGrey had morals, and wasn't into women.

She tried so hard to write it off as Commander Tanaka just trying to make the mission pleasant and enjoyable for everyone. She didn't want to let it get to her. When the countdown was finally in the last couple minutes, the commander finally got down to business. He sat forward in the captain's chair.

"Mia, adjust the thrusters to fifty percent once hyperdrive is disabled. Tyler, I want the weapon system online just in case we run into an unfriendly ship passing through. I'm going to need communications up and open, Hans. HQ will want to know how the Alphecca handled her first space jump."

She opened up the command window and had the long strings of code inputted, ready to be entered into the ship's system. If she entered it now, it would be too soon and it could cause a continuous loop of conflicting commands in the ship, possibly destroying the hyperdrive. The last thing Mia wanted to be remembered for was breaking the new ship on her first day.

Once the Alphecca came out of hyperdrive, the view screen changed from blurred colors to vibrant definition of the solar system and space dust in front of them. There were three seconds before the ship would stall and Mia needed to submit the thruster coding into the system. She hit the enter button and felt a little bit of panic rising up. The ship wasn't responding. It should have excelled forward instead of coasting. She turned to the commander, looking for further instruction, when the ship picked up the speed and thrusters leveled out to fifty percent. The starship's system must have had a built-in protocol to ensure smooth maneuvers.

Mia gave a sigh of relief. For the first time, her gaze found the outside world and it was beautiful. Whatever star was in this solar system was illuminating the clouds of dust in vibrate hues of reds, golds, and purples. The few planets visible ahead of them were large and as mysterious as Junpiter's surface or the core of Neptune's frozen world. Everyone was in awe.

"Any word from headquarters, Tanaka?" She turned to see Commander McGrey stand at ease next to the captain's chair. At least someone got to avoid the tension Commander Tanaka's behavior caused.

"Not yet, but the communications are just being re-established from the hyperdrive. I am reporting back on the Alphecca's first successful jump as well as having the ship's diagnostic report relayed back as well. I'm sure HQ is anxious to know how their new baby is doing."

Commander McGrey's expression faltered for a second. If Mia hadn't been watching the two commanders closely she would have missed it.

"I see you have everything under control. I'll report back when it's time for my shift."

"Heather." Commander Tanaka reached out and grabbed her wrist when she turned to walk away. "We need to talk."

Commander McGrey shook her head. "There's nothing to say, Tanaka. You don't have to explain anything to me."

The look on the commander's face was clearly defeat. He let her go, but didn't watch her leave. The bridge doors swooshed open and then closed as the other commander took her leave. Mia tried not to stare at the scene that just unfolded. No one else seemed to have been close enough to overhear the interaction.

Something just didn't seem right. The mission had just started and Commander Tanaka felt the need to explain something to Commander McGrey. Their reactions and body language didn't read as completely professional – and body language was something Mia really worked hard at knowing and projecting, being a dancer. There must be history between the two. But what kind of history? She didn't know. Given the kiss-ass cadet from earlier, Mia was willing to bet that it was something along the lines of something romantic.

"I think there's something going on between the commanders."

Mal glanced up from his plate of boring space rations to see Mia taking a seat across from him. "What?"

"I think there's something going on between them. I'm not trying to be a gossip, but there was stuff that happened on the bridge." Mia took a bite out of her quesadilla. "First, this cadet brings Commander Tanaka coffee, which he's probably mildly interested in, and then he's up there making her laugh while we're about to exit hyperdrive."

"So the fucker isn't doing his damn job?" Another reason to be pissed off about the dick.

Mia shook her head. "No, he did his job. There was thirty minutes until arrival when we were paged and this cadet was gone long before that. But then Commander McGrey came in to check on things and that's when it got weird."

He was beginning to be over this conversation. If there was nothing useful to blackmail Tanaka then it wasn't worthwhile to be listening. Mia was probably tired from her shift and wouldn't be down to fuck, so it was hard to give her the time of day. "What? He started to flirt with hard-ass McGrey?"

"No," she said slowly. Mia leaned in slightly. Damn, she had a pretty mouth. It would look nice around his cock. "But Commander Tanaka said they needed to talk so he could explain something. He reached out to stop her from leaving even, but she blew him off. The guy looked devastated. That's why I really think there's some kind of history between them."

"Okay, so maybe they fucked in the past." He really wasn't getting what Mia felt like he needed to know.

With a sigh, she gave up. "Yea, okay. Just guess you'd be more interested in who our commanders are. I'm pretty sure there's like half a dozen rules about fraternizing and inter-mission relationships, and they both seem to want to go by the rules... Just thought with your family that you might know something about them."

What Mal didn't know was that she just wanted to talk about McGrey because there was a small bit of idol worship going on. What he finally got though was an idea. Either McGrey meant something to the prick or he'd fall into the trap of being set up for rule violations. Maybe Mia wasn't only good for a fuck, and she seemed to be willing to talk and play friendly.

"You want to bring them down a peg?" He asked. Maybe that conversation had been enough to make her resolution waver. But she just shook her head.

"I think that's going a little far. They like each other or had sex. That's all." She now shrugged it off. "Just feels petty. Especially when everyone on this ship is probably having sex."

"Are you?"

It caught Mia off-guard and had her face turning into a tomato. So, under the tattoos and talk, she was just another shy, nice girl. He had been right to wait. Mal would have broken her over bruises on her body or something that would come out of his mouth. Mia was an after-fuck fuck – like a dinner mint after a meal.

"No," she said one word, barely audible,

He couldn't help a smirk and half-chuckle. "Why not?"

Her face got even redder, if that was possible. Her eyes refused to make contact. He was making her squirm, and the power trip over being able to do that was stroking his ego.

"Just 'cos I'm not... Are you?" That last question seemed awfully hard for her to ask. Like she didn't want to know, but she did. Maybe little Miss Goody-Good liked him, or at least his body.

"I hooked up yesterday." She ever so slightly peeked up at him. Her expression, he couldn't figure it out. "Hey, I'm always up to fuck. I'm a dude."

That didn't seem to make things go easier. He could still feel something awkward between them. Somehow, lying about fucking around probably would have been worse, or at least Mal thought so – and yes, he could actually fucking think sometimes. If he had a pussy, he'd probably realize that he wouldn't want a crush fucking around, let alone hearing it straight out.

"Mia, we're good." He was going to give it to her straight. "If you need it, I can give it to ya."

"S-stop." She actually held up her hand to him. Probably because her voice was basically not there. He could make his move and Mal doubted that she'd really stop him. He had an effect on her, and she wanted him bad. "That's... I'm not..."

"Just think about it." He leaned across the table and kissed her cheek. "Nine inches. Thick and uncut." Literally. Just how he like to fuck.

He got up and threw out his trash, leaving Mia all hot and bothered at the table. He headed back towards the bunk hall, hoping she'd stop him any minute to take him up on the offer. The further away from the cafeteria he got, the more he just fucking knew she couldn't walk or was so hot and bothered she couldn't think straight or... or she was finger-banging herself under the table. Yea, that was it.

Mia got his blood pumping. Now he needed to find someone to fucking give it to.

CHAPTER SEVEN

Alex had really fucked it up. She wouldn't even talk to him now. He should have realized it was a risk and gone about it differently. He could have just met her somewhere else on the ship – and, hell, he knew all the good places to hide out – or he could have gone down to the cadet's room. He could have played it off as some spot inspection of their room or bullshitted some story.

No.

Instead, he fucked her two feet from Heather and walked right into their little run-in. He was so damn stupid! Now Heather wouldn't even listen. He might have just lost her because he had thought with the wrong head. He needed to find a way to make her hear him out. He needed to tell her all that he felt.

The problem was that he was stuck on the bridge now. Sure, they had come out of hyperdrive and basically had set a short-term auto-pilot to get them the rest of the way. It wasn't like he needed to be confined to the bridge. A commander was free to walk about and handle the every day-to-day operations. It was just that they'd be preparing to make an approach on the planet soon and he'd need to be on the bridge for that. He'd feel a lot better knowing that Heather was on the bridge too. Even if he'd only admit to himself that it was for selfish, personal reasons. Alex groaned as he slouched in the captain's chair.

"Alphecca, send transmission to HQ base," he commanded the ship.

"Connection to HQ base established. Message to proceed."

"Commander Tanaka, Starship Alphecca. Departed hyperdrive in vicinity Zenox 5. System diagnostics one hundred percent operational." Alex watched as the com device on his wrist picked up the message. There was a circular loading icon as the ship transmitted the device.

"Sir, there's a communication incoming from HQ base," Hans announced. He seemed to know how peculiar that was, giving their transmission just went through. There were no additional reports needed, seeing as the ship would process and automatically send along the diagnostic report.

Alex sat up a little straighter. "Patch it through to the view screen."

The vision of space flickered away, only to be replaced with an aged man in uniform. "Commander Tanaka?" Alex gave a nod of his head and the man proceeded. "The tracking location of your ship does not located you within Zenox 5. It shows a location in the Mytrops galaxy, exact coordinates are being determined. You, commander, are severely off-course."

Shit... How the hell did that happen?

The immediate thought was that Heather was in command at the time of hyperdrive. She would have been the one to give the commands, but she hadn't been the pilot. The pilot was a new cadet, but surely Heather would have been watching closer than normal about what was going on with the ship. Even then, it wasn't Cadet Ha's responsibility to input the coordinates. At least, not in this stage of her career and with this crew. There was another that handled that, but he was a veteran who knew the procedure for assigning arrival coordinates. Even if he wasn't, the Alphecca would have already had their mission inputted into the system and it would have taken just a few minutes to upload and activate the back-up programming to get them there. Logically, the mistake would have happened back on-planet with whoever built the Alphecca. But she was run-through thoroughly and deemed in perfect working order. Something wasn't adding up.

"HQ, the crew followed protocol and used exact coordinates for Zenox 5. The ship's reports have come back with nothing less than perfect and operational. How could this have happened?"

The man on the screen seemed at a lost too. "We have people here working on determining exactly what happened."

"So what are our orders until then?" Alex asked. It seemed like nothing, not even a straight-forward, easy mission, would go his way.

The man had muted their transmission as he took a call from a radio. Maybe it was the tech team there and the problem was an easy fix that could be transmitted now and sending them on their way. He could only imagine what Heather would say if she was still here. She'd probably blame him and call him unfit to command. Yea, in the whole scope of things it was a small worry but, to Alex, it was another strike against him in the quest for Heather.

"Commander Tanaka, orders are to hold coordinates and await further instruction." With that, the view screen went dark before someone decided that the outside world was a better image to view than the black emptiness.

"You're all dismissed until communication is re-established with HQ base and new orders to proceed are received. Keep your com devices on and remain at the ready for duty."

There was no point in keeping the crew on the bridge if HQ had no clue what happened. With a mostly veteran crew, it wouldn't take long for them to reassemble when the communication came through. Until then, he might as well let them break to get something to eat for lunch. And, now, he definitely needed a cigarette.

Just down the hall from his room, Alex tumbled, off-balanced, into the wall. The ship had lurched! The thrusters weren't supposed to be running. The ship rocked again, throwing him against the other wall and down to the floor.

He needed Heather.

"Emergency personnel report to position. Bridge personnel report immediately," Alex all but shouted into his com device that echoed throughout the ship's announcement system.

Alex got back on his feet and ran to her door.

She had locked the door to her room and went to lay down on the bed. Heather hoped that he wouldn't bring it up. There really was no need to. There was no relationship back home to guilt him over, though she really hadn't done much of that. And it wasn't a secret that he had got around, and she wasn't a saint either. Heather just didn't see the point in bring up their sex lives.

It was time for another dose. Heather hadn't been late in a long time, but yesterday's episode was enough of a reminder as to why. She pulled out the case from the desk drawer and set it, opened, on top of the desk.

Seven neon green vials rested on the packing foam with the few syringes. It was coming to the point where she'd be out soon. Heather had avoided bring it to the medical department to see if someone could multiple the liquid. She doubted the general would approve of Force resources going into cloning drugs. The bigger reason, though, was that she didn't want General Ruthesford to know what was in those vials and she definitely didn't want to come on his radar again. She had managed to survive him once, but Heather wasn't sure she'd be as lucky a second time.

She'd had to give up a full vial in the hopes of someone working some chemistry magic to create more. If it failed, it meant life was going to get unbearable faster. The most logical thing would be to take time off from work to return to the planet and get more. The only caveat in that was that the planet where the drug originated from was an active war zone and travel was now because of the civil war its inhabitants started. Heather would never see the old physician that had handed her the vials nor the pale green translucent aliens that occupied the jungle-eques lands again.

Heather lifted the hem of her shirt and tucked it into the band of her bra before tugging down the waist of her combat pants. When the ship lurched, she fell over the back of the desk chair, feeling it jab into her ribs. Something had broke. Heather heard a loud crash and a thud and something felt wet beneath her fuzzy sock covered feet. She pushed herself off the chair and looked down to see green seeping everywhere.

Every vial had shattered!

Her case lay on the floor, glass everywhere. Syringes rolled under her bed and desk as the ship rocked again. Iridescent liquid ran and spread across the floor. By the time Heather could get her bearings, she was being tossed again. Something struck the back of her head and, for a moment, she saw nothing but stars. There was a pounding in her head... a pounding... the door.

Heather swayed and slipped and staggered her way to the door, forgetting that it was locked. She tried to force it open, throwing her shoulder into it twice before realizing what happened and turning the lock. Alex threw open the door and she fell into his arms as the ship tossed them again.

"What's going on?" She desperately asked. There was panic in her voice, but not all of it was over the current state of their ship. Heather was screwed.

"When we came out of hyperdrive, we weren't where we're supposed to be. HQ gave us orders to stop. Everything was fine, but..." The words got lost as the ship turned again.

"We got to get to the bridge."

They clung to each other, each bracing one arm against each wall. It was still an impossible struggle and, once there, it was chaos. Only half the bridge crew managed to make it back. Mia Ha was in the pilot's seat, trying desperately to get the ship responsive. It was like every minute, the status of the ship was getting worse.

"Tanaka, see if you can get the ship online again. See if there's any place we can land." The last thing they all needed was to be spiraling through space – until they hit something, got shot down, or everyone became too ill to continue. If the ship was spinning out of control, they were a lost cause. No rescue ship – if HQ sent one – would be able to couple with them and tether them back home.

Heather staggered over towards the pilot's seat before the ship's bucking tossed her to the ground. She crawled the rest of the way. She gave one order. "Move."

There were tears streaking down the girl's face. She was frozen in place until Heather gave the order louder. Then the cadet hurried out of the seat, tripping on something and landing in a crying ball next to the navigation station. Pulling her body up to the keyboard was extremely taxing after the fight to get to the bridge and fishing to stay standing. Then, to add to the problem, Heather could feel the withdrawal starting – and she knew some celestial being out in the universe really did hate her.

Her fingers flew across the keys as Tanaka yelled orders over the sounds of chaos plaguing the bridge. A few crew members had stumbled in, demanding answers, and added to the background noise. Alarms and beepers started going off at the various stations while the Alphecca hurled itself towards doom. Heather was running into dead-end after dead-end with each command code she entered into the system. Nothing seemed to be responding. All the codes for this starship had been exhausted. She started throwing out every systems command for every starship in the fleet, hoping something worked.

Suddenly the ship bowed back, and rocked back to a level position. She was still moving, but at least the tossing and turning had stopped.

"You got her under control?" Tanaka yelled from across the bridge. The bigger, unspoken, question was *how*.

The last command on the screen was for a starship model that had just been taken out of operation. The only reason that she knew of it was because Heather had been the last to pilot it, and that mission would never be forgotten. It had been what started everything.

Things on the bridge finally calmed down. The crew started to straighten up their stations. Emotions were leveling out. Heather got out of the pilot's seat and started to head back towards Tanaka. She needed to tell him that she wasn't going to be able to stay on the bridge. She needed to get back to her room to try and get some of the drug soaked up and into something so she could inject it into herself. Heather could already feel the internal shakes starting, even though it physically didn't look like she was rattled. Her legs felt weak as she walked over, then everything started spinning in her head.

"Heather, are the..." Tanaka stopped, staring at her. Then his arms reached out to hold her up. "What are you covered in?" Heather flinched when he touched her forehead. "And your head is bleeding."

She touched it herself, even though she knew the sting was coming. Her finger tips were red when she took them away from her forehead. Maybe it wasn't withdrawal then...

Alarms started going off. "Engine malfunction. Code Red." The ship's announcement kept repeating on the bridge.

"Heather... Cadet Ha, can you run the system diagnostic?" Tanaka seemed to have thought better halfway through. She must look worse than she thought. He leaned in, almost as if to kiss her.

"Are you alright?" He asked quietly. "And what are you covered in?"

Her brow furrowed together in her confusion. Why wouldn't she be alright?

"Heather, how many fingers am I holding up?" He held up his hand, but when she didn't answer he changed up the question. "Can you tell me your name and where you are?"

She tried to push him away. If he wasn't going to kiss her then there was no point dealing with him. "Why so many questions? I'm fine," she grumbled. At the same time, her legs gave out... and gave Tanaka a reason to hold her again.

"Signh, take Commander McGrey to the medical bay. Make sure they check for a concussion."

61

Heather tried to fight the crew member that touched her and tried to get her off the bridge. She needed to… do something important right now. She just couldn't remember what it was. Leaving the bridge, she heard Tanaka ordering reports and something to be done with the engines. Maybe even something about emergency landing, but Heather wasn't sure what he was saying anymore. She was just really tired and starting to feel a lot of pain.

Alex watched her being led off the bridge. It didn't feel right to him. There really was something going on with her, and now the ship's engines were failing. Two things he cared about – only one he could address at the moment. He needed to have faith in the medical crew to be able to take care of Heather until he got things handled here.

"Mia, get back in your seat and get ready to code emergency procedures." He took a deep breath. There was only so much they could do with dead engines, but at least the ship wasn't careening through space anymore. This… this was something he could work with. "Carter, bring up coordinates of the nearest land-able planet."

He could tell that the crew was really rattled after what happened. Hell, he was too. It was just that he had hundreds of eyes watching every move he made and relying on him, solely, to get everyone through this. That's why he needed to land this ship and get everything right, and fast.

"There's an uncharted planet at 5.02320 beta, 9.51255 selt, 9.21006 rhu."

That wasn't far from their current location, but it was the fact that it was uncharted that bothered Alex. They had no idea what they were getting themselves into by landing there. The planet's coordinates were in the database, which should have been a good sign.

"Any information on inhabitants and ground conditions?" He asked.

Carter took a couple moments to scour the system. "No, sir. Just basic observations gathered by satellite. Solid core, poor oxygen atmosphere, life-holding."

So there was solid ground down there and there was something walking around that didn't need as much oxygen as they did to survive. Alex could restrain all non-essential personnel to the ship. A small group could explore for resources in the limited number of external spacesuits available in the landing bay.

"Set the ship for those coordinates and watch her very carefully. For some reason the Alphecca isn't holding position." A warning was all that he could give. "Hans, try to re-establish a connection with HQ base once we land. They'll need an update on our status."

Alex began thinking there was a reason that they weren't ordered to land there. Then again, the engines were busted and any move of the ship was probably going to cause more damage. There was just one thing left, and he was more worried over that.

"Mia, I need you to ease the ship towards those coordinates. Handle it as if the engines are offline. I want to wait until we've breeched the top of their atmosphere before dropping landing gear. We don't know how rough that will be coming through there and we definitely need those wheels to touchdown."

The cadet didn't give him a verbal acknowledgement of what he said. She just started doing what he ordered. Alex knew – if he was more like Heather – that he needed to correct her and get her to follow starship operational procedures on communication. It might not cause a problem now, but she had a long career ahead of her... hopefully. They'd need to fix this ship and get back home for that.

The ship's trajectory slowed and began to turn towards the purple-hued planet. This was going to be a first for him, and for everyone on the ship. The enormous mass was slowly getting closer and, on the view screen, it looked like a sick cinematic joke showing the slow, impending doom to come. As far as Alex was concerned they still had all their guns and weapons on-board, so there was nothing to fear down there. But it was eerily quiet on the bridge as they inched closer, even after the view screen when white as they entered the atmosphere.

When the landing gear started to drop, a god-awful sound resonated in the ship. Something was very wrong. Alex could hear murmurs amongst the crew – they didn't believe they were going to make it. Those same murmurs grew louder, and now the thoughts about dying started up.

"Refresh the view screen," Alex ordered, trying to keep himself in check. He needed to really be a strong commander for the crew. He knew that they didn't see him as the strongest. The strongest one was recovering on the other side of the ship.

CHAPTER EIGHT

Her hands never stopped shaking. She couldn't believe how inept the commanders were. First, Commander McGrey entered flight codes without considering the repercussions and ship functions. For all Mia knew, one of those commands put the engines in a coding loop that destroyed them or another code ordered the engines to run both in normal and reverse at the same time. There were paths and flowcharts for the coding that she didn't think the commander took into account. Then her general appearance was unprofessional, between the fuzzy socks and whatever was splattered all over her shirt. And then there was the way she had spoken to Mia. Not once did either commander ask if she was injured or alright.

Commander Tanaka only proved the point of how little they could lead. He was ordering the ship to land when HQ said to stay in position. Their engines were down, yet he wanted to make them work – probably destroy them – to land on an unknown planet and strand them there until they perished. He wasn't even addressing any of their concerns. The only thing he had done right was to refresh the view screen.

Outside, it looked almost like a forest on Earth. The colors of greenery were just brighter and saturated. There were a few trees that, instead of leaves, looked spotted with giant cotton balls. There was a stream a few yards from where they had landed. But the strange part was that there was no movement outside, no sign of life. Back on Earth, there was at least a fly or bird flying by.

There didn't seem to be anything, even though the ship's information said it sustained life.

"Hans, has a connection to HQ been established?" The commander's voice pulled her from her thoughts.

"No, sir. Seems that communications are cut. I lost them when the engines went down."

Mia was still staring outside, but listening to all that was going on around her. This didn't look like that bad of a place to die.

"Try to restore them. Track back the root cause – electrical, coding, whatever. I want a report in an hour."

It was more beautiful than Earth. This was probably how everything looked like before the big cities popped up, and it had that kind of magical feel when she looked at it. Like, at any moment now, an unicorn or a fairy might come by.

"Help!"

Mia looked around the bridge, trying to figure out who needed help. Maybe… no, they had what they needed and their station was already put back together. Maybe it was someone off the bridge, calling through the bay doors. The voice had sounded faint anyways. By now, someone closer had probably helped him… or her… Mia forgot if the voice was male or female.

"I want everyone to run a full diagnostic test on their station and the systems you're responsible for. Fix everything you can, note if something's missing. I want a full report from every station in an hour. If another emergency comes up, call me on the com." With that, Commander Tanaka took his leave.

She watched him walk off the bridge and couldn't figure out where he was going. The bridge was a mess, there were a dozen reports he just asked for, and the ship was broken.

And he just left.

Mia lost what respect she had for him then. Mal was right. Commander Tanaka was shit.

Mal held his head as he walked back towards the quarantine room where he fucked himself into the Interstellar Club. Whatever bullshit was going on had tossed him around like a marble in a tin can and he cut open a gash across his eyebrow. It was bleeding bad enough that he might need a stitch, but it was knowing he'd look like a badass that got him to actually get someone to look at it. No stitch meant the chicks wouldn't believe he was a bad boy. He'd look like the loser of a fight, not the guy who started it.

"I demand you release me!"

He rounded the corner to find three medical cadets holding McGrey's ass on a cot.

"Commander, we cannot discharge you. Orders or not. You're in no condition to walk out of here," the doctor told her sternly.

For a second, Mal believed that someone could actually have authority over her, but it didn't last. She went right back to arguing before folding over in pain. It was fucking pathetic. How did some pussy become commander anyway? She couldn't handle a fucking period. That's why women shouldn't be in the Force. She probably slept her way up to that position, and that's *why* women should be allowed on the Force – for entertainment.

"Hey! Guy bleeding his fucking life out over here," he called to the group. They obviously didn't know a helpless cause when they saw it – because McGrey was hopeless.

"Take a seat, sir, and we'll be with you in a moment," said one of the nurses.

Now that was interesting. Mal hadn't noticed her at first because she was in one of the side rooms, but he definitely did. She wasn't human. Her skin was a deep blue with small black dots. There was a smooth spot where her nose should have been and atop her head were two small faun-like horns. He wondered what else was different under that white lab coat.

He watched, with more delight than he should have shown on his face, as McGrey was sedated.

"That should do her for a few hours. Hopefully by then she will have calmed down and the medication would have gotten a chance to work on that pain."

Mal could only imagine. There was a bandage on the commander's face, so she must have hit her head when the ship was throwing everyone around. Other than that he couldn't imagine that she was in any real pain. It probably meant his cock would tear her apart and make her cry... and he liked that idea.

"Okay, so what's wrong with you?" It was a normal nurse that came to check him out. Unfortunately, that nurse also had a cock.

"Need a stitch in my head, idiot. I'm fucking bleeding."

The nurse rolled his eyes. "Got a concussion too?"

It was a wise-ass remark in response to his wise-ass remark... and it was getting another wise-ass remark in return. "No, dumbass, and stop making me do your whole job."

If there was any question about stitches versus a bandage, they were gone. The nurse looked like he wanted to punch Mal, but that was the opposite of his job duties and there was a commander laying not even ten feet away. He'd be a fool to hurt Mal. Well, in any non-medical way. There was no local anesthesia given, not even a topical one. The stitching needle bit into his skin with each one adding, and the prick decided that he needed three stitches on his brow.

"Lay down and don't move."

Tsk... like he'd listen. Mal would do what he wanted. He just so happen to want to lay down. He kicked up his feet and watched as the nurses and doctors in the medical bay started looking at more and more people that walked in injured. It was about to be a full house in the medical bay it looked like. Across the way from him, McGrey hadn't stopped whimpering.

She really was pathetic. He sat up. "Hey," he called. When she didn't say anything back, he got up and walked the few feet over to her. "Hey... commander," Mal said that last work thick with sarcasm.

McGrey groaned as she tried to roll over and look up at him. The sight and sound of her like this really got that sadistic side happy; only, it wasn't by his hand. She tried to speak, but let the pain cut her off.

"What?" She finally croaked out.

"Need anything?" He was trying to taunt her. He'd make her beg and then walk away. It was completely out of spite. Mal wasn't ready, nor expecting it, when she reached out and grabbed his cock through his pants.

Her hand ran up and down the outside of him. He was ready to get down, but something Mia said came up to bite him. Commander Dick had a thing for McGrey. The best way to get revenge was to do it through her. He hit a button on his com, pretending that all he was doing was putting his arms behind his back and pushing his crotch into her hand.

"You want my cock?" He asked, knowing he needed to set her up. He needed it to be obvious to what was going on.

"Yes," she groaned.

Mal smirked, not that she seemed to notice. Her gaze was fixed to the growing bulge under her hand. "You want it bad?"

Her hand ran up higher, trying to find the zipper. "Yes! Just give it to me!"

She was trying to speak and demand through the pain. He'd give her brownie points for that. But what his ears heard – and what he was betting on – was that she sounded desperate and craving his cock.

"Where do ya want it, McGrey?" He watched as she found the zipper. Halfway down, though, she gave up and moaned in pain. She wasn't able to play his little puppet any more. It meant he was going to have to speed this along and improvise. He doubted it was actually going to happen, and that bummed him the fuck out. But the blackmail from it would be priceless. It worked for revenge on Tanaka and could be used for favors from McGrey, who definitely wouldn't want anything tarnishing her reputation.

"You want it there?" Mal grabbed her between the legs. She didn't disappoint with a moaning "yes", although it was starting to sound more like pain. "You like that, baby," he sweet talked. "Yea, you take it all."

Heather groaned and moaned, but it had nothing to do with him. Her hand had long fallen away from his cock to wrap around her stomach as she folded up in pain. He kept with the dirty talk a little longer until he thought he heard someone coming.

Mal quickly turned off the recording and got back on his cot. He laid down, like he had been ordered, and pretended like he didn't know there was a huge boner in his pants with a zipper now imprinting a fucking zigzag pattern on his cock.

"You're free to leave," the nurse from before said without as much as a glance his way. His attention was on the commander writhing in pain.

He smirked as he left. Those fucking idiots would get what was coming to them. On the way out, he saw the blue alien nurse. He winked at her and noticed she was watching him. Could he? He nodded towards his junk.

"Quarantine."

Just one word. If she was down to fuck and liked what she saw, he'd be there waiting. If not, she'd probably show up just to kick him out. Either way, she was going to get a load of Mal.

Chapter Nine

What the hell was going on?

Heather struggled to figure out where she was right now. A moment ago, she had been on the bridge – the rest, she didn't remember. The all too familiar urges were starting up. Her body was begging – demanding – to be filled. There was the pain, yes. Painful cramps like she never experienced before and a pain so deep inside her that just needed a hard dick to reach. She felt hands on her and wondered just how many there were this fucking time...

"Commander, do you understand us?"

She tried to open her eyes, but the light was too bright and she had to close them again.

"Commander, give us a sign if you can hear and understand us."

Heather managed to move one hand enough to tap someone's wrist a few times. Hopefully that was enough of a sign. If not, then her situation was worse than thought. She couldn't move more than that. The pain just kept growing.

"Heather!" She heard a male calling her name.

"Sir, you can't be in here. She's not in a good state and we need you to get those engines back to be able to help her properly." There was cussing and then nothing.

"Commander McGrey, I'm Doctor Oden. We're going to run some tests on you. We believe there may be something wrong with your baby. There's nothing in your medical file from your pre-flight physical noting your pregnancy and I'm not sure how the doctor on-base missed it. But we're going to get both you and the baby checked out. Okay? Just hang on and we'll get you something for the pain."

Alex couldn't fucking believe they wouldn't let him into the room. He was the fucking commander! He needed to know how everyone on his crew was doing!

"Can you believe that about McGrey?"

"Yea, it's a pity. I think she's lost it."

Alex stopped his frantic pacing when he heard what the two passing nurses. He reached an arm out to stop them.

"What's that you're saying?" They seemed frazzled. Probably because they weren't supposed to be gossiping about patients, but for this time he'd allow it and was grateful for it. So he pressed on. "Is the concussion that bad?"

"Concussion?" The alien nurse on the left asked.

They exchanged a glance with each other before the other yellow striped one answered. "She's not crazy, if you're taking the words like that. We were feeling sadness that Commander McGrey may have lost her baby. The pain is no good."

Baby?

Alex stared at them, completely at a loss for words. Heather wasn't pregnant. She... she couldn't be. She would have... No, she probably wouldn't have told him or said a thing to anyone. Knowing her, she'd keep taking missions and have the kid mid-hyperdrive on a starship. That also meant there was a baby daddy. There was some man in Heather's life already, and here he was trying to get in.

"Commander?" He must have had a look on his face. The two alien nurses looked concern, and probably wondered if they'd be checking him out soon too to see if he was well.

"I'm good... I'm good." It wasn't too convincing to his ears. "I just... I need to go see about this thing. I'll be back for a report."

He hurried out of the medical bay. His mind was in a million pieces. Never had he imagined that Heather would be a mother, outside of the thoughts of her starting a family with him.

"Commander Tanaka, communications with HQ base are still down. There's damaged wire in the engine room that needs to be replaced before the waves can be opened up for communication again." His com buzzed alive with another blow.

"Send technicians to repair it. Over and out." This was turning into a mission from hell.

"Commander, life has been detected outside." He hadn't noticed the cadet walking towards him until he was right in front of his face. "Lieutenant Gregor wants to take a scouting group to the surface."

Gregor was old as dirt. He could remember the first time that he ran into the ammunitions expert. It had been a while after his career started and they were entering potential hostile space territory. They hadn't ran into anything in the skies, but the moment they landed the attack started. Gregor grabbed a bunch of new cadets and he – and his two veteran weapons specialists – headed off that ship and defeated the whole lot revolting their presence. Alex had gotten pulled into that excursion. He hadn't a clue what to do to or what was going on, but everyone made it out alive and bullet-free because of Gregor. Afterwards, the guy always seemed more like a fatherly figure in his mind.

But now there was the subject of a scouting group. It wasn't a bad idea, and something they would have gotten around to sooner or later. It was possible that there were resources that could be used on the ship and a village – or town or some kind of habitat – nearby where they could get information from the locals. If there was anyone that Alex trusted to do the job, it was him.

"Tell Lieutenant Gregor to assemble a small group and see what he can find for us out there." The cadet nodded at the order and hurried off.

Alex knew that he needed to get a report on the navigation system and get the engines back. There were other reports waiting too, but his mind kept going back to Heather. Before hearing the cause, he had seen how much in pain she was and her tear-stained cheeks just about broke his heart. Seeing her like that was unbearable. But the doctor said getting the engines online again would help her. He needed to focus on that.

Everything was hazy. The lights were dimmed a little, making it easier on the eyes. Somewhere off to her left, something was beeping. There was an odd feeling in the region where the pain was supposed to be. Dried drool irritated her face and she tried to rub it away with the back of her hand, only to feel the tug of an IV line.

"Oh, good, you're awake." She registered movement in the corner of the room and realized that a nurse had been sitting there. Heather watched as she set down a book and walk to the bed's side. "I have orders to remain with you until you woke. Can you tell me how you're feeling?"

"Strange..." She felt the need to close her eyes for one really long minute. "I don't understand why I'm here." She knew what was going on. She was going through drug withdrawals.

"You're here so that we can monitor the baby."

Heather shook her head. "I'm not pregnant."

Not anymore.

It was years ago and it was the worst time of her life. There was no way that she was pregnant right now. Heather was too careful. Even when the urges struck, she always grabbed a pill the next morning to make sure nothing stuck.

"Oh, no, you're wrong. You are pregnant. The doctor noticed the spike in your bloodwork and we just took an ultrasound that proves it." The nurse seemed confused over why she was denying the possibility. "You're at least four months along, commander. You should have notices changes in your cycle."

That was the thing. She didn't have one. It had been years.

Heather just let it go. It was easier than to try to explain and end up getting herself killed. Maybe those tests were the reason she was numb down there, or maybe she finally got some drugs that worked.

"The doctor wants to know why it wasn't picked up in your pre-flight exam. They should have been monitoring this on-planet and limiting your missions. A baby is a delicate thing, commander, and trust me when I say that none of us want harm to come to either of you."

Harm couldn't come to the baby because it was dead. Heather knew it and she felt it every day for three years.

"I'd like to rest now. Can you see if the doctor will discharge me to my room instead? I'd rather take up space there instead of the medical bay where someone really might need it."

The nurse had a sad smile on her face. "I'll talk to him."

When she left, Heather rolled on her side and faced away from the door. Her hand instantly went over her stomach where the baby had been. It was where she should have felt him kick, but never had the chance to. She wondered if he would find out. If the doctor managed to get a message through, her life would be ruined. A baby wasn't supposed to exist. It couldn't. Not after everything, and it seemed that time had been frozen inside her. Four months. That had been when she told him.

CHAPTER TEN

Mal got the summons. These coms were fucking annoying when they were issuing out orders. He sulked his way to the docking bay and then veered off down a hall towards the munitions room. Inside was already a group of five guys. They were jacked, just like him.

"Harrison, you'll take left guard on the group. Anything that looks suspicious to your virgin eyes, call it out." Gregor gave the assignment as he fastened the spacesuit around his waist.

"Who you calling a virgin?" Mal quipped back.

"Psh, that's about the only thing virgin on him," one of the other joked.

A short guy in the back with a blonde buzz cut spoke up. "That's not what Raidar's sister said!" That earned him a punch to the arm.

"Watch what the fuck you're saying. That's my sister you're talking about, and we both know she's a virgin." There were a few snickers at that. Mal guessed that one was Raidar.

Buzz Cut passed him what looked like a flimsy suit. It was not at all what the teachers projected an astronaut's suit to look like. It wasn't bulky. Mal just hoped that it protected just as well as it was supposed to.

He pulled it on while Gregor gave them a rundown of their mission and what they were looking for. Once everyone was suited up, the fun part came. Gregor inputted the access code and started handling out gun after pistol after rifle. Mal had a handgun on one hip, spare magazines on the other. Around his ankle was a knife, and in his hands was an assault rifle.

"Alright, boys, move out!"

They stepped inside the loading bay, hearing the doors to the ship seal shut behind them. Mal could feel the pressure changing around him, and suddenly the spacesuit seemed to fit differently. It was like the flabby thing was suddenly shrink-wrapped to his body. When the ship's door open, he swayed like his legs were going to give out. It was the strangest fucking feeling.

"We're going to head straight west for a mile and mark out a perimeter. We'll circle our way back to the ship and report in. Stick to formation. Do not break under any circumstance." The voice came in through the spacesuit's helmet.

The group moved forward and, for once, Mal didn't try to go against the pack. He didn't even crack a fucking joke. This was his job and it was fucking awesome. Fucking around now would mean that he wouldn't have this. He'd be a fucking dish boy with pruney hands from all the damn dishes he'd be washing. That and they were on some strange fucking planet with who knew what was out there. It was time to be serious or he'd be in a black bag in the cargo bay.

There was nothing at first. "Unknown target to left, appears friendly."

Mal glanced over and didn't see it at first. All he saw was a plant, and then it moved slightly. It reminded him of a venus fly trap, only it wasn't just reacting to touch. It was freely moving. He couldn't see any eyes but he could feel like he was being watched. It was unnerving.

One of the guys in formation held out his wrist and let his com scan the creature. "Catalogued, sir."

They continued their scouting for a mile before turning the formation. They saw more of those Venus plants until they got close to the river bank. With the river in their path and no immediate way to cross it, Gregor ordered them to turn back towards the ship. They ran into two different, smaller creatures –

both seemed to be friendlies. So far, there was nothing threatening. Maybe they got lucky and landed on a planet of fluffy bunnies and cotton balls.

The river ran up along the ship and passed it. There didn't seem to be any bridges or fallen tree to walk across, or even a point where the river was narrower to wade across. While it looked like crystal clear water, there was no way to know if that's indeed what it was. For all they knew, it was a new kind of acid or something that would eat through their suits and then their bodies, if they didn't suffocate first.

They jogged the perimeter along the river. The further from the river they got, the more of those Venus plants grew. And then they didn't. Instead, there were prickly bushes of nothing but thorns. One of the guys carefully tried to slice off a sample with his knife. The thorny bush wouldn't cut through and, when the branch got nicked, it leaked some kind of liquid that dissolved the blade. Definitely not a friendly.

Out of their entire scouting mission, there wasn't a single creature that was classified as truly hostile. There also wasn't anything bigger than a loaf of bread. They rounded back and boarded the ship. While most of the group stripped out of their spacesuits, Mal hung back. He wasn't ready to go back to the fucking boring life on-board. He knew Gregor's word was absolute – as their lieutenant – but he wanted to break orders. He wanted to get out there and scout more... or more or less to play around with his unfired gun. Mal would gladly go and shoot those couple creatures to bring back for research, just as long as it got to be him shooting.

Gregor logged all their rifles and pistols and knifes back into the armory. The wire gate slammed shut and it was a definite "no" in continuing the scouting mission. It was with a lot of reluctance that Mal had handed over that rifle. The spacesuit was gladly returned when it was back to the flabby suit version. He zoned out a bit as he watched the suits being hung back up and logged into the inventory. That's when they were dismissed. The guy that had scanned the creatures and plants left to upload the data into the ship's system. Gregor was off in search of Commander Dick to give a field report. Mal wasn't sure what he was going to do now. He didn't want to head back to his room, and he wasn't hungry, and he didn't want to get in another workout. He didn't even want to fuck. This fucking pissed him off! Mal wanted to be out there scouting and shooting shit. Again, he never got what he wanted.

Mia debated stopping by the medical bay to see Commander McGrey. It seemed that something more serious was going on with her. The commander hadn't bothered asking if she was okay after the ship tossed them, so she decided against it. Instead, she decided to explore more. With nothing better to do, she spent hours wandering the halls. The ship was bigger than she had thought it to be, but there was no place that really held her interest. There was a gym – which was great she guessed – and then just rooms of equipment and supplies. There wasn't a library, which probably made sense because everything was in the ship's data system. There didn't seem to be any room for entertainment, which made her wonder how people kept themselves from going insane on the long missions. Sex. That apparently was how

Sex wasn't something she was a prude about, but Mia didn't feel the need to screw anything that moved. And none of the guys on-board really made her get the urge to rumble in the sheets, and none of the guys really took much notice of her except Mal. She didn't want sex to fill the void. That wasn't really healthy.

"I'm not sure how, but it looks like someone tampered with the engines. I know none of us did it, but there was no way it just happened all of a sudden. It doesn't make any sense."

Mia paused by one of large open doors. Glancing inside, it seemed to be the anteroom to the engines. She continued pass the door, but stopped and leaned against the wall next to it. Eavesdropping wasn't something to be proud of, but it was something interesting and – because she was stuck on this ship too – impacted her.

"Then who could have done this? Ain't nobody got the know-how to do the damage that's been done. It'll take us a week just to fix 'er. We don't got the parts."

"Help."

Again, she heard that strange voice. It must have been one of the engine repairmen that she heard earlier. It made sense now that she heard the voice when she was next to them and they were talking about the problems. She didn't know how she'd help, but she'd try.

Mia took a deep breath and stepped into the doorway. "Is there any way I can help?"

The three guys turned and looked at her, confused either about who she was or why she was there. They stared at her for a while before staring at each other. It seemed like they hadn't been talking to her, but that didn't explain what she heard then.

"Ain't nothing you can do. You're what... medical?"

She shook her head. "No, I'm navigation."

Again, empty stares.

"I'm just going to go. You're probably right and there's nothing I can do because I don't know a thing about the engines."

They didn't say anything and the silence really got awkward. Mia backed out of the room and kept wandering down the hall. It didn't make any sense. She'd heard someone ask for help, but then the person asking for help didn't want her to do anything when confronted. She was sure that she wasn't just hearing things. They weren't in space long enough for Mia to go that crazy.

Chapter Eleven

Heather slipped out when the nurses changed shift. There was no point in staying in the medical bay when there was nothing that they could do to help. The pain had subsided – with the help of the cocktail of drugs they had pumped into her. There was still the problem of the doctor contacting HQ once communications was re-established. If she could just take command, Heather would order him against doing so. Then, if he broke orders, she could use force to detain him and try to undo the damage of simply inquiring.

She made it to her room without incident. Once inside, there was no way anyone would know that she was there. Heather could hide out until it was her shift and then take control back.

"Heather?" The voice behind her made her stop dead.

Tanaka was the last person that she wanted to see right now. He would send her back to the medical bay. He had sent her off for a bump on her head and – knowing there was something more than that wrong with her – he wouldn't hesitate to stick her in a room of doctors.

"I just want to be in my room," she said without turning around to face him.

"Are you alright?" He asked quietly. "I... I read your file and I, um, know, Heather."

It almost sounded like he was hurt. How did she hurt him? Tanaka wasn't involved with her and they barely spent the time together to be close friends. Even though he snooped through the medical bay's notes, she wasn't really upset. It just meant that she wouldn't have to explain anything to anyone.

"You don't know anything, Tanaka." She opened the door and went inside her room. Heather wasn't quick enough and he came in after her – or maybe she really wanted him to.

Tanaka closed and locked the door behind him. "I know you're pregnant. I... Do you know who the father is?"

That was rich. Her hands balled up at her sides. Was he seriously going to lecture her about sleeping around and getting knocked up like he was her father? "Yes, I know who the father was. The baby's dead."

"What? Oh, god... I'm so sorry, Heather. I didn't know. It wasn't in the file." He genuinely seemed mortified, even though a moment ago he was ready to lecture her.

"Tanaka." She sighed as she sat down on the bed. "It died three years ago."

She watched as he sat down beside her. Tanaka took her hands in his, gently stroking the back of them with his thumbs. He hadn't forced her to look at him, which was a good thing. Heather had a feeling that she was going to have to tell him everything and trust in someone else for once. If the threats were real, at least she could have some security in knowing that Tanaka could defend himself.

"Do you remember our last mission together?" It was a start.

"Yes," he said slowly. "Oh god, you got pregnant then..." Tanaka paused, thinking about something. "It's not mine. We didn't have sex."

God, he really thought that... "No, we kissed and that was a mistake. We were both really lonely and I think you had a little too much to drink that night. But that's not what I'm talking about..." She really didn't want to think about that. "It was the mission I signed up for after that."

She didn't know if she should tell him everything or just keep it to the basic details. Yes, the simple facts would keep him safe and fuckable... Shit! The urges were coming back and Tanaka had locked himself in here with her... and he was holding her... and he was close enough that she could smell his cologne... and if she just leaned in a little she could...

"Heather, what happened on that mission?" He asked gently. "Heather?"

She snapped out of it. Maybe that's something she should start with first. Then they could fuck and she could... no. She had to focus. Sex wouldn't do anything but satisfy the cravings for a little while. Then the urges would come back and Heather would be screwed again, literally.

"Tanaka, I first need to tell you that I'm having strong urges to have sex with you right now."

He stared, blinking at her and her admission. "Um, I, well..."

"Before you overthink it, it's because of what happened and the drugs I've been taking. I wouldn't be going around having uncontrollable sex otherwise." She wasn't sure what Tanaka was thinking. When she risked a glance at his face, he was unreadable. "The vials I had of the drug broke when the ship went into emergency, and that's what was on my shirt."

"Well, that's romantic," he said sarcastically. "So you only want to have sex with me because of some drug?" When she nodded, he had another thing to ask. "So you've never thought about being with me before?"

Heather stared at him, unsure what to say. "You were with Maggie."

"Before Maggie, then. We've known about each other since the academy. What if you told me that you liked me and I'd had done whatever I could to be with you? Think about it like that. Was there ever a time you wanted to actually be with me, without these drugs?"

She didn't want to think like that. Of course she had liked Tanaka, but the idea that all she had to do was say the word and they would have been together was insane. He wouldn't have just dropped a relationship to take her out on a date or go to a work event with her.

"Yea, I have," Heather admitted quietly, "a couple times."

"Heather, I've wanted to be with you for years. That's why I was really excited to be assigned this mission with you. It meant that I'd get to spend time with you and – now that you know it's over with Maggie – maybe see if we had a chance."

"Tanaka –"

"Heather, please just call me Alex." He rolled his eyes. "I've been asking you for years to call me that, but you're just so stubborn."

It felt like the tension broke a little. "Ok... Alex."

"You have no idea how good that sounds coming from you, Heather." He leaned in and kissed her. She started to kiss him back and then moved to straddle his lap. His hands went to her hips as she ran her fingers through his hair.

"Heather," he spoke her name between kisses. "Heather, we need to stop."

She stopped, but barely. "What do you mean stop, Tana-Alex?" She caught herself with his name, only because she thought that if she called him by his given name that he'd let her into his pants. Heather trailed kisses along his jaw, down his neck, hoping that he'd give up on the idea to stop.

"Heather," his voice wavered. It was working. "I want to know..."

How bad she wanted him? That she could easily say. "I want your dick in me so bad, Alex. I need it. I need you. I don't want anyone else. Please, I need it so bad."

Fuck! Alex was so close to pinning her to this bed after tearing those damn clothes off her. He had wanted her so bad for so long and this was a dream come true. The sound of his name on her lips was fucking awesome. This dick was ready to burst through the zipper of his pants.

He wanted Heather, but why was she going to be his now? What happened to her to make her want him in the last five seconds? "Heather, please... need to know," he begged.

When she finally, reluctantly, moved away from his neck and then off his lap, Alex regretted it. He was so damn stupid! He could have asked her after sex. Now he had a raging boner and couldn't focus on anything other than having her beneath him. Then again, if something happened to her and there was a chance of him triggering a memory, Alex wanted to know. Something happened to her. After sex, there was little chance he'd be awake long enough to ask and that was a horrible way to leave things. Especially when Heather had finally gave him a chance to be in the loop.

"I took a mission right after ours with General Ruthesford. I thought it was a great opportunity for me to prove I was a great commander and to show that I was ready to be promoted to something more. We were exploring territory and monitoring a planet's civil war. They were advanced enough to reach space and the Force wanted an update on the likelihood that they could become a threat to us."

Heather folded one leg in front of her on the bed and then started to pick at the fuzzy socks on her feet. These had little orange carrots and white bunnies printed on a purple background. Either this was a highly classified mission – where she was breaking protocol telling him – or she had embarrassed herself in front of General Philip Ruthesford and it was her pride getting in the way of the story.

"The mission was to be six months long. Two and a half months for travel and to set up observations, and then the main objective of the mission. The starship wasn't allowed to hyperdrive too close to the location, due to the war and their ability to detect our travel. We had to come out of hyperdrive almost half a galaxy away and drift through a dozen solar systems. It was all so that we could take advantage of the stealth gear on the starship and make a base within observation range while being undetected. It was a long trip make longer and you know what happens on long trips..."

Oh, he knew where this was going. Like how he already found someone to hook up with on the first day. It made him feel stupid for not realizing that of course sex was coming into her story.

"I was the only pilot, so I was always on the bridge. General Ruthesford doesn't like to use the auto-pilot features and ordered me to stay on my station. It was alright the first few days but then it started to get to me. I didn't have any time to myself and I guess I wasn't thinking right. I should have known better and told the general that I wouldn't have sex with him."

Wait, what? It was General Ruthesford!? Married, straight-laced, by-the-book Ruthesford? He was the only one more anal about rules and protocol than Heather. It just... it didn't make sense.

"The first time was fine. I had thought it was a one-time thing, but he ordered me to meet him the next night. I asked about his wife and doing this behind her back... and he told me to shut the fuck up because I was a worthless cadet on his ship and that this was the thing we do in space – that everyone knew that. He said that he had mistresses, but I was going to be his space bitch. The second time, it was rough. Really rough. I had bruises on my legs and stomach and... and I was so sore that I almost started crying because I had to sit on a hard pilot seat all day. Then he ordered me back the third night. I didn't go. I broke orders and went to my room. He... he came and found me. Ordered my roommate gone and then..."

She had stopped looking at him long ago, but this made her head hang lower. The blood was boiling in his veins. He knew what the general did to her, what she was trying not to say out loud. He raped her that night. Well, it sounded like all but maybe that first time. Alex wondered how long it went on and if she told anyone. He couldn't imagine Heather just taking that, but she suddenly looked so fragile in front of him. He realized, then, that something really had changed about her since their last mission. After you tore down the walls, Heather was missing inside... and that was incredibly sad.

"How many times did he rape you, Heather?" He asked softly. Alex hoped that she wouldn't close herself up now. Not after she opened up this much already. He needed to know more.

It took forever for her to say anything. Her hand had stopped picking at her fuzzy sock. She reached up to brush away a couple tears, and it ate his heart. "Almost every night until I told him I was pregnant."

Fuck! That could have been weeks, maybe months. It probably didn't cross her mind until signs started - well, stopped – popping up. In space, she wouldn't have the routine physical and bloodwork that would have caught it. General Ruthesford had raped her for weeks and got her pregnant. But... Heather said the baby died. The baby that she said was still inside her.

Alex felt like he was going to vomit. For three years, she carried around his dead baby. Why didn't she do anything?!

"I walked into his office room on the ship and told him that I was pregnant. He told me to get rid of it and not to tell a damn soul. He said that if I didn't get rid of it that he would. I was scared. He made threats on my grandma if anything went wrong. I knew I couldn't go to the medical bay because they would probably ask me who the father was for consent. I didn't want to kill the baby because... because it was just a baby. I..." Heather's tears had started to streak down harder and faster. "I couldn't kill it."

He wrapped his arms around her and let Heather cry into his shoulder. It didn't take long for his shirt to be soaked, but he never stopped gently rubbing her back. "Heather, I couldn't blame you. It's just an innocent baby. It didn't know anything."

While Alex rubbed her back, his mind wandered while she cried. If she didn't get an abortion, then how'd the baby die? If she didn't do it, did the general? Why was the fetus still inside her? That didn't seem normal. And why was she taking drugs? Shit... when she said they were because of the pregnancy, Alex had assumed that she needed them to heal because of it. He hadn't thought that she was taking drugs because she was still pregnant.

Now he wondered what Heather had gotten addicted to, and how he could help her.

"What is that drug?" He asked once she had calmed down a little. It still took her a while before she answered him.

"I don't know. The village doctor gave it to me after General Ruthesford sent me on-planet."

"Wait, what?" Alex felt his jaw drop open. "He sent you to a planet knowing there was a civil war going on?"

Heather nodded.

"I think it was his way of taking care of it," she said quietly. "He set me to pilot down a pod with three other cadets. We were supposed to deliver supplies and get someone out – I can't remember who. But I was the only one who could pilot the pod."

"And the ship," Alex interjected. "Guess the general didn't think of that."

"We went down but it was an ambush. Rebel fighters grabbed me and threw me in a prison. They saw the uniform and tried to use me as a hostage to bargain with HQ, but you can imagine what the general did. They had the village doctor in the cell with me. She saw my condition and the bruises from trying to fight the rebels when they took us – well, took me. She made a promise to give me medicine but in the prison cell there wasn't much she could do to help.

"She patched me up the best she could and kept trying to tell me things would get better. After two weeks, I didn't see how anything could get better. I started to get these horrible cramps and then I'd start bleeding. The rebels would tease me or hit me or strip me down to gawk at an alien body... It wasn't long after that when the camp was raided and we were freed by the Libertarians."

She seemed to have calmed down some, even though these must have been painful memories to bring up. If anything, Alex was the one reeling now. The general raped her, backed her into an abortion, sent her to a war-torn planet, and then left her to die. That wasn't what should have been done. Everything he had done was against everything the Force stood for and what they all signed up to do. Alex felt disgusted over what he was a part of – even if it was just being enlisted.

"How did you get off the planet?" Alex wanted her to tell him that they send a pod and a rescue team for her, but he somehow knew that wasn't the care.

"The guys that got deployed with me were waiting back at the pod. I don't know how they escaped and I never asked and it never made it into the mission report. But they were all waiting there when I went to the spot we landed. None of them knew how to pilot. It was really awkward returning back to the ship, and the whole crew seemed to know something wasn't right. I think they all knew we weren't supposed to come back."

Heather just rested her head on his shoulder. The tears had stopped. Now, he really was at a loss for words. Everything just played over and over in his mind on a loop.

"So this alien doctor gave you drugs and you took them because she promised they'd help. It stopped the urges and killed the baby, which is still inside you." He was just trying to process it and ended up saying it all out loud.

"It's not my choice to carry it around," Heather said quietly. It was almost eerie how calm she sounded now, but maybe it was just exhaustion from letting out so much. "I couldn't explain to a doctor why I needed an operation, which would go on my file and he would find out. And I didn't know where to go for a shady surgery."

Alex tried not to crack a smile. "You're not supposed to know where to get a shady surgery. That's not something you should want to have."

He could understand her train of thought. It would be undocumented and done quick. The problem was that it could be done too quickly and too many vital steps overlooked. That was riskier than whatever the general was threatening. A shady operation was almost guaranteed to take her life, and that wasn't something he could ever allow to happen.

"Heather, I want you to know that I'm never going to let anything happen to you. If the general has it out for you, I'll figure out a way to get you out of this. I'll find a way to make it so he can never reach you again. I want to gut the bastard for what he's done to you. Heather, I..." Alex trailed off when he realized that she had passed out.

He sat with her in his arms for a while, just watching her sleep. Since the trip started, this was the first time that she really looked at ease. Alex leaned down to kiss her forehead. He made promises to her, even though she might not have been awake to hear them. She had let him in tonight, and he'd let her into his life tomorrow. Tomorrow, he'd hope and pray and beg her to be his.

"Goodnight, Heather," he said softly.

CHAPTER TWELVE

It was day two and nothing really was changing.

The engines were still down and they were no closer to leaving this planet than they had been when they landed. There were parts missing from spare inventory on the ship, which was probably due to the fact that no one expected the Alphecca to have a problem on her maiden voyage. The scouting group had gone out again, recovering more data and samples. One mineral sample seemed almost a compatible match to some missing wiring, but the crew was unsure how to refine it down to use it. Communication lines were re-opened to HQ, but it was only a one-way connection – at least that's what the technicians reported. They could communicate out, but there was no one responding to know that things were actually working. The crew was a little tense, but the veterans had stories and put their trust in the two commanders to get them safely back home.

Heather hadn't left her room.

Alex said he'd cover her shift. There really wasn't much to do, but there needed to be someone the crew could reach and who could handle the reports. He hadn't stopped worrying about her. Last night, he had stayed in her room, just to give himself the peace of mind by watching over her. A painful wave stuck and turned Heather into a crying ball for an hour. It was probably that pain that knocked her out the second time. She had fallen asleep, but it hadn't been restful. She had whimpered and cried in her slumber. Knowing there was no way to help or ease the pain, Alex laid beside her – his heart breaking and bleeding for her.

"Sir, a cadet's been reported missing. Attempts to reach them by their com device failed."

He rubbed his brow and snubbed out his cigarette. With everything going on, Alex didn't hide the smokes. With Heather holed up in her room, he could smoke on the bridge. He sat up in the captain's chair and turned to address the cadet reporting to him.

"Who has gone missing, and are we sure whoever reported it knows that they're definitely missing and not just somewhere else on the ship?" They hadn't allowed anyone to leave the ship without a spacesuit and, even then, only the scouting party was permitted use of those. Lieutenant Gregor hadn't reported any missing when he departed this morning.

"Yes, sir. It's Cadet Mia Ha and it was reported by Cadet Malcolm Harrison."

Okay, that had his attention. He knew Harrison had an interest in Ha, so if he couldn't find her then there was some legitimacy involved. The guy was a brat, but he didn't come off as the type to file a false report like that. Besides, what could he gain from doing so?

"What's the full report, cadet?" He asked.

The cadet opened up his com device so he could read the notes. "Cadet Harrison was to meet Cadet Ha for breakfast before he departed with the scouting party. She did not show at their designated time and was not in her room when he check. Her roommate reports that Cadet Ha was there last night but didn't see her in her bunk in this morning. Search of the medical bay, cafeteria, and open access areas proved fruitless. When communications attempted to reach her via com device, Cadet Ha was unresponsive."

"She has to be on the ship. There's no spacesuit missing and there's no way she wandered out into the alien atmosphere and lived. Her body wasn't found by the scouting party, so we can rule out her leaving." Not that he expected her to do that or break all these protocols. "Sweep the ship once more. I guess as a precaution, check the docking logs to make sure there was no unauthorized openings."

"Yes, sir." The cadet took his leave.

Alex knew he probably should inform Heather, just to keep her abreast of what was going on the ship. But he knew that she was shoulder-deep in her own issues at the moment. He could handle this and give her a bit of a rest.

"Commander Tanaka." His com device buzzed to life.

"Answering."

"I just left the docking bay and there was an unauthorized opening in the ship's log. Video surveillance picked up a dark haired female leaving at 0200 hours without a spacesuit. Video never shows her returning."

So that meant that she left without a spacesuit and survived longer than she should have. The scouting party hadn't encountered a body and their radius of exploration was expanding. Besides, where could Mia Ha have gone? She couldn't have gotten very far on this strange planet.

Alex headed back towards the commanders' rooms. He debated if it was to check in on Heather or to just relax in his own. He knew that he felt drained. A cadet missing didn't help the situation he was already in, and he was blowing through the packs of cigarettes he'd taken for this trip. He paused outside her door for a moment to listen in. He didn't hear a sound, then he remembered how thick the doors were. There probably wasn't anything short of screaming that would be able to be heard through the door. But he should probably tell Heather about the cadet. If the shoe was on the other foot, he'd want to know.

He knocked on the door, giving pause for a moment, and went inside. She was curled up on the far side of the bed with a warming pad over her stomach. Alex walked over to the bed and laid down behind her. She didn't even flinch or move. Maybe she was asleep.

"Heather?" He spoke softly, just in case she was passed out. Alex knew how hard sleep was to come by right now. "Are you awake?"

"Mhmm." It was a tiny noise, but at least he knew that Heather was awake enough to listen to what he'd say.

"I got a report that Cadet Ha is missing. It seems that last night she left the ship without a spacesuit and hasn't been seen or heard from since. Lieutenant Gregor is out with the scouting party right now. I'm going to have them keep an eye out for her." He felt her move back against him, and he wrapped an arm around her. "I just wanted to let you know what's going on."

He wished the circumstances were different – the reason why he was laying here with her. Everything about it was shitty. He didn't want Heather to be in pain or for a cadet to have gone rogue. He wanted to place a kiss on her neck, hold her tight against him, and talk about their future together. He wanted to turn this shitty moment into a romantic one, but the time just wasn't right. Heather must know by now what he wanted, with him coming around and being this close with her. She must know that he wanted to be more than friends; although, being super close friends was the ultimate low that he'd accept, but only because he'd still have her in a way.

So instead, he asked only the things a close friend could. "How you doing?"

"Little better," Heather said slow and low. "Still get jabbing pains. Got in a nap. I'm just..." He waited for her to continue, but she didn't. Alex thought she might had passed out from exhaustion again, but she started talking again. "I'm just tired... and hungry. Can't go out."

He knew that. There was no way that Heather would make it to the cafeteria, much less a round trip, with food or without carrying food out. She probably didn't want any of the crew to see her like this. It would tarnish the hardcore shell she wore.

"What do you think you'll be able to eat? I'll go get you something." He offered. "They had spaghetti and meatballs on the buffet or sesame chicken and rice. The chef even put together mini cheesecakes."

"Rice."

"Just rice?" She'd starve if she stayed stubborn. "How about just a little chicken? You need the protein and the energy to feel better."

It took a moment, but Heather gave in. He was getting up and heading to the door when she rolled over to look at him and asked him a question that made him stop dead.

"Alex, what are we?"

He knew that she was asking him to define what was going on between them now. For all intents and purposes, they were a couple. They looked like a couple and acted like a couple now, with him taking care of her and how they just were on the bed. But the label was never defined and, excluding Heather's hormonal kiss, they hadn't shown affection for each other.

"We're commanders on the Alphecca, Heather. How could you forget that?" It was a smart ass remark, but it also dodged the question. What if he said they were together now and Heather corrected him? She could make him see that he had all this wrong between them. That was something Alex wasn't sure he was going to be able to handle. He just finally succeeded in getting her call him by his first name. Knowing that nothing could ever exist between them would make that too bittersweet to handle.

"You know." She didn't even try to rephrase the question. Yea, he knew and she knew that he knew. There wasn't really any bush to beat around.

He dropped his hand away from the door and turned to face her. "I want you to be in my life and I want something real. I've wanted that for years. So I'm not going to go screw that up by sleeping around or pushing you too hard and too fast into being something more with me. That's why I don't want to answer that question... Well, that and I don't want to hear your rejection. I just want to take care of you, get you back on your feet, and see you smile again. Without pain."

Heather just stared at him the whole time that he spoke. It was hard to read what was going on in her head, on a good day. Now, pain always had a mask on whatever she truly thought and felt.

"I want to be with you, Alex."

He didn't think he heard her right. Those were the words he waited years to hear. "You want to be with me?" She nodded slowly. "You want to be with me completely. In a relationship. Just the two of us. With me. Dating me?"

Again she just nodded. Heather had opened her mouth to speak but a jab of pain struck her and had her curling back up. He walked back over to sit on the edge of the bed and gently rub her back.

Heather McGrey wanted to be his girlfriend. He could hardly believe that.

Mal heard Gregor take the transmission. He had been standing next to the guy and literally heard the man talking over the com, but he couldn't hear what was being said by the person on the ship. Then the suit's radio crackled on for their scouting group.

"Men, we have an emergency. A cadet has been reported mission. Her photo has been sent to your com devices."

He raised his arm in front of him and activated the hologram sphere on his wrist. Mia's photo from the Force Academy hovered above the device. Shit. She hadn't just blew him off for breakfast. He thought that she was having second thoughts about talking to him or was off screwing some other guy. Shit, man, he hadn't wanted her to really be missing.

"Cadet Ha was reported missing this morning. Surveillance video of the docking bay shows that she exited the ship at 0200 hours without space gear. She's been unresponsive to communication via her com device.

"Because we haven't evaluated the atmosphere's oxygen content, it's unknown if life can be sustained without space gear. We're going to assume that she's still alive, but prepare for the worst. If you see tracks or any sign of Cadet Ha, radio me before continuing. I want us to break into pairs and take paths north, south, east, and west of camp for two miles. Report back. We'll maneuver clockwise and return on the minor compass axis."

Gregor started to name off pairs. He knew that he had to be the one to find Mia. He just had to.

Chapter Thirteen

She groaned as she tried to open her eyes. The spot above her left eye just throbbed though, and the sound of clicking just made it worse. Mia tried to reach up to rub the spot and use a pressure point to alleviate the pain, but her hands were bound. It seemed like she was tied to a post and forced to stay standing. A rope wrapped around her ankles, another was around her hips which trapped her hands, and a third kept her shoulder and back upright against the hard wood.

"He... hel..." She tried to call for help, but her throat was so incredibly dry. Her tongue stuck to her dry, cracked lips.

It was the clicking noise that was worrying her the most. There were a lot of different pitched clicking sounds... and some were getting closer. It took real effort, but Mia was able to open her eyes. She wasn't sure if that made things worse or not. On the post closest to her left, there were four small lizard-humanoids chained and shacked at their wrists. On the post opposite them was a larger, darker-colored version. That one had a muzzle around its mouth, but it didn't look any less threatening. Mia wouldn't doubt that the monster could tear that muzzle to pieces if it wanted to.

But at least she was able to tell that most of the clicking noises were coming from what she guessed to be its offspring, which roamed the length of their shackles. Where they had hues of tarnished gold and seaweed, the parent had flecks of crimson that Mia wasn't entirely sure was natural. It looked to her that those flecks amongst its darker skin were souvenirs from a fight. That had Mia thinking that she might just end up dinner for one of these monsters.

"Stop calling us monsters."

That mysterious voice was back. She hadn't seen anyone else standing around them but, then again, her sight wasn't the best right now. Mia had no idea how they knew she thought of these things as monsters, because she knew that it hadn't been said out loud. Her voice hadn't been able to come out to scream for help, and it wasn't going to suddenly start working to hold a conversation.

"I can hear your thoughts, little one. Call us Dragouul."

Mia turned her head back towards the adult... Dragouul. She just had a feeling that it was that one doing all the talking, but she didn't really know how to communicate with it. Sure, it said that it could read thoughts, but how did one go about talking like that?

"Just think and I shall hear. I am the one who called you, but you seem to know that."

Mia wondered why. Why her? What good was done by getting her caught? Why didn't she remember anything about leaving or whatever caused her head to hurt?

"When I called you, you left on my command. Your mind was weak... no, silent. They fought you when you untie my babies. Sorry they hurt you."

Okay, so that seemed to explain little but, yet, Mia wanted to accept it. It was better than anything she could have dreamt up. Buying a story and believing it were two different things, but if she knew only what she was told then the commanders couldn't punish her for that. It seemed like she had no choice in the matter.

Mia looked around their site more. It looked oddly like a campground site back on Earth. Only, there were strange plants and she couldn't see their captors. Maybe there were none. Maybe this was just a trap. She might be bait for the whole crew and these Dragouuls were going to eat them all.

"No trap. Not for you."

Could Mia even trust this one? There was no way to know if anything it was saying was true or not.

"I am called Azvark. My mate is Cryzka. He is hurt but safe on ship. He is peace talker... diplomat. You trust us. Need your people to free me."

And how was she going to do that? Mia doubted anyone knew that she was gone. At best, Mal would look for her, but that was only because she didn't make it to breakfast. Other than that, no one probably knew that she was gone. No one was going to come looking for her. Even if they left the ship, they had no idea where she was. Hell, Mia had no idea where she was and there was no way to communicate back. She didn't... She had her com device still on. She couldn't reach it, but it was still on her wrist. If Mia could get her hand free, she could operate it and hopefully get a message back.

Growling started off to her left and she realized something big was coming. Two large bear-like elephants with large claws came into their camp area. They caused the babies to stop clicking and growl instead. Although, it looked like the odds were vastly against them, even if the sheer numbers supported them. Mia had no idea how these creatures caught them nor tied them up, but she knew that nothing good could come of it. Either they were going to be killed, or sold. Mia wasn't betting on being the latter. What were those things?

"They're the eidonga. Killer for hire in this part of space. They want my mate. Use us as bait."

One of the eidonga shoved a kid out of the way. It fell to the ground and started to cry. Mia heard the – what she guessed was their mother – click noises as it. She could almost feel the pain and angst over not being able to reach the little kid.

They needed to get out of here. Mia looked over at Azvark. Her hands were also bound behind her and to the post. The only difference was that she had a tail. It might not work, but all Mia needed to do was get that arm free. If Azvark's tail was more

100

prehensile and less like an Earth lizard's tail, there might be a way out of this yet. She wondered what that tail could do.

"Not like these monkeys you think. But I can try. Wait until they go hunt. I try then."

Mia didn't want to think about what these eidonga did for hunting. She knew with claws like those and their actions towards that kid, it couldn't be good. Luckily Azvark didn't elaborate. It seemed like she was a fountain of knowledge too.

Night was falling, it was only a matter of time until they could try to get the com device free. They just had to keep calm and hope they could survive that long.

Chapter Fourteen

The scouting group didn't find anything. That meant that Mia had gone farther than anticipated and outside the parameter they had set. Two miles seemed like a long way to go for a midnight walk. He called in for a scan of the atmospheric oxygen levels when things came up empty. It seemed that there was enough oxygen in the air, just a little less than that of Earth.

Alex paced on the bridge. Communications were still down. Engines were damaged. Mia Ha was still missing. The best they got was a partial footprint but the trail had gone cold too fast. The truth was that they had no idea where Mia Ha was. They didn't know if she was even alive. But, if she was dead, it wasn't because she suffocated.

"What's your plan?"

He turned to see Heather walk onto the bridge. She had a cup of coffee in one hand and the other looked ready to grab onto anything if the pain crippled her. It seemed that getting some food, rest, and lots of coffee into her system worked wonders.

"I've had air samples tested and the air is safe to breathe. I have Gregor taking inventory of our weapons. Outside of the tactical team, I can only ask for volunteers to go out on a recon party. We're going to try to pick up Ha's trail where they found a footprint. It might mean we set up camp for the night, but we need to get out there and find her. Protocol gives her 96 hours before being deemed lost on an alien surface." But Heather probably knew that from the general's mission.

"Hello?" Their wrists crackled with a static voice.

"Was that Cadet Ha?" Heather asked. She brought up her com device and started to run a voice analysis. "It is her!"

"Don't reprimand her yet. We don't know the circumstances," Alex warned. He could already see that she was ready to cite protocols and rules being breached. "The thing to remember is that we need to first find her and then get her back to the ship. Whatever happens after that is going to happen then. It's all priorities."

He tinkered around with his com device, trying to get the thing to trace the location of the call. "Mia, we're here. We hear you. Can you tell us where you are?"

Hopefully the com device would be tracking the call and able to locate her. He glanced over at Heather and noticed that she was still tinkering around with hers. The next second though, the view screen came to life. A crude map pulled up on the display and a large blinking ring signaled Mia Ha's location. The longer they could keep her on the line, the longer their equipment had to triangulate her, and the more exact they were in finding her location and getting to her.

"Held hostage by eidonga. They have a family of dragouuls too. She said her husband is a diplomat. Don't have much time until they get back. We're all tied up."

He caught Heather pacing out of the corner of his eye. He hoped that she was coming up with a plan, because he had nothing if this GPS system didn't pinpoint a location. Maybe Mia could give them some more information to help them locate her faster.

"Mia, do you see anything around you that could help us find you faster?" He waited. Had she gotten the communication back? There was a chance that these eidonga overheard the com device and where taking some kind of action. If they were, then Mia's time was running out.

"No, sir. There's nothing but woods. We're in some kind of camp but I think they made the clearing. They're huge."

Shit. That wasn't good, even not knowing what huge fully meant. They might not have enough bullets to take these things down.

"Heather, can you -" He started, but she cut him off.

"Already on it. I'm having the ship scan the database to see if we have any record of these lifeforms."

The view screen populated the alien profiles, complete with images, when the system found the information files. The dragouuls were easily twice the size of a human, but they were enough of a humanoid that they probably wouldn't cause a huge wave of fear amongst the recon team. The eidonga were even bigger than that, and more ferocious looking too.

Their bite strength was four times that of a great white shark. They had sixteen long, razor-sharp claws, in all, and the strength to slice a person in half. The Force database recommended zero contact with these alien lifeforms and "if crossed upon, nuclear detonation is only approved method of extinction".

The Alphecca didn't have nuclear weapons, but she did have the most advanced defense and targeting systems on any starship. If nuclear detonation really was the only way to deal with these creatures, they were screwed. They couldn't launch a sneak attack and be off the planet by the time these creatures realized Mia wasn't their hostage anymore. Besides, a nuclear detonation would devastate this planet. The wildlife – though alive and a danger – was too fragile to withstand that. They'd end up dooming this planet to a barren existence as a space trash wasteland.

Maybe it wasn't as bad as Alex was thinking. "Mia, how many eidonga are there?"

It was a while before she responded. "I saw two this morning. Azvark says there are three."

Three? Shit... With one, they could risk it and slip them all out under its nose with a bit of luck and some stealth. With two, they could distract one or pit them against each other to escape. A third eidonga just added too much unpredictability.

"Cadet Ha, does this Azvark know of a way to attack and fight these alien lifeforms?"

It was Heather that stepped in and asked that question. He had forgotten that there was another source of information on the other end of the com device. Azvark was probably how Mia knew what these aliens were called, and it definitely was how she knew how many of her captors there were.

There was radio silence again as they waited for Mia. He could just see it happening now – she was compromised, caught, and murdered. This was too much of a risk to have put her life in and now it was all over. It would be the first time Heather or he had lost a cadet or member of their crew.

"She says an acid can blind and burn them. It sounds like citric acid." So an orange could wound these monsters? Alex hardly believed that. "She says titanium bullets... but if you shoot anything enough times it'll die."

Alex glanced at Heather. She had stopped pacing. They had oranges. But titanium? He didn't know. And who was to say that this information from that Azvark was correct? People still thought carrots improved your night vision or how breaking a mirror would curse you with bad luck.

"What do you think?" He asked Heather. "Think we can round up a few dozen oranges?" It was all in jest.

Heather rolled her eyes. "I'm not sure if we should take that seriously or not. They are alien lifeforms, so who knows how non-lethal things will react to them. It wouldn't hurt to rinse everything with orange juice. The worst is that we look like complete imbeciles to the crew."

She did have a point. They were supposed to be veteran commanders that knew how to lead and were supposed to know everything. The crew looked up to them and sought them out for knowledge on everything.

Alex glanced up at the view screen. The blinking circle had gotten much smaller, but it still gave them a quarter mile radius where she could be. They were just going to wing it and hope Gregor could come up with a plan.

"Mia, try to stay calm and avoid suspicious. We're cutting communication in case we give you away. Lines will remain open. We're assembling a recon squad to come get you. You'll get out of this."

Alex hoped that reassured her. When he stepped down off the platform the captain's chair sat on, Heather caught his eye.

"I don't know if she's going to last. The odds aren't good."

She was clearly trying to put a brave face on. It was just that there was no other option. He wasn't going to let Mia become his "Heather".

"Maybe not, but she needed to know that she wasn't alone. I know you probably wished that you had known if anyone was coming for you." That seemed to be the wrong thing to say. Heather turned away from him and started to walk towards the bridge doors. "I just meant that it's nice to be reassured sometimes that things are going to be ok, even if they aren't. The odds aren't horrible – three against like ten."

Heather actually gave a small laugh. "Three that are like the size of ten. Each."

"Okay, but that's beside the point." He walked alongside her, unsure of where they were heading. Heather seemed to have some destination in mind.

"I know, but it still needs to be factored in. I'll put out a message to the ship and see what kind of volunteers we can get. Why don't you go find your weapons man and meet me in the armory in about fifteen minutes?"

She started to walk away, but he stopped her.

"Why are you going to the armory?" That didn't really make sense. There was only one reason to go there than, say, the bridge where everything could be monitored and directed.

Heather tried to give him a glare but, with her current health status, it wasn't as convincing as she probably thought it to be.

"Because I'm volunteering for this mission. That's one of our cadets out there and she's the pilot."

So they were going to risk both their pilots on this mission? Alex wanted to point that out to her, but thought against it. With a broken-down ship, it really didn't matter how many pilots they had. They weren't going anywhere for a long while.

"Fine." He knew that he'd never convince her to stay behind. "But I want you in the rear, away from the scouting lines. If you get another painful attack or feel less than par, I want you to take two cadets and head back to the ship. You can supervise and run the mission from the bridge. Do we have a deal?"

From her silence, Alex knew that she wasn't too happy over it. It was extremely realistic to ask of her, but what made more sense was to lock her in the medical bay. After all, they were still looking to re-admit her. It was only the fact that she hadn't gone to that part of the ship that she managed to be walking free of IVs and tubes.

It was begrudgingly, but she gave the one word response: "Ok."

Chapter Fifteen

Gregor had assembled the scouting party, equipping them first with the munitions. They were the most skilled and probably the only fucking decent shots on the ship. But Mal couldn't argue that there was safety in numbers. They may have said he was stupid, but he was tactically smart when he wanted to be.

Mal watched as people he never saw before came to the docking bay to grab a gun or knife or anything. It was good that so many wanted to help find Mia, but none of them knew a damn thing to actually find her. If anything, they'd just hold his team back.

"Gregor, we can't take these people out. They don't know shit!"

"That's enough, Harrison." The lieutenant was obviously a little tired of hearing the same thing over and over. "Your crew members just want to help. If you were out there, wouldn't you want to know that everyone was on their way to save you?"

"No, sir. I'd want to know that an experienced tactical team was on the way. There's a guy over there with a broom. What the fuck's a broom gonna do?"

It was a slight exaggeration. It was some kind of tube or pipe. It could have even have been a baseball bat, but what it wasn't was a gun. There was no way they would be good for anything except being bait or sacrificed in case of a chase. Mal wasn't the one getting eaten. If it was anyone but Mia, he wouldn't be sticking his neck out.

He gave up for now and went to join the rest of his team. They were more okay with the idea of dragging everyone out for a little walk than he was. This was a bunch of bullshit and he was the only one that was able to realize it.

By the time everyone got equipped with something, the two commanders had joined them in the armory. Commander Dick kept making eyes at McGrey, like he was expecting her to do something like bend over and take it or drop to her knees and suck him off. She didn't look right though, but what did he know?

"We got a transmission from Cadet Ha. She's being held captive with a group of the alien race of dragouul. We've send each of your com devices an image of this race and Cadet Ha's photo." For some damn reason, the fucking prick was being awfully official sounding.

People started gasping as they brought up the images on their com devices. Apparently, these dragouul things weren't all that pretty to look at. Mal watched as a few decided to hand in their weapons and stay behind instead. Maybe they should have sent out an even worse image to scare people away. Mal didn't bother to look at it. There was nothing he wouldn't face and fucking kill. Besides, Mia was gonna be his and that would be hard to do if she was dead.

"Alright, guess now is your last chance to turn back. There's no shame in that. Most of us aren't weapon experts." Commander Prick gave it a couple more moments. Only one or two people had second-second thoughts and left.

"Okay, so we'll get a move on just after a quick word from Lieutenant Gregor. He'll be the one in charge of this mission. Everyone is to listen to his direction." The prick finally stepped aside and let the shorter dark-haired man have the spotlight.

"I am Lieutenant Gregor. I am ex-special forces and a hostage rescue is something I'm very familiar with. Based on your profiles in the Force's data system, and the availability of munitions, you have the weapon that you have. If you notice something, call it out to the team via your com device on your wrists and myself or one of my team will make a decision on action needed to be taken." He paused for a moment and gestured towards Mal and the group. That was how you included and introduced someone, not the fucking pathetic way Commander Prick did.

"Do not shoot unless you're being physically attacked. We do not know all the lifeforms on this planet and cannot risk mistaking an ally as a hostile. The rescue mission also includes that of an alien diplomat's family. Injury or harm to them can possibly result in an intergalactic incident. And, for that, you don't want to be held responsible.

"The goal of this mission is a quick in-and-out job. Stick together and do not wander. Once we're out there, keep talking and communication to a bare minimum. Stealth is what's going to be on our side. Especially when we have three confirmed hostiles, all bigger than a grizzly bear.

"Now, we're not asking you to engage in combat." Gregor paused, probably going over what needed to be said. They weren't fucking training to be in their group. "My team will lead and be held responsible for the actual combat. I am appointing Commander Tanaka and Commander McGrey in charge of securing the hostages. If the opportunity arises, you will lead the group into the camp and free the hostages, returning them to our ship."

He stepped out of the center of the group of people and walked over to grab his combat helmet. "Everyone is to report back to the ship. In the case you become separated, head for the Alphecca. In the docking bay, report to the ship's data log that you have returned by stating your name and rank. She'll catch all your com device identification numbers on the way out, so this way we'll have a roll call of people with us."

Gregor didn't say it but it was so they knew if anyone was left behind. Or dead.

With that, he hit the hatch button to open the docking bay doors. The tactical team fanned out behind him and led the crew forward. Gregor had the full terrain map on his com device, but each of his team had a simpler version to track their location and Mia's. Mal occasionally glanced down to look at the two blinking dots on the screen. They were getting closer, but it was still a long way to go before they got her.

The grass of this planet squished down beneath their feet and, as it started to turn to dusk, the blades got slipperier. It was like the grass was squirting out water or something. The worst part though was how quiet it was. If Mal was a jumpy person, the eerie silence would have put him on edge. He could hear a couple people behind him talking about it. A quick glance over his shoulder shut up the idiots though. Did they not fucking listen to Gregor back in the docking bay?

For a group of almost twenty, they moved pretty quietly. The blinking red dot on their com devices that indicated Mia's location kept getting closer to their own blinking dot. But the closer the group got to Mia, the further they were from the ship... and that started to make whispers of regrets. Mal wanted to fucking groan. Didn't these idiots listen to what the fuck they were signing up for? Damn... He wanted to turn around and tell them to head straight back to the ship, but would have meant he was disobeying orders to stay quiet, and it would disrespect Gregor and his authority. As much as it pissed him off, he kept quiet.

"Something growled over there," he heard someone all but scream into the com device. Seriously? Did they not know a damn thing about how they worked? A whisper would have fucking done it. No! They had to panic and basically tell everyone without using the communication device.

"Roger. Keep voice low," Gregor responded.

The lieutenant's pace slowed, and so did the group. Mal could sense something now. It felt like they were being watched. Everyone – finally! – shut the fuck up. But it was the look on Gregor's face that made him worry for a second. It seemed their leader was a little worried, but then it passed.

"Tactical team, left flank coverage. Potential hos-" Gregor didn't get the chance to finish giving the order to change formation.

Out from the woods on the left came a thundering growl as the beast charged. People screamed and started to run. Mal, the tactical team, and the commanders held their ground. The hairy, spotted beast let out another awful growl. Someone – not pissing their pants scared – verbally confirmed it was one of the eidonga. The good news was that it was alone. The bad news was that it was fucking lethal. They had no way to know how these fucking things attacked. It was large enough that it didn't need to use smart ambushing tactics against small humans.

Mal pulled out his service rifle and got the beast in his scopes. He was best as a sniper, but the damn thing wasn't going to give him a chance to set up and put the thing down. He lifted the gun and took aim, waiting on the orders to fire.

The beast was charging them, getting yards closer every second, but Gregor wouldn't give the command. Mal could see the fucking whites of its three eyes and see the blood stains on the razor-sharp looking claws that just cut through the ground. It was tearing up the place and it was going to tear them up. His finger itched on the trigger, ready to disobey orders.

"Now!" The order finally came.

All eight of them emptied round after round into the big – fucking ugly – eidonga but it was still coming at them. It was charging straight towards the center of the remaining group, which was right where the two commanders were. The prick, Mal couldn't care less about. But that tight ass McGrey, he didn't get to bang her yet and it would be a pity to let that die. If he saved her then she'd have to fuck him to show how damn much she appreciated him saving her life.

He tucked the butt of the rifle against his shoulder and aimed for the eye socket on his side of the fucker's ugly head. He pulled the trigger and a bullet ripped through the target, popping the eye in a bloody mess. The beast stopped dead... then turned and started charging Mal.

Shit!

He had thought that its skull might be like a human's and that was the weakest spot. The bullet would tear through and blow up the brain. That wasn't the case this time.

Mal pulled the trigger to put the beast down, but nothing fired. Fuck! His magazine was empty. He reached for the extra one on his hip, but the eidonga was already breathing down his neck. It spun and kicked him with its back legs. Mal went flying. A tree stopped his trip, but broke at least one rib. He landed on top of his rifle. There was no way he'd be able to get it out from underneath him, reload, and fire off a shot before that bloodthirsty fucker was on him again.

It came at him, slightly slower as if it was stalking a wounded creature. Mal struggled and tried to get his rifle free. He wasn't going down without a fight. The eidonga reared up on its back feet, freeing its claws to attack and finish him off. One blood-stained paw drew back to swipe at him. Shots rang out and the next time Mal looked at the thing, it was on dead on the ground. Behind where it once stood was McGrey, pistol still raised.

Well, fuck him. The last thing he expected was for one of them to step in. Gregor, yea, but only because they were on the same team. He knew the prick didn't have it in him. But he hadn't expected McGrey to be able to take a shot. He was happy and more than grateful to be alive, but there went his plan to get for to bang him. Unless she was a fucking dominatrix, he couldn't see how being on his knees to thank her would lead to fucking. Although, there was an image...

"Are you okay, Cadet Harrison?" She had holstered the pistol and held a hand outstretched to help him up.

He didn't want to take her help and come off as a weakling, but he also didn't want to put her off. It seemed like maybe a step forward in getting her to like him. So Mal took her hand and let her help him back onto his feet. He winced though, but she hadn't caught it. The prick did though.

"What's wrong Harrison?" He came over to ask. The question drew the attention of his team and Gregor.

That was the last fucking thing he wanted on him right now. He'd rather have McGrey riding his cock and cracking a whip over his ass. If Gregor didn't think he was fit for duty or that his judgement was clouded in pain, he'd be ordered to return to the ship and end his mission. He couldn't take a risk on that.

"Bruised rib." Commander Prick eyed him. Mal knew it was broken. He'd felt this pain before, but he couldn't let the fucking idiot know. Out of the corner of his eye, he could see the look on Gregor's face. His commanding officer knew what was going on, but it looked like he was going to let Mal slide with this. At least for now.

Commander Dickwad threw back. "Can you even walk?"

"Tanaka, he said it was a bruised rib," McGrey interjected. It seemed like taking her help had been a fan-fucking-tastic move. "Lieutenant Gregor will make the call to send him back to the Alphecca. We need to get to Cadet Ha."

The look on his face was clear – he hated the fact that McGrey stepped in and cockblocked him. Mal grinned as he took the moment to reload his rifle. He was loving this.

"Harrison, you hang back a little and stick with the group," Gregor ordered.

He glanced around to see that some of the crew had returned. They probably felt safer with them than running off to who knew what the fuck in the woods. Any other time, Mal would have fought the order, but he was able to recognize it for what it was. Gregor would let him stay, but his duties had been cut to babysitting. He'd just have to man up.

"These eidonga are dangerous creatures, even with our weapons. We're going to need to take a slightly better tactic to get the hostages free," the weapons master spoke, mainly, to the commanders. "Harrison's the best shot on the team. We get him to set up his rifle and snipe out the hostiles."

The commander seemed to agree with that minor detail of the plan. It was one of the crew members that had ran away that spoke up now.

"What if one of those... things, attack us again? We don't have time to do anything."

A valid point, but it seemed that Gregor already had something in his head about that. He turned to McGrey. "How'd you take that monster down?"

"It turned and I had a clean shot at the base of its head. I took a risk."

"A risk that paid off." Gregor walked over to the dead alien's body. He made a loop around it. "Bullet wounds to the torso seem to be non-lethal and impact dampened by the thick fur. A few strays found homes in the legs and paws, but nothing there. Shot to the eye appears to have stopped at embedment in the skull. Their anatomy is a hard one to find weaknesses. In the case one attacks again, we empty all we can from our guns until it stops moving."

He turned to Mal. "Take a quick look at the body. Find your targets, but keep in mind what Commander McGrey said."

With that Gregor commanded another cadet to take samples from the dead eidonga for research aboard the ship. He also had the cadet pull out an orange they were carrying to see if the citric acid was a rumor or not. Gregor squeezed the orange over the eidonga's body – open wounds and untouched skin. The places where the orange juice hit sent up little bits of smoke, like someone had started a teeny tiny fire on the beast's skin.

"It seems that the information was correct." It surprised them all, and it made them look like less of a fool now for sprinkling orange juice all over their ammunition now. "We're to proceed with caution. Get a move on!"

What was left of their rescue party followed after Gregor and the team. Meanwhile, Mal struggled to keep up with his broken rib. He had to push himself now that everyone knew how fucking bad he was needed on this team... on this mission... everything. Someone finally acknowledged what he was trying to tell them all the fucking time – he was fucking awesome!

This time, nobody was saying a word. He kept his eyes open for tracks and ambushes, but nothing seemed out of place since the last time they scouted. Then they were out of the scouting loop and into new territory. The terrain was basically the same as it was a quarter of a mile back. They kept moving silently forward until someone whispered into their com device that smoke was sighted. It was a faint grey line against the darkening blue shy. It was probably a camp site where they had Mia. Everyone else seemed to think so too.

"Harrison, Trebold, Veiner... scope out the situation. Set up to snipe if it's our hostiles. Report back immediately."

All three nodded to Gregor's orders before moving out. Trebold and Veiner were two of the best guys on the team, and two guys that weren't sporting broken ribs. It made it hard to keep up with them, for once, and they didn't give Mal any special consideration. They were real fucking men. Their "tough love" kept Mal going and pushing himself.

They slowed about two hundred yards back from the smoke. They couldn't just go running in and bang around the place. That would ruin any chance of sneaking up on these fucking eidonga. With two left, they needed the element of surprise more than they had thought. Those beasts didn't drop easy.

Mal pulled up his rifle to his face and looked down the scope. He tried to see if he had a clear line of view to the campsite. There were a couple trees that would give him problems, but he couldn't really make out any hostages.

"I'm getting nothing," he whispered into his com. "Gotta move closer."

The group inched up a few more yards and Mal tried to scope out the area again. He had a line of sight that saw the little aliens and Mia next to a bigger, uglier version. He could also see one eidonga at the site next to the fire.

"I got a visual on one target and the hostages. Clear line of sight. Setting up," he reported to the team.

"Let Trebold and Veiner get closer and report back. Take the shot if you need to before then. Identify the location of the second hostile." Gregor's voice came in over the speaker in their helmets.

While he set up his sniper station, his two team members slowly proceeded towards the site with guns raised and ready. Mal got on his knees and then laid on his stomach behind his rifle. He inched up and into position so that his eye was just glancing down at the scope. He turned the rifle in its stand towards Trebold and Veiner, who were approaching from the right side of the camp now. Mal watched as they circled around to where the hostages were.

"Second hostile not in campsite. Tracks led off to the north. Hostages within reach. Orders to proceed?"

Mal moved the sights away from his team members and back onto the eidonga still in the camp. He had a clear shot. It was just to wait for the order.

"Take the shot. Initiate hostage recovery. Proceed with caution and rendezvous with rescue party."

That was all he needed to get the blood pumping. Mal could feel the excitement building over being able to do what he fucking did best – blow away motherfuckers. He planted the crosshairs between its outside eyes. Taking a deep breath, he let it out slowly. Once all the air had left his lungs and he was calmed, Mal pulled the trigger.

The fucking beast let out a god-awful screech. Even being as far away as he was, it still hurt his ears. Half of its head was blown away from the heavy sniper round, but that hadn't been enough to kill it. Mal lined up a second shot when voices crackled over the headset.

"Second hostile incoming."

"It must have heard that fucking thing."

"Can't get hostages."

"It's coming!"

Mal swung his scope and saw the second fucking alien. It must have spotted Trebold and Veiner because it was heading towards that side of the camp. If it kept going, he'd lose the clear line of sight and end up having to shoot around trees blind.

The thing had its back to him but he knew where McGrey had shot, so he wasn't going to watch two guys of his team being shredded to bits. He planted the crosshairs at the base of the fucking alien's skull and pulled the trigger. It dropped with one shot, while the other one screeched louder having realized what happened.

"Ain't no fucker coming to save you. Damn alien..." He lined up another headshot and finally silenced the screeching.

"Good shit, Harrison," he heard Trebold over the headset. "Rescuing hostages now."

Mal knew that he should dismantle the sniper setup, but he couldn't resist something. He lined up the scope and slowly moved it over all the little alien dinosaur people. Then he put the crosshairs on the big ugly one. Slowly he moved it to Mia. Her face was full of fear, but he watched it change as the two guys moved into the campsite and untie them. He needed her to know that it was him that fucking saved her. At least one woman on the Alphecca was going to be on her knees praising him over being their fucking white knight.

He waited a couple minutes longer before dismantling the sniper station and heading back to rejoin the rescue party.

Mia couldn't understand what was happening at first. The eidonga guarding them had suddenly started screaming and she swore it busted her eardrums. It was so painful that her whole body cringed, trying to curl up to protect itself. She had closed her eyes and hadn't know it was shot, but she had felt the ground rumble as the other one came running back into the camp. It sounded like a bunch of other things happened, and then it was silence. Well, except for Azvark's babies who were frantically clicking messages between them and their mother.

When Mia felt like she could open her eyes again, she saw two dark figures coming into the camp. At first, she panicked thinking they were more aliens coming to do worse things to them. She realized they were from the ship and were talking to their com devices. It seemed like forever, but one of them finally freed her. Her arms tingled as blood started to flow again and she wasn't sure that her legs could stand.

"There's a another one... don't know where." She needed to warn them.

"We know, Cadet Ha. Commander McGrey took care of it back with the rest of the rescue party."

So there were more than just these two guys? It took her a moment to realize that of course there'd be more people on a rescue team and that, of course, she'd be rescued.

Mia just nodded that she had heard him and followed the guy as he got the others freed. Her mind wasn't all there as they headed back. She kept thinking of hundreds of things. She hadn't noticed that they had caught up to a third dark figure, let alone that they were walking next to her.

"You ok?"

The voice startled her out of her thoughts. She glanced over to see Mal next to her, and it didn't make any sense. She couldn't think of a reason that he would be here. He wouldn't risk his life for hers. Would be?

"Mia? You alright up in there? You're kind of zoning out on me."

"Yea," she tried to snap herself out of it, "I just can't believe you're here."

He chuckled. "Of course I am. This is my team, and I couldn't let you die." His face grew a huge shit-eating grin. "I'm the one that downed those two huge fuckers that had you. Those beasts aren't easy to drop either. I'm just that good."

She just nodded in agreement. To be honest, she wasn't processing all that he was saying. Mal didn't seem to notice anything other than her agreeing with his self-compliment. Not that she was still in shock. Like how she had no idea when their small group doubled in size or how they managed to get back into the ship. She had no idea how she ended up in his room or how she ended up naked or what happened. But she woke up with two big arms wrapped around her in the middle of the night.

CHAPTER SIXTEEN

The pain was getting unbearable again. Heather could barely make it ten feet without having to slow her pace and breathe through it. All the while, she had Alex watching her. There were other people watching her, but mostly because they wanted the chance to walk beside her and thank her for killing the eidonga. She tried to focus on each crew member as they replaced the last one, just to focus on something other than the pain.

"You're in a lot of pain, little one."

She heard something, but dismissed it. No one could see that on her face in the semi-darkness of their walk back. Besides, Heather didn't recognize the voice. For all she knew, it was a trick of her mind or a delusion caused by the pain to make her think about her pain again. And it had worked. Her mind remembered the pain, focused on it, and it got harder to make it through the journey back to the Alphecca.

"Let me help you."

Again, she thought that she heard something as they were walking in through the docking bay doors. This time, Heather actually glanced around. Most of the rescue party were men. While the voice didn't sound male, it didn't exactly sound female either. She could rule out Cadet Ha. The poor girl seemed to be in a fog the whole way back. The other woman that was in the party was talking to someone else. And the dragouuls hadn't made a sound.

"I don't need to talk for you to hear me."

The hair on the back of her neck was standing on end. She turned around too fast to try and catch the source of the voice. It did nothing but cause her midsection to twist and spike up the pain. She actually cried out as she lost her balance and started falling. Alex caught her and helped her to the floor.

"Everyone's dismissed after they give their reports to Lieutenant Gregor. So go report to the armory," Alex ordered.

People were reluctant, but they did eventually dispersed. It left the two commanders alone, with the dragouul family. He took it as they didn't understand English. Besides, they appeared to be harmless.

"Heather, I can try to get you back to your room and get a heating pad from the medical bay. Do you think you can last that long?"

It had been what helped before, but she was too far gone for a heating pad to help this time.

"Don't fight us."

"I'm not fighting anything," she groaned.

"Heather, what are you talking about? No one's asking you to fight something." Alex stared at her, confused. "I knew I should have made you stay on the ship," he deadpanned.

One of the little dragouuls walked over and placed a scaled hand on Heather's forehead. She moved to push it away, but everything started to feel warm and the pain lessened. Heather started up at the tiny creature, so confused as to what was going on.

"My... daughter has touch abilities. She wants to help the little one."

The little one? Heather couldn't understand how they could help a dead baby. But the voice corrected her. She was the "little one" to them, even though she was taller than the children. For now.

The pain started to disperse, or at least go back to a manageable level. The little dragouul turned to the mother, chirping, and walked over to hug the large alien's leg. Heather could picture it as a little child getting praise from a parent for doing a good job. The little girl certainly did a good job if Heather felt like she was good to try moving again.

"Thank you."

Alex's confusion was written clearly all over his face. "Thanks for what? I didn't do anything, Heather."

"Not you." She moved cautiously and got back to her feet. "Thank you for whatever you did. It helped a lot," she told the little dragouul. Hopefully she'd be able to understand what Heather said. Although, it seemed like they could understand her thoughts, and those were in English.

"Heather, let's just get you back to your room to lay down. You need to rest." He secretly thought she was crazy. The family hadn't said a word the whole time, only some clicking noises that no one could understand. "I think you're just tired."

She started to walk away with him, hearing him tell the family that he'd be right back to help get them situated on the ship. Maybe she was just tired and all this was in her head. Shit! That meant that she just made a fool of herself – and in front of a diplomatic family too! People didn't just hear voices. Cadet Ha had talked to the adult dragouul, but Heather hadn't heard any real words so she must have been crazy. Crazy and a fool.

"*Little one, I can hear your thoughts. Not fool.*"

The voice was quieter this time, barely more than a whisper. If they could read her mind, then that must really be how they communicated. So why hadn't they talked to Alex? She tried to will her thoughts to Azvark, but realized maybe it was the distance that weakened and quieted the voice. She slowed her feet to a stop to try and buy her some time within the radius of Azvark's mind reading ability.

"Heather, come on. We need to get you laid down before you have another attack," Alex tried to coax her along, but she was determined.

"*Can hear male thoughts but can't speak. They close their mind.*"

"You can't hear the dragouul talking." It wasn't really something directed at Alex. It was more of her mind talking out loud. "They can hear what you're thinking but they can't talk to you because you're a male."

She turned to face Alex. "You know what that means, right?"

"That I can't hear anything?" He offered. It just made her story seem that much more certifiable.

"No. You can't hear them. They've only talked to Cadet Ha and me." Heather wasn't sure why that idea stuck with her.

Alex managed to get her moving again while she was distracted with her thoughts. He got her all the way back to her room before she came out of it. She could see that he still didn't believe her and that was what hurt the most. He had so easily accepted her story about what happened on the general's mission that landed her in a painfully semi-pregnant state but not that an alien lifeform could communicate telepathically only with females.

It was a long shot, but maybe there was one way to convince Alex that she was sane. "Can you go check on Cadet Ha? Just talk to her… make sure she's okay."

Alex nodded. It was an easy enough request. He'd go check in on the status of their cadet and Ha would let it slip that the dragouuls read her thoughts. It would all work itself out.

"I'll swing by and check on her after I go get you a heating pad. I know I haven't been around you long enough to really say, but I know you're going to get another one and it's going to be worse. They always come in pairs."

It really was too soon for him to know anything about what she was going through, let alone to expect what was coming. So far, Alex had only been around for the first smaller waves. The last one that had her crippled on the floor was a bigger one. It wasn't the worst she ever felt, but it was painful and it didn't come in pairs. It just never stopped.

How was he going to explain in his ship log that Heather had gone insane? If he logged that, it would be on the record and damn her career. It would follow her onto every mission until they stopped assigning her missions altogether. She'd be passed through the Force's psychologist and therapist, and that might not even help her recover. It might cost Heather her career. The only thing logging this would do would be to ensure that she hated him.

Alex couldn't do that to her.

He headed back to where he had left the alien family. They were all sitting on the floor in the docking bay, waiting around like it wasn't a big deal. At least they were reasonable, unlike Heather and her delusions. Maybe it was the alien air of this planet that made her mind slip. No, because then his would have had to start cracking, which it hadn't. No one else seemed to be affected by it either.

"Sorry that took so long. Right now, I'm not sure there's a room big enough to accommodate you all. I'm going to see what we can do to make sure you're all together. I don't know what your kind typically eats, but we have a cafeteria on-board that I can show you to. I'm sure those eidonga didn't exactly feed you while you've been held hostage. Then again, I'm probably sure that you wouldn't want to eat what they had."

Alex stared at a room full of silent alien beings. Even the kids weren't making a sound. In a way, what Heather said sort of made sense. If they did some mind reading thing, he might not hear what they were saying. But that couldn't be what it was. Maybe it was a language barrier.

"We understand, human male," the large one finally spoke. "We hear you but you don't hear us."

Shit... Heather wasn't crazy.

"Lots of words on here bad for my babies' minds."

Shit! He meant *crap*. He meant... Whatever they could hear or read in his head had made a couple of the small ones chirp between themselves. Or maybe it was just a coincidence.

"So you can understand English... right?" The large one simply nodded. "And your name is Azvark... right?"

"Yes. I am called Azvark and my mate is called Cryzka."

Something to that story was missing. So Alex asked, "Where is your mate?"

It took a moment for the alien to respond. It almost did seem to want to. "On our ship. I sense he is hurt but will live. The eidonga attacked us to get him. I do not know if it is safe."

Okay, so they were here on a ship and there was at least one more of these dragouuls somewhere. It was reasonable to assume that Azvark would want to meet back up with her mate, but that was something that Alex knew he couldn't guarantee. He had to worry about the safety of his own crew first, and no one might want to volunteer for this mission. Then there was the fact of not knowing where this other ship was. The scouting party hadn't come across it, so Alex knew that it had to be located far from the Alphecca.

"I can't make any promises, but we can try to contact your mate. Our techs should have communication lines open soon enough and we can send a message to your ship. Your mate can at least know where you are and that you're all safe."

"Then we cannot stay." Azvark glanced at her babies for a moment. It was as if something was on her mind that took a while to decide upon. "You say something wrong with ship. If you get my mate, we will give you our ship for parts. All you need to do is promise to take us home."

It was the solution to their problems. Reunite a family and then they'd be able to go home. Do nothing and these dragouuls may leave them abandoned on this planet. It was risky. They were flying blind either way. Then there was always the possibility that the dragouul ship wasn't compatible with theirs and everything would be pointless.

"The little one. One you call Heather. You care about her. Is she your mate?"

That was out of left field. "Uh, um..." How was he supposed to answer that? And why was this being asked? It was awfully odd and personal, but then he remembered they could read thoughts.

"My baby can keep pain away. We can't fix but we can help your mate."

Alex realized how far from left field it actually was now. Azvark was bringing more to the plate to get the deal to swing in her favor. He had to hand it to her, though. For only being a diplomat's wife, she sure knew how to get the deal she wanted.

"First, I want to contact your ship. You need to let your mate know that you're alright and we need to know his location. Any insight as to the general surroundings would be great, and he might be able to warn us of any dangers we might find." He didn't want to make this a fool's errand if the alien wasn't alive.

Alex heard a couple of the kids chirping and he would even say that it sounded sad – then he realized that he had accidentally thought that these children's father was dead and they heard that.

Sorry.

He needed to continue saying what his plan was, quickly, so that he could get away from these dragouuls and not feel guilty over the not-so private thoughts he was having. At least he wasn't thinking about Heather and how she'd feel like underneath... *Shit!* Azvark – he swore – gave him a death stare. Okay, so he wasn't the only one that desperately wanted some space between them.

"Once we get in touch with your mate, I'll assemble a team to rescue him, much like the one that rescued one of our cadets and your family. They'll escort your mate back to the Alphecca – our ship – and our medical crew will attend to whatever wounds he may have. After everyone's safe, then we'll see about repairing our ship with parts from yours and getting us all home."

Azvark nodded, but she glanced again over at her children. "I want one to go with your team. Cryzka needs to see us. He do not know you. My baby will take him home."

"Send one of your children with my tactical team?" That was complete ludicrous. "We just saved your children and you're willing to send one back out there in harm's way?"

She nodded. "The eidonga are no more. My baby will protect your team. Cryzka see baby and won't attack."

Alex hadn't really considered that part. He'd guess if a bunch of aliens – to these dragouuls – with weapons stormed aboard his ship that he'd feel hostility too and probably try everything he could to take them out and defend himself. Even though the dragouuls seemed to be on their side, if they walked through the docking doors in any other scenario that would probably be what he'd do.

"As long as your child listens and follows what my men tell it. I also can't be held responsible if it gets itself hurt. My team will defend itself, but they're not babysitters." He watched her stare long and hard at her children. Probably thinking that what he said was a risk and really not a guarantee of anything. Alex had only meant it as if they got a papercut or some small injury that he couldn't be held to blame because at least they weren't shot or mauled or eaten by some plant creature.

"It is agreed. Bilfa will go."

He watched as the one that helped Heather stepped forward. Maybe it was his own stupidity or maybe Azvark was really much better at this bargaining thing than he first thought. Bilfa was the only one – that he knew of – that could help Heather. If something happened to her, Heather wouldn't get any relief. The stakes were just raised.

"Let's go to the bridge and see if we can make contact then." He couldn't help but feel a bit outsmarted. Alex didn't have an ulterior plan or motive. It was ridiculous to feel this way other than his ego was bruised a little as how quickly his weakness was known and how wrapped around their claws he was now.

Crewmembers that weren't on the rescue team stood and gawked at them as they passed by in the corridors. Alex could overhear a few things they were saying, enough to know that everyone was frightened of the group following behind him. That meant that everyone behind him also had heard what he had, and probably more because they could also hear the thoughts that didn't escape their mouths. He just prayed that the alien family could hold it together and ignore them. There was enough tension already between the crew over the crash – then add this alien family and their missing, wounded father.

Unlike the rest of them, Alex had the extra burden of knowing the state of his girlfriend. Yea, if he was doing all this – a significant part for her – then he thought he earned the right to call her that. Whether Heather like it or not, she was his girlfriend.

The large doors to the bridge swooshed open and allowed the group to progress. The bridge was empty, except for two technicians working up front by the view screen. Out of habit, Alex went to sit in the captain's chair, only he was outran by two little dragouul children who started to climb all over it, chirping at each other. It took a moment to compose himself.

"We need to make contact with another starship on this planet. Have you opened up the communication lines?" Alex addressed the two men, both of whom were now staring at the dragouul children fighting over his chair.

One of the men seemed to register they were being questioned. "Yes, sir. We've restored on-planet communications and local space lines. In approximately thirty minutes, all communication lines will be open and we'll report archived transmissions back to HQ Base."

Not the best news, but it was still good enough for what Azvark needed from him. Although, that last part about reporting the archived transmissions worried him a bit. Alex knew that each transmission that they had attempted to send to HQ Base was archived until the system was functioning again or in range to transmit. That was just standard-issue protocol on starships these days. What worried him was what someone could learn from those reports – if they were the ones behind the sabotage. They could find out their current state and send something else their way to ensure they didn't return – which Alex was going to assume was their goal. If someone actually *did* sabotage the Alphecca. It was hard to believe that a brand new starship would break down on her maiden voyage.

"I want all transmissions sent to my com device before being reported back to HQ Base. I want to ensure they follow protocol and aren't hour long messages of frantic screaming or dead air." It was a small lie to cover his tracks and ensure the correct information got out. Besides that, he had no idea what medical or any of the other officers could have reported out about Heather. For now, he needed to protect her.

Azvark gave him a knowing glance. Of course she would know his motives. At least he could assume that she was sure that he wasn't the one to have sabotaged them, if she truly could read all his thoughts.

"There's a dragouulian starship on this planet. I need a full communication line to it with two-way audio and video displayed up on the view screen."

The men didn't make a move, at first. It wasn't an impossible request, just a difficult one. They'd probably need to consult with the translator on-board to find out speech patterns and maybe the navigator to determine possible exit coordinates the starship may have had, assuming it came in the direction of the home planet. At this stage in the Alphecca's system renewal, it probably would put her at full capacity to do a planetary lifeform scan of those parameters to locate the dragouulian starship. All that would take an enormous amount of time.

"Now," Alex pressured. He worried that time wasn't going to be on their side.

The men turned and hurried the work they had been doing before one called on his com device for the navigator. It took him a moment to realize that the cadet assigned to navigation was Mia Ha and, of course, the veteran member of the crew to supervise was Heather.

"Fuck," he muttered under his breath. He couldn't help it this time, no matter what Azvark thought of it.

The curse also caught the attention of the men, who stopped and stared at him for a moment. Both Mia and Heather weren't available. There was no telling if anyone else aboard had the necessary training to complete the scans. Cadet Ha definitely couldn't make it to the bridge in her condition to get the system running. That only left Heather, but she was probably doubled over in pain and incapacitated without that heating pad he promised her.

His eyes glanced over towards the dragouul children. One of them – unfortunately he couldn't remember which – had been able to ease the pain. It had been a temporary fix, but it still could give Heather enough time to get the scans done without anyone else noticing that their co-commander was unfit for duty.

Azvark caught his eye and gave a nod. Of course she would understand his longing gaze over her children and know what he was thinking. It was just a minor problem of getting Heather here without breaking apart.

"Ghani, I need you to escort one of the dragouul children to Commander McGrey's room." One of the men paused, setting down a wrench and wiping off his hands.

"Sir, I do not understand. Your orders were to complete the repairs and establish communication lines. I cannot do that and take that child to the commander. I do not know why you are asking this."

Of course he wouldn't understand. "Now your orders are to take one of them to McGrey. Doing that gets us a navigator that can find the dragouul starship. Cadet Ha is in the medical bay and not going to respond."

Alex could see that the man was reluctant to go anywhere alone with one of these aliens. It's not like he could be blamed. Under different circumstances, Alex would feel the same way. However, the dragouul family had already proved what side they were on and were giving up a lot just to aid them.

"Try to keep your mind clear or at least PG," he called after them. It was probably a futile warning. The mind was a hard thing to keep clear and decent.

"And we now wait." Azvark uttered his thoughts with a simple glance his way.

Alex nodded. "Now we wait."

Heather wasn't hunched over in pain nor was it anywhere on her face. He watched her walk in with the dragouul kid and a very confused technician. Chances were that there had been a lot of screaming before Heather left her room. Of course, there probably weren't any answers given. The alien children were too young to verbally speak our language and the commander definitely wouldn't want anyone else knowing her business. Alex hadn't – and wasn't – going to offer up an explanation.

"Bilfa told me a little of what's going on," Heather told him quietly after approaching the captain's chair that he had just reclaimed from the bickering children.

He was watching the technician return to his post, but gave a quick nod. "Yea, we need a bio-scan of the planet to locate dragouul genetics and route the ship's communication lines on those coordinates and hope we get a signal." Alex glanced up at her. She seemed to be ok. "You know, easy peasy lemon squeezey."

Heather rolled her eyes. "Should I enter the coding blindfolded too?"

He knew that the task was far from easy, but he had hopes that Heather could do some magic and make it work. Turns out it was still a tall order if her sarcasm was coming out.

She walked over to the navigation station to reboot it. From his perch, he watched the monitor run a system scan, but he mostly watched her. Alex wanted to believe that she was okay. He wanted to believe that the past few hours were all a dream and that he never saw her face contort in pain. Whatever the alien kid did was almost too good to be true.

Heather got the computer up and running, but the screen was far from what he was accustom to seeing it display in-flight. Maybe that was just because they weren't in space. Maybe it was just because they couldn't get the starship's system back running. Maybe this was all a lost cause and Heather couldn't even pull out this miracle.

A bunch of clicking came over the bridge. It would have meant nothing to Alex, but he saw all the dragouul kids stop dead. Everyone's attention was on the front view screen. It took a moment before a visual could match the audio, and Alex almost regretted it instantly.

The huge face of the dragouul male blipped up on the screen. More sharp prawns lined his jaw and crowned his skull than his mate, Avzark. His coloring was darker and grittier, like a camouflaged killer unafraid to spill blood. The glowing ember eyes against the darkness didn't dissuade that instinctual feeling.

Alex had heard Heather gasp when the view screen jumped alive. The technicians had actually screamed out in surprise before backing far away, as if the dragouul could simply reach through and grab them. Then there were the children – all of whom had ran up to the screen to get closer to their father. Loud clicking to his right caught Alex's attention, startling him for a moment before realizing it wasn't the intimidating male but Azvark making the sound. It was the first time that he heard her communicate in a way that wasn't verbal English. Their telepathy obviously couldn't work over communication lines, or at great distances. For once, that worked to his advantage – the male had no idea how terrified Alex was of his appearance.

"Cryzka said he stopped the bleeding of his wound but finds it hard to move. He expresses gratitude to your crew for the rescue and has agreed to part with our ship." She spoke for a moment before clicking more. "If you can spare a pilot, the ship can come closer."

Spare a pilot?

Cadet Ha was still in the medical bay and in an unknown condition, seeing as he never got around to check up on her after putting Heather to bed. Of course their starship wasn't moving, so that freed up Heather for the mission. Even if she doubled-over in pain, Azvark had requested one of her kids go with the recon team so that her mate wasn't startled by aliens invading his ship. Although, her mate could see what these "aliens" looked like now via the view screen and should be able to figure out not to attack the things that looked like him, Heather, or the cowering technicians. But that meant putting Heather in harm's way again. She already had him worrying enough and now he'd be knowingly sending her out in that condition. He could wait an hour or so until command was scheduled to shift back to her. As commanding officer, she couldn't leave her crew and ship unattended. Screw the stunt he pulled last night to get Mia Ha back.

"Tell him that we do not have one to spare. We're aware that he's a distance away but, for him and the ship parts, we will make the long trip." Alex had turned to the large alien and waited for her to translate that to her mate on the screen. Instead, more clicking was broadcasted.

"He understands and advises that it will take almost a day to reach our ship and then another to return. In lieu of your mate, I request that you send one medical person to attend his needs. My mate is stubborn," clicking cut her off for a moment and she paused, "and he'd also like to advise that he knows your language. His voice causes his embarrassment and he wishes not to vocalize to you. You can, however, speak straight to him if you wish."

Shiiit...ake mushrooms. Alex caught himself in the mental curse and quickly turned it around. The last thing he needed was the kids ratting out his vulgar language.

"I can find someone to send from the medical bay, with supplies." That wasn't the problem. Neither was assembling the recon team and providing protection on this mission. It was still the fact that the alien ship was a full day's journey away. It would put a strain on the mechanical team to figure out what was needed and transport parts back. There had to be another way to get that ship closer than sending Heather out.

He turned to address Azvark, out of habit. "How were you navigating your ship beforehand? If you had a pilot, can't we use him?"

"Dead defending my mate and the ship," she commented, eyes straight ahead on Cryzka. "The eidonga tore him apart. It is why they were not hungry until you came to get us."

A shiver ran down his spine with the knowledge that they had almost been too late. Alex wasn't sure how he would have handle the fact he lost a cadet, and in such a gruesome way that they probably would never have found her remains.

"Is the navigation system IGS standard, HYPox, or planetary based?"

He turned to see that Heather was actually approaching the view screen up front. All she got was clicks until Azvark translated. Her words were just as scary as seeing Heather walking towards the devilish figure.

"HYPox with a planetary back-up." She walked up next to Heather. The vast difference in their heights was obvious. Heather was at least four feet shorter. "I could translate our language but I do not know how to use it. It would be worthless."

"I know HYPox. It's a grey area in the interstellar system standards. The Intergalactic Alliance decided on starship operational systems to have at least one common control system in case of interspecies emergency operations. HYPox just isn't the favored one, but I do know it."

What Alex, nor the dragouuls on the bridge, didn't know was just how riddled with coding bugs and infinite loops the HYPox systems operated. Nor did they know that it would cause some pushback with the Alphecca's IGS standard operating system until every data port on every repair part could be manually override. He was just focused on what this really meant.

"Heather, you're about to assume duties of commanding officer. You cannot depart the ship and leave it vulnerable if something were to happen." It was a plea more than anything. A bluff.

She just shrugged her shoulders. "I could leave you in command or just leave before it shifts back to me." Heather glanced over her shoulder. It was a challenge. He wasn't completely sure that she would have done this before Alex had admitted his feelings for her or not. She knew where he stood and could exploit that if she wanted. "Logically, we need to get that ship closer to ours if we hope to salvage from it and double-check our systems. There's a chance that their starship may be more operationally sound than ours and having it closer would eliminate risk of crew transfer if we needed to abandon the Alphecca for theirs to get home."

He hated her logic.

It was something that he hadn't thought of – the fact that the Alphecca might be broken beyond repair. Reasonable, timely repair. They had rations for only so long, and a trip home they had to survive. Sure, this had happened at the beginning of the mission and they'd be making a trip straight back to Earth, but they couldn't waste a long stay on this planet to fix an infinite amount of components to fly again. If their starships really were compatible, it would make more sense to repair the lesser damaged one and use that to leave even if it wasn't on the Alphecca. That meant that someone had to go retrieve the other ship.

Fuck!

Alex ran a hand over his face. There was no way around this. He had to let Heather go. Not only that but he just promised one of the medical personnel too. He couldn't take that back now that Heather volunteered. Heather, a doctor, and one kid. That's what he'd be asking his tactical team to take with and watch out for. That's three extra bodies that would be on his conscious if anything went wrong. Three bodies that weren't trained for this.

As badass as Heather wanted to play, she didn't have the stamina for something like this.

He pinched the bridge of his nose. "Commander McGrey, a doctor, and Bilfa shall join the tactical team. We'll send a transmission when they depart. Just transmit the coordinates of your ship."

It was a shitty way to end the call, but Alex needed this to be done with so he could get some air. The whole thing had fallen out of his hands. Sure, he could play it off as doing his interstellar duty to rescue a diplomat in need, which could only better or create relations with Earth. That would sound better than failing in negotiations and bending too much to the will of two dragouuls. Then there was the fact that he could be reporting back with a short crew and without a girlfriend. The latter could happen anyways if things just didn't work between them. As much as he wanted Heather and had pined for her, it didn't guaranteed that she felt the same or that they'd work out in the long run. He knew it – again, that logical thing he'd rather ignore – but he could hope and plan for the best.

There were clicks all around the bridge when Alex cut the line. It was reasonable that the kids wanted to talk to their father after the grown-ups were done, and he had robbed them of that. They'd just have to wait a couple days before he arrived to do all their talking. Azvark hadn't said a word, so either she was talking to Heather or just choosing not to say a disapproving thing to him. She wasn't his mother or wife, after all, and that's really the only two that could have a place in saying how childish he acted.

He left the bridge and headed down the hall. It eluded him how this really would work out. He had set himself up with an escape plan, then Heather had taken that out of the equation. The dragouul starship was a gamble – either with parts or as an escape. He hated the fact that he didn't play the hardass and –

"Hey."

He stopped when someone grabbed his arm. He knew who it was. He just wasn't sure he could face Heather at the moment. She stayed behind him for a moment, probably expecting him to turn around to face her.

"Alex, it's the only way." Straight to the point. She knew what was wrong.

"But why you. We could have delayed it a couple days until we could evaluate the ship and the parts. It wouldn't have put you at risk. Now we're taking a risk when it might be completely worthless."

"It's not going to be completely worthless. We still have to get Azvark's mate."

He groaned. "Yea, her mate. To reunite a family." And then what would happen? Either they'd all die after wasting the Alphecca's food rations or because the dragouuls hijacked their ship in a huge Ponzi scheme. "If something happens to you then we need to rely on Cadet Ha. She doesn't have half your experience and that could doom us trying to fly whatever deathtrap back to Earth. Not only that but she's never done a real, full atmosphere re-entry. She could burn us all miles from home."

Though the chances of that were slim, given the Academy's training. Alex wanted her to at least admit that she overstepped, that she unnecessarily put herself at risk.

"It's not going to happen," she simply put. "Communication lines are up. Data logs are being reported back to HQ Base. They're going to know that we interacted with the dragouuls. If anything happens to us, it's a declaration of war."

"But I could still lose you!"

Alex hadn't meant to yell that. He could force himself to admit it, but he hadn't meant to raise his voice. His shoulders dropped in utter defeat. The dragouuls had beaten him. Heather had pulled the rug out from under him. He had slipped up.

"I could lose you, Heather," he repeated. "I don't care if the Force would avenge you. I don't care if every last dragouul, eidonga, or whatever the fuck out there is erased from the universe. I would still have lost you… and I don't want to lose you."

There was nothing she could say, and nothing that she did say. It felt like an eternity standing there, staring into her eyes. As if silently plead with the other to let them do what they had to do.

Chapter Seventeen

It would have been nice if the voices had stopped. If anything, they had gotten louder. Not only in Mia's head but around her. There were enough beeping machines to know that she was in the medical bay on the Alphecca, even if she hadn't opened her eyes.

There hadn't been anyone by to see her, not even one of the commanders. They were probably looking after the dragouuls and playing politics. That didn't explain why Mal hadn't come by. She had expected him to once he was done with whatever debriefing he'd have, but he hadn't even bothered. She hadn't seen him since last night when he went to her room. Sure, he knew that she was alive but he couldn't be bothered to know if she was doing okay. This whole thing had her rattled, and that's probably why she had to check in with medical. They were making sure that she was okay and Mal couldn't even make sure that was the reason she was skipping their breakfast routine.

"Alright, Cadet Ha, your vitals have sustained a stable level for 12 hours. The pain in your side from the attack is being tempered with the pain medi-pack." Yea, one huge-ass pill that was, literally, hard to swallow. "But you've been complaining about voices."

Scratch that. She *had* been complaining about voices. That was before she realized the dragouuls weren't just in her head. Not if they would need the commanders to help them once they got on-board. The fact that none of them came looking for her, or really reached out directly to her, meant that they could get by on their own with just anybody. The error for Mia was in mumbling to herself when stupidly listening to voices which got herself caught, rattled, and fucked by who was turning out to be an asshole – Mal. Okay, maybe not as asshole because he did come and help rescue her, even if it was his job, but he really did suck.

"I'm not hearing voices. I was just tired, and mumbling to myself, and got confused that it was really me talking to myself. I just needed to get some rest and down some coffee." It was a lie, but at least Mia was hoping the nurse could relate. The nurses back on Earth certainly were overworked and knew how easy it was for their minds to play tricks on them.

"Regardless, it's on your record and I need to check you for that."

Mia had no idea how that was going to happen. It wasn't like they could attach an electrode to her head and it would blink if she was crazy.

"I'll come back and you can talk to me again in a couple hours. It's going to be the same." She rolled her eyes. "I'm fit to return to duty and I'm not crazy. The only thing I am is a little sore from where that beast punched me." That was putting it lightly. The force that eidonga had with its paw when it nabbed her. "And I'd really like another medi-pad with a pill that wasn't the size of my com."

"Medi-packs are large so they can cover an array of ailments."

Great. She was being treated for things she didn't even have. Yet, they focused on the one thing she did have before she knew she wasn't crazy.

"Talk to Commander McGrey. She'll clear me and tell you that I'm fine." When in doubt, name drop. She was the only one Mia could assume heard the dragouuls and was in any position of power to help her out.

The nurse turned off the tablet with her file and stood. "Unfortunately Commander McGrey is not on the ship. She left about an hour ago on a mission and it is unclear how long that would take."

Shit.

141

"Well, how about Commander Tanaka?" There was a small chance that he knew she wasn't crazy. Then again, she had left the ship even if she had no recollection of it and now there were aliens on-board after a shoot-out rescue mission... which was all because of her. He might just say she was crazy to get back at her.

"Cadet Ha, the commanders can't be bothered with every little medical need. You're under observation. If the medical staff deems you competent, only then will we allow you to return to duty." She headed for the door. "Until then, just try to relax and enjoy the break from work."

Mia groaned. She wanted to just get up and walk out after the nurse left, but she knew that it wasn't that easy. It also would accomplish nothing. She'd just be ordered back to the medical bay and any refusal would be disobeying orders. That was one thing that she didn't want on her record. Mia was just starting her career and insubordination was a swift death to anyone.

Instead, she booted up the menu screen on her com device and typed in her password to access the hidden file. If anyone found out that she hacked the device to install Tetris and Mario Bros, she'd be court-martialed for tampering with the standard issue device. They would cite that she could have compromised the integrity of the security sensitive device through the coding she had entered to pirate the games. But she wasn't about to die of boredom either.

The psychiatrist didn't take too long to show up, which was both great and horrible. It meant that she wasn't stuck waiting around long but it also meant that she hadn't the chance to beat her high score. That meant that when she got home and the game updated that she probably wouldn't be scratching the leaderboards anymore. But at least she hadn't been caught, so there was a tiny win. Oh, and the shrink decided that she wasn't crazy either...

Now was the problem of what to do. The commanding officer was not on the ship, there was nothing to pilot, and she didn't want to see Mal. It eliminated her room, the bridge, the gym, and, probably, the cafeteria right now. She couldn't stay in the halls either and risk bumping into him. There was nowhere to really hide out and kill time until she got orders.

"Come with us."

"Play with us."

Mia stopped dead. She knew that voice. Well, voices – even if they all sounded the same. It was almost ironic that the shrink said she wasn't crazy and then she started hearing voices right after that. Although, if the crew didn't already know, it was just how the dragouuls communicated. Well, at least some of them. It seemed like age and gender played a big role in what they could and couldn't do.

"Where are you?" Mia thought. Why not play with some alien children? That was probably the last thing anyone on this ship would be doing.

"We smell food. Big room."

They smell food but either didn't have it or see it where they were. That had to mean they were close to one place that she was avoiding. A big room... that could have been the cafeteria if she hadn't ruled that out from the first thing they said. There must have been a large conference room or something near the cafeteria and – as Mia headed in that direction – she tried to think of what was pointed out on the starship tour. Short of bring up the Alphecca's layout on her com device, there was nothing to do but take a walk over there and poke around.

It wasn't hard at all to find the room the dragouuls were in. There were enough people whispering in the halls to get an idea of where to go, and then it was narrowed down to either the library or a multi-purpose room. It was the latter. The intent of the room was probably to hold crew meetings or have a conference call without interrupting operations on the bridge. Now it was covered in mismatched mattresses and random pieces of bedding. In one corner, it looked like someone had made a pile of pillowcases and fashioned it to look like a bird's nest. Given they were reptilian in appearance, Mia probably shouldn't have been surprised to see that they tried making little nests to curl up in. She had to carefully step over one such nest on her way into the room because the youngest – and smallest – had decided right there was where it needed to sleep.

"Who wanted me to come?" She thought into the room. Mia didn't want to tip off the other kids that she was there to play with them in case it started a riot. She wasn't sure if their thoughts transmitted to everyone or if they had control over what was heard, like Mia did if she sent a text versus talking in a crowded room.

Two kids waved to her from the back of the room and she took that as a sign it was them that summoned her. They made room on the floor for her and she sat down between their eager-looking faces.

"What do you want to play?" She whispered.

The kids stared at each other for a moment. If they were talking, they weren't saying anything to her. At least that answered one question about their telepathy.

"Human game?"

A human game. Well, that was easier said than done. Most of the ones that Mia thought of off-the-bat were ones where you actually had to say words, like *Duck, Duck, Goose!* There wasn't any playing cards in the room for games like Crazy 8's or Go Fish, and she doubted that she could find someone who had packed a deck in their luggage. A human game that was simple, didn't require talking, and didn't need much…

Tic. Tac. Toe.

Mia looked around for any scrap of paper that she could find. Because the room had been intended for more than an impromptu living area, there were a few supplies that she could commandeer. One of those happened to be a white board and markers. That was all they'd need and they could play the game for hours without worrying about running out of paper or having to find a pencil sharpener.

144

"It's called Tic-Tac-Toe and it's one of the human strategy games." She wasn't sure why she was trying to sell the idea. Maybe it was because, from their short interactions, Mia knew the dragouuls were a more advanced species than they were.

"These are the lines of the game, so you always start by drawing them first." Mia drew two horizontal lines intersecting the two vertical lines. "You pick a symbol and that's how you know what moves you make. There's a cross and a circle. You decide who goes first and then you take turns putting one of your symbols in an empty space. To win, you need to get three in a row." Mia drew in the symbols, alternating which ones she drew, as she talked to show them how a mock game was played. At the end, crosses won because, well, crosses always won.

She gave the kids a moment to take in the game and realize which symbol won before erasing the board and drawing a new hashtag sign, smiling to herself knowing that it was called an octotrope, but it was a bit of trivia that would be lost on these kids. It was lost on basically everyone back home but it was a nugget of knowledge that made Mia feel a smidgeon smarter than everyone else.

"So who wants to play me first?"

CHAPTER EIGHTEEN

Mal wasn't sure if he should go after McGrey or Commander Dickwad. Seeing McGrey walking ahead of him didn't help his decision any. He had the opportunity now to blackmail her, but she knew everything. Including every damn rule and fucking protocol. She'd find a way to flip it ass-backwards and end up blackmailing him. Then there was the prick. He was back on the ship, but he was the one that would take it harder. Mal was willing to bet he hadn't fucked her. It would turn McGrey into sloppy seconds and ruin her for him. Or if they were fucking, it would destroy whatever fucking good thing they thought they had going. Plus, McGrey might know the recording wasn't real. She might remember that she was high on something and was all talk. Commander Dickwad wouldn't…

"Well, humans have relationships and then they decide if they want to marry someone." He overheard a small bit of what McGrey was saying to the alien kid. It wasn't enough to keep his interest. He rolled his eyes at their stupid chatter and shifted a couple feet to the left to talk with one of his team buddies.

"You bang Leeda yet?" Mal just had to ask. She was the next girl on the crew roster, so that meant she was going to get nailed sooner or later. It would just have to be later if his buddy was still after that. This team was like family after all.

The guy sighed. "No, met up with her last night. Got all hot and heavy on the bridge. But get this, I stuck my hand down her pants to do a little foreplay and she ain't even telling me that she's on her fucking period. Pulled my hand out and it looked like I was in the war. At least she had the mind to be embarrassed though. She'd probably let me bang her later."

"You didn't have the balls to fuck her now? Duuude, it ain't nothing. Bitches make a big deal out of it. I woulda wore that shit on my dick like a bloody fucking badge of honor."

His buddy just chuckled. "Yea, you would."

Mal didn't take it as anything but a complement. A fuck was a fuck. And his buddy seemed good-natured enough about it that he probably could fuck Leeda when they got back and he'd never know by the time she was done bleeding that he was getting the seconds. Besides, he needed to work through the roster at least once before he went back to his favorites. And his dick was fucking craving some Tiffany Eldridge. Busty fucking redhead that could actually keep up with him.

"So who's the next target?"

Leeda Bheru. Not that Mal would admit that to his buddy. The one after her was Hylux, a harder target to nail down. She was a nurse in the medical bay and always working. Word around the ship was that she really like alien dick, especially alien-human dick. Some people had a hard time ignoring the fact that her skin was blue and speckled with an unnatural color, but pussy was pussy. It was just another bragging right to have fucked one more species than the next guy.

"Hylux. Can't figure out how I wanna do it. Heard they got this third opening. Might actually take my time to explore that one." He chuckled.

Lieutenant Gregor dropped back in the formation, completely hushing them. They were family, but there's just somethings you don't tell your "father".

"We're at the edge of the scouted zone. I want tighter forms for the next five miles. Harrison, take the lead with Bragis. Thomson, I want you to drop back to the rear. I'm going to have the other guys flank. I'll be joining you when I finish giving out the orders."

147

"Lucky you," Mal teased once Gregor was out of ear-shot. "Get to handle the rear with the big guy." He made to grab an imaginary ass in front of him. Anything to get his buddy's goat.

"Fuck you. I'll take the rear if it means not getting fucked and shredded by the first plant you sniff." He was referencing the plants they saw on their first scouting trip. It didn't scare Mal. No fucking plant could get the best of him.

Mal started to pick up his pace to get to the front when his buddy asked him something that kind of irked him. "You fucked that crazy chick we brought back. How was it? Got her next on my list."

He didn't want to think of Mia getting passed around by his brothers, but she really didn't mean much to him. No one did. Whoring her out or hanging onto her for himself didn't really help El Numero Uno, aka himself. There was no reason to stick up for her. "The only crazy thing about her is what she can do with a dick. Ain't seen a chick take it like her in a while," he gloated.

She might always be "the crazy chick", but Mal liked to think he helped her out of this one. It was better to be known for being a good fuck than a nut job. And if he talked her up, so what? His buddy didn't have a shot. Mia had a taste of his dick and there was nothing better than it in the universe. She'd be on her knees begging for it just like every fucking chick on that ship. No one else was going to touch her now that he used her. No one could come closer.

Search. And. Destroy.

Maybe instead of Hylux he should be working down McGrey while they were away from the ship.

Mal passed her on the way to his position in the front. He had to keep his eyes peeled for anything he could shoot. Bragis wasn't the talkative type, so the rest of the jaunt to this alien ship was going to be boring as fuck. He'd rather be watching paint dry. And when there wasn't even a fucking hungry plant around, the mission dragged on. He was practically dying with boredom by the time the deep galactic purple ship came into view just over the top of the hill. The setting sun made lighter colors shine on the ship. It almost looked like a bag of melted Jolly Ranchers. Mal groaned, thinking about the candy. He fucking missed having anything he wanted when he wanted.

The alien ship was twice the fucking size of theirs and clearly fit in better on this planet with that color scheme. The alien thing next to him chirped and started down the hill in front on the group.

"Hey! Stay the fuck behind us!" He yelled at it, but it didn't stop or slow down. McGrey ran passed him. Groaning, Mal decided to follow everyone else and take back the lead. He ran down the hill to get in front of them and cut the alien off. When he stopped, the thing ran into him and fell back on its ass. He couldn't help but bust out laughing. "That's what you get for not staying in the back."

"Cadet Harrison!" McGrey took a while to catch up, and then she was out of breath. It just made the way she said his name sexier, especially because she was pissed at him. She probably thought this fucking thing needed to be handled with baby gloves just because it was small. Size didn't matter unless it was tits or dick. "You do not... talk to her... like that..."

Wow, the commander really was struggling to catch her breath. Guess age was really starting to show. Then again, it would mean even a quickie would be enough to fucking rock her world. Maybe that's why Commander Dickwad had a chance. Small dick for no stamina. But he saw Lieutenant Gregor jogging up and snapped to attention. McGrey could bust his ass, but the only way he'd care what she said was if it was through Gregor's mouth. Luckily it was just an apology – that he didn't mean – and cleaning duty – which he didn't mind. So what if he'd have to disassemble every gun, rifle, and weapon to clean them to a sparkle only to reassemble and log everything back into the armory. It wasn't like he wouldn't be happy playing around with some guns.

McGrey took the thing's hand and started towards the bay doors of the big ship. For having been attacked and hosting a diplomat, it was odd that the doors were wide open. He made a comment to Gregor, which only got a warning to keep his eyes open for hostiles. One eye stayed by the scope when they scanned and approached the ship. The damn thing next to them kept clicking. Didn't it fucking know that it could give away their position if there was an ambush waiting!?

The tactical team took point and led them into the ship. Gregor hung near the back to cover their rear, not that they were expecting an attack. An ambush within the ship was the more likely scenario. McGrey would every once in a while give them directions to the ship's bridge in hushed tones. The alien thing stayed quiet, and stuck to her side. Around every corner and into every room, Mal and Bragis first had to clear it before the rest followed. There weren't many rooms that they had to pass through, but plenty of corners and hallways. After what felt like an eternity, they came to a thick, closed metal door.

"Bilfa says he's in there. That's the bridge," McGrey quietly said. Either she was keeping her voice down for a reason, or out of habit, or she assumed they could all hear her over the silence they stood in.

Gregor walked up to the door, examining it for a point where they could get a hold to pry it open. There didn't appear to be any weak spots. "Any magical words or ideas on how to enter, commander?"

"She's talking to him now. He's entering commands to open the door. It seems that their electrical systems were slightly damaged in their crash."

Mal groaned. Great! They came all this fucking way for a damaged ship that couldn't probably fix their own fucking mess, but listening to some alien kid irked Mal more at the moment. It hadn't said a damn word but somehow it was calling the shots.

"We should send someone to scout the rest of the ship for hostiles, sir," Mal suggested. He was basically volunteering, if it meant getting away from this bullshit.

"No," Gregor shut that idea down. "We need the full team in case this turns on us. I can't ensure anyone's safety if we don't secure the bridge and ensure no traps are activated on the ship,"

It wasn't something that had crossed his mind. Then again, that wasn't his job – to think. It made sense, even though Mal didn't like the answer. He just had to fucking nod and go along with the boss' orders.

Gregor walked back over to McGrey and the alien thing. "Is he managing to get the door to disengage and open?"

Heather nodded. "It seems like he overheard us and ran a bio-scan. We are the only ones on the ship."

"And at his door." The way Gregor said it sounded like there was something else on his mind now. Probably the fact that if the alien ran a bio-scan, it knew exactly where they were and how many. Something handy to know if you wanted to ambush or trap someone. "Well, we're ready just in case that's not completely accurate." He meant, in case there were a couple guards or crew members inside that were prepared to attack us when this huge door moved.

There was a hiss of air slowly being released and an awful smell that crept up to their noses.

"Bilfa says it's their atmosphere and should dissipate soon. It's not toxic." McGrey was definitely trusting these fucking aliens way too damn much. "They have a higher mineral content in their air because they survive deep underground. The starship saturates the recycled air with mineral particles. The one that is causing the odor is called himpoflorix, essentially harmless to us."

Essentially harmless didn't mean it really was harmless. She was so fucking doped up on talking to some alien fuckers that she couldn't stop fangirling to realize that they were at risk. Essentially harmless his ass.

"Good thing our atmospheric unit is still fully functional," McGrey commented. That actually got a chuckle out of the lieutenant.

"Good thing." Gregor raised his laser pistol in front of him – leaving the larger rifle strapped across his back – as the door opened. "Have the kid tell her father to raise his hands and not to move until we cleared the room."

McGrey stared at him for a moment after he spoke, then the kid. She turned back to Gregor, not having said a word. "He knows and he's complying. This is completely unnecessary though."

"Extra precautions are worth it if they protect my team."

Gregor motioned for him and Bragis to take point. He took up the left side of the doorway while Bragis had the other. Peeking around the edge, it was dimly lit inside the room. There was plenty of space to hide half a crew. Perfect setup for an ambush. At first, neither of them spotted the diplomat. This clearly was a setup, and a damn good one if they believed a computer simulation and some kid. But then there was a tiny shift in the shadows and eventually Mal could make out two darker circles staring at them. He turned on the flashlight of his scope and finally the dark-colored diplomat appeared in the room. The huge fucker was all dark dirt-brown and deep green like camouflage. The huge thing looked more soldier than politician. It definitely was a reminder that they didn't know as much shit about these fucking aliens as they thought they did. For all they knew, they were going to end up turning on the Alphecca's crew and slaughtering them after Mal went and saved their tails. Literally.

"Lieutenant Gregor to Alphecca. Do you copy? Over." Gregor had one hand on his pistol and one on his shoulder radio.

It took a moment before the radio crackled back. "Alphecca here. We copy. What is your status? Over."

"Arrived at target. Secured starship and diplomat. Setting camp and will report back to base in the morning after tracking beacon is confirmed transmitting. Over."

"Roger. Will await transmission of beacon and provide confirmation. Enjoy your night. Alphecca over and out."

And with that, the radio went silent.

CHAPTER NINETEEN

"Tell me about your mate again. Did you really chose him?"

Heather knew the question was nothing but innocence. The concept of falling in love and actually choosing the one you wanted to be with was as foreign an idea as Bilfa was herself. "We've liked each other for a long time and decided to start a relationship now that we're both single."

Bilfa understood the concept of being single. She was unattached right now, even though a mate had long been decided for her. As a diplomat's offspring, it was even more expected that she follow tradition and that the union be advantageous. She explained that her future mate was almost six years her senior and was actually originally betrothed to her older brother. What happened was that Azvark became pregnant and the family set the arrangement when the other female was announced pregnant. Only they both birthed males and the agreement passed onto the next female child Azvark would birth, which was Bilfa. It was obvious that the other family wanted the power and honor of being linked to a diplomatic family immediately – not almost a decade later and to the second oldest child. It was understandable that Bilfa felt a little worthless as the second place prize.

"You said yesterday you mated before and he mated before. How can you be mating now?"

That definitely wasn't a question that she wanted to answer out loud. Especially with how the mood was now walking back to the Alphecca. Everything went fine with getting the beacon transmitting back to the ship. It was this morning when everything went downhill. Lieutenant Gregor's team had thought certain things that the two aliens took offense to, not that the tactical team knew the dragouuls possessed telepathy. But either way, it was human nature to think certain things based on being raised without alien lifeforms everywhere and it was common sense – which most of us humans have – not to say our thoughts out loud. The thoughts were something that Bilfa and Cryzka refused to repeat, and they wouldn't call out who thought them. It just left a painful tension in the air amongst them as they headed back.

"Our society allows you to openly love someone, even though some people don't approve. There's no law against it. Sometimes it's a mistake when you're growing up, and you think that you'll be with that person for the rest of your life. Sometimes it's because you're feeling lonely or just because sex actually feels really good. Sex – mating – has also been used for revenge, to hurt people and prove to a loved one that they really didn't matter at all, or to break up an ex-lover's new relationship."

Heather knew that she probably was saying – thinking – too much to a kid. But, in reality, Bilfa wasn't so much a kid. Her hatch date was coming up soon and she'd learn firsthand what sex was all about. Only that she'd be married and, potentially, stuck with one dragouul for the rest of her life. It seemed like divorce was an even bigger mystery than casual sex. Heather liked to think that if she was crossing a line that Cryzka would tell her. So far, he acted oblivious to their conversation. Then again, maybe he was just as interested as his daughter as to the ways of humans.

Bilfa was quiet for a moment. *"So sex can be used as a way of war."*

That was definitely an abstract way of thinking about it. Not that it hadn't been used in the past just for that reason. Want to start a war amongst tribes? Claim one member of one tribe slept with someone important of another. Want to start a coup for power and money? Sleep with the CEO and take it all.

Heather nodded. But maybe she should clarify more. *"Usually people end up choosing one person by the end of it all. They're always someone special to them and they decide to only mate with each other. That's what love is. It's more than just mating. It's also being best friends at the same time. Alex is that for me."*

"Love can be learned." The voice felt heavier, somehow. It didn't take much to determine that Cryzka was the one with that thought. While true, she didn't want to dash Bilfa's dreams. There was a chance that she could have both an arranged marriage and love for someone that'll be her best friend. It seemed like her father was more of the traditional sense.

"It could be real love with your mate too." She glanced over at Bilfa. *"It may just be destiny to meet each other like this and fall in love at first sight."*

Bilfa didn't think anything else, at least not to her. She probably didn't want to talk at all anymore now that her father had stepped in with his opinion on the matter. Love didn't matter when it was tradition. Earth had seen that for centuries with its own arranged marriage cultures. Heather was sure that going against a father's wish was severely against the acceptable social norms. Knowing that, it was almost hard to encourage the child to go after what she wanted for herself.

Without the girl's company, the journey back was really lacking. None of the tactical team spoke to her; not that she expected them to. They had their duties to perform and it was their responsibility to ensure the safety of the entire group. They either spoke quietly between themselves or to Lieutenant Gregor for orders and reporting. And he didn't have a need to speak with her as the mission was a simple trek back to the Alphecca. It left her mind to drift back to Alex.

Alex really was an all-star, even with his incredibly laid-back approach. He kept nailing missions and had people talking about making him the next general – a dream that Heather shared. He was her perfect match, professionally, and it was clear that they complimented each other. The problem was that she never heard of him getting anywhere near to commitment, romantically. There were so many rumors about his exploits and – she wasn't going to lie – it was hard to hear the stories that she knew weren't fabrications. Then there was her lack of trust that prevented most from getting close, even on a friendly basis. And there was the fact that Alex thought she was pregnant. In the very least, he knew that she had survived something and had a few scars on her soul. But, if she took into account her own rumors, they were an even more perfect match.

She was the one to whore around with every man, woman, and alien being for so many years. Every officer had already had a taste of Heather McGrey, and they claimed that was how she rose so high before plateauing. Now she was more selective of her bed partners and the men in power didn't like it being a competition or sex being a favor system.

To be chosen – one of the few – meant that you were better than the rest. It was just as good as a promotion to a cadet. It was getting a piece of a hot ass that had taken every powerful man in the Force, and that was where you ranked. You were better than your fellow cadet. A member of the elite. And if you performed well, there was no doubt that Heather McGrey would remember your name and move you up in the ranks, just like she had. There was no person that could claim to have been with her twice, so there was always something more prestigious to obtain. But in the chance that she left you a lowly cadet, there was the chance to blackmail or ruin her reputation with the knowledge of her body or kinks – actual or fictional.

Heather had heard the lore about her and knew that – like Alex's – there was more truth in it than she cared. She had whored herself out years ago. Anyone and anything that could get her off would ease the pain for a while before it came scratching to the surface. While she hadn't slept her way into her rank, the general had targeted her for sex. After that and the failed attempt to end her life when she wouldn't abort, sex was a side effect of the strange alien medication. It made her body crave it when she needed another green vial. She was still trapped and forced into physically filling a void. Heather was more "selective" now because she had grown accustom to the medication and the side effects weren't as strong. There were other ways to live than beneath someone else.

Alex and her both had too many sexual partners to really deserve being with anyone else. Two degenerates – a word one she had heard addressed to her before, preceding "whore" – that belonged together only because they'd cause less trouble for the rest of the worlds. It was something that she had taken heart to in the past, but not so much anymore. Time had a funny way of hardening you.

She felt a tingle in her palm and glanced down to see Bilfa. She had thought that the girl had left her but apparently what had occupied her thoughts had ended up back to the girl.

"I'm fine," Heather said quietly. Something the alien girl wouldn't understand – just like every human male.

CHAPTER TWENTY

"Permission to board."

The cadet on the bridge verified that it was Lieutenant Gregor on the view screen before opening the docking bay doors. Alex watched as his girlfriend and two dragouuls entered, surrounded by the tactical team. From this side of the monitor, he couldn't tell if Heather was in any pain or not. She had spent the night away from him and he damn near smoked all the contraband cigarettes he had just to calm himself down.

"Fenrir, we got a group of eighty on-board and heading your way for a hot meal," he warned the ship's cook through the chair's communication system.

"Ain't got that many bodies left to feed, commander. Dinner just wrapped up."

It was just the kind of remark Alex had hoped for. It meant the cook wasn't expecting anything and he could mess with the guy; you know, pay back for the cold chicken nugget prank on the last mission that happened over April Fool's Day – a tradition not lost to the times.

"The tactical team just returned with Commander McGrey and two dragouuls. I'm expecting them to be very hungry after an overnight trip on-planet."

The groan from the other end was audible. Eighty was an exaggeration only in the physical number of people needing substance. A hungry tactical team could really put it away, but that was nothing compared to what one dragouul would eat apparently. Luckily, this wasn't going to be a long mission with them aboard or else the whole crew would be starving to death within a week if they were keeping to their original plan. Headquarters hadn't gotten back to him with official orders to return, but they could always add in the diplomatic aid that drained their supplies as an excuse to get home. Nobody would argue that without bringing up talks of war, and there was enough of that already without Earth getting involved again. Lesson learned.

"Gregor!" He called into his com device as he got a move-on towards the bridge doors. Again, there was an audible groan.

"Yeah?"

The smile just grew on his face. His buddy was tired from the trip and Alex being cheerful would just kill him.

"Glad you guys finally decided to show up." He headed down the corridors towards the group. "After you pack up your gear, take everyone down to the cafeteria for a hot meal. I already got Fenrir on standby."

"I bet he's fucking thrilled."

Alex chuckled. "Almost his exact words, friend." He took a left and realized too late that he had gotten too lost in his thoughts over seeing Heather to focus on the Alphecca's layout. "Hey, you let me know if he pulls some crap and throws sandwiches at you. I told him to serve the best."

Gregor laughed over the com. "Then sandwiches are exactly what we're getting." It went silence for a few minutes as Alex got back on track. "I might be a little late in getting that report in to HQ. Got little sleep last night. There were no incidents to report and nothing was encountered on the trek back."

"Don't worry about it then. If it's late, I'll just claim the ship's communication system isn't completely back up and running and it was a glitch in the system's back-up communication hard drive. We fixed it; they get the report."

The guy worried about doing his job way more than Alex did. On that note, Gregor was just like Heather. Both by-the-book and

159

strictly professional. For a moment, the idea of his friend and girlfriend being together crossed his mind. Heather was a better match with him, any day. So why was she with Alex? He tried to push it from his thoughts. Gregor was single and he couldn't cook. Heather's food would probably kill you if you ate it. Yea, there was no way they would last long together. That's why Alex was better…. Yea. He tried to remind himself of that as he went to surprise her.

Along the way, he had materialized a cup of coffee, hopefully to Heather's tastes for this time of the night. She had been without it for almost two days and must be going through withdrawals. That and he didn't want to show up empty handed. Alex needed some way to remind her that he was great for her. Surrounded by men in the corridor in front of him, he needed something to stand out.

"Thought you might like this," he said, coming up behind her in the group.

She was startled at his voice and looked a little surprised to see him. She couldn't have thought that he wouldn't come to welcome her back. "T-thanks."

Heather took the cup and quietly sipped at it. It was a little unnerving to walk beside her in the silence. He wanted to ask her so many things. How was she feeling? How'd the trip go? Did she want to go back to his room tonight? He wasn't sure if he should ask her back to his place. Well, he wanted to order her back into his bed – as much as he'd love to slowly strip her down and give her another reason that he was the best boyfriend in space. But then he'd seem no better than General Ruthesford. What he really wanted was just to have her in his bed tonight – to hold her close and to know that she was alright. It had been unusually hard letting her go yesterday for the mission, and it was unbearable now to know that she might have suffered another painful attack as well. As his girlfriend, he had to be there to protect her – even if it was from herself.

"Want to come over tonight?"

He could see that she that she was stalling. Maybe to give herself enough time to come up with an easy letdown. He wanted to take her off that hook, but at the same time felt like she shouldn't be turning him away. She also shouldn't feel obligated to be around him. After all, their first priority should be the ship and the crew. That seemed to have taken even more of a backseat in his mind after re-establishing communication with HQ.

"I think that I would rather just sleep in my own bed tonight," Heather said quietly. There was an undertone of regret with a touch of fear, at least to his ears.

"It's ok, Heather." It did knock down his ego a bit. "I'll take the long shift tonight and do rounds. You should try to get as much sleep as you can."

Alex started to walk away, but she grabbed his hand. "I didn't mean it as if you couldn't come to my room. I just want to be around more familiar things tonight and your room still feels strange."

"Well, if you don't mind me and my snoring, I'll see you back at your room after you get something to eat."

"I won't be long," she said quietly.

"Already spent too much time with the dragouuls?"

That probably wasn't something he should be thinking in this general area. One of them might hear him, either out loud or mentally. The idea of constantly having to guard his thoughts in order to get through a mission was enough to drain him. He could only imagine how Heather felt and what she had to frantically cover up. Then again, she probably had more mission specific thoughts and not the kind of distracting thoughts and ideas of debauchery that crossed Alex's mind frequently. Those children were going to learn a lot from their time aboard the Alphecca; albeit, it probably wouldn't be anything good.

Heather shook her head. "No, it's just I'm feeling drained by… well, everything. I just want to do what I have to and then get away from it all."

Alex knew it was a risk – albeit, a small one – but he leaned in to kiss her. It caught her by surprise but she ended up melting into him. The longer he lingered on her lips, the more she forgot. Warm coffee splashed his leg when the cup fell from her hand so that she could bury her fingers in his longer-than-allowed hair. His own pulled her flush against him and instantly moved to find skin when a soft moan escaped her lips.

If they kept up much longer, they'd both end up a spectacle on the floor. Heather must have realized the danger they were flirting with and tried to step back. His hands firmly kept her in place. Not only was he not ready to be apart from her, but he also had a large problem that would be visible if she moved.

"Alex," she quietly whined. It was a pained warning of desire. Heather probably hadn't realized the awkward position her body had put him in, and she probably was losing resolve the longer they stood together.

He kissed her forehead and lingered close. "I want you so badly. Just give my head a moment to remind certain parts that it needs to calm down." Literally.

It seemed like she finally noticed the part of him pressing urgently against her and blushed. Her face buried into his chest and Alex couldn't help falling a little more in love with the hardened commander.

"Hey," he whispered against her hair, "isn't that a good sign? Means I'm completely and hopeless in love with you."

Crap!

He felt Heather stiffen a little in his arms. It wasn't that he lied, but it was far too soon to be using that word. He didn't regretted it but he wished that Heather was more comfortable being loved. Then again, she had been through a lot of terrible shit. Did she think that she would never be loved?

"I'm not going to apologize," Alex said firmly. "I know its fast but we've known each other for years. I don't think I have to wait to say so."

"You can't love me, Alex," she mumbled into his chest.

162

It just made him chuckle. "I don't think you really have a say in that."

And she didn't. She couldn't change how he felt about her. He just wished that he could have admitted to himself earlier what he wanted and actually pursued it. It would have saved him a long of annoying mornings and the daunting task of compiling excuses to kick out his one-night stands. It also would have meant that the years with Maggie had been for nothing; however, he had learned things about himself and, actually, grew as a person. It wasn't a regret, but he wondered if he would have been the right version of himself to be with Heather now if it wasn't for his ex-girlfriend.

"I need a cig." It broke the building tension. "While you get something to eat, I'll go grab a smoke."

"We're on-planet, Alex." She spoke as firmly as something she had felt a moment ago. "Take it outside or I'm going to have to start reporting you."

Alex chuckled. He smoked; she followed protocol. Guess when things got awkward they always fell back to their default. "And taint the pure air of this planet? This is a rare, untouched ecosystem that could easily be thrown off balance."

"By a single cigarette?" She clearly wasn't humoring him on that idea.

He nodded. "Yea, I could accidentally wipe out a whole species with secondhand smoke. It would be an interplanetary incident that could put us at war with this world."

She stepped away. "If you end up wiping out those creepy Venus flytrap plants, then you have nothing to worry about. I'm sure the locals wouldn't care. Plus, they got the whole "war" thing under control."

That was probably true. They did shoot down a diplomat's starship and hold the inhabitants of two planets hostage. A little puff of smoke was going to be nothing compared to that. But still… it could be chilly out there, and it was so nice and cozy in his room. Plus, Alex had already been taking smoke breaks on his bed so the damage was already done. Heather had to have noticed the scent left in the air the last time she came to his room, but said nothing. It was such a difficult choice. As commander-to-commander, he could take his smokes wherever he wanted and file a report stating his defense and reasons it should be permitted. As girlfriend-to-boyfriend, he'd lose no matter what logic he pulled out of his ass. Heather said outside; she meant outside.

He grumbled, but complied. He'd take his smoke outside... for now.

Chapter Twenty-One

"So who's a good lay on this piece of junk?"

Mal shoved half a burger – with all the fixings – in his mouth. After that mission, he was fucking starving for some real shit. He was only half listening to his team as he destroyed the tray of food. He just wanted to eat, fuck, and sleep tonight. That's why he listened to what the guys were talking about. He had a list, but it was always nice to know if things needed to get mixed up or not. Taking it alphabetically was almost boring, even if every chick could pose a new challenge.

"Saw my roommate on the way back. Said he had this chick last night that blew him fucking away. Got these tats, though, so you gotta be into that shit." The blonde guy leaned into the rest of the listening team. "But she not all like that he said. She's got a fat ass and some nice tits, and she's down to give you whatever."

That definitely was his type. Mal wanted something nice to pound. A little extra cushion would mean he could go harder on her.

"Hairless?" He asked, kind of surprising the guys he was actually joining in. Usually he was the one with all the scoop.

The blonde shook his head. "Naw, but its mowed. Just enough to give your dick a tickle before you plow the field." He laughed at his own stupid joke. "The real good hit is this chick bends and is so fucking tight. Took the D twice and still tight as a virgin."

Mal groaned, but it wasn't from imagining fucking her. "No way she's real. Name or your full of shit."

165

"Seems like playboy missed one." The blonde smirked. "Mia. Ha."

A couple of the dragouul brats started crying and scurrying over to their big-ass parents. His blood felt like there was ice running through it. He wanted to kill his teammate for talking about Mia like that. He wanted to rip off the ears of the rest of his team so they couldn't hear about her. He wanted to fucking kill this guy's roommate for fucking her. But he really wanted to hunt Mia down, throw her up against the fucking wall again, rip off those combat pants and fuck her into oblivion, and make her realize that she was his thing. She wasn't anyone.

But now his whole fucking team knew what she got.

He got up and threw his tray at the trash can, startling McGrey as she walked in.

"Cadet Harrison, clean that up immediately!" She barked the ordered.

He ignored McGrey. She'd get it later. She moaned for him in the hospital, but he'd have her moaned and underneath him. For now, he needed to take back what was his and make damn sure Mia never tried that shit again.

People parted in the halls, trying to avoid his temper, and were left whispering in his wake. His feet brought him to Mia's door and it was the pounding of his hand on it that brought Mia. She opened the door, startled by the deadly look.

"Who is it?" A female voice called from inside. If it had been male, Mal definitely would have lost his shit more than he already had.

"Get. Out." He ordered Mia's roommate.

The pale blue chick started to get up and grab her bag, hands shaking. She was on Mal's list, but it wouldn't be for a while. Even if she was scared now, she'd have forgotten by then. Although, it would be fun to hear her scream and beg for him not to fuck her before she got a taste and cried out, demanding more.

"Klira, stay." She stared, unafraid, back at him. "This isn't his room and I'm not going to talk to him anyway."

"Like hell you aren't!" Mal shoved his boot between the door and the frame as she tried to close it on him. "You're fucking around and that shit stops."

If a woman ever had the chance to scare Mal, the look Mia was giving him might have done the trick. But no woman ever scared him and, frankly, no fucking man ever did either.

"You're one to talk. And it's not your business what I do." She tried to push the door a little harder, but it wouldn't budge with his foot there.

"Like hell it's not!" He put his hand on the door and easily pushed it wider. "You're fucking mine, Mia. You don't fuck around! That pussy is mine," he growled.

It came fast, and he didn't have time to reach. The left side of his face stung where Mia slapped him. It just made his blood boil and his dick harder. She played around last time like she had claws, but she rolled over and fucking purred for him. Mal knew that she didn't have the bitchy bone in her bone, and no fucking bitch-ass was going to bone her to do so.

"You're going to regret that, bitch!"

He plowed into the room, knocking her over. For the first time, real fear was in her eyes as she fell on her bed. The blue chick had screamed, ran out, and left them alone. It probably was a matter of time until a commander came. It probably wouldn't look too good for McGrey to catch him balls deep in another chick but, then again, it might make her want him more – or get her to join in. Or it could make the delicate little commander scared, and he wanted to fuck her before she'd hide from him. Fuck her and make Tanaka break.

Mal kicked the door shut behind him and flipped the lock. A commander could get in with the right key card, but it would buy him some time. "You're mine, Mia. You ain't nobody else's and you can't go fucking around on me."

She had made it to the edge of her bed and seemed to hesitate on getting up. Either way, she was fucked.

"Y-you don't own me, Mal." She tried to sound brave, but he had already seen the chink in her armor. He scared her as much as he could excite her. Mia was smart enough to know that it wasn't a kink he was showing now. He'd be more inclined to snap her neck versus edging her to an unbelievable high.

"Awfully brave words for a whore." His smile grew as he noticed her bottom lip shake a little. "Maybe I should treat you like what you are instead of a person. I could do much worse things to your body. I could break you."

She tried to move further away, but her back was up against the opposite wall. A few photos she had taped up there got bumped and fell to the floor. Photos of Mia laughing and smiling.

"I'm not a whore!" She tried to yell back, but it was like a kitten trying to roar. It was pathetic.

Mal closed the gap between them. He could hear the hitch in her breathing as she fought to keep in the tears. "Then don't fucking act like one," he growled.

His hands dug into her sides as he forced her body in place and pinned her. Only her hands were shaking. The rest of her body must have remembered what he could do to her and how much she loved it. Mal pressed his groin into her and smiled as he heard Mia fight her instincts. He forced his body harder against hers. He was going to fucking love teaching her a lesson.

"I'm going to treat you like a fucking whore." He grabbed the waistband of her combat pants, tearing the fly open. "And you're going to fucking beg."

"Mal, no... please."

She squirmed, trying to get away as he yanked her pants down past her knees. There was no way that she could run away from him again like that, but he still flipped her over onto her stomach. He fisted her panties with one hand – tearing them apart – while he downed his own fly and pulled himself out. Mia's crying already had him hard.

"This is fucking going to hurt."

CHAPTER TWENTY-TWO

Every part of her ached by morning, long after he left. Mal had been rough last time, but it had been consensual. Just some light restraints and spanking. Last night had been an utter nightmare. The more Mia cried and begged for him to stop, the more it seemed to have turned him on. She didn't want to think about what she looked like right now. Her voice had barely come back, and it was still raw. At one point, his hand had been around her throat, but everything after that is a blank. Judging by how some parts of her felt, it was a blessing.

Mia hated the idea of it, but she had to leave her room. Not only had her roommate not come back and she was starving, but also the pain called to her better judgment. The thought of anyone seeing her – in as bad of shape as her imagination thought up – was terrifying, but Mia hoped that sneaking to the infirmary at five in the morning would limit the number of people awake.

She didn't run into a soul until the infirmary bay doors swooshed open. Then it was like entering another world where no one ever slept. Everyone seemed to rush by her as if she – in her condition – was invisible. Then again, that's what people did to those that were homeless – ignored the problem until it went away.

One of the nurses finally noticed her in his rush to somewhere, a medical chart half-open. "Um, you alright?"

He was staring and it really started to feel awkward. She wanted to be like those homeless people back on Earth and turn invisible. Mia just wanted to shrink up and wait until her body fixed itself. All she managed to do was shake her head, but that was enough. The male nurse set down the medical chart and gently wrapped an arm around her back, probably to stop her from bolting. Was it that obviously she was having regrets about coming here?

"Please sit on the cot here. I'll grab a doctor to come see you." He started to walk away, but paused at the edge of the curtain that split the small room into two private parts. Mia had seen that the other half of this room was vacant. "Is there anything I can do for you in the meantime? I can't get you any medication until you've been seen, but I could bring an ice pack for that bruise on your cheek."

It was like his words materialized the injuries. She hadn't realized that there was anything wrong with her face – minus her eyes – until he mentioned it. If he wanted to bring an ice pack, then there had to be a reason. The more she thought, the more she sort of remembered Mal punching her. It wasn't something she wanted to be thinking about now. The very thought was making her stomach heave, and remembering was hurting more than the aches plaguing her body.

"Yes." The voice that came out sounded so small to her ears. "And w-water, please?" The four words cause her throat to feel like sandpaper.

Mia stared down at her hands in her lap. She was trying to figure out how she let this happen. Was there something she said that made Mal think that she was his? It was just a one-night stand and she thought that was obvious to both of them. Mia wasn't a fool and knew he got around, even that he had a list. That part hadn't really bothered her because at least they had been together early on before he could catch too many diseases. But none of that really opened the door for last night. All she wanted to do was curl up, just thinking about it.

"Miss?" The male nurse had come back while she was caught up in her thoughts. "I brought you some water and the doctor will be with you in a moment. Can you tell me your name so that I can bring up your file for her?"

Mia took the paper cup and sipped the cool water. The thought of giving a wrong name and bolting crossed her mind, but she was already here and the damage was done. "Mia Ha," she admitted, staring down at the little bit of liquid left.

"Thanks, Cadet Ha. I'll go get Dr. Ahme."

She took a few more sips of the water before it was gone. It barely changed how her throat was feeling. If anything, it reminded her that it wasn't enough. The water was just a temporary fix, a bandage. But no bandage would be enough to fix her...

"Cadet Ha, I'm Dr. Ahme." A middle aged elf-looking woman pulled up a stool to sit in front of her. Her neon purple hair and eyes distracted Mia at first from the depressing turn that her thought had taken. "My nurse briefed me on your state when you walked in and, per protocol, we had to inform your commander. Commander Tanaka will remain outside of this room, but he does need to be briefed as he is ultimately responsible for your squad of cadets.

"I know that right now, you probably don't want anyone to touch you and that you don't want to think about the incident, much less talk about it. However, you're going to have to say something. It can be as simple as a head nod, for some questions. Do you understand?"

Mia didn't want to talk about it and she definitely didn't want to think about, so the doctor had that much right. She also didn't want Commander Tanaka to find out. Who knew how he would react? Would he say it was her fault? He was also Mal's commander, and a man. They always say that the woman provoked them or dressed a certain way which meant she wanted it, but they all wore the same standard issued space fatigues.

She nodded, which made the doctor continue. "I'm also going to need to touch you during my examination. I will need to see the extent of your injuries and apply any treatment needed. I will

171

erect a privacy force field during that time so you can be assured that no one will ever see nor hear you. You experienced something horrendous and it can pull out emotions that are hard to handle."

The doctor was trying to be gentle in her bedside manner. The effort wasn't completely lost, but it wasn't enough. Nothing would be enough. Nothing could erase what was done.

"Where's my cadet? I'd like to see her, talk to her."

Mia could hear Commander Tanaka, and he sounded close. He also sounded more concerned than bothered. Maybe he wouldn't put all the blame on her.

"I'm sorry, commander, but you're not allowed to see her. The doctor is with her right now and due to the fact that this was at least an assault – possibly a rape – we're not to allow anyone near her unless it is requested or permitted by the cadet. The doctor will report to you the findings so that the correct action can be taken."

It was the same male nurse speaking that had taken the time to get the cup of water. He hadn't blamed her for this, she just realized. Maybe not all men on this ship thought the same way.

"Please, just tell me if she's... I guess she's not ok. Shit." Mia could imagine his hand slowly running down over his face as he tried to figure out what he really needed to ask. "Did she... was she able to make it here on her own or was she found somewhere?"

"She walked in on her own, commander. She's visibly hurt and I can tell that's she's afraid."

Was she?

Maybe she was. She was afraid of what Commander Tanaka would say and do. Afraid of what the doctor would find and where she would touch. And yes – she realized – she was terrified of Mal and of him finding her.

"Alright, the privacy field is up. Please remove your clothes and set them on the cot." The doctor stepped away from the wall where there was an activation keypad. Mia hesitated. "Was the nature of your attack sexual?"

There was an odd colored clay on her boots, Mia noticed. She didn't want to – and couldn't – meet the doctor's eye. She didn't want to even nod her head. It was debatable whether or not what happened started because of a sexual reason. Mal had assumed things, confronted her about sex she had days ago, then decided he had to…

"Yes." The voice was even smaller than the last word she said.

The doctor nodded, seeming to reassess something. "Have you looked at your body for injuries of any kind and bruises?" No, she hadn't even looked at her face. Mia shook her head. "I can tell that you're not bleeding from any open wounds. I can use our diagnostic wand to get a body scan for any critical damage, but I am going to have to take a vaginal swab."

Mia knew that it was the same as an annual exam, but the idea terrified her now. While it was something that she had done a bunch of times, this was all new. She didn't know how much the spreader would hurt, and the brushing of the swab would probably feel like steel wool. All she could do was shake her head.

"That isn't negotiable, cadet. A vaginal swab is mandatory."

There was no way that she could do it. "What if it wasn't rape?"

The question seemed to confuse the alien doctor. "You were attacked and it was sexual. You are reluctant to remove your clothing and seem to be adverse to physical contact. While you could have gotten into a situation rougher than you wished, you would be acting differently and would have been able to state that you just needed a check-up to make sure that you were alright and maybe ask for something for the pain." The doctor sighed. "I understand that thought of an exam is terrifying but I can make it as painless as possible. You wouldn't even need to be awake for it if you're afraid. My duty is to treat you and that's what I'll do. Please, cadet, remove your bottoms and lay down on the cot."

It felt like she was getting scolded. It was a stupid thing to say, but Mia was desperate. She just didn't want anyone touching her. She thought that if it wasn't rape that she wouldn't have to go through with it. It wouldn't remove the threat of Mal or his anger, but it would at least make things less awkward. And what would an exam really do? It wasn't like they could test the sample and find out...

Mia froze halfway through complying. She must have gone pale because the doctor asked if she was alright. "C-can you... can you tell who... who it was?"

"Of course. It's their DNA. A quick genetic test and analysis in our database will tell us who attacked you," the doctor calmly said, pulling on a pair of latex gloves.

It would come out that it was Mal and he'd be brought in to be questioned. He would say that Mia asked for it. There was her roommate, but she had left before anything really happened. All she could say that Mia got into a fight with him last night and she was kicked out. The only people who really knew what happened were her and Mal. And, of course, he wouldn't say that he raped her. Maybe she should try to say it was consensual again.

"Before you say or think anything more, you will be protected from him and he will face punishment when we land on Earth."

That wasn't much of a relief, and the explanation of being protected was vague. They were on a starship. How protected from him could she be?

It was something that she just had to put out of her mind right now. Mia needed to force herself to take off the sweatpants and her underwear. It was unnerving to have the doctor watching her every move. Mia pinched her eyes tight and laid down on the cot.

She tried to distract herself when she heard the doctor drag her stool over. She started shaking when she left the weirdness of latex on her skin. There were tears running down her face when the doctor nudged open her knees. The doctor was saying something but Mia couldn't make out any of the words. Her sobs great worse and worse until her whole body was shaken with each new cry. At some point, the doctor had taken the swap but Mia was in hysteric, and didn't notice. She didn't notice when the doctor placed a blanket over her lower half nor when the bite of a needle came on her arm.

Alex paced outside the room. He didn't know what to think. This was bad. This was worse than bad. At least he was the commander handling it. If Heather had been involved, there was no way Malcolm Harrison was going to walk away breathing. But it still wasn't a position that Alex wanted to be in.

The Harrisons and the Tanakas weren't strangers. Malcolm's father was a fast rising politician, and his father was the decorated militant. Two respected men in their own right. Two stubborn men that made life unbearable. It was the Academy that brought them together and their love of parties, either crazy keggers or black-tie affairs. Malcolm was more or less a strange to the latter, but Alex knew the high expectations that were required of them. He was to become the youngest general in the history of the Force; Malcolm was to become a ruthless businessman. It would go against everything their families had strived and groomed them for if one was to be the folly of the other. If only the cadet had thought about that. There was no avoiding the discipline that needed to be handled, and he could hear both their fathers telling him to cover this up – make the problem go away. If Cadet Ha ever said a word, it would be a scandal that would destroy both of their families – more so the Harrisons. But that was all theoretical because Alex had no intention of letting this slide. It was morally wrong and he couldn't dehumanize his cadet by making her attack and pain meaningless. Then there was Heather. Her attacker never got brought to justice.

"What do ya want, fucktard?" Malcolm came around the corner, looking pissed off just for being asked here. He probably didn't know that Medical connected his DNA to Cadet Ha's attacker... but he would.

Alex held open the door to the starship's conference room. It was large enough for a medium sized table and ten people, but it was private enough for this. He gestured for the cadet to step inside. "Stop calling me that and address me properly or you'll only make things worse for yourself."

He laughed. "Okay, Commander Fucktard McTiny-Dick."

Alex tried to brush it off. He tried to think of the yoga and meditation that his grandmother tried to teach him as a kid – to calm himself so he wouldn't be such a terror around the house, running wild.

It wasn't working much.

"There's been a report of a sexual assault on the ship. In fact, there was the one I'm going to talk about and then another report days ago that seemed awfully similar, but not nearly as brutal." Alex locked the door and went to take a seat at the table across from the cadet. "One of your fellow cadets was raped last night and I thought that you should know it was someone you personally knew."

He just shrugged. Like it was no big deal. Like it didn't affect his life.

"Cadet Ha's roommate admitted that you visited her last night and ordered her out of the room. She said you made threats. Then I get a call from Medical about a female cadet being sexually assaulted. She has bruises where no normal person should have laid hands. Her windpipe was damaged from the force someone exerted to hold her down and her throat is raw. She has a fractured rib... black eye... cuts in her mouth from being slapped..." Alex paused for a moment to see if anything affected the man across from him, but his face was one huge blank. "Someone tried to break Cadet Ha. As a person on the protective detail, it should at least trouble you a little bit that there's someone like that aboard. I'm sure Lieutenant Gregor would want to be informed so that he could increase on-board security."

"Cut the shit, asswipe. You think I did this and you're, what, trying to scare me? Why don't you go fuck around with someone else and blame them? Hell, blame everyone on this fucking ship." Malcolm leaned over the table. "Because you got nothing on me and – if you did – you're a good little boy who wouldn't break his daddy's heart. What do you think he'd say if you threw the old family friend under the bus?"

"Probably that you deserved the ultimate punishment for abusing a woman, but that was better left for behind closed doors. I know your father would take much pleasure in the task. He still hate you for killing his wife?"

Malcolm struck the table with his fist. "Don't fucking talk about her! It wasn't like I asked for it. Think I wanted to be born? It was that fucker and his black-hearted, infested cock that killed her. It's his damn fault that he shoves off on me!"

He knew it was a nerve. Malcolm's mother had been the sweetest woman he knew – other than his own – when he was growing up. She always had little sweets that she'd share with him, and she'd talk about how soon Alex would have a little playmate to have fun with and pass the time when their fathers had business talks. She hadn't deserved to die in child birth, just like Malcolm didn't deserve the blame. But at least the man could show some kind of emotion, even if it was just unresolved anger.

"She'd be ashamed of you, Malcolm, and you know that. If she survived you, she would have raised you the right way and you wouldn't be abusing other people, physically or verbally."

"Aw, did I hurt little Alex's feelings? Oh, boo-hoo!" He mocked him and feinted crying, twisting his hand at the corner of his eye. "Poor wittle Awex!"

He wanted to snap. Throw a threat or fist at Malcolm, but he couldn't unless he wanted to mess this up for Cadet Ha. Her justice wasn't worth the price of his ego. "They took samples of the semen inside her. It came back as yours. We have proof. We have witnesses. When we get back to base, you will be court-martialed for rape and your fate will be whatever the General and council deem appropriate."

Malcolm laughed. He actually had the gall to laugh! "You're such a fucking retard!" He couldn't stop laughing. Like he had just been told the world's funniest joke. He was gasping for air. "The General is basically family. Ain't no way that's ever touching me!"

It was like a vacuum in space opened up inside his chest and everything went rushing into oblivion. Alex knew it had to be true, not that he knew there was a connection before. Malcolm was more untouchable than he was. Malcolm was untouchable to him. And worse, Malcolm would make sure his father knew that Alex had betrayed the family's friendship by perusing this. Nothing would come from it other than more hatred. It didn't really matter – being a grown man now – but Alex had wanted this to mean something. He wanted giving up family bonds to mean something for Cadet Ha. She deserved justice.

"But what's really funny is your fucking face! You actually think you could get me with something." The laughing had died down but there was still amusement on Malcolm's face. It was like that smirk was permanently glued to his face. "You're not untouchable, fuckwad, and I got you."

The smirk only grew as he lifted his arm and turned it so the speaker portion was aimed more towards Alex after he brought up the audio file. "Just like I got Commander McGrey moaning out my name, begging me to fuck her." He hit the playback button and Heather's voice filled the silence of the room. There was no mistaking those moans. There was no mistaking the name she was calling out.

"You didn't –" Alex started.

"Oh, but I did and," he cut him off, "she. loved. it."

He was flying across the table, ready to fight. Alex threw a punch but the smug brat dodge him, putting a chair between them.

"She fucking wanted it," Malcolm taunted. "She needed to be fucked by a real man… got tired of giving pity fucks for you and being your sloppy seconds."

Alex pulled the rest of his body over the table, knocks chairs over as he fell into them on the other side. "I'll kill you for that!" He got to his feet, shoving one chair into the wall to clear a path to Malcolm.

"Oh but you won't." The cadet stopped the recording and stood with a bigger smirk. "How would your precious Commander

McGrey feel knowing that you're the reason our sex tape got leaked? Yea, that's right. It gets sooo much better than this little part. The second night she came begging for it, and we did some fucking great shit."

While the rage built up inside him, so did the hopeless feeling. Heather wouldn't have cheated on him – but that recording. Heather would know that he tried to stop Malcolm if anything got out. The kid had to be lying about a sex tape and that audio could be anyone….

"It's sinking in now, huh? Bet it's a bitch." Malcolm laughed. "But I'm not above letting an old family friend buy my silence. I'm thinking that he needs to be my little bitch on this ship. I'm thinking the first fucking thing he's going to do is get rid of that damn rape report. Sounds like a fucking good way to apologize for being such a fucking ass."

He wouldn't. He couldn't. That was taking away everything Cadet Ha endured and her bravery in the medical bay. He'd be robbing her if he wiped Malcolm's slate clean. He'd be letting another rapist go free just like Heather's had. And Heather… she'd never be able to look at him again. Then again, he couldn't look at her either. She had destroyed his heart and the worst part was that it had been Malcolm. She picked Malcolm – who had known about them and purposely recorded it to torture him as some sick payback for something stupid that probably happened when they were kids.

If Malcolm ever knew about Heather and the fact that she still carried the General's baby, it would catastrophic. They'd both be disciplined for being colleagues having a relationship, but it could possible mean Heather's life was over. Literally and metaphorically. He might hate her now for what she'd done, but he couldn't do that to her either. Alex would have to keep her secret, knowing it would kill him to protect the one person that hurt him the most. He wanted her to hurt as badly as she hurt him, but he couldn't stoop that low. He still felt the need to protect her.

"I'll get rid of it, but you have to leave Heather alone. She stays out of it. You don't touch her again." It was hard not to let his emotions get to him.

Malcolm chuckled. "You think I'm going to give up that fine piece of ass?" He started towards the door. "You're the one who's fucking insane. She's the one craving my fucking cock." He unlocked the door and flung it open. It hit the wall so hard that Alex jumped from the sound of it. "And McGrey is going to fucking get it. I'm going to fuck her so hard that she can't walk. Every. Fucking. Night."

And he left.

On the floor was the piled remains of a too-broken man.

CHAPTER TWENTY-THREE

Heather was surprised when he never showed. It wasn't like Alex to say that he'd be somewhere and then to flake, especially with her. He hadn't been in his room when she stopped by this morning on her way to the bridge. If he had, he didn't answer and she'd rather believe it was because he was passed out, asleep. But it was her shift and there wasn't much time to debate what was or wasn't going on with her co-commander. She'd see him later and they'd grab lunch together. A night back in her own bed was just what she needed, but she also missed the warmth and safety of being wrapped up in her boyfriend's arms.

It was mostly deserted in the cafeteria when she walked in to drab her first cup of coffee for the day. It seemed like her addiction for caffeine had grown since the withdrawals started.

The liquid was scalding but it was a welcome and familiar feeling. The three spoons of sugar and dash of cream was a good way to ease into the morning. It also gave her step a little pep as she stepped onto the bridge. It was relatively empty, minus the officer monitoring communication with HQ. There was a technician tinkering around and installing the recovered parts from the dragouul starship.

"Any good updates on getting her running?" She asked the technician, taking a sip from her cup.

He shook his head. "Not yet. We're got a handful of parts to install here but then there's the mess down by the engine room with the main navigation and control system."

That would be secondary to installation. It didn't sound promising that they'd be leaving this planet anytime soon. "Do you have an ETA on when that would be?"

Again he shook his head. "It's tricky converting some of these alien parts into our ship and there's been some things that needed MacGyvering. I wouldn't trust any of the junior technicians with this. So it'll at least be another day or two for me and Hans. Once we move down to the engines, maybe another two days. Then we gotta reboot the system and throw some coding around… a week?"

That would feel like an eternity.

"Let me know when you hit the coding. I'll take some shifts and get us through that."

"Yes, commander."

With that, she headed to the commander's chair to log the details given by the technician and to switch command duties back over to herself. There was a draft report lingering in the system. That was so unlike Alex. Even though he was lax on some things, he wouldn't just leave it in limbo. She'd have expected him to submit a short report and then an addendum to fill in all the missing gaps of his first. Curiosity got to her and she hit the playback button.

"Oh-five-oh-nine. Medical bay notified me that a cadet was sexually assaulted. Her injuries range from bruises to possibly a broken rib. Emotional state is poor… understandably. Reporting to Medical now."

The recording paused for a moment and she assumed he'd be walking to that wing.

"Cadet Mia Ha was sexually assaulted. Medical collected DNA and is analyzing it to identify her attacker. Awaiting to speak with her before establishing a protective detail. Wait, the doctor is saying the guy was…"

The recording ended there. Maybe that's where Alex was now. Cadet Ha. If she wasn't mistaken, that was the new navigator for the mission. The girl had been a little nervous, but it was understandable on her first time behind the coding wheel. She had eased up and became a natural. Then this happened. Heather hoped that they wouldn't end up losing her. She didn't have to imagine what the cadet had gone through, nor imagine that quitting the Force was probably on the girl's mind.

It was debatable whether or not Heather should reveal that she was also a victim. Back then, there had been a few other woman to commiserate with. It hadn't felt like much help at the time, but looking back it was probably the thing that got her through it. Heather could be that for the cadet. It was just that she couldn't give too many details and risk letting out who her attacker had been. It was an internal debate that lasted the whole trek over to the medical bay.

Heather stopped one of the doctors on duty. "I'm looking for Cadet Ha. She would have come in early this morning."

"Cadet Ha is in the third room, but she's still unconscious. The attending doctor sedated her and she's been kept under observation. The psychiatrist still needs to talk to her and determine what help needs to be provided. I'm sorry, but I can't advise that you see her right now."

Heather nodded. That was understandable. She was sure that one of the doctors would inform her when Cadet Ha awoke and was ready to talk. That just left one unresolved thing.

"Is Commander Tanaka still here?"

The doctor shook his head. "No, I'm afraid that he left soon after the cadet was admitted. The doctor on duty gave him the name of the attacker and he left to handle that." Something seemed to be bothering the man. "It's got a few of us worried that someone like that was allowed on our ship. It would be nice to know that it was taken care of and can't happen to anyone else."

"You and I can both agree on that. That's why I'm trying to find Commander Tanaka." Well, one of the reasons now. "We'll make sure whoever did this is held responsible. I don't like the fact that this happened on my ship either." Nor to another woman on her watch.

Heather stepped away and headed out the bay doors. "Tanaka," she spoke into the com device. She hoped that he would realize that it was important. After all, she hadn't called him by his surname since they got together.

The radio was silence. "Tanaka, answer. This is important." She waited a moment, hoping he'd respond. "We need to discuss the attack."

But he didn't respond at all.

That was odd. It was like Alex just disappeared from the face the world. She pulled up the docking bay data log but there had been no openings since she arrived back with the dragouuls. So Alex hadn't gone on-planet. She brought up the data system in her com device and opened his profile. No, his device was online. That meant he had to have heard her transmissions. Ok, so then he was choosing to ignore her? Why would he do that? It didn't make sense why he couldn't answer and was hiding from her. A man didn't hide unless he was doing something wrong, and Alex...

She didn't want to think about that. There was plenty of opportunities for him to cheat on her, but that just didn't seem like something he'd do. Not after Alex told her how much she meant to him and how happy he felt now that they were together. She could... Her finger hovered over the sub-routine to track the com device. It wasn't hard to justify – there was a crime aboard their ship and they needed to handle it. Protocol. It wasn't that she was a jealous or clingy girlfriend, and it wasn't that he said he'd spend the night with her and then disappeared.

It was too tempting. Alex had a past that should have been making her worry and act a lot more than she was now. The doctor had confirmed that he was awake and went to deal with the attacker. The unfinished log meant that he must still be handling it. By reason, she should then track with com device to locate him. Either she'd join him in the discipline of the attacker or she'd find him knocked out from a fight. That settled it then. He could be in danger. She hit the bio-tracker for his com device and couldn't believe where he was.

He was in his room.

She had knocked and there hadn't been any response, not even a hint of movement. There was no way that he was asleep. The com device would have been loud in that small room. He was ignoring her. There was no way around that. That or he left his com device, but that was only shadier than plainly ignoring her. She didn't want to believe that Alex could be cheating.

Instead, she went back to his room and knocked. Again, there was no sign or sound of life. "Alex, I know you're in there. Please, talk to me."

It didn't seem like her plea was going to get her anywhere, and Heather didn't have the time to track every com device to make sure that he was in there alone. The upside was that he'd have to come out eventually to either use the bathroom or get something to eat. It was only a matter of time before that door opened. And then it did, but it made her heart drop.

"I don't want to see you, Heather. Go away." The voice came out of the smallest gap.

She jumped at the chance to see him, trying to budge the door open more. "Alex, we need to talk. Let me in."

"No." Heather searched the sliver of his visible face, trying to understand. That's when she realized his eyes were red. "We don't need to talk."

"Alex, what's wrong? Are you..." She didn't want to ask if he was high. He smoked cigarettes against protocol, but she wasn't sure that he hadn't packed anything else.

"Just go away."

"Not until you tell me what's wrong."

"You!" The loudness of his voice startled her. "You're what's wrong. You! You! You!"

All Heather could do was shake her head. She couldn't have heard him right. How was *she* what was wrong? The only thing

185

that she could think of was her asking to spend the night in her own room, somewhere familiar. But that hadn't meant he couldn't have come over.

"Alex, I don't-"

He let out a half-hearted chuckle. "You understand. You knew what you did. I can never forgive you for that."

Alex tried to close the door but she forced her boot into the gap. He still tried to force the door closed, knowing her foot was there. It hurt. He was hurting her.

"I said you could come over last night. I just wanted to be in my own bed for once," she tried to explain it to him again.

"Like I'd care about that?" He sounded so cold all of a sudden. "I know you cheated on me. So cut the shit, Heather. We're over."

When he kicked her boot out of the way, she didn't fight him. When he slammed the door, she didn't try to stop him. She was in shock. She was so confused. It didn't make any sense. By the time her wits came back, it was too late to try and stop Alex. His door was closed to her, in more ways than one.

Chapter Twenty-Four

Mal kicked it up a notch in the gym room. It was the second time he upped the speed on the treadmill. His muscles were starting to ache from the long run, but it cleared his mind. Things weren't exactly fucking perfect. He hadn't expect Mia to fucking go to that fucktard. The bitch should have fucking learned! What kind of girlfriend – no, she was just a whore – does that shit and snitches?

Someone came in the gym, letting the door slam behind them. The last thing Mal wanted was to be around someone. Especially a tiny little thing like the girl that got on the treadmill next to him. All he could think about was working his anger out on her. Anger over that whore. Anger over having to fucking deal with fucking Tanaka. The recording he had of McGrey in the hospital was enough fucking blackmail to give him a free pass for any fucking shit he wanted to do.

"Hey." Maybe all he needed was to be fucking balls deep in something.

The girl glanced at him, gave that head nod thing to acknowledge him and kept on running. Guess that was his answer about fucking her. He brushed it off. If she was on his Fuck It List, then he'd pound that later. He headed for the showers and let the place steam up before getting inside. The water scorched his back, but it felt fucking good. It eased some of the tension. In a towel, he headed down the hallway to his room, earning him stares. And let them! They can just be fucking jealous of what he got – and they hadn't even seen his cock yet!

He changed into his uniform, pulling a white tee on instead of the camouflage combat shirt. They weren't fucking fighting anyone, much less going on-planet. Not that he knew of. Mal strapped on his com device and downloaded the communication files that he had missed during his shower. He almost expected a message from Gregor saying he was suspended from duty, but there wasn't any. Tanaka really didn't have the fucking balls.

Talk about putting a fucking smile on his face.

That just left what he'd do with McGrey – minus fucking bending her over and pounding that piece of ass. He didn't have blackmail on her to get away with shit. If anything, he owed her and that pissed him off. Malcolm Harrison didn't fucking owe anyone anything. If she hadn't stopped that fucking alien from eating him alive, there wouldn't be a fucking problem. But she saved him. The best way he could play it was to get that fuckwad to override anything she fucking did to him. All he had was that recording of her moaning in the hospital bed for god knows why. If she ever heard it, she might know what it was and call his bullshit. Then he'd be fucking screwed. Somehow he had to make sure that never happened.

He knew right now that the fuckwad was a crumpled blubbering mess and no fucking use to him now. It wouldn't make sense to go to him now and make demands. The fucking idiot probably was still on the floor where Mal left him.

Pathetic.

And it was only poking the bear to waltz right up to McGrey and make demands. He wanted to do that when he was sure she'd end up on her knees. He couldn't go there either.

Mia was a loose end. She had talked and had to pay for whoring around. Why did she fucking get it in her head that she could fuck around on him? That was bullshit. He said she was a good fuck and wanted that ass later. Wasn't that obvious to her? It was far more than any other bitch on this starship got or would get. She was the trophy on his Fuck It list. Now he had to handle things before they got back on-planet. He needed to make sure that she didn't say a damn word to anyone else. If anyone but that fucking idiot knew what he did, then it would be a mess and the Harrisons didn't tolerate messes. He'd hate to get his father involved – the fucking prick – so that fuckwad Tanaka had better pull through for him. If not, there was one sure way to make sure Mia never talked...

"Fucking Christ!" He rounded the corner and ran into one of the giant fucking aliens. Mal jumped out of the way, feeling disgusted that it had touched him and creeped out that he couldn't see its eyes through the skull piece it wore on its face. "Fucking alien shit," he mumbled under his breath as he walked away.

Mia opened her eyes slowly. The doctor had finally left the room and there was no need to play dead any longer. They probably had some kind of monitor hooked up to her to know if she was awake or not. Probably something monitoring her pulse or heart rate.

The ceiling above her was pure white and it gently curved down into the wall at the head of her bed. Her sight had been bedazzled with stars and swirling colors the first time she opened her eyes and the nightmare of it all struck her. There was barely a faint smell of vomit left in the room, probably thanks to some automated cleaner bot. But noting the lack of stench just reminded her what caused it in the first place and she felt her stomach retch, only nothing would come out.

She just wanted to vomit out the pain, the memories, the disgusting feeling that was burying itself inside her. She wanted to run and escape this prison of a body. She just wanted everything to disappear. She wanted to disappear. Maybe if she could get out of this bed, Mia could just...

No. She couldn't.

Her mom had escaped the late stages of cancer that way instead of suffer to the end. Mia had hated her for it at the time, before she tried to understand why her mom would take her life. It was tempting… to stop the pain. Mia could see the storage drawers that probably had scalpels or at least a syringe, shelves of medications all above that. She could lock the door and be gone before maintenance could open the lock.

No. She had to stop thinking like that.

A strangled groan tore out. She didn't want to be constantly feeling him. She didn't want to constantly be thinking about him, fearing him, dreaming of him… it.

That groan betrayed her and the door opened to one of the last people she thought could help at that moment. There was no hiding the fact that she was conscious and losing herself.

Commander McGrey shut the door behind her and drew over a chair next to the bed. It was so strange to see her take a seat and act so casual. She expected to be lectured about protocol and procedure, hearing about the charges or penalties against her for fornicating with a few crew members. But that's not what it seemed like the commander was here to do.

"The doctors turned me away before, but I need to be here and to talk to you. I know nothing I say can ever change what happened and probably not how you're feeling right now. The pain he caused is going to last and it'll take your whole life to train yourself to push it all away." The commander's voice was oddly soft – almost nurturing – and Mia found it hard not to, at least, listen. "The doctors, here, can heal your body. The therapist they send in will try to get you to cope. There's no one that can heal your soul."

"Commander, I know you're probably trying to make me feel better or something, but it's not working."

"I don't understand, right?" The commander shifted in the chair and, after a moment, leaned closer. "I was raped three years ago on a mission. Nothing made me forget what he did to me and how I felt. Nothing could make me whole again. I had other women with me that suffered from the same man, and that's the only way we survived. But it wasn't really surviving. It was just trying to get to tomorrow."

Mia stared at her. There was no way someone strong like the commander could have gone through that. That just wasn't possible. She wouldn't have allowed herself to be that weak, unlike Mia.

"I was able to face my abuser but I never was able to call him out publically. He tried everything to kill me."

The commander had to be exaggerating that last part. No one would actually attempt murder if they got caught. Thinking of Mal, even though it hurt, she didn't think he'd actually try killing her. He may attacker her again, beat her, run her and her reputation through the mud, but Mia didn't think he'd actually go that far.

"It's no easy task to confront him and it doesn't make the pain go away either. But it's worse to watch from the sidelines as he laughs and goes on with his life like nothing happened. In public, he'll pretend you don't exist, but it'll be every time that you're alone that you'd fear... fear him suddenly being there. It's impossible to feel safe if he's left out there."

Mia felt for the commander, and herself. She hadn't been conscious long enough for it all to sink in yet, but she could feel the fear waiting outside these four walls.

"So it'll never be over," she whispered, more to herself.

"Only if you let it. All I need is a name and I can make sure he never gets near you again. I can protect you on this ship and when we return to Earth, I can make sure that he does his time."

Protect her? The commander had already failed to do that once. But still, the idea that McGrey could make it go away – at least as far as Mal – helped that growing pit of fear and loathing. After all, Mia had been the one to go to Mal that one night. It was her fault that he thought she was into him like that.

"No offense, commander, but you let him be on this ship when there's something clearly wrong with him. He's not normal. The background checks..." Mia hadn't realized how much her hands were shaking in her lap until a hand gently covered them.

191

"I know we already failed you, Mia, but I don't want to fail you again." She couldn't. "I don't know how he got through the background checks but, if you tell me his name, I can stop this right now. Can you do that?"

She shook her head. Saying his name aloud was impossible. Mia could barely stand to think it, let alone say it.

"Alright." To say Commander McGrey was disappointed was an understatement, but she knew the struggle to speak up and keep living after something like this. She couldn't fault the cadet. "Then I'm going to let you rest and I'm going to figure out how to catch this guy."

Mia didn't say anything as the slight protective warmth left her shaking hands. The commander paused by the door, almost hoping that she'd change her mind and speak a name. It was one last shot to be brave and strong.

But right now, she was anything but.

Chapter Twenty-Five

"Have you ever thought about dying?"

The look in his eye clearly said that he had, many times. Just knowing that General Ruthesford had imagined – and probably fantasized over – her dying sent a chill through her whole body. She was shivering now and it wasn't due to the fact that she was standing in front of the general stripped down. He had the room set to 50^0F to watch her skin turn blue before he'd beat and fuck her red. It wasn't that that chilled her bones, it was the lusty desire in his gaze to make her death a reality.

Heather shook her head in reply when he stood. The general hated to be kept waiting. He hated when his questions weren't answered.

"Did you know that I chose you, Heather?" This time she quickly shook her head, and he continued. "It's because you know every rule, protocol, procedure, and detail. I could ask you what I could be found guilty of when I bend you over my desk and you could recite it verbatim."

He was doing all this just because she was good at her job? Because she could follow orders and knew what procedures needed to be done? That was fucking insane! He was fucking insane.

"You would use that pretty little mouth to tell me all the ways that I'm in the wrong."

The general circled around his desk and came to a stop in front of her. Heather flinched when his hand reached up to stroke her cheek. It was the same hand that punched the wind out of her to force her to double over and be in position for him to finger fuck her. The taste of which Heather could still make out on her bruised lips from where his hand demanded to be sucked clean.

"And while you're accusing me and citing everything I've done wrong," he yanked her body against his clothed one, "I would be rewriting every rule. Everything out of your mouth would be a fucking lie. You wouldn't know a damn thing. There wouldn't be a damn thing that you could do." He shoved Heather across the desk, grabbing her hips and dragging her back to the edge. "My position gives me anything I want."

Heather felt his hand trail down over her hip before a sharp slap broke the momentary silence and made her ass scream in pain.

"You're in a perfect position, Heather." His words sounded saccharine sweet. "Let's explore our options." She didn't need to see his face to know a wicked smile was there.

His knee shoved her legs wide as his hand gripped the nape of her neck to hold her down. She realized exactly what option he was looking to explore this time. The fear of the pain made her panic and she fought to get out from under him. But the more she fought, the tighter he squeezed.

"You know I just love a fight. Makes me so fucking hard," he whispered into her ear. "Let's see how long I can make you scream."

CHAPTER TWENTY-SIX

Alex paced his room, two enormous problems on his mind. The first was Heather. She played the fool, weaving such a great story about how she always wanted to be with him. Then she goes around and fucks a cadet behind his back. Malcolm Harrison, of all dicks! The fucking rapist on board.

That was his second problem. He'd love to watch the piece of shit burn, but it was all a political dance between their families. That all rounded back to Heather again. What would she do when she found out her fuck buddy was the one who raped Cadet Ha? It was bound to happen sooner than later. She never could let things go, which was obvious by how she kept trying to feed him her lies. With it being another space rape, she would never let it go. Heather couldn't destroy her abuser, but she could definitely destroy Malcolm and the Harrisons' political aspirations. That meant, as a Tanaka, he needed to step in to dissuade that by any means possible. This would surely earn him the general's position when the time came.

Yet, he couldn't think of a single reason to step in front of Heather's warpath. The feelings were still raw and overpowering. All he wanted was to protect her from reliving her past. As much as he hated it, Alex was still in love with her. He didn't want to try and understand it. If they were back on Earth, he'd be numbing it out in some seedy bar with his best friend, who probably had some minor misery of his own to drown.

"Call from... HQ Base."

Alex tried to ignore the call on his com device. It was against protocol to keep headquarters waiting and, if Heather, was here he'd be getting a lecture right about that.

"Call from… HQ Base."

The com device gave a little vibration on his wrist. Probably a special features woven into the coding for when HQ Base called so the call couldn't be ignored.

"Commander Tanaka," he answered, hitting the round yellow button on the bottom right of the device. He wondered if he could feint a dropped call with their remote destination and get back to the bigger problems at hand than some late progress report HQ Base was calling about.

"Commander Tanaka, you have an order from General Ruthesford. You are to detain Commander McGrey and isolate her to the medical bay of your starship. She is to be removed from communication with other crew members. This is for everyone's safety. Her latest medical report shows anomalies in her system and, if needed, you can journal her as "In Quarantine" in the ship's log."

Heather was sick? Well, he knew she was sick if she thought she could go around playing these games with his heart. But it sounded like she was sick-sick. Was that why she ended up fucking Mal? She had mentioned that the injections that helped with the pain and tapped down certain urges. Seeing how he hadn't gone on the recon mission to get the Dragouul diplomat, maybe she lost control and took Mal in desperation.

That still didn't excuse her behavior though.

"Understood. I shall detain Commander McGrey to the medical bay and wait for further instructions."

"Roger. Over and -"

"Wait! One question." Alex cut off the operator before he could end the call. "Has there been any update on the orders for evacuating the planet? The last transmission should have contained the information of the Dragouul diplomat's rescue and acquisition of their starship. We've began retrofitting the

Alphecca's damaged parts and there's no ETA for departure. The last transmission was not to attempt relaunch."

The com device went so silent that he could hear the light hum of electricity in his room's light. Did they hear him or was his question ignored? It was already suspicious that they told them not to attempt returning. Of course, their ship was severely damaged and re-entry into space may simply be disastrous. Yet, HQ Base hadn't sent anyone to rescue them. While the Alphecca was the newest starship out there and leaving her off in the universe was a travesty, it was worse to lose a whole crew. There should have been somebody from a nearby planetary base or passing starship that could come to their aid. Instead, they had been told to do nothing.

"Sorry, Commander Tanaka. At this time, the order still remains to standby."

Alex grumbled his thanks as he rubbed his temples. They weren't leaving anytime soon and he had to face the music – well, face Heather. He knew that she was just going to keep feeding him lies instead of owning what she did. She was desperate to talk though. That he could use to make this ordeal easier on himself.

He left the safety of his room and headed down towards medical. Cadets walked passed him, cheery and chatty. Word clearly hadn't gotten out about Cadet Ha, which was fortunate. That meant that one problem was contained for now, but it was a ticking clock. Mal could literally fuck that up at any moment. He needed to contain that cadet and then make sure the other one was properly taken care of. He needed Cadet Ha to get all the medical treatments she could get to physically erase what was done to her and then he'd need to arrange a therapist to meet with her for the mental and emotional damage. It felt almost callous to think of her needs as just another item on his list to check off. In truth, he really didn't know any other way to help her other than to bandage her up and get rid of Mal.

"Commander." One of the doctors acknowledged him as soon as he entered through the medical bay doors. "I'm assuming you're here about Cadet Ha. She's woken but hasn't said much. Her injuries seem to be healing… although she did need to be restrained after Commander McGrey left her."

"Heather – um, McGrey – sat with her?" That was not good. She could know who raped the girl and already be on the warpath. Then there was no way that he'd get her to meet him in medical and follow through with his orders.

The doctor nodded. "Yes, and I'm not sure what they discussed. She was not supposed to see the cadet and it was only when she left did anyone notice her. I can't say if it was something the commander said or if the realization of what happened came over the cadet. She's sedated now, so I'm not sure how helpful she'll be in your investigation."

Alex nodded along, taking note of what the blue man said. "I'm glad that she's on the mend." There really wasn't much more he could say, so he didn't. "I'm actually here because of McGrey. Orders came from HQ Base that she needs to be detain in isolation in the medical bay. I need to see that it gets arranged. There's no problem in getting her here. I just need to know that there's personnel ready to restrain her and do what needs to be done."

The doctor looked like he wanted to argue. It was another time that rank came in handy. "Understood. We can have a room arranged in the back in ten minutes. Is there anything we should know about why she's being detained? I'm not sure what you are at liberty to say, commander."

Even to a medical professional used to seeing strange, it sounded like an odd request. "I was told there was a medical anomaly in her last report from after the crash. I'm guessing they're just being safe instead of sorry."

"I can pull her last medical report and make sure it's nothing that poses a serious risk to my people. If you'd like to wait up here by the nurse station, we'll get the room ready for Commander McGrey."

He nodded and walked by the nurse station, then decided to take a detour. He stopped outside the cadet's room. The doctor had said that she was sedated, and Alex should have known that it meant not to disturb her. After all, his brother ended up a doctor. Alex tried to think of how he'd feel, being the one trapped in a medical bed. He'd want to know that someone was out there doing something.

Alex overrode the code on her room – probably an added safety feature after Heather's stunt – and pushed the door open. The cadet looked even smaller in that bed since the last time he saw her. Her eyes were glazed over and half-dead when her head turned to look at him. Alex wanted to tell himself that it was only due to the sedative.

"Cadet Ha..." He hesitated but finally decided to move to the chair next to her bed. "I don't want to upset you but I want you to know that we're actually doing something."

The words he knew that needed to say just got jumbled in his head and he wished – for a moment – that Heather was here to pass on the news. She always knew what to say. But she wasn't and he needed to get it out before someone came and shooed him from the room. "I know it was Malcolm Harrison. I am in the process of locating him and, when I do, he will be detained. I am filing the paperwork for a court martial. Once we get back to Earth, he will be arrested, tried, and locked away."

He saw a tear roll down her face. Even sedated, he had managed to upset her or maybe it was out of relief or – dare he say – happiness. He had said his peace, and now the space inside the smooth-walled room just felt awkward.

"Well, that's all I wanted to say." He got up slowly, trying not to take another look at her. It was gut-wrenching that this had happened on his watch. He couldn't look back and see the pain she was in. He couldn't look back because he was afraid he'd see Heather in her place.

"Heather, can you come to medical?"

She jumped at the voice coming from her com device. It was the last one that she thought she'd hear right now. Then again… medical? It had to be something about Cadet Ha. It meant that it was all professional, which was a slight disappointment. Heather couldn't understand how he could suddenly not care about her.

"Is this about Cadet Ha?" If so, she really saw no reason to walk all the way down to medical. The com devices were secure and any transmission possibly recorded by HQ Base between them was a moot point, seeing as the rape was already recorded and the report sent in. So if their com devices were bugged and it recorded Cadet Ha's current status, it made no difference.

"Actually, no… I, um… I just want to meet you in medical." Alex sounded a little off. Then again, the only reason he was down there was probably because of the cadet. Rape was enough to shake anyone.

"I'll be right down." Heather signed off.

She sat up from where she was moping and reached under her bed to grab her boots. It would break protocol, but she left on her fuzzy socks and just stuffed the tops into the boots. They were the only bit of comfort that she brought, and the only thing she had to cling to during this break-up. Well, that and coffee, which she could use another dose – and it was on the way.

It took almost five minutes to get to medical with a steaming cup of half cream, two tablespoons sugar, and a dash of cinnamon – coffee. It was hardly liquid "courage" but it did give her some comfort and it could keep her hands busy while they talked.

She walked through the sliding medical bay doors and didn't spot Alex anywhere. She walked over to the nurse station and asked the cadet there if he'd seen Commander Tanaka. The cadet said nothing, and then everything happened so suddenly.

Someone came up behind her, wrapping an arm around her chest, trapping one arm against her side. The first thought that passed her mind was that it was Alex and he was acting affectionate because he realized she was telling him the truth. But the arm was scaly and blue. The second thought was, in a moment of panic, that she was being attacked. Heather tried to kick behind her but nothing connected with the attacker's legs. Training taught her to thrown her head back in an attempt to break the attacker's nose and take advantage of the moment of pain and shock. But another set of arms had latched on to restrain her, only this time they belonged to the nurse she was just talking to.

"I order you to let me go!" This made no sense! Heather kept fighting, dropping her coffee in the process, feeling it scald her leg. "Let. Me. Go!"

"Heather."

It was one word from a disembodied voice. It made her pause for a moment. It was like God coming down and choosing her as the special one to speak to. It was the ray of light in a gloomy word. It was Alex's clear voice in this confusing situation. It was the distraction as something bit her arm.

She felt her body being moved through the lobby area. They took her into a room, and then she finally saw him. He was standing just inside the door. His face was a storm of emotions. In that instant, Heather knew that he hadn't asked her here to talk about their relationship or about the ship or about the cadet. He was a bystander, casually watching everything happening. He knew.

He *knew*.

Her face felt hot as tears ran down it. Alex knew this was going to happen to her. He was the only one that could have given the order!

"Let me go!" They had her on a medical bed now – two of them were trying to hold her down while the third got the restraints. "Alex, stop this!"

The more she struggled, the more the two large bodies forced her down, crushing her. The more she struggled, the more indifferent Alex looked. He wasn't going to help her; that was clear. He was the one doing this. All because he thought she cheated on him? That made him the worst person ever. He said he loved her. How could you do this to someone you love?

"Alex, don't do this," she begged.

Her left arm was strapped to the bed, the cuff digging tightly into her wrist.

"I didn't cheat on you. I swear on my grandma's life that I didn't!"

It was harder to fight off the large men with only one arm. When she reached over to try and work off the cuff, they seized her wrist. They squeezed it so hard and yanked it away that she couldn't do anything but scream in pain.

"A-le-ex…. pl-ease," she begged between sobs. Her body ached, but she just couldn't stop fighting. Her legs would never be able to unlatch the cuffs, but that didn't stop them from tying them to the bed.

"Shut up," he snapped. While it got her mouth to snap shut, it just made the tears run harder. "She's to remain in isolation. Remove the com device. Code lock the door."

Alex started to walk away. How could he be this cruel?

"I'm sorry… I'm sorry, Alex. I'm so, so, so sorry." She couldn't move. Everything hurt and it felt worse when one of the nurses removed the com device from her wrist. She would be completely alone. "Don't leave me, please," she begged. "Please don't."

He stopped at the door. His face was hidden from her, but then he turned around and walked to her bedside as the nurses disbursed. His face got close to hers, enough that she could smell the lingering cigarette smoke on him.

"I don't care how much you apologize, Heather. It's not going to fix anything. You. –" Alex pulled away and started pacing the room. "You destroyed what we had. You destroyed me, and nothing you say is ever going to change that!"

He let out a frustrated breath, running a hand through his hair. "You're here because you have to be here." Alex had calmed himself, but barely. "You're stripped of your duties. You're to remain here in isolation, and you'd best think about your decisions."

This couldn't be happen.

Alex didn't give her another look at he walked out.

This wasn't real.

The door swooshed shut and a digital beep announced it was locked.

This was just a dream... a nightmare.

She needed to wake up. All this would be over if she just woke up. All this would go away if she just woke up. This couldn't be real. This couldn't be happening to her. Her body tried to fight. A strangled scream tore out of her, but it died before it could escape the soundproofing of the room.

She knew that she needed to find someone. Heather always listened so patiently. If not, then her mate might be helpful. There was just so much anger and violence aboard this ship. Azvark worried that gaining these aliens' help would end up causing harm to her family. Two of her children already had night terrors from things they overheard in the crew's minds.

Her raptor-sharp gaze searched everywhere for Heather. She didn't seem to be present in any of the rooms where the others congregated. Reaching out with her mind proved fruitless. It seemed that the girl was just too far away, but something else was close.

Azvark felt it long before she saw him coming down the corridor. It was a fury of pain and anger and confliction. Nothing was coherent in his thought for her to pick up on. Just bits like "following orders" and "for the best", followed by "betrayal" and "Heather". It was all out of order and surely would give her a headache if she tried to piece the train of thought together. One thing was clear though – this was Heather's mate and the other human in charge of the ship. He almost ran into her large being before noticing her. In a moment, fear and panic rolled over his facial features, but then was replaced as fast with indifference.

"I'm sorry I... I almost didn't see you there." She watched as he ran a hand over his face, trying to gather his thoughts. In his mind, she could at least hear things taking on more of sentences than garbled messes. "Did you need something or just taking a walk?"

"I was walking but to find you or your mate." She wasn't sure why he asked her a question that was the answer. "While my children suffer from your crew's thoughts, I'm more worried about physical harm. Earlier a male passed by me and I sensed the worst, most violent thoughts from him. He wished to kill someone."

Something registered on the male human's face. Words like "Mia" and "Mal" and "must stop him" were filling his head now.

"You thought of a word... Mia. This was a word the male thought of as well. I do not know what a "Mia" is but I think that it is in danger."

"Yea, I think so too," he mumbled to himself. If Alex had nothing to worry about before, this definitely was something. With the dragouuls being able to read emotions and minds, it was the scariest realization that Mal would do something crazy. "I have a plan and I'm on my way to handle it, so don't worry."

He started to walk away when she asked about Heather. He tried not to think of the truth. He tried not to think of where she was or how he felt about her. He tried to think of nothing.

"I haven't seen her, but it isn't her shift so she might be in her room."

Chapter Twenty-Seven

Philip Ruthesford paced his office. He had the initial report and the launch dock photo laying out on his desk. There was something not right about Heather McGrey. Something not right but also something that irked him and drew his attention back to his mistake. She had not only tried to keep his child but also tried to keep her life. At least one of those things he knew that she succeeded in. The child was what didn't sit right with him.

In the photo, that bitch looked nowhere near pregnant. Maybe a little fatter than his tastes allowed. But to any other, she was a tall, thin woman with long hair. In no way did she appear months pregnant as the blood tests indicated. That's why he needed a bioscan and additional testing done on that bitch. He needed to be sure. For one, he didn't want to think that she had kept something of his. Philip knew of her exploits, having kept tabs on his loose end, but nothing would have matched up. That and the fact that she had mysteriously disappeared on that planet he abandoned her on made for strange math when it was later known that those species had what could be thought of as black magic.

"Status update on McGrey," he barked the order into his com device.

It hummed to life a millisecond later. It was hazardous to keep him waiting any amount. "She's been detained in the medical bay aboard the Alphecca. Her blood is currently being analyzed by the on-board system. ETA on results is three minutes. Her bioscan is scheduled in an hour due to the fasting requirement for an accurate diagnosis. Per request, she's not been sedated."

He smiled to himself at that last part. It would have been wonderful to have a direct link to the ship's system to watch her in that isolated medical room. She must be going mad and struggling against the restrains. Her body must be bruising, and she was always one that bruised beautifully.

"I want to be notified the second the tests are completed."

The General walked over to the built-in bar in the wall opposite the panoramic office window. He went for his favorite brand of whiskey and poured himself a double, neat. He needed to keep ahead of this situation with that bitch. No one wanted to be responsible for killing a pregnant woman. Fifty people, give or take, no problem; but, for some reason, the moral line in the sand was drawn at pregnant women. He could care less about whether she was pregnant or not – he had someone on-board that could finish the job. It was guilt and what it could do to people. It could make certain folks turncoats and confess to tampering with a brand new ship. That would be a travesty. Especially after the trouble he went to make such a competent crew. It really would seem like the crew that could handle anything thrown at them just couldn't survive – that it was all just a hopeless situation – instead of disposable pawns meant to remedy a problem.

Philip wondered if she thought this was all about her and in part, it may have been – initially at least. That bitch had done well to avoid him, but her silence wasn't guaranteed like the other whores.

"General Ruthesford, the results are in from the Alphecca."

He tossed the rest of his drink back and dropped the tumbler off on his desk. "Proceed."

"The blood test confirmed that McGrey is pregnant. The hormone levels are elevated; however, they have not increased since the initial test. The on-board doctor filed it as inconclusive because hormone levels typically rise as pregnancy progresses."

The feeling of unease sat heavy with him. The death of a pregnant woman could spark certain rights groups to demand an investigation. It might become too obvious if someone looked at the roster and deduced that a politician's son, career threat, and loose end were casualties with connections to him – amongst a few others. A devastating mission would give reason to increase funding for "safety", but a sabotaged mission for personal gains would destroy reputations and careers.

A reminder to pick up his wife flowers after work popped up on the holographic screen over his desk. He dismissed the message and had it snooze for another week to remind him to cherish his wife. She was a saint after all and the apple of his eye.

"The notes in their record indicate that they are waiting for the bioscan before proceeding with their official report."

Philip checked the time. He really didn't have all day to sit wasting it over a used whore. "Email the findings of the bioscan, both the official report and whatever the crew keeps on their end."

"Roger."

He muted his com device before pulling off his tie and laying it across his desk. He dismissed the holographic screen and pushed his chair all the way against the wall. Walking back to his office bar, tumbler in hand, he refilled his drink before heading to the door. Sitting just outside was his second favorite whore from the good ole days. He didn't need to say a word. All he needed to do was step aside to let her pass. She stripped at the other end of the room and held his tie in her hands, ready for his game.

"I've found one of our friends from the Mecurian." He locked the door as he watched for her reaction. "She's on the starship that's gone down and the report's come in that she's pregnant. Tasha, do you remember your friend Heather?"

The tiniest bit of recognition played on her face. She remembered. She also must have figured out that it was at his hand that the ship went down; otherwise, why tell her? It would add another layer of fear to the remaining whore. She would know

207

that his power reached beyond this planet. He could reach her anywhere.

"Do you know anything about this?" He stalked closer.

In her years as his office bitch, she'd become quite loose in the lips – figuratively and literally. She stretched them around his cock and she passed on the gossip heard in the halls. But more importantly, she told him everything he needed to know about that mission and where the other girls had been hiding. So, when Tasha nodded, he knew that something was said between the whores on the ship.

This was about him.

CHAPTER TWENTY-EIGHT

"I have to tell him."

Her friend put both hands on her shoulders and tried to physically stop Heather from walking into the general's quarters.

"You can't," she begged. "Please don't, Heather. You'll only make him angry and he'll just end up taking it out on one of us."

Tasha had shown up at her room one night with a black eye and angry handprints around her throat. Fear had separated them for so long, but one sexual rampage had secretly revealed to a handful of women aboard the Mecurian that they weren't special to General Ruthesford. When he had made his rounds that night, Heather had been left for last. He almost completely broke her that night – in every way imaginable – and it set into motion what was happening now. Rather, what Heather was trying to confess?

"Tasha, the baby is his. He's going to be angry either way." There was no doubt in their minds that the publically "model gentleman" and doting husband would never be seen as having an affair. Even if someone stood on their side, the general's rank could make it all disappear. "I can tell him now and he'll be angry, or he sees me getting huge and puts it all together."

She dropped her hands from Heather's shoulders. It was a valid point. They were in the middle of a long mission. Either way, the general would be furious and they'd have to deal with his wrath. Everyone would feel pain over this. The idea that even the general couldn't get away with mass murder aboard his ship was the only tiny ray of hope that they could cling onto.

"I have to think about my baby, Tasha. I can deal with what he does to my body, but I can't let him hurt my baby." Memories of being choked unconscious only to be slapped awake and have that repeat over and over sent a shiver up her spine. That had been gentle for the general. "He's almost killed me before. A baby can't survive that. I'm just hoping that telling him will make him less rough."

Hope.

No matter how small, they all learned to hang onto it. If he tied up Felicia and whipped her, there was the hope it was out of his system by the time he ordered the next of them to his quarters and that they'd be sparred. If Mikata endured rape while being water-boarded, the rest of their fates were that much better. If Hanya's lip piercings scratched his cock, the sex would be excruciatingly painful for her and brutal for the next woman, but it would be out of his system for the next day.

A baby was worse than a scratch on the cock. A baby was permanent and told the whole world of the shame. His reputation would be tarnished. If all the women then stood up, his career would be ruined. They could finally destroy the general the way that he destroyed them every night.

"Heather, he could try to kill you again – get rid of you and the baby now. He'd send your body off into space and cover it all up."

Grams would be devastated when her granddaughter – and great grandchild – didn't return. "He could do that at any time though. We both know he's more than capable of that."

"So you wait to tell him. He's not going to get around to liking the idea of being a dad. You're going to be forced to get an abortion."

An abortion was out of the question. This baby didn't do anything wrong. Heather could raise it by herself. Well, with her grandma to babysit while she worked. A family was something

Heather always dreamed about having. The circumstances were shit, but half of this baby was her.

"The best you could hope for is him not finding out until we're back on-planet. You can just disappear for a while. He won't be able to touch us at home. We'll be free. Just... please, Heather," Tasha begged. "Please don't tell him now."

CHAPTER TWENTY-NINE

McGregor stood in front of Alex, stone-faced. He couldn't believe one of his own men would do something like this. He knew his commander though and knew it wasn't something that his friend would make up. A lesser man would expect Alex to cover it up, knowing their families' political friendship.

"I understand. There's a holding room adjacent to the armory where he can be kept."

Alex shifted back and forth. He was worried about something. "And your men can do this? You always talk about your guys as a brotherhood instead of a team."

McGregor nodded. "Many of them are veterans and act professionally. Besides, this is a proven rape by one of our own. We'd want to handle that personally."

Luckily Alex didn't ask for more detail than that. It was best to let the commander think that only meant detaining Harrison. It would help with the deniability of it, and leave hope that Alex would help cover for them. Plus, it was easier to ask forgiveness than permission with matters like this.

"I'll notify you when he's been detained and file the appropriate paperwork." Alex thanked him, then left him to take care of things.

For Harrison, he wanted three men. The target was most likely in his room still, judging by the GPS in his com device. The room was roughly an eight foot by ten foot room with tuck-away beds.

There wasn't much combat space and three men would overcrowd the room, making taking Harrison a breeze. While he was of a large athletic built and had surely been a strong member of his team, McGregor knew the cadet's size could be used against him now.

"Camaroo, Sidek, Sharma… meet me at command in five minutes. Full combat gear. Detain mission." McGregor dialed in the three men he trusted most for this mission over his com device. By the end of the short transmission, he had three affirmatives.

As he turned the bend in the hallway and saw his men standing alert outside command. He walked passed them and through the door of the room allot to them for tactical operation discussions. McGregor walked to the head of the modest room.

"A rape has occurred on this ship and the attacker will be detained by the four of us. I've told Commander Tanaka that we will detain him and handle the situation. I don't need to tell any of you the severity of this offense, especially when it was done by one of our own." He noticed three different degrees of reactions – all changes over the men's faces, nothing verbal. "Cadet Malcolm Harrison will be detained in the holding room adjacent the armory. Are there any objections?"

There were none. If anything, there was more resolve on the men's faces. Camaroo volunteered to take the left flank that would move in first. Sharma wanted to be the one to take him to the ground. It seemed that he had made the right choice as he listened to the plan come together. Seeing as they were all on the ship and in tight quarters, there was no stealth needed. They walked down the hallways, two across, and took their stations outside the cadet's door. McGregor counted down on his hand and gave the signal. Sidek kicked in the door and quickly moved out of the way for Camaroo.

"What the fuck?"

It was something they expected to hear, but it wasn't the scene they expected to encounter. Harrison wasn't upset at the intrusion. He was upset over being interrupted while with a woman. It infuriated McGregor. That a person could hurt another the way he did and go on about his day.

His men pulled Harrison off the woman and pinned him to the ground, although there was grumbling about his naked ass. McGregor reached over to the wardrobe panel and pulled out a shirt once it opened, offering it to the woman. She didn't take it at first, probably in shock. Not only had their interaction been interrupted in a semi-violent way with their entrance but she also stood stark naked in front of four other men. McGregor unzipped the shirt and wrapped it around her shoulders, trying to cover her body.

"Get the fuck off me, Sharma!" Harrison was thrashing on the floor, but that was just to his liking. It gave him a reason to dig his knee into the cadet's back.

"Maybe you should have thought about that before being a piece of scum," Camaroo dug right back.

His men lifted the cadet off the floor, which was no easy task with the fight Harrison was putting up. With the woman here, it had foiled their plans on crowding the room and, instead, they gave him a berth. Being a combat brat, Harrison knew to use it to his advantage, even if it was at risk of potentially harming the woman with his trashing. Clearly her well-being did not matter.

McGregor put his hands on her shoulders and gently moved her out of the line of fire as they dragged him out. He knew that he should have ordered someone to cover the cadet, but the humiliation was a minor punishment that could be justified. Harrison was dangerous, especially in the situation they found him in. He needed to be detained as quickly as possible and that did not include dressing a thrashing man. It was defendable if they were questioned. What wasn't acceptable would have been if this woman got hurt in the process.

"Are you hurt, miss?" She didn't give him an answer. She didn't even look at him, just at the door where Harrison had disappeared through. So, he asked again. "Are you injured?"

Finally, she shook her head. It seemed like she also just realized that there wasn't anything covering her body, minus the shirt he had wrapped around her. She clenched onto the material, trying desperately to pull it closed over her chest.

"Do you think you can get dressed and make it back to your room alright?" He waited for what seemed like a long time for the woman to nod. Hopefully she was just in shock and not slow in the head. The latter, of which, he wouldn't put pass Harrison to take advantage of – now that he knew what the cadet was capable of doing.

McGregor took her at her word and left her to join up with his team. While they had been unseen arriving at the cadet's room, they had apparently caused quite the attraction hauling him away. McGregor passed many small groups of cadets gossiping about the naked man and chatting about people being hauled off, much like the terror groups of primitive planets. He kept a straight, stern face as he took the route back towards the armory. It was a relief when he saw his men outside the holding room, joking amongst themselves.

"Can you believe him? Thinking he could buy us off." It was Camaroo's voice. "He was on our team! He should have known that we couldn't be bought."

Sidek was shaking his head. "Two grand would have been nice though, but it's not worth destroying our reputation over. I mean, the guy's a rapist. It would be one thing if the kid was caught stealing a pack of gum."

"Gum, Sidek?" McGregor couldn't help but be amused. "You are sounding like an old man and, take it from an old man, even I'm not old enough to say something like that."

Sidek, like the other two, were at least ten years his junior. Unlike many things in life, years didn't mean experience. These three were unmatched by men half their age. They had skills and values lost on the younger generations.

He could hear the muffled curses and death threats coming from inside. "I'm guessing none of you had the nerve to gag him?"

"Naw, sir. None of us wanted to risk catching what he's got if he bit us."

McGregor knew there was a slim chance of someone hearing his pleas and releasing him. No one other than his team should be around the armory. If they were, it was either for some dubious plan or they were really lost aboard a new starship.

"Tell the rest of the team that Harrison's been discharged and removed from his duties. It is a direct order to have no interactions with him and not to release him under any circumstances." He was going to have to let the risk exist. There was too many other things that needed to be addressed. And, honestly, if he was released from the holding room, they could also deport him from the ship. It took a lot less effort to open the bay door, so there was a greater chance that karma would have her way with him if he was stranded on alien soil.

CHAPTER THIRTY

Azvark found herself waking up to a slumbering ship. She wasn't sure what stirred her. None of her huddled up children nor mate were roused. The slumber of the human crew was duller than their conscious thoughts. There was no bodily functions that she needed to perform. The only thing her mind could process was that Heather's absence was a lingering bother. She was in charge of the starship yet nowhere to be found. The male had lied to her, that much she knew.

Carefully, she eased herself out of position amongst her family and slipped outside the large room that Heather had gave them for use. She wandered the hallways, trying to push her mind out. There were no signals that Heather had picked up on her presence.

"Azvark?"

The voice was weak and so very small. She knew that it was Heather's. It would be the only female one that would know her name, if the sound of the female's voice wasn't obvious.

"Help me find you."

Silence came after that. Silence shouldn't be what she heard. Heather had to be somewhere close now to be in her range. The voice was so small, and she needed to speak again so Azvark could walk towards the sound.

"Heather?" She needed to find the female commander. Something inside just told her that it was important. Too much

was occurring on this ship, and she hoped Heather would be the solution to all of that. *"Talk to me."*

It seemed to be an eternity before the voice came again. It wasn't anything that she'd call words. More like small moans, as if Heather was half asleep or something. She waited until she heard the thoughts. Walk, stop, listen. Walk, stop, listen. Azvark found herself outside the medical bay.

"Heather, are you ill? I'm at your medical place." A little whimper came into her thoughts. Heather was inside.

She waited for the doors to swoosh open before making her way inside. Unlike the rest of the starship, the medical bay had standard height ceilings. It wasn't like patients would be standing on beds or the doctors would need additional room. Unbeknownst to Azvark, that lower headspace allotted additional storage. However, she did realize that it was more difficult to walk in this room due to her size. She had to duck her head to avoid knocking it on the doorway and from dragging her spines along the ceiling.

A nurse easily spotted her and came rushing over. "E-excuse me, but you c-can't be in here."

The woman was nervous and, from her thoughts, Azvark knew it was because of her species. "I'm here to speak to Commander Heather." She hoped that she had said that the right way. She knew that just saying the woman's name didn't always get her where she wanted.

"The commander is not here. You need to leave though. Visiting hours are over." The nurse ran through so many thoughts at once that it was a jumbled mess. Although Azvark did pick up a couple interesting bits. The first being that Heather was here but in isolation. The second was that the medical crew were up to something.

"I will go then." She didn't want to argue with this nurse. After all, leaving the medical bay didn't mean that she couldn't talk to Heather. Once outside, Azvark found a portion of the hallway where she last heard Heather's thought clearly.

"Heather, I know you are here and they are doing something to you. I will get you out. I will tell the male human."

"No." It was weak in sound but not in tone. Heather did not want her going to the male commander for help. It didn't make any sense. He was the only other person that had power, and the only other one that could get her out of medical and stop whatever was going on.

"You are friend. They are hurting you and your baby." It was more of an emotion than words that came. *"I do not know how to help you. I must go to the male human unless you tell me what I can do."*

"My baby?" It definitely felt like there was reluctance and pain that Azvark could barely understand. "Baby" seemed to be the word that caused so much anguish with Heather, and she could almost read why. *"Alex did this to me."*

She heard – felt – Heather flinch in pain and realized that her own emotions had transmitted back on accident. It was the first time in over a hundred years that she hadn't controlled herself. But it was over the thought of such betrayal by a mate, and her imagining for a moment of what it would feel like if she and Cryzka were in Heather and the male human's place. She would rip off Cryzka's face with her teeth as she slowly snapped his bones.

Azvark apologized for the pain she caused. She tried to talk more with Heather but it seemed like there was still something in the way of them truly connecting, and it wasn't just the wall. Slowly, she found out some of what happened – including Heather being drugged. There was still a lot to the story that she couldn't piece together and that just didn't make sense. Every question took more out of Heather and seemed to only cause her more upset, not that she mentioned it verbally. It was a taxing turn of events so - instead of trying to find the truth – Azvark took the motherly approached and just talked to her softly about the things going on outside her prison cell. It seemed to calm Heather's mind enough that she finally was able to fall asleep. That left Azvark alone to think about how to handle this situation.

As the wife of a diplomat, she did have some power, or at least the humans would perceive her to have power. Cryzka would definitely say something to the male human if she mentioned this to him. Being Rights was a big topic on their planet and, from diplomatic visits, she knew it was an area of concern on every planet, just with a different name. She decided that she would seek out the male human in the morning and confront him first. Even though he tried to shield himself from her, Azvark knew that she intimidated him to some extent. If playing the bully was what was needed, then she would have to do so in order for her friend to gain freedom.

When the solar orb crested the horizon, Azvark was already outside the male human's door. He was just stirring inside and his thoughts were becoming more guarded. He had taken his time getting ready and it seemed like many hours passed before the door to the room opened. Once again, the male human failed to notice her and almost ran into her.

"Oh, sorry. I... sorry." He was rattled and shook his head, like he was trying to shake himself out of a fog. He didn't think anything of it and went to step around her.

She blocked his way with her tail. "We need to speak. You will tell me where Heather is."

The thoughts cycled through his mind before he caught himself and remembered that she could read them.

"She's not on duty." He said it slowly, avoiding the question. It was as if he still thought she'd fall for the words coming out of his mind.

"I know where she is and spoke with her." That certainly caught his attention. There was confusion over how that could have been possible, and then more guilt. "You know what you've done."

He had the sense to hang his head in shame. "It was a direct order from our headquarters. She's supposed to be detained and isolated."

"Did you ask why?" Azvark could read that he hadn't thought to because his emotions clouded his judgement. "She is not sick but doctors are doing scans."

"Scans?" For once, the male human seemed genuinely surprised. Something went through his mind and it felt like pieces out of the past more than a memory. There was the feeling nagging at the back of his mind to check on Heather, but it kept getting shut down.

"Is Heather not your mate?"

That got him stumbling in his thoughts as well. "Well, no... we broke up."

"You do not love her?"

The male human didn't say anything, so she asked again. He still refused to say anything and kept his mind focused on the floor so his mind was shielded. It definitely was a soft spot and, after speaking with Heather last night, she needed to poke it.

"She believes you hate her. She's in pain and hurt in that place. But worse is that you have betrayed her. You broke her."

If it needed to be described, Azvark could only compare it to the small snaps made in a thin layer of ice when walked upon. That's what happened inside the male human at that moment.

"I didn't betray her. She betrayed me." Anger was filling in the cracks of his soul. "You don't understand what Heather did."

The flashes she picked up explained what he claimed Azvark didn't know. The pain in his thoughts kept growing and the longer it went on the more she felt a headache coming on. Azvark knew that her mate would be upset and worried about her meddling in the relationship between these two humans. There was a lot more at state for a diplomat if something turned south and it was reported. But this was just something right to do.

"She did not betray you. If you would speak to her, you would know that. You let your fear blind you!" She had to push to get through to him. She had found the soft spot and just needed to push. "She carries a baby and you threw her away. The pain in her heart is huge and the pain in her body crushing. You are the cause if it and a coward for not speaking with her. You only tell me lies when I already know the truth.

"I know that you just dreamt about her. You took Heather with you someplace warm with water and mated on the sands. You can't say you love her because you are full of shame and guilt. She deserves a better mate than you," she stepped closer.

His voice was barely a whisper, "I didn't know she's still pregnant."

In his mind, images of the sitting on a bed aboard this starship flashed by and was replaced with a crash scene. Broken glass. Strange liquid. Pain and addictions. Times of mating. Times of anger and thoughts of revenge.

"They are scanning her and keeping her like a prisoner; and you never ask why? You go ask before you hurt my friend more." She leaned down to stare him directly in the face. Azvark had made sure that her bone mask had been on her face. It was more intimidating close-up when you could see the blood stains on the ivory that hadn't worn away yet.

"I'll... I'll go see her," he mumbled.

"If you ever loved Heather, you will." She left it, and him at that.

His very soul was shaken. The dragouul had been in his head and he knew that there was nothing he could have done to stop that. But it wasn't that which shook him. It was the fact that she was so adamant and sure that Heather hadn't betrayed him. If she had spoked to her last night, that meant she got inside Heather's head. It should have been the most definite proof that Heather hadn't cheated on him, but he still couldn't completely accept that. Believing it would mean that he was wrong, and he didn't want to be wrong. He had been cruel to her, and there would be no coming back from that. They would never be how they were.

He held his com device to the panel next to the door and overrode the security code. The door gave a single beep before unsealing and sliding out of his way. The man inside glared up from the floor at him.

"Have a little accident?" Alex tried to stifle a laugh, having found the cadet face down on the floor.

"Shut up, fuckwad!"

The cadet had a split lip and a black eye. There was a hint of bruising on his torso that Alex was just going to ignore. Someone had thankfully put some G.I. briefs on Mal but – for the most part – he was still naked. He could "assume" that the cadet, in a fit of rage, had thrashed about and self-inflicted these injuries. He also had a feeling that the cadet would gain more by the time they arrived back on planet.

"That's not the way to talk to your commanding officer."

"You always loved being a fucking cocksucker!" Mal scoffed and rolled onto his side, revealing darker bruises. "You finally sucked enough dick to get a tiny bit of power and it's gone to your fucking head." He let out a laugh but it quickly turned into a coughing fit.

"You know that would hurt so much more if it didn't sound like you were dying." Alex realized that his anger was rising but it didn't necessarily feel like it was towards Mal.

Sure, the cadet had slept with Heather. Mal would fuck anything that moved. Heather at least had limits and rules, or so he thought. The real difference was whether Heather sought him out or accepted his advances. That was Heather's fault, but he had the chance to take it out on Mal now. It was so tempting. There were already bruises on the cadet's body. What was a few more or even a couple broken ribs? He wanted to make them both suffer for the pain he was going through.

The realization that Mal would get justice during his court marshal and there was no way his daddy could buy Mal's way out should have been enough. It would have to be enough. Mal would no doubt tell his father that abuse came from his hand and then it would be a punishment dealt upon him from Alex's own father for tarnishing their families' relationship. Unfortunately, this was as much as Alex could get away with and still keep the shit from hitting him. There was one way that he could make life worse for Mal.

"As you pointed out, I do have a bit of power. That means I could offer you a deal. You know, help you get out of this place." Alex made the gesture of glancing around the room and taking in the stark nothingness that was the holding room.

"Fuck you," Mal grunted out. "You can't fucking do shit."

As stupid as the kid was, Alex knew that this probably wouldn't be all that easy. Mainly for the fact that they hated each other. He needed to make the cadet believe that a deal could be made, even if it was completely out of his control. He needed Mal to think that he was suddenly as corrupt as their fathers.

"It would be in our families' best interest for me to make a deal with you. If I just override the reports sent to HQ then your family would be in debt to me and mine. We both know that your father would hate that." He crossed his arms over his chest and tried to seem indifferent. It would come off as arrogant to the cadet, which would piss him off. In anger, Mal wouldn't be thinking straight and realizing this was a trap. Mental warfare. "And we both know that your father would hate you for not taking a deal to keep the score even when offered. Imagine what he'd say to know that you wouldn't even hear me out. Do you really hate him that much that you'd fuck your life up over it?"

A glare was all that he got for the longest while. "Fucking say it so I can say no."

Defiant asshole.

"If you want this over with, I just need you to tell me everything you and Heather did. I want every single detail."

Mal rolled on the floor, literally, laughing between coughing fits. "You want me to fucking what?" He couldn't stop laughing. "You're a sick son of a bitch," he got out between laughs.

"You said you fucked her, so it shouldn't be a problem then." He needed to think of a reason, quick, for why he'd want to know. It needed to be believable. "I need to know if she really fucked me or just fucked around with my head."

He took the bait, thinking Alex was just a sensitive guy that needed validation. For once, his weakness would work to his advantage. "I don't think you can fucking handle it, but that's your fucking problem."

Mal forced his body into a sitting position and, if his hands hadn't been bound behind his back, they probably would have been interlaced in front of him like some villain.

"She came to my room, knocked on my door, and when I opened it she pushed her way inside. She told me to get on the bed and tried to act all tough. We both know she ain't nothing but a bitch with no real fucking power. But I did it to let her think she had it, because bitches these days like that." Mal smirked at something in his head that he found funny. "She said I had to fuck her and couldn't tell nobody. Needy bitches aren't my thing so I really didn't get my shit up over this and she got pissy. Grabbed my cock and started blowing me, finally using that pretty mouth for something good. And hey, she spoke to my dick so it was ready for that old snatch."

Alex shifted, visibly uncomfortable, and Mal took it as a reason to continue. In Mal's mind, this was now revenge for fucking locking him up and having his ass beaten.

"I pulled her off and pushed her on the bed. Yanked off her pants and tore her panties off with my teeth. And I shit you not, that slut loved it. Got her fucking wet. That pussy was glistening and she was begging me to eat her out, but I ain't like that. I wanted her to beg and scream my name. So I teased her with just the tip which, just saying, is more than some bitches can handle. And she's on my bed, head back, loving it and begging for me to fuck her hard. She wants it rough and raw, so I fucking rammed into her. And dude, she was trying to fuck me with her hips while I plowed. Grabbed my ass and dug her nails into me so I'd fuck her harder. But I needed to see those tits. Always loved that ass but I wanted those tits too. I fucking tore that shit off her and, damn, the old bitch has a nice rack. I just had to taste those. I sucked one in my mouth and got her moaning. I had to record that shit. Her moaning for me, that is. And I just fucking wanted to see what she'd do so I bit her nipple. Took her in my teeth and gave a little bite. Those eyes flew open and rolled into the back of her fucking head. That bitch came so fucking hard on my dick. Guess she never had a real man before." He tossed in that last part just to take another stab at Alex.

He wasn't sure what to think. It was playing out in his head just as Mal was saying and he could almost imagine Heather doing everything he was saying. He knew that her injections had long worn out and that sex soothed the pain. It was her addiction, and that used to mean Alex was her fix.

"Tell me more," Alex begged. "I need to know everything. I need to know if she let you take her up the ass."

Mal chuckled. "Yea, she fucking asked for it after cumming so hard. She said she wanted to feel completely used. Said she wanted me to fucking destroy that ass and, hey, I am always one to oblige. Can't leave a bitch unsatisfied. That would ruin my reputation, and bagging a commander is way up there."

He started to talk about how he rolled Heather over because her body was done but not her demands. Alex couldn't listen anymore though. He just couldn't stand hearing it anymore. He walked out the door, hearing Mal's voice get louder as the raunchy details poured out of his mouth. Alex enabled the lock on the holding room door and stormed down the corridor.

He had heard all that he needed to and his heart was torn into pieces. More than anything, he wanted Heather out of his mind and out of his life. He knew what it was like to be cheated on and his heart knew the truth before his head most of the time. And his heart knew it needed to heal, it needed something. If Heather could cover up the pain with sex, then so could he. She was always jealous of that cadet of his that he assigned to coffee duty. She was pretty in all the right ways but not overly sexy.

"Find Anita Bienz," he ordered the com device on his wrist. It took a second and a half to locate her on the ship's GPS system. She was in her room.

Perfect.

He hadn't exactly recited any grand speech or pick-up lines in his head on the walk over. He just knew that he would put out the offer and make sure he definitely got consent.

When Alex knocked on the door, it took maybe a heartbeat before she answered. She was surprised to find him at her door but, then again, maybe it wasn't that much of a surprise to her. Maybe it was just a surprise that it had taken him this long.

She tucked back a stray piece of hair behind her ear. "Commander Tanaka," god, the breathy way she said his name went straight to his dick, "is there something I can do for you?"

"Invite me inside and I'll show you want you can do for me." Alex licked his bottom lip, imaging devouring the sweet cadet and every inch of her body. "But that's only if you want me and what I'm offering."

Anita looked up at him with the most innocent doe eyes he'd ever saw, but she was far from innocent. She knew how to flirt. "And what exactly are you offering, commander?"

"Me."

Her eyes slowly ran over his body, lingering just below his belt line at the growing presence there. She took one step back, allowing him enough space to enter.

And he did.

Chapter Thirty-One

Azvark did not like this. She had tried to gain access to the medical bay again, even telling the medical staff that she knew Heather was here. It only resulted in the men who rescued them coming to escort her out, and then having the door's sensor programmed to ignore her genetic type. For all intents and purposes, she was locked out. Once again, she took up her position outside in the corridor where she talked to Heather last night.

"Heather, I am here. Are you okay?"

She was worried that maybe overnight something had happened. Nothing about how this was being handled seemed right to her. She could feel the woman stirring and had a small pang of regret over waking her. Heather must have spoken aloud first because the thought seemed a little distant like a faint echo. Having caught herself alone in the room, she switched to conversing in her mind.

"Tired and sore... can't feel my left hand... but okay."

"I told the male human to come to you. He needs to make this right." Nothing came from the other side of the wall and she knew that it hadn't exactly pleased Heather to know that she talked to the male commander. *"I will make him release you."*

"Azvark, you've been a good friend... but I don't think there's anything you can do for me. Alex hasn't come and he won't. The doctor said they're waiting for HQ to examine my results."

The male human never went to see her? Azvark was sure that she had intimidated him this morning enough to warrant a visit.

228

The day was practically over. It did not compute. She would need to pressure the male into releasing Heather. There was nothing wrong with her and… she could just hear her mate lecturing her now. The idea of that gave her pause.

"You said you felt my baby and I know you don't know." There was a great deal of pain in Heather's thoughts. Flashes of a thatched hut, old alien shaman, sounds of guns sparked for a second before Heather thought again. *"I used to have a baby but it died. It never left me. It's been dead for years and when you said you felt it, I wanted to believe that it was still there somehow. I always wanted to be a mom and I thought maybe I could after I left the force… I don't think that will happen."*

She could not begin to understand the complex emotions and thoughts that must have plagued Heather for those years. It was a terrible thing to lose a child, which she had experienced once or twice when one of their eggs failed to hatch. It would be a tremendous burden to carry that pain around, literally, every day.

"Heather, you will get out of there and you will be a mother."

"The baby's father is in HQ… and he wants me dead."

There was a chill that ran down Azvark's spine with that last thought. There was something about it that just sent a freeze through her mind. Heather was being held for no reason because HQ ordered it. HQ was going to decide her fate when they reviewed the testing. If HQ wanted Heather dead…

She took off to find the male human. She needed to make him see reason, now more than ever. On her way through the corridors, she reached out to her elder son and asked him to stay outside the medical bay to eavesdrop on the medical crew – a fact that only filled him with glee. But that odd act was met with a message from her mate, meaning they had just been together.

"Love, what is it you doing? We are not to play with humans."

"Heather was taken, unwillingly, and put in danger. I must interfere, love, because she interfered for us. Without her, you wouldn't be with me in this existence."

He was irritated with her. *"What is your plan?"*

He wasn't agreeing with her actions – that she knew. He had merely asked so he could grant or deny permission. This could always become an interspatial conflict and he – being a diplomat – would take the brunt of the punishment.

"I will tell the male commander and make him do something."

It was the truth. Azvark would simply talk to the male human. She shielded her thoughts from her mate so he couldn't catch just how she would go about that. She had already decided that she'd force him into rescuing Heather, no matter what it took.

Given the time, she assumed that the male commander would be returning to his room. When she found herself once again outside his room, there was no drifting thoughts inside. If he wasn't there, there was only two places that she could think he'd have gone. Reaching out to her child confirmed that Heather's bedside was not where he currently was located. The bridge of the starship was the other logical location. While she wasn't entirely sure of its location, Azvark headed down the corridors in search of it anyways.

By great fortune, she ended up walking pass the cafeteria and noticed a man from the rescue party that seemed to have enough rank to possibly help her. As she approached, she watched him take her in but there was no fear in his thoughts. It was the way he responded to her imposing form that made her realized this human probably had seen worse things than her. It was a little unnerving to be in his presence, and it definitely ruled out intimidation.

"Need help," Azvark chose to speak aloud in their language.

His hands rested on his hips. "What do you need help with?"

"Find male human called Commander." She could read his thought that the male wasn't actually called "Commander" but a brief image in his thoughts proved that they were talking about the same male human. "Need talk."

"Tanaka, pick up." He spoke into the device on his arm. His message was met with silence but he calmly repeated himself into the arm thing again.

"McGregor... is it an emergency?" The voice seemed out of breath in a way and he definitely wasn't alone.

Something triggered in this McGregor's thought that confirmed this commander was not alone. It was something like a post-mating sound – as best that Azvark could decipher – where voice and demeanor changed.

"The diplomat's wife wishes to speak with you." McGregor's mind played an imaginary version of what he believed was being said on the other end. It seemed that cursing was mostly likely not transmitted.

"Kinda busy with some... thing right now." A lightly strained sound – as if someone stretched their body – and then a sigh transmitted. "Can you just help her?"

The man took his hand away from the arm device, stopping transmissions from his end. "Is this something I can help you with?"

Azvark felt pity for this man being between the commander and herself. He had done much for her family and seemed to be a good being. This was an uncomfortable spot, though, for him to be in. When she shook her head, he just sighed. His mind thought to ask what it was that she needed to speak to the commander about, but he didn't seem to think that would be enough to get the commander to meet. It was something McGregor knew would be put onto him.

He pressed the button on his arm device and held it up towards her face. "Tell him, if you can, why you need to talk."

She knew that this man was giving her a way around the circumstance and that the commander wouldn't listen long enough. She hoped that this rule bending wouldn't get McGregor in too much trouble.

"Heather in danger. Release her. Wrong to lock her away."

A frustrated sigh came from the other side. "I told you that she is fine and that I'm following orders. Those orders come from someone higher up than me or you. You need to stop harassing me. There's nothing I can do."

Nothing the male said was true and he was choosing to ignore her warnings. He was weak and, in her mind, never deserving of being Heather's mate. This coward was just going to hide from her on this ship until it was too late, refusing to understand and save Heather.

Azvark let out a guttural growl that rattled the nerves and bones of those standing around her. It had transmitted through the arm device and echoed off the room's walls where the commander was hiding. The man in front of her – McGregor – had a worried thought about the crew's safety as he took his hand away from the arm device.

"Thank you for your help. I am angry that he does not help his crew. We will not hurt anyone but I will save my friend." She turned and walked out of the cafeteria, dead set on finding the male human.

"The body scan doesn't make sense. It shows Commander McGrey's pregnant. There was nothing in her pre-flight physical saying this, and she never reported it."

"It doesn't matter what the pre-flight report said or not. HQ is the one that wanted this and they're the ones that get to decide. We just have to figure out how to follow orders without causing a panic on-board."

"They really want us to terminate her? That seems a little extreme. All she did was lie on a form."

"We're not allowed to question HQ. They must know something we don't."

"Did they include any reasoning, doctor? Maybe any further direction for handling this?"

"They ordered it to be handled quietly and suggested laying blame to a medication reaction or death by natural causes."

"But she's not on any medication, right, Sue?"

"No, the head doctor never prescribed anything. Just blood work and a body scan."

"Nothing was passed onto me about that, but it's a story that probably wouldn't cause too much of a stir. No one besides our group knows that she's even in medical. I think that a reaction to a sedative would be an easily explainable cause of death. Most people are never sedated to know, whereas, there might be a question why we didn't know that she was allergic to a prescription."

"I don't like the idea though that HQ can just do this."

"Yea, doc, like I don't really feel safe. Like how do I know I'm not next?"

"We signed over our lives when we enlisted, but this isn't something typically requested by HQ. There must be extenuating circumstances that have lead up to this. None of us should worry about meeting this fate on our own. It's just an unfortunately thing for the commander and we should try to make it as painless as possible for her."

"Yea, it's the least we could do. She was a good commander... I liked her a lot."

Azvark scanned the adjacent rooms as she roamed the corridors. It would only be a matter of time before she picked up on the male commander's thoughts or that of the female he was with, which was an assumption gleaned off McGregor's mind. If the commander's thoughts weren't clear, perhaps the fear from her roar would still be on the female's mind. It had been on the minds of everyone in the cafeteria.

The corridors were essentially deserted, save for the rare, lone strangler making their drowsy way into a room. It was what made Azvark realize she had interrupted the evening meal and that neither her elder son nor she would have ate. Maternal instincts took over for a moment and she reached out to her child.

"News?"

"Doctor's talking about ending life. Picking lies."

It was even more urgent that she find the male commander. Heather had not been wrong, but Azvark's warnings had fallen on deaf ears. The male human would need something more to be convinced and, luckily, her elder son had a useful gift.

"Come to me. You will need to show to male commander." Azvark hoped that her son would be able to use his gift well, and for that long.

Her family was typical of their race. Many dragouuls possessed gifts but it still wasn't too common. Only two of her many children had gifts; although, the youngest twins weren't of age yet when the signs could manifest. While females were the dominate gender in their race, their gifts weren't typical of the dragouul characteristics. Telepathy was the main language of her people; yet, it was the submissive male class that held more mental gifts. Her son's gift fell amongst those and, honestly, could be troublesome. Although, his sister, Bilfa, had an equally troublesome physical gift that afflicted emotions.

A visiting diplomat had once explained the dragouul race perfectly: *"The males are dragouul and the females are strong."* The males were what you expected but the females surpassed even that.

A door on her left suddenly opened to allow a female with fire-hair to come out. She looked a mess to Azvark but she let the thought pass – accrediting it to the human's late hour – until she heard the small female's thought.

"Oh, no! It's that thing. It's going to kill me. I got to get out of here... tell Alex."

The girl glanced over her shoulder, estimating her escape time. It didn't take a clever being to know her plan and it was tempting just to follow her to the male that had been eluding her all day. Azvark whipped her tail around her body and used it to trap the female in the corridor with her. It only made the small human's thought run quickly into each other to become a jumbled mess.

"Commander Heather is going to die. Tell me where the male is so he can stop them." Something flickered across the female's mind when Heather's name was spoken. A weakness. "You were with him and keeping him from saving her. You are guilty but you can make me find him."

"He's still in my room. I left to use the toilet while he had a smoke. Honestly, I didn't –"

"You lead now," she cut off her rambling. An apology for sleeping with Heather's mate wasn't something that Azvark needed to hear nor was there time for it.

The female did as asked. She led Azvark to the door and the thoughts inside confirmed who was there. She sent a quick ping to her son to help him find their location before she opened up the door.

"Hey, baby, you took longer than –" A startled, naked version of the male human frantically searched for something to cover his body as a slew of curses poured out of his mind. "Fuck, Azvark, this has to stop! I'm going to call your husband."

"They are to kill her." She stared the male human down, daring him to say something. "My son has it recorded. A message from your HQ that I can show you." It seemed like that statement was giving her warnings more traction with the male human. At least his mind was considering hearing her out now.

"I project for my son and you will see." As a female, Azvark had a physical gift, but it was also one she was trying to train herself to mentally do as well. It wasn't always successful – done mentally – and had only worked once. The risk was too great to take for Heather when it was in the name of training and science. "I touch you and my son. Then you see what he has seen and you will save Heather."

She could hear pattering of feet getting closer until a puffing dragouul showed up in the doorway.

"How should I?" He asked his mother.

Azvark directed him to sit on the bed next to the male human. The close contact between him and the two dragouuls cause him to flinch instinctively – which gave Azvark a small bit of joy for all the trouble this male human caused her. Her son held out his hand for her to take, and the male human followed suit. Instead of holding the human's, she covered his forehead with her lizard-like hand only for the purpose to set him at ill-ease.

She coaxed her son's mind to open and recall the memories he had stored. It was like walking into a library and seeing everything recorded upon a shelf. The young dragouul directed her to where she felt the memory swirling around her being. Azvark visualized it in her hand and urged her gift to push it into the mind of the male human. The instant the memory started, it felt like a zap of electricity stinging her palm. It wasn't painful, just uncomfortable and she could see that the human felt it as well. While the memory was in playback mode, Azvark could still see him as the memory only appeared opaque in her vision. She could see the pain and regret grow on his features, and then the wave of fear and sadness in his heart because he believed it was too late.

Azvark removed her hands and thanked her elder son. He had done well not only following her directions but also at focusing his gift to capture all the details of the conversation. His memory had trapped the different voices of the medical crew and even the tones and inflections when they spoke.

"You save her now," she continued to insist.

The male human just shook his head. "I can't. I'll be too late."

Azvark growled and leaned down close to his face. "You will not know unless you try. If you fail to do that, I skin you alive and tear the flesh from your bones."

He wanted to give up, and the defeatist attitude oozed off him in such a way that her son decided to leave. Well, between that and his growing hunger. Azvark did the only thing she could muster and grabbed the male's shoulder, pulling him to his feet.

"You save now," she repeated as she pulled the sheet off the bed to wrap around his body. "I make you."

"Alex, you have to. You just gotta go do it," the female behind her spoke up.

It was enough to get the male to pull on his pants and run out the door with his shirt in hand. Azvark was the only one to follow as he ran down the corridor towards the medical bay. Try as she might, she couldn't get into Heather's thoughts. The only hope was that they were too far for the thoughts to get picked up. She still had not picked up on any when medical knowledge started to pour into her head. The bay doors opened for the male human but quickly slammed shut in her face when the bio-scanner picked up on her presence.

CHAPTER THIRTY-TWO

Alex had managed to pull on his white tee as he ran through the corridor. His mind was split between the crushing depression and guilt over losing Heather while the other half was hopeful that he'd make it there just in time to save her and his past actions would be completely forgiven. He knew that he had deliberately ignored every warning that Azvark had given him and didn't even question the original order himself. He hadn't made clear-headed decisions and didn't protected his crew as his rank and position dictated. Even worse, he had threw his relationship with Heather out the window and then treated her like trash. To make it all that much worse, he then went off and had sex with a cadet under his command to drown the pain.

The doors had swooshed open for him, letting him run into the nearly empty medical bay. A sole voice from somewhere scolded him for running but he ignored it as he turned the corner and headed towards Heather's room. It was the room they restrained her in when he had given the orders, and he prayed that they hadn't relocated her. If they had, then he'd never find her and it definitely would be too late.

He threw his shoulder into the door and forced it to open before the air seal had completely disengaged. Alex half fell into the room, stumbling in between two nurses. The doctor at Heather's bedside paused for a moment at the interruption.

"Commander?"

Alex was out of breath from the run and held up a hand to ask the man to give him a moment. "Get... get away from her..."

"We have orders to sedate the commander," the doctor said and moved to grab the intravenous cord again.

If he stuck that needle into the cord and pushed the plunger, Heather would be dead. The fact that the doctor was just making that move meant that he had shown up in time. However, if they didn't obey his orders, Alex wasn't enough to overpower the two nurses and take down the doctor.

"I order you to stand down." He needed to hold his ground. As much as he wanted to take a look at Heather's face, he knew that he couldn't.

"Commander, our orders came from HQ. I'm sorry but you've been overruled on this." It sounded like the doctor didn't completely agree with the orders but was still following through with it.

He needed to think of something. If he had been fully dressed in his uniform, there would have been a pistol on his hip and he could have definitely made them see that they needed to follow his fucking orders instead. Unfortunately, there was no pistol. It was unlikely that Alex could get ahold of HQ and, even then, it was highly unlikely that they would change their orders. After all, someone there wanted her dead. If he had to bet on what Heather had told him, this order came directly from the general, himself. There was no one else coming to Heather's aid, and he had already ruled out physically overruling them. His diplomatic skills left something to be desired and it wasn't a guarantee that he could buy time that way.

"I just got an order from HQ that she's not to be terminated." That seemed to catch the doctor's attention. The man hadn't said a word about termination, only that they were sedating her. It seemed like that tidbit gave his lie more creditability. "They've reassessed their order and decided it was something that needed to be handled on-planet."

Slowly, the doctor lowered the syringe. Turning towards one of the nurses, he asked, "Who got the original transmission? Maybe we should ask them to confirm with HQ."

Alex understood the man's reasoning, and he would have questioned it too if someone suddenly gave him a contradictory order through a different means. It meant that he probably only bought himself a few minutes munless he could throw his weight around. If not, then he'd have to figure a way to get Heather out of medical.

"*Azvark, can you hear me?*" It was a desperate ploy, but if he had bought time then he could get that back-up. But no voice came into his head this time. Was she even still there? Maybe she couldn't hear him.

"*Yes. You do poorly.*"

Great, a critic. He didn't see her in here trying to stop them from killing Heather. At least he was trying to do something.

"*I need you to find McGregor and tell him to report to medical with his men. I need them to back me up and force the medical crew out of the room. There's two nurses and a doctor.*"

He heard nothing in his head after that and can only hope that she would do as he asked. Alex really had no reason to believe that she would do it, seeing as he completely ignored her warnings. Although, she did take a liking to Heather and kept claiming to be her friend. Hopefully Azvark would do it for her.

"Are you questioning your commander?"

The nurse closest to him gave Alex the once over. He knew that he was a mess. It probably lowered his creditability, but he was still the commander in charge. While it was clear that they didn't completely trust his word, they couldn't as easily openly say that they questioned him.

"No, but we should confirm that our original orders were correctly given. If there was some internal error that resulted in Commander McGrey being marked for termination they should be made aware." The doctor seemed adamant, but at least he had set down the syringe.

There was no error. There also no way in hell that he could let the doctor make that call back to HQ. It would tip them off and get them asking questions. The first objective was to secure that syringe and make sure that Heather was safe. The problem was that he needed to do it casually and not draw their attention.

He stuck his hands in his pant pockets and walked up next to her bed, opposite side of the table that held the syringe. Alex made the move to look at the monitor behind the bed. Her vitals appeared stable and steady to him. It was a little reassuring to know that he had arrived just in time.

"Seems like everything's good. Huh?" He glanced over at the two nurses. Neither of them seemed interested in the monitor though, but they were interested in him. "Is she currently sedated? I can't imagine she's sleeping through all of us talking."

The shorter man nodded. "Yes, we've kept her sedated per your orders."

That definitely proved they had lied when Alex showed up. He tried to casually walk around to the other side of the bed. There needed to be an excuse to do so though. He needed to think fast and come up with something before they got suspicious. There was only one thing that he could think of and it was a pretty weak reason.

"Did you take off her ring?" Alex went through the motions of grabbing her hand and holding it in his. It was almost too much. Her skin was still soft and warm, and it brought back memories that he wished he could go back and live in. It only made him long for her more. "She wanted to keep it quiet, but she married just before the flight and hasn't reported it yet. If she were to die in space, Jason would want it brought back."

He hoped that adding a name would give more creditability to his story. So far, no one had tackled him to the floor and he was close to grabbing that syringe. The only hiccup was that the doctor had left the room long ago to call HQ on the console at the nurses' station. It was a slightly more even fight, but it was still two against one and Alex knew that gender meant nothing with how

241

the medical crew was trained. The female nurse was just as capable as the male one in the room.

"No, sir," the young woman answered. "No one removed anything. I don't think anything was even logged in for her. She was just in the general clothing she's in now."

"Shit... I don't know what we'd tell Jason when he asks for it. Hopefully she had taken it off and left it in her room." Alex tried to appear pensive while he shifted his body to block their view of the small side table. His hand closed around the syringe just as the doctor walked back into the room.

"There was no new order from HQ," the doctor said, point blank.

So this was it then. There was going to be a struggle. They were going to take back the syringe and Heather would be gone. The report would be filed with HQ and they were know of his interference. Court martial would be awaiting him when they made it back home.

The nurses seemed to change their perception of him and started towards him. That was until McGregor walked in and placed a hand on either of their shoulders. "I wouldn't be going after the commander. He is in charge of this starship when in intergalactic space."

The doctor simply stood next to the door until he was join by his two nurses. That seemed to give him some courage. "Commander, we were only following orders but we understand that there may be some punishment awaiting us – as you see fit. We have not submitted a report to HQ, but they will be looking for a report. I'm not suggesting that you submit our report but can you at least allow me to file one locally on the Alphecca's log. If we return home... I'm just concerned for the sake of my crew."

The doctor was worried that a death sentence would come down on his head as well. Falsifying an official report to HQ was a serious offense, and claiming the death of a commander wasn't something that could easily be swept under the rug if she happened to show up somewhere. The doctor's report surely would contain the first orders and then the chain of events that resulted in failing to meet those orders. If the general took exception to that, the medical crew would have the local report on file to show that they had complied with orders. It could save their lives. Finally glancing over at Heather – helpless – in the medical bed, he wasn't so sure they deserved their lives when they were so quick to take hers.

"Fine." Alex didn't hide that he didn't like this. "And I want your word that nothing like this will occur again. *If* orders like this come from HQ, I want to be made aware of them first. I also want your word that no harm will come to anyone else aboard my ship. Your loyalty is supposed to be to this ship and her crew... and her commander."

The three in the room had the decency to look shameful. He truly believed that they regretted their actions, as by-the-book as they were.

"We all took oaths to do no harm." Which was laughable in the current circumstances. "None of the medical crew will act outside of preventative and emergency care. I apologize for not notifying you of the order."

Alex left it at that and waved them out of the room as the large mass that was Azvark shoved her way into the room and to Heather's bedside. The alien seemed solely focused on her friend and he hadn't expected her to speak out to them.

"She has child. In pain."

He knew but the words still got to him. The poor thing inside her was what had caused Heather so much pain. It was a reminder to her every day that the general had fucked up her life and she could never escape his attacks. It was extremely risky, giving what almost happened, but he glanced over at the doctor and his team.

"I'm sure you saw the bioscan. Can you remove it?" Alex asked.

The doctor gave a slight shrug. "I can't say if it's completely safe to remove. It started to calcify and it's webbed out from the corpse along the umbilical cord. It's hard to say how much of the commander's body has also began to calcify. Couple that with the fact that the infant could have been in a state of decay before the recent calcification began could mean that her blood is tainted and it's already too late."

"Recent calcification. That must have been when the injections stopped," he thought.

Alex hadn't meant for it to be a conversation, but Azvark chimed in. *"Yes, I do believe so. Heather has pain but I think she should decide what happens."*

That was probably true but Heather wasn't awake right now. She couldn't go on with living her life in pain, and she shouldn't have to live with the constant reminder of the general either. It had to be something that fucked with her mind over the years. More than once, he had listened to her nightmares and had it ate him inside.

"I need you to try. If it can be safely removed without taking her life or maiming her, then get that thing out." Alex looked down at her sleeping face. He knew that she was sedated, but she looked so peaceful and so beautiful. He knew, deep inside himself, that this would be the last time he ever saw her this way. "That's an order."

He left the room and the medical crew to take care of preparations. McGregor had followed him out, and the silence of his friend was a question to everything.

"I need you and Azvark to stay with Heather. She needs to be there to read their minds and make sure that they don't try anything. I don't completely trust them after the stunt they tried to pull. And you need to be there because someone needs to have a gun and make shit happen." The medical bay door swooshed open, but a hand on his shoulder stopped him.

"She's going to be angry with you when she wakes up."

He sighed. "I know."

"I meant about making this decision for her... but she's also going to be mad at you when she wakes up."

"I know." And this time McGregor didn't need to clarify. Heather would hate him not only for deciding what happened to her body but also for fucking around with the coffee cadet. He could argue that they were split, but they were only split because he had her detained. Even so, Alex knew it was wrong inside his heart. He had cheated on the best thing to walk into his life.

"Can you do me a flavor though?" The older man mumbled something and he just took it to continue. "Keep an eye on her and watch out for her. I don't think it's right to ask you to tell me everything she does."

"No, it's not," he chimed in – like a father trying to reaffirm a lesson to his son.

"I just need to know that she's safe. She... she's still important to me." I still love her.

McGregor just gave a nod and then went back towards Heather's room. That was the best he was going to get out of the man.

It was one thing to know and another to hear it. Right now, Alex need to hear it straight from the horse's mouth. He needed that asshole to know that nothing he did mattered because Alex had seen through the lie, even if that wasn't completely true. He wanted to break Mal like he had been broken.

Once again, Alex overrode the security code on the holding room door and stepped inside. The stench was strong and, clearly, the cadet had no issue of defecating all over the room. Whether it was to prove the point that he wasn't fazed by his circumstances or whether he accepted that he had no option, Alex didn't know. It was probably a mix of both but that didn't mean his nose wasn't being tortured.

"What the fuck you want, asshat?" Mal grumbled from the corner.

He made his way across the small room and kicked the cadet over. "You know what I fucking want. I want the goddamn truth out of your mouth about Heather. I know you fucking lied to me. You're a lying piece of shit just like your father."

"I'm nothing like that cock-sucking prick!" It seemed to strike a nerve, just like Alex knew that it would. That hatred would be all-consuming if he didn't pull back on the leash.

The cadet tried to push his body back into a sitting position, which prompted Alex to kick him over again just as he accomplished the goal. A string of curses came out of the kid's mouth. He needed to make Mal listen to him. He needed to make Mal treat him with some kind of respect, or fear at least. He needed the kid to spill every last drop of truth about Heather out of his mouth. He needed to know that there may have been something he could fault her for – if only to be petty in an effort to make himself feel better about what he'd done. Alex stepped on the struggling cadet's hand as it tried to push off the ground. A strangled scream, curses, and then silence as Mal waited for him to speak.

"Tell me what really happened between you and Heather," he demanded.

The cadet grunted as he tried to pull his hand free, failing. "Go fuck yourself!"

"So, that's a no?" Alex put more weight on his foot. "Are you sure you don't remember now? There's only so much a hand can take before it breaks." *Just like a heart.*

"Fuck. Off." Mal grunted, clearly biting back the pain.

Alex started to twist his foot, knowing it would cause a new kind of pain without snapping the bones just yet. It make the cadet scream out, but no confession. He didn't really want to break the cadet's hand and he was sure there was only so far he could push things before Mal realized torture wasn't in his blood.

"Tell me and I'll see about getting you a deal out of here. You'd like that, wouldn't you?"

"You're a fucking liar," Mal growled.

"I have the power to wipe reports from the ship's log. I could just say someone got into the system and thought it would be a funny prank. Hell, I could even call our fathers and they could have everything sorted out by the time we land back home. You could walk off this starship a free man with a hooker waiting for you in a hotel room."

Alex knew how to paint the picture. He knew what Harrison would fall for. It was the perfect scenario to have everything wrapped up and tossed out with the trash, then topped with a bow where he could run off and do the same ole shit.

"Didn't fuck her," he grunted out.

"Sorry, what was that? Couldn't quite hear you." He wanted to make sure that he heard exactly what Mal said.

"I didn't fuck her!" The kid tried to pull away. "Get off my fucking hand."

Knowing it would remove the threat of pain and broken bones, he lifted his foot. The kid was already talking. Alex had to give him something to keep it coming.

"More," he demanded. He tried to make it sound threatening, hoping that he had pushed just enough to seem more of a threat than he was. Mal had made it clear when he first broke the news that he was less than a man.

"She was in medical... moaning in pain." There was still a defiant look on Mal's face as he told his story. "Thought I'd record her just in case it could be useful."

Mal was a horrible human being. Only a sick fuck would purposely twist something for the sole purpose to destroy something or someone. Mal was just like his father.

"Did you ever touch her?"

He shook his head, but there was a smile on his face. "Naw, but she begged me too. I wanted to hold her down and destroy that ass. I wanted to fuck her raw," he dragged out that last word. "But the nurse came in and I can't fucking stand blue skin."

Alex doubted that was the problem. He knew the cadet messed around with aliens. He heard about it on-planet and even in the halls as gossip amongst the crew. If he had to wage a bet, it was probably Nurse Krolox. Algeon. Blue skinned. Male.

Alex couldn't stop himself. "Why'd you do it?"

The kid just laughed. "Why the fuck not?"

Of course he wouldn't get an answer. Alex should have known better. It was one thing to know there was always a target on his back, but there was the chance that maybe his actions were directed at Heather instead. Maybe it was her dictation of protocol or some citation she issued against him. It could have been any petty thing to trigger Mal – probably just the fact that she denied him.

Turning, Alex headed towards the door and fresh air. He'd been in this cesspool too long and was thinking too seriously on crossing a line. He had gotten his answers and learned just how similar he was to Mal. They both acted out and hurt someone – manipulated the truth and found themselves just.

"Hey! Fucktard! Get me out of here." Alex heard shuffling and knew the cadet was trying to get himself off the floor. "A deal's a fucking deal."

His com device unlocked the door and he pushed it slightly ajar before glancing back over his shoulder. Alex knew that in a different life, he would have ended up like the scum on the ground, covered in his own feces, who would destroy a life at the blink of an eye. He knew that he owed his path in life to his mother's heart and how he learned at a young age what was right and wrong.

Glancing up at the ceiling, he made a show out of it. It was about time that Mal got a taste of his own medicine. "See, I said that I could do all those things but I clearly remember never promising a damn thing. You are a repulsive human being and deserve everything that's coming your way."

"Tanaka!"

It was the first time the cadet called him by his name. Alex wasn't fooled though. He could have called out anything but chose to call out his last name. It was a desperate reminder of who he was and what the familial duty was. It didn't stop him from walking through the door though.

He was going to enjoy watching Mal burn.

Her body ached and a persistent beeping was causing her head to throb. She wanted to find the source and stop it, but her legs and arms felt so heavy. Heather didn't think that she could manage to sit up, let alone turn off the noise.

But then it suddenly stopped.

"You are safe now, friend."

Azvark. Of course!

She tried to move again, but her limbs still wouldn't budge. Was she strapped down to the bed? Trying to sit up only caused pain in her lower abdomen to shoot up her body. That was something new.

"I can't move."

She hoped that Azvark would explain when even her eyes struggled to open. It felt like forever before a reply came.

"It's the medicine. You will be alright." It felt like there was a smile in her brain. *"I made male human see truth."*

Well, there was only one male human that earned that name from Azvark. Even though the proud words had come into her thoughts, Heather still didn't believe that Alex had done anything to help her. It was his fault that she was ripped from her ship and locked up to die. He had no reason to help her and had made it clear that he wasn't going to either.

"I want to get up." Even though Azvark made it clear that some medicine – a sedative for all she knew – was keeping her in bed. *"I can't open my eyes. I want to see what's wrong with me... why I hurt."*

Heather could feel a largeness in her mind. Obviously something was going on in her friend's mind and Azvark was trying to condense something down to a short explanation. But what came was a hand on her shoulder to stop her from trying to sit up and see why her lower half throbbed so.

"Why do I hurt like this? Tell me, Azvark," she begged. One word strained to get out through her dry throat. "Please."

The alien looked away, focusing on some imaginary thing on the wall. Why wouldn't she just say it? What could have happened that was so bad? The last Heather remembered was being sedated and hearing someone say it would be over soon. She was still alive. So did that mean whatever they did ended up paralyzing her? No, if that was the case then she wouldn't feel this kind of pain. Maybe she lost a leg or... No, Heather could see the two lumps under the blanket where her feet were. Besides, this pain was higher. It felt like the worst menstrual cramping she ever had mixed with the pain attacks that she suffered from after the crash destroyed the vials of serum. Was she stabbed in some struggle to save her life and that's why there's pain?

"P-please."

Her friend's shoulders dropped. Guess it didn't matter what race you were, the tell-tale signs of defeat were the same. *"I asked him to wait until you woke but he decided for you. I want you to know that I tried."*

Heather nodded, even though she didn't understand. She knew that General Ruthesford had tried to kill her, but she wasn't sure what Azvark had tried to do. Maybe she really did end up paralyzed and this was just phantom pain or maybe she was stabbed and lost a kidney.

"The male human," Azvark corrected, hearing her thoughts.

Alex? What would he have done to her that she should have been awake for? Heather tried to piece everything together but still felt like her mind was in a jumbled up foggy state.

"Your baby was long dead and hurting you. It made rock of your inside. Doctor said it was bad. The male human decided it should come out. I wanted you to wake and decide because..."

She couldn't quite see where this was going. There was a feeling of dread inside her, as if her body knew before her brain could process. *"Because what?"*

"Because you never can have babies now. Everything is gone."

She felt like all the blood suddenly evaporated from her body.

No.

"I'm sorry."

No.

Why would he do that? He knew that she wanted to have children. How could he do this to her? Did he hate her that much?

It wasn't fair.

Heather didn't bother brushing away the tears streaming down her face. She knew it was pointless because they wouldn't be ending any time soon. This was *her* body and *her* decision – and it was just ripped away. He didn't even have the authority as commander to order this. He didn't even have the authority as her boyfriend to do this. He was worse than the general. At least he had let her escape and she had a chance to rebuild. She'd never be able to rebuild what Alex stole.

"I want to be left alone."

"Heather, I don't think-"

"No," she thought firmly, *"I want to be alone."*

Slowly, Azvark rose from the chair beside her bed and walked towards the door. She paused there and Heather could feel a light tug on her mind. She didn't ignore it nor invite it. She just turned her head away from Azvark and stayed that way until long after the room door had swooshed back into place.

She had refused any and all visitors for two days. Being stripped of her rank shouldn't have permitted her to do so, especially when Alex had tried to come in. The medical staff had stepped in and said that she refused visitors. Perhaps because it was a doctor that wasn't involved in her attempted murder, Alex listened and stayed away. Azvark hadn't returned either and no more messages invaded her brain.

There was no way that Heather could ever get pass this but it was getting unbearable to be stranded here. If only she was home, she would have her grandma then and maybe the pain would lessen. Her grandma had lost her only child – albeit after living life and having Heather – but the pain must be the same. Maybe there was a way to cope. But first, she needed to get off this planet.

Slowly, Heather pushed her body up to a sitting position and took a rest. Her breathing was already heavy. Carefully – to avoid sudden motions that would jerk her abdomen – she hung her feet over the side of the hospital bed. On the wall opposite her was a computer panel that she could access and find out the status of the ship. Even if her rank and authority were taken from her, Heather was one of the best navigators on the fleet, and that came with a good deal of programming knowledge. It might take a few tries, but she was sure that she could hack an authorization code to get that information.

Her feet inched closer to the floor as she eased out of bed. The reintroduction of her body weight on her lower half was more shocking that she'd have thought. It was an instant bolt of pain up and down her body. If the bed hadn't been in arm's reach, she would have ended up on the floor, doubled over in pain.

"You're better than this, Heather," she told herself. She was the only one left on her side. She was the only one that was going to pull her up and get her going again. She needed to stay strong and fight.

Her left hand reached for the vacant chair next to the bed, then her right hand followed and grabbed onto the back of it. There weren't wheels on the legs and it was sure to alert the whole medical crew that she was out of bed if it scrapped along the floor. Then she wouldn't be able to get her answers. They'd put her back in that bed and give her another round of pain meds until her body adjusted. There were no open wounds to show that she needed to heal, so she should have been grateful for that. Her body was practically as good as new – minus certain things – thanks to the technology.

Heather inched herself around the chair and toward her next target – the medical cabinet. It was a little bit of a stretch from where the chair was to reach the countertop. Her fingertips just grazed the edge of the counter. It wasn't much to hold onto and – the second she let go of the chair – she would have hope her legs had enough strength to take an unaided step. Taking a deep breath, she braced herself for the pain and let go. Her balance waivered but held. Maybe she didn't need the crutch after all. Gingerly, she took small steps along the cabinets, keeping the sturdy structure as her back-up. It was a moment of triumph and relief when she reached the wall panel.

Out of habit, Heather tried using her own entry codes. They unlocked the system but didn't grant her access to any of the information that she needed about the ship. In the Alphecca's eyes, she must just be a lowly cadet looking up the lunch menu or weather report, but at least she had access. There were two options – try to work around the protocol coding to grant herself access again or hack in with someone else's clearances. Obviously granting herself access would be the easier of the two, but it could also send out an alert if someone was monitoring her. Heather had no idea if the general knew her condition or not, which probably was something else that she should look into.

Opening a new command window, she plugged in the personnel identification code of the one person that she knew would be simple to impersonate. While Alex's passcode was something of a mystery to her, Heather knew the answers to the security questions would be basic knowledge. It was a simple identification check that was standard for this class of starships. It would only be one foot in the door, and she would still need to hack the rest of her way in.

What street did you grow up on?

It took a moment before the answer came to her – Locust. It was a street downtown, in one of the nicer neighborhoods. Alex had mentioned that his family had been in the home for centuries, and his family connections would have justified and sustained such a nice place.

What was the name of your first girlfriend?

Heather cursed under her breath. For as well as she knew him, this wasn't something that really came up. He had mentioned a girl back in high school that he dated briefly, but it could have been so briefly that Alex didn't count it at all. And how many girlfriends did he really have? He was more of the serial dater without the committing part. The number had to be very low. Before Heather, there was Maggie. That relationship lasted a while. If he had submitted these security questions before the Alphecca departed then Heather was ruled out. She could go with Maggie and hope that there really wasn't anyone serious before her. At best, she would have three attempts at the answer. Realistically, she only had one name to try.

She entered the name and couldn't believe that the system accepted the answer. This damn ancient security system was going to be the death of her. How anyone in the past managed to get through this torture was a mystery to her.

And there was one more.

好きな食べ物は何ですか？
Sukina tabemono wa nani desu ka?

"What the fucking hell?" Heather stared at the last question between her and gaining access. She had no idea what it any of it meant. Not the symbols and not the English version of whatever the squiggly lines meant. If she still had her com device – one, she wouldn't need to be hacking into this – Heather could have scanned the language and translated it. She had no idea what any of it meant, other than Alex was an asshole. He must have written in this question specifically instead of using the given prompts.

"Suki... na... tabem... ono... waaa," she slowly tried to sound out the English translation, but nothing registered in her head. There might be a chance that Azvark could translate, seeing as she seemed to have learned English as part of her diplomatic wife duties. It would be a long stretch, given how many old languages were still around.

In the main city, there was still Spanish, English, Afrikaans, Chinese, and Russian. Those were the five main languages that Alex might have learned. She doubted he'd have taken on Afrikaans, seeing as he was Asian and it was more of a race language. At some point all African and dark skinned citizens had decided on one common language of their race, just like Asians had with Chinese. Heather knew from a couple flight manuals during basic training that Russian had more of English looking characters in their language – and this definitely wasn't English. That really only left Chinese, and she had no hope left if that was the case. Part of her didn't think that Alex was Chinese and something was nagging at her mind about how he described being homeschooled. There were more non-traditional Asian lessons, as she recalled. He wasn't Chinese, so he was...

Ugh! Not that it mattered. If Heather could figure out what he was, it still wouldn't help her in answering the question. She didn't know anything other than English and like three phrases in Spanish for when she ordered lunch from the Spanish food truck on base. Knowing the language wouldn't make a difference. That meant she had to think of what question he'd have asked.

Heather knew the generic prompts, seeing as they had been options for when she entered her security questions as well. Now that she thought about it, there wasn't anywhere that a written question could be entered. So that must mean that this prompt was one of the choices she had been given, just in a different language. That narrowed it down... to about thirty options. Three attempts before system lock-out. An alert that would get her caught.

The only ones that she could really remember had to do more about family – mother's maiden name, where your parents met, name of oldest sibling, etc. From Alex's stories, he didn't really fit into the family mold and it had caused a bit of a rough childhood for him. She doubted that he would have picked a family question. There were ones about first jobs and school mascots, but those were too easy. He had gone to the Academy – which had no mascot

255

– and this was his first job. The majority of the other ones were about favorites. Favorite color. Favorite season. Favorite food. He must have picked one of those prompts.

But which one?

Color. Season. Food. They were the only three Heather could remember and each one was worth a shot. Three prompts and three attempts. If he entered anything other than what she thought, it would be over too.

"Favorite color is green, so…" She entered that into the system and got a red error. Green was his favorite color, so it meant that this wasn't the prompt. Not unless by changing the language of the question, it would also change the language of the answer. Then there was no way in hell that she could get the right answer. She would have an easier time trying to hack in with someone else like McGregor.

"Ok, well, his favorite season is summer because he hates being cold." Another red error popped up on the screen.

"Last one's the charm." His favorite food was chocolate. There was a stash of it in the kitchen that he reserved for himself. Cigarettes, chocolate, and whiskey were his vices. Heather entered in "chocolate" but her finger hovered over the button on the screen. If she got this wrong, it was all over. And something about entering "chocolate" didn't seem right to her. These were supposed to be security questions and Alex – for as laidback as he came off – would have taken it serious. He wouldn't have put in something that everyone knew. The other two answers weren't easy. Guessing his street could have been a stroke of luck for the random person trying to hack his account, but not his first girlfriend. It was common knowledge around the base that Alex was a short-term dating option only. So why go from an easy question to a harder question only to get with one so easy that it could be quickly guessed? There had to be something more to it, but like the language was something.

"If the language is related to what he is, then maybe it's also a hint as to what food it could be." She had to believe that this was the favorite food prompt. That much she couldn't afford to waiver on. "There's nothing really Asian on this ship, except maybe sauces. Fenrir does like his teriyaki chicken. But sauces aren't a food."

If Heather believed that her legs could handle it, she would have been pacing now. The answer to this must be something he had at home. Seeing as he was constantly on missions and before then living at the Academy like every cadet does, it had to be something from his childhood. That meant that knowing the language could have helped her narrow down the typical foods and decide if she ever remembered Alex talking about them or not.

His favorite season was summer... He did bring up one time where his brothers thought it would be fun to push him into the swimming pool even though he didn't know how to swim. According to Alex, he had almost drowned. But there was no food in that story. He did mention that his brothers were jealous because their mother would spend more time with Alex, seeing as he was the baby of the family. He would get bullied more often and never really stood up for himself. His father would force him to go outside and play anyways but his mother... his mother would allow him to stay inside and cook with her! He would stay inside... during the summer... and... She felt the train of thought slip between her fingers.

Japanese!

Alex was at least some part Japanese. While he was homeschool, he learned the old language and tea ceremony and kendo. His mother loved the spring when the cherry trees would bloom and they'd pick the blossoms to make sweets for the summer. Alex mentioned something about one of them and he had to explain it because it was something she had never heard of and the name didn't make it obvious. When he'd get bullied, he'd go inside and his mother would give him a sweet to cheer him up and he'd ask for "more cheese"... No, that wasn't quite right. He said that he'd get teased when asking for more.

"More cheese…" She tried to imagine what a little boy with a full mouth would sound like. "Mo chee… mo chee…Mochi!"

She deleted the "chocolate" and entered "mochi" instead. This was her last chance. She hit the button and the screen went dark for a moment, then refreshed with the Alphecca's logo on the background.

Heather had full access.

She when to the ship's log and brought up the mechanical status reports. It seemed like the borrowed Dragouul parts had been integrated with the Alphecca's mechanics. Diagnostics still needed to be ran and there was a lot of programming to do. It seemed like the parts were a match but the operating language wasn't. It was more of a tedious task than an actual problem. With the crew they had, it was maybe a week or so away from being completed. They had enough rations, even with the dragouul family, to be able to make it that week and then the short trip back to Earth. After all, their original mission was supposed to last a couple months.

It was tempting to restore her access and watch Alex trip over himself wondering how it happened. It was tempting, but first she needed to see why her access had been cut. Stripping her of the commander rank shouldn't have limited her that much.

Heather navigated to the personnel files and pulled up the ship's roster. Her name wasn't listed alphabetically like everyone else's. She kept scrolling towards the bottom, noticing that the Dragouul family was listed there, and then – finally – was her name. It was next to Malcolm Harrison. Where his was colored red, hers was grey. She knew from past missions that persons aboard a ship that were considered dangerous were color-coded red so that the crew would be able to know and establish countermeasures. Grey wasn't a color she was familiar with. Her finger moved over her name and tapped the screen.

Heather McGrey – **DECEASED**

Deceased?!

She stared at the screen, not truly believing what she was seeing. Heather wasn't dead. If she was dead, then she wouldn't be here. She wouldn't be standing at this wall panel hacking into a ship if she were dead.

Or was this the afterlife? Maybe this was what death was like – one giant simulation. Maybe that's why beings weren't afraid to die and welcomed it. Or maybe this was a construct of the mind and it created a scenario it thought best to deliver the unfortunate news. If this was, hers sucked. So far it was all about Alex and her being in pain, which would have been a great simulation and metaphor for the breakup. Having the security prompts for Alex could have been her mind's way of pointing out how much she cared about him, how real their connection was, how she knew so much about who he was, how much she loved him.

The lights in the room dimmed and two soft notes chimed over the announcement system. This wasn't the afterlife if the ship was notifying her that it was evening and it was entering power-saving mode. No, this wasn't death.

Heather opened her records and scrolled through the summary page to find her cause of death. It seemed that HQ was notified three days ago that she was deceased and the cause of death was an allergic reaction to a sedative. Report was filed by medical and Alex signed off on it. Body was cremated and disposed on unknown planet.

Her body was very much not cremated. So that meant that whatever happened the day before she woke up was reported incorrectly to HQ. According to Azvark, it was Alex's helpful doings. She would never have imagined that he'd file this huge of a false report. It was one thing to fudge some details on a report, but to file a death report on a person that was going to be walking off this ship at HQ's docking bay was another thing. There was no way to hide the fact that she was alive. All this would do would start proceedings back on Earth and her next of kin would be notified... Heather felt sick at the thought. Her grandma was going to get a knock on the door and find out that her only family was gone. She'd be devastated. It would be too much for her.

She needed to get a message to her grandma that she was still alive. There was no way in hell that Heather was going to put her through another loss. All Heather was going to do was send her a little transmission to let her know that she was alive but when she opened up the transmission log all her resolve drained away. There were so many transmissions from HQ from the day that she allegedly died. Curiosity got the better of her and she started to read through them. By the last one, she knew that it would be impossible to send her grandma a note. The Force and, more importantly, the general thought that she was dead. It would put her grandma back in danger to know that she was alive. As depressing as it was, Heather had no choice.

But what would that mean for her when the ship departed the planet? If she was a literal dead woman, then she could never walk off the ship. It was listed that her body was cremated, so she couldn't even leave in a makeshift coffin and disappear afterwards. Alex may have stopped her death but his actions were still so strange and that was suspicious. Was he planning to kill her himself? Then there was the crazy idea that she'd go to the Dragouul planet when they dropped off Azvark and her family. Surely she'd be safe there, but there was the matter of reporting immigration. The big hiccup was that Heather didn't want to be forced into whatever life that would be. She had been forced into enough things in her life and she'd already had so much taken from her. It wasn't fair, and this world was all about that mystical balance.

Heather closed out of the personnel files and pulled up the medical bay reports. She was listed as deceased there as well, but it wasn't her record that she was after. It seemed like Cadet Ha was released yesterday and put on restricted duty. Even if the ship was fully operating, a navigator didn't have much physically demanding work. She was probably just taking it easy and recovering in her room. Heather wondered if she was going to be able to mentally recover. She knew that their last conversation had gotten personal and, seeing as she was dead now, it wouldn't be stepping out of line to give a name to the one person affected the same ways she was. Cadet Ha deserved to know how brave she was and that she was doing the right thing by holding Harrison to it. She deserved to know what could happen if you kept it a secret and that person gained enough power to make you, literally, disappear.

She logged out of the system and used the hem of her medical gown to wipe the screen of her fingerprints. Instead of using the cabinet and chair as a crutch, Heather slowly walked back across the room, making it to the bed a lot fast than her first journey out of it had been. She just eased herself down on the edge and sat with her feet still grazing the floor of the room. It was then that she realized that she still had her fuzzy socks on. She still had her socks. She was still her.

Chapter Thirty-Three

He needed to pluck up the courage to face her. This was ridiculous. Heather was calling the shots when she had no power. The worst part was that it overruled his orders! The crew was insubordinate but he couldn't actually discipline them without letting HQ know by whose order. That would just cause chaos, and he needed everyone to keep a level head and think about going home. If there was a fear of returning, then Alex doubted anyone would waste their time repairing the ship. He, for one, wanted outta here.

"There's something on your mind."

He dropped his head over the back of the commander's chair on the deserted bridge. Work here was already complete, minus the final programming that would come when they finally launched. It was the quietest place he could think of to relax and escape.

"It's nothing," he said dismissively. This didn't concern his coffee cadet. She was nice enough but this wasn't a place for her to step in.

Alex felt her shoulders shrug against his thighs and sighed as she took him back into her mouth. He knew that this should stop but he was so desperate to make himself feel good in any way possible. Heather was alive because of him, but her and that alien treated him like it had been all his fault. His heart ached over what he'd done by following orders, and then by sleeping with the woman between his legs. There was even guilt now as she knelt before him.

He knew that he needed to talk to Heather and explain things before she found out some other way. Azvark, for as much as her hearts are in the right place, would probably tell it in a way to cushion the blow for Heather it but also paint him in a not-so-great light. He needed to be ahead of the narrative on this one. He needed to explain why she couldn't run this ship on its return nor have any part of bridge operations. He needed to explain to her that she was dead and decide, together, on a plan to get her out of the city. There was no way that she could ever return back to her life once they departed.

For a moment, a breeze caught him and caused him to shiver. For sure the cadet was about to chime in again. He knew that – with his mind elsewhere – that her goal of getting him off was lofty. But then he felt her weight on his lap and her fingers wrap around him.

"No." He moved to grab her hips and stop her from sinking down on top of him. She already had her uniform skirt hiked up around her waist and her panties were gone.

"Alex, you need this. I know you do."

She wasn't wrong. He'd been with her the last two days which made it obvious that their relationship was now sexual instead of flirty eye candy with menial tasks such as coffee runs. It was just that Alex had always stopped it before it went this far again. When he found out that Heather never fucked Harrison, his one-night stand with the cadet crushed him. The betrayal and guilt were too real. He always thought that maybe Heather would understand a blowjob here and there. After all, he was basically an addict and it wasn't entirely different than her getting a fix when she needed it. Fucking the cadet again would make the betrayal all that more real. It would be deliberate now and not the result of some misunderstanding. This was a choice now.

Heather will never forgive me.

His hands traveled up her sides and around the front to cup her breasts. He had never needed a commitment before and everyone had been happy knowing that. The cadet knew that – this was not serious. There was nothing wrong with how he'd been in the past and even Heather had accepted that without forcing him to change. Things would just be how they used to be, but he wasn't sure why that made him feel so empty.

"Take it all."

Alex walked into the medical bay and headed straight towards the room in the back. Heather was going to open up that damn door and she was going to listen to him. She was going to accept that he was in charge and calling the shots now. She needed to understand that everything was done to keep her safe and alive. Heather would need to accept that she wasn't in control anymore.

"What the hell?" He stared at the wide open door. It was cleaned and sterilized, and there was nobody inside. Just a crisp bed and the lights dimmed. Glancing around, Alex noticed the blue-skinned nurse from before and grabbed their arm to get their attention. "What happened to Heather McGrey?"

"Oh, the commander discharged herself this morning."

Discharged? He didn't even want to address the fact that she wasn't a commander anymore. The idea that Heather was out there, walking around, was an open can of worms. It meant that Azvark could have ran into her and told her version of what happened or that Heather accessed a panel on the ship and made it known that she was alive. This could be bad.

He ran a hand through his hair, trying to gather his thoughts. "Okay, and where is she now?"

The nurse shrugged. "I dunno. Somewhere on the ship, I suppose. She didn't say where she was going."

And she didn't have a damn com device for him to track her either. This was bad. He needed to find Heather and the only one he knew that could do that was with the one person he hoped she wasn't with. Alex hurried out of the medical bay and towards Heather's room. Maybe she simply went back to her room to rest or to change. It would be amazing if that's all she really did.

He got to her room down the hall from his and knocked. Giving it exactly two seconds, Alex knocked again. Two seconds later, he knocked again – knowing that if she was inside that she would probably just now be reaching the door. But he couldn't wait. He held up his com device to the door's access panel and overrode the code. It swooshed open and inside was a vacant room. Nothing had been touched, which meant that she hadn't come back here.

The only other logical place where she'd have gone was the cafeteria. If not to eat, then she'd have gone to get a cup of coffee. With how much she normally drank, there was no doubt in his mind that she must be going through withdrawals. Alex hurried off that way, slightly slower than before. Guilt was pulling him back.

The cafeteria was a little busy, but it wasn't hard to pick out faces. There was a group of first year cadets in the back corner playing cards. A couple of McGregor's men sat around one table nibbling on something. Heather's face wasn't in the crowd. That didn't mean that she hadn't been here.

He headed into the back kitchen area. "Fenrir, got a question for you."

The stout man turned. "If it's if I got more of that spicy dark chocolate then the answer's no. I ain't mixing more of that up. Gotta save the chilies for dinner."

"No, it's not that but you certainly know how to hurt a guy," he joked. "I'm actually wondering if Heather McGrey came through here today. Just trying to track her down and check up on her."

Suddenly, Alex was suspicious of how much he knew. It wouldn't take long for a rumor to spread around the ship, especially with most people being off-duty because the ship wasn't operating. What if Fenrir knew exactly where Heather was? What if she was here right now, hiding?

"Naw, I ain't seen her for a long while. A few days I'd guess. Strange too because she hasn't raided my coffee supply." He paused to scratch the back of his skull. "Probably a good thing you're looking for her. She must be sick or dead or something to not be drinking coffee."

If only he knew...

"Hey, thanks." Another dead end. Strike two. "If you see her, ping me on my com. You know she's too stubborn to come find me on her own."

Fenrir chuckled. "Ain't that the truth."

He headed out, dreading his last stop – Azvark. Then it hit him. There was no way Heather could be on her own. One, the doctor said that she was probably going to be in pain. Secondly, Heather had to eat at some point and – if she hadn't shown up here – then someone was getting food for her. It was a long shot but it could delay the inevitable.

"One last question... has anyone been taking a lot of food out of the cafeteria?"

The man rolled his eyes. "You mean practically everyone who wants to eat a-lone."

Alex shook his head. "No, well, yes... but no. I mean did it seem to you like anyone was taking out food for someone else? I'm thinking if Heather's not feeling well that someone might be helping her."

"Aw, I see. Playing like a real detective now, commander. Hmm, let me thinks." He walked around to the front of the kitchen where the pass-through window was. "The only ones really taking out food are those lizardy ones we picked up. The small blue-ish purple one's been coming in a couple times more, but I just figured they were loving my cooking."

Bilfa.

"I'm sure that's exactly why. You are a wonderful chef!" He headed out the door. All roads were leading to one place.

"You're a fucking liar!" Fenrir chuckled. It was never openly said, but everyone thought his food was mediocre at best. It was just that no one else wanted the job or the trouble of feeding so many.

If Bilfa was taking more food, then it was a very good chance that it was for Heather. The little Dragouul had already been a huge help when the pain attacks started. She was Azvark's daughter and, from McGregor's report, they were close on the trek back to the ship. There was going to be no avoiding it. He headed towards the large conference room where they were staying and opened the door to almost black-out conditions.

"Wha... hello?" The ship was never this dark. This was a sign that something had malfunctioned.

"How can we help you, commander?" The voice sounded large and firm. It must be Cryzka.

"I, um... just give me a moment. I need to get someone to see about fixing these lights," he turned to walk away when the voice came again.

"We asked for them to be off. On our planet, we live underground and away from the solar rays. I filed the correct forms to request them to be disabled in this room for us. We're more comfortable but I do apologize for the disadvantage you're experiencing now because of it."

That was one way to put it. This was exactly how every alien horror movie started. Dark room. Mysterious sound. Stupid guy. Death.

"I'm looking for your daughter, Bilfa. I believe she knows where Heather McGrey is and I need to find with her. She left the medical bay and I want to make sure that she's okay."

There was a long pause before the voice spoke again. *"Heather McGrey is fine. She is being taken care of."*

"Yes, but I'd like to see that she's okay for myself. I just need to talk to Bilfa and-"

"You do not need Bilfa. You have the answer to your query. Please go. Your voice will wake the little ones."

Alex wasn't sure whether or not he believed the little ones were sleeping or not. He wasn't exactly in a place to judge, seeing as he could see nothing in the room. There was even the chance that no one was in the room and they were just sending him telepathic messages from across the ship. It meant that he was going to have to take up a post outside the cafeteria and follow Bilfa to find Heather.

"The commander is looking for Heather McGrey. He may follow you. I wish for you to not meddle in their affairs unlike your mother, but you must make your own decisions. One day you will need to know what should be done."

Her father's voice was clear in her mind. The commander was searching for Heather and they couldn't really understand why. Not completely anyway. Mother had said that their people wanted Heather to die and disagreements happened between the two humans. Their people said that she was dangerous. But the woman sitting next to Bilfa didn't look dangerous and she knew that the human had never tried to harm her or her family. If anything, the woman was more sad than before.

"What are you doing now?" She stared curiously at the human hands working with a few snipped wires and some kind of tool.

"Someone had cut these. I need to fix them." Before Bilfa could ask why, she continued. "These send messages from the engine to the power converters. It steps down the output to a manageable level for the biosystems to operate without having a separate unit on-board."

It really was all too boring, but Mother had asked her to watch over the human again. In truth, it wasn't so bad when Heather had been talking about her life and how humans are. These matters with the ship and these fixing things were what made this difficult.

"Mother doesn't want me to ask, but what happened with you and that male human? He asked father to tell him where you are. Father wouldn't tell him."

Emotions were coming at her from the female but Bilfa wasn't as skilled yet at sorting them out into memories and thoughts. It just felt like a large weight, filled with whatever unlabeled emotion Heather was experiencing.

268

"He took something from me that I can never get back. He betrayed me," she spoke quietly. "Alex is the type of man that will do anything to make something right if he realizes that he's at fault. But this... this isn't something that can be made right."

"Why not?"

Bilfa didn't expect an answer. For some reason, the female was being as vague and puzzling as Mother usually was. It was probably a human thing used to distract from the subject. But in her limited experience, everything could be made right. Even if something was lost, there was always a way to find it again.

"He cut out a part of me." Heather set the tool on the metal grating beside her and let the wires hang free, now that they were repaired. "I always wanted to have a baby and I held on so long to the one I did have. It caused me the pain that you helped me get through."

Bilfa started to speak, but held her tongue. It was hard not to explain to her that it was a foolish thing to do. You must never keep something that is causing you pain.

"He let the doctor take out the part of me that makes babies. He never asked me what I wanted, and he took away the only thing I ever did want."

"This is sad."

It was a statement and a question. Bilfa was sure that "sad" was the correct human emotion to assign to this situation and it also was "sad" that Heather would never have what her mother and she would. Never having little ones was something Bilfa had never thought about and didn't think it was possibly not to. Everyone was mated and every mating brought little ones. That was life and that was the way things were.

"I don't want to talk anymore about it or about him."

That would only leave boring ship talk or silence. Neither seemed pleasant to Bilfa. Besides, Mother was just worrying anyway. Heather seemed fine and no one was going to find her down here. Half the time, Bilfa had walked right passed the galley door on her way back with food. Food – that was it!

269

"You are hungry. I will get food."
She got up, not waiting for the female to reply.

Her body ached, but it was the aching of her face that woke her. Heather sat up slowly, realizing the odd pain in her abdomen was disappearing. It was a relief to be able to get around more, but also depressing. It was the last remaining piece of her baby. Without the pain, she feared that she would forget the little thing that she had loved so much and would never have again. She hadn't even seen what it looked like or held it in her arms. It was bad enough that it had died, but Heather never got to tell it how much she had loved it.

She rubbed the side of her face, trying to ease out the groove imprints left behind from her nap on the metal grating in the engine room. Except for coding, there wasn't actually much left to do here either. Most of the hard work of mating up the two ships' parts had been done and all she really could do was to check the connections to reassure herself that sabotage wasn't going to happen again. The rest was programming, which she could do from anywhere, but she wanted to be left alone. It wasn't exactly quiet here, with the constant humming of the engines, but no one knew where she was. Heather just needed to keep her hands busy so she didn't think too much.

Bilfa was a godsend. Motivating herself to go back up the levels of the ship to get food was too daunting. Plus that's where the rest of the crew was. Did they know that she was stripped of her duties? Technically, she was the lowest ranking being on this ship. Even the Dragouuls outranked her. It was petty to think about what others may say. Nothing probably changed and they'd still refer to her as their commander like the medical staff had.

Heather let her feet dangle over the edge of the metal grating above the engines below as she pulled up the monitor to work on the programming. It wasn't much, but it was the only thing that she was left being able to do on the ship. If it got them home faster, then it was worth it.

"Heather!"

She froze and listened. She thought that she heard her name being called but it was muffled over the sound of the engines. It had to be a figment of her imagination. Bilfa and Azvark always used their telepathy instead of vocalizing their thoughts. Ignoring it, she went back to the task at hand.

A hand grabbed her shoulder and she nearly jumped out of her skin. In the very least, she had almost left off the grating. Heather stared up at the face just inches from hers. It was like seeing a ghost. Perhaps she hadn't woken up yet at all and this was another nightmare. Perhaps this dream version of Alex was here to push her down into the engines below and finish the job the general wanted done.

"Heather, what are you doing?" When she didn't say anything, he made a move to pull her up. "Come on, let's get you out of here."

She felt her body be lifted up and led out of the engine room. The silence in the corridor outside was almost deafening compared to living in a constant mechanical hum. It really sank in that this wasn't a nightmare or a ghost. Neither could have dragged her out here. That meant this was really Alex and she wanted to punch him so badly. Striking her commanding officer would come with consequences. It would be reported and forever be a stain on her permanent record. Then again, she was technically deceased as far as the Force was concerned.

"Why are you here?" Heather tried not to glare up at him.

"What?" The question caught him off guard. Had he thought that he was rescuing her? Being down there was her choice. "I've been looking for you for days. You checked yourself out of the medical bay and, before, that refused to see anyone. I just wanted to make sure that you were alright."

Hmpf.

"I'm alright. You can go back to whatever you were doing." Heather turned away from him and started to head back inside the engine room, but a hand stopped her again.

"I don't think you are. Actually, I know you're not alright."

"Yea, and what would you know about that, Alex? Do you know why I might not be alright?" She turned around to face him. "Do you think that maybe something happened to me? Do you think that might be it?"

"Hey, I did what I had to for you." He was holding up his hands. It was a sign of surrender, but his words didn't sound like he was backing down.

"You did this for me? What part of it do you think was for me?!" Was he crazy? This wasn't what she wanted at all. There was no way that she could ever have the life that she wanted. Everything Heather had worked for was for nothing now.

"Yes, I did," he started to defend himself.

"So locking me up in the medical bay was for my own good?"

His hands dropped to his side. "I was following the orders from HQ. I didn't know what they were going to do."

"No, of course not. For once you followed orders without questioning them. And why do you think that was? I've had lots of time to think and I realized that you were done with me. You couldn't handle a real girlfriend and wanted to go back to your flings. You hated that you were tied down with me. It was that control that bothered you. That's why you stripped me of rank and fought me every time something came up with the ship. You never wanted to be co-commanders." She took a step closer. "You heard one lie… got one order… you took the chance to dump me and then toss me completely away."

Alex was getting angry. His hand was twitching for a cigarette, or at least to run his hand through his hair. All signs that he was stressed. She had him. She was right and saw what kind of man he was. The fact that he didn't try cutting her off just fueled his guilt in her mind.

"You only stopped them from killing me because Azvark made you. She told me how many times that she tried to warn you but you just wouldn't listen. You didn't want to get involved. It would look bad for your career if you stood in the way of the general. Wouldn't it? It took a diplomatic threat to get you to do anything, and then you were almost too late!"

She didn't realize what she was doing until her fist connected with his chest. He didn't move, didn't make any motion to stop her. Another fist came down. And another. It felt like she was the one being chipped away, broken. Tears streamed down her face but she was too busy hitting him to spare a second to brush them away.

"And then you did the worst thing possible. You took it all away for me. You might as well have let them kill me."

"No." He stopped her fists. "I could never let them kill you, Heather. Never ever."

Her legs felt so weak by those words. It was if all her fight just left her. Heather knew that his feelings hadn't been real. Even though everything they were had been a lie and he showed her nothing but hate when he abandoned her, it was hard to hear that he never wanted her dead.

"Just leave me alone, Alex." She pulled out of his hands and started back towards the engine room.

"Heather, I'm sorry." She stopped. There was no way he had just said that. When she didn't turn around, he said it again. "I'm sorry for what I've done to you. I never wanted to hurt you. I lov-"

"But you did. You hurt me so bad… and I can't forgive you."

This time, when she walked away, he let her go. The metal grating felt uncomfortable as she took a seat again and started to program in the processes for the new parts. Heather knew that it was expected to forgive someone when they apologized, but she couldn't. If those words had left her mouth, they would have been lies. And those last words that Alex tried to say. She couldn't. She just couldn't. If you loved someone, you didn't put them through what he did. Heather had meant what she said to him. Alex was more in love with the idea of her than actually being in love with her. The fact that he also just left meant that she wasn't worth fighting for.

Heather brought up the auxiliary power systems and finished translating over the operating codes. In the back of her mind, she knew that she couldn't hide down here forever. And that's exactly what she had been doing before Alex found her – hiding. There were better places to program, like the bridge. It at least had comfortable seats... it was quiet... it was some place that Alex wouldn't expect her to go.

She ran a test sequence on the new coding and waited for the diagnostics. That would decide it. If the test came back functional, then she'd go to the bridge. If the test failed, she'd stay down here where no one missed her. It took less than a minute, but it felt like hours. The icon in the bottom right corner of the screen was green. Their back-up power systems were fully functional and now compatible with the new parts. If the engines malfunctioned this time, they'd still be able to run on this and get home instead of plummeting out of the sky again.

And that settled it.

Heather tucked the monitor back into place and hibernated the terminal. There were no personal items lying around down here and Bilfa had always taken the plates back upstairs when she left. There was nothing left to clean up and there'd never be any sign that she was here at all. It was quiet as she walked back up through the corridors. It felt like she had walked into a distant memory or alternate reality because of that. Heather was disoriented in such a familiar place.

"Hey, commander." One cadet smiled at her as she passed. That answered one of the questions on her mind. Maybe she could still be a commander, even if it wasn't official.

She ended up stopped, outside her room, staring at the code panel. She wasn't sure that she was ready to be back here. Too much had happened in this room. Heather knew that she smelled and needed a change of clothes, so it was unavoidable. She punched in the five digit code and the door swooshed open, granting her access.

It was like nothing ever happened here. No memories came rushing back. Everything was orderly and smelled disinfected. Maybe everything was one long nightmare spawned by the injection withdrawals. She placed a hand timidly on her stomach and felt the tinge of pain.

This was real.

She pulled out the trunk under her bed and grabbed a change of clothes. There was no way that she was going to look in a mirror until after she washed up. There wasn't a doubt in her mind that the cadet in the corridor was being nice and avoided telling Heather what a mess she was. Heather grabbed her shower caddy and headed out of the room. The goal for today was to just try to feel human again.

Chapter Thirty-Four

Mia hated this feeling. She was completely alone on this ship and nowhere felt safe. In the medical bay, she wasn't allowed to see Commander McGrey when she came in. When she got out, the commander's location never showed up on her com device. That last conversation they had just kept replaying in her mind. She couldn't stand this. She felt weak and scared all the time. McGrey said that she knew what it was like because she lived through it. If she could survive and come out that strong, then there must be a secret to make this pain go away.

She didn't want to leave her room. Her com device kept alerting her to poor nutrition and it was only a matter of time before someone from medical came around to check up on her. It was probably a safety measure to make sure the crew was healthy and not injured somewhere where they couldn't get to the medical bay. Mia just didn't want to eat, and she couldn't sleep.

It was six o'clock in the morning. Almost no one would be awake right now, seeing as the ship was stuck here and no one really had to work. She couldn't blame everyone. If she wasn't feeling like this then she'd probably sleep in and take a vacation too. Instead, she had to worry about running into people and playing the game chicken with medical.

Mia decided on an orange juice and maybe a plain bagel as she pushed herself out of bed. She had changed into her combat uniform pants and wore a hoodie over her t-shirt the whole time she had been discharged. It was the safest clothing option that her mind thought of in order to stop anyone else from attacking her, as irrational as she knew that was. Besides, she never opened the door or went near anyone else. That's why she was surprised when she walked into the cafeteria and didn't think twice about sitting across from the only other person there.

"Hey, commander," she spoke quietly. McGrey glanced up. Obviously she hadn't seen her coming and was probably lost in some thought. "I haven't seen you in a while…"

"I know." She didn't try to hide it or make small talk. There seemed to be something different about her. "How have you been coping?"

Mia had rehearsed the answer in her head so many times, but no one ever asked. No one was ever let close enough, but it was easier to let the truth slip out. "Not that great. I'm still having nightmares and I can't eat and I don't want to be around people."

"I threw myself into work and didn't stop until I passed out. With the ship down, I can't tell you to try that." McGrey went back to staring at the cooling coffee in her hands. Yea, there was something different if coffee was still around while McGrey had a mug. "How good are you at programming interstellar time warp units on a hyper-glyconian synchronization?"

She shrugged.

"I'd honestly avoid it if I could. I'm not horrible but it takes a long time with the calculations and converting the parameters within the interface." It was such a strange question that Mia couldn't help asking. "Why?"

"I've spent the last… god, I don't even know how long. I've been down in the engine rooms aiding in reprogramming the spare parts of the Dragouul ship to work with our interface. I've gotten the basic systems online but there's a large portion of the overhaul that involves the hyper-glyconian synchronization. I thought that if you did want something to get your mind off things that that would definitely be a distraction."

"Oh." Mia left the silence sit between them for a while. Having something to do might be enough of a distraction. It sounded like McGrey was using the ship's repairs to distract her from whatever happened. "I'll help."

McGrey nodded and finally took a sip of the coffee in front of her.

"So, what happened?" Mia asked. She wasn't really expecting much of an answer, even though McGrey had started opening up when they last talked. Maybe this had nothing to do with that and maybe she was so far out of line to ask her commanding officer.

"General Ruthesford was the man who raped me. He deserted me on a war-torn planet to get an abortion or die, but I was captured by one faction. The abuse they put me through killed my baby. I got very sick because my body never rejected it, so they sent me to their local medicine worker... a shaman. I've been taking injections for years to stop the pain and symptoms, but the crash destroyed that. Ruthesford tried to kill me before and now he got Alex – um, Commander Tanaka – to detain me.

"The medical crew were supposed to kill me but the Dragouuls stepped in. The doctor noticed that the baby was still inside me and apparently was fossilized. Tanaka decided to order them to take it out." McGrey hadn't looked up once. It wasn't hard to see the pain and torment on her face as she spoke. Mia wished that she had followed protocol and held her tongue. "I'll never be able to have a family like I wanted. I don't know what talk got around the ship but Tanaka and I were dating before this happened. In less than one day, I lost my boyfriend, my ship, my rank, my life... I'm reported deceased and the only person I care about is suffering with that back home, alone."

She reached over and covered one of McGrey's. "I'm sorry."

It wasn't original and it certainly didn't make any of that go away. It was the only thing Mia could think to say. She knew that she wouldn't want someone defending Commander Tanaka if the roles were reversed, so she couldn't say that he probably didn't know what he was ordering. And now she knew who McGrey couldn't bring to justice or even say his name before. Mia wasn't so sure that she'd have the guts to stay in the Force if her boss raped her. She knew that the woman in front of her seemed defeated and weak right now, but the truth was far from that.

"I saw that Cadet Harrison has been detained and restricted from any interaction."

Mia wasn't sure whether or not that was meant to gauge how she was coping or not by mentioning that name, but she took back her hand. It hurt. It hurt a lot, and it brought back a lot of what she wanted to forget. But it also was good to know that she'd never run into him.

"He's going to be court-martialed when we get home. The report that was filed had a lot of evidence against him. You should know that. For all the wrong Tanaka has cause me, he at least did right by you. He was the one that filed the report"

It seemed like McGrey just defended him, which didn't make a lot of sense to Mia. Not unless McGrey still had feelings for the commander, not that she could blame her. Commander Tanaka was a good looking guy, but he also did something horrible to her. It was probably just too soon for McGrey to sort everything out and decide how she felt about it all. Mia knew there were still moments were she was confused over how she felt about Mal. He had been fun to hang around because he could laugh things off and was easy to talk to. Even when she showed up at his room that one night, sex with him had been great. But he'd ended up way too possessive and then forced himself on her. There was a good side of Mal and a bad side of Mal, and she had seen both.

"When do you want me to help programming?" Mia tried to change the subject back to something neutral.

"After you get a chance to eat something." McGrey stood and tossed the rest of her coffee in the trash. "I'll meet you on the bridge. We can use the terminals there."

When she started to walk away, Mia noticed the woman's wrists were bare. "Where's your com device?"

"A dead woman doesn't need one."

Chapter Thirty-Five

"This is fucking stupid, Tanaka."

That wasn't what he expected McGregor to say after he filled the man in on everything that transpired. He figured the guy was going to pull from some deep pool of experience and lay out the perfect solution on how to get Heather back home and off the ship.

"Well the other option was to let the bastard have her killed and, obviously, I couldn't let that happen." He ran a hand through his hair. "None of the crew knows what almost happened, and everyone in HQ thinks she's dead. The bigger problem here is solved."

"I think you're looking at this the wrong way. You're like a boy trying to hide a frog in his room from his mother."

Alex stared across the table at him. He sounded like an old man but smart things weren't coming out of the guy's mouth. Just sarcasm and negativity. "Then tell me what you think should be done. We can't just leave her here."

"No, but she's close friends with the Dragouuls. When we deposit them on their home planet, she could remain with them and seek refuge there. The male on-board is an ambassador and can see to her asylum."

"But she'd be the only human there and that's hardly a life she'd want." Not that he hadn't already robbed her of that. Being the only human or not, it wasn't like she could start a family. At least Heather could have her life.

"Well, everything ties back to General Ruthesford. Handle that and you can bring her home."

And therein laid the problem. How was he going to do that? The general clearly wanted Heather dead, and he knew why. He hadn't told McGregor but – he wondered if the other knew – if that would change his mind.

"He wants her dead because he raped her and that thing that medical just cut out of her was the baby he killed. I'm not sure how you're expecting me to handle that." He made air quotes around "handle that", more to mock the man.

The surprise registered on McGregor's face for a moment. "Then she should file a report for court-marshal and let the courts take him out of the picture. Your report about her death could be said to have just been a precautionary measure to ensure her safety after you found out the plot to murder her and the truth about their relationship."

"The statutes of limitations has passed. Even if they didn't, we both know that the general would buy his way out of this and somehow make himself to look like the victim." That was the worst part. Heather was the true victim. That bastard would spin everything around to make it look like she asked for it and then decided to use his name to find fame. He'd probably claim that he wanted to break it off and she's accusing him of rape as payback or in an attempt to keep him.

"I feel like you already have an idea in your head, Tanaka. So why don't you just say it instead of making me guess what you want."

What he wanted wasn't practical. "I want that bastard dead. If he's dead then Heather can get her life back without living in fear of the next fucking thing he tries to pull."

"You know that's treason."

"He's not the god damn president, McGregor."

281

"No," the man paused to cross his arms over his chest, "but he might as well be. Are you going to tell me next that you want to be made general instead?"

It had always been his aspiration to reach the rank of general, but Alex never expected it like this. If the situation presented itself, he wouldn't say no to it. "No, I'm not going to say that."

"Tanaka, why are you willing to put so much on the line for McGrey?"

That was a loaded question and he knew it. The truth was that he still had feelings for her and there was a tremendous amount of guilt on his shoulders after what he'd done to her. He wanted to make it up to her somehow, to pay her back. Options were limited, and this was such an extreme. Murder, that is. It came back to the feelings that he realized were still there for Heather. They hadn't changed. Even though McGregor probably knew about the fling he was having.

"Because she deserves it and so much more. The Force isn't about this. It's supposed to be a place for justice and peace – everything we stand for out in those galaxies! The system abused her and let her fall. We're supposed to be a family and yet we've turned our back on our sister. That's why something needs to happen, and if I'm the one that needs to do it then so be it."

"Well, if you're planning on shooting the general, you will not survive. If you don't get shot right away, then they'd destroy you behind closed doors. I don't want any part of it." He made a move to the door.

"Do you think that Senator Harrison has enough pull to get his son out of a murder charge?"

McGregor stopped just short of opening the door and walking out. "He's already going to be busy trying to get that scum out of the rape charges."

It must have peaked the man's intrigue. Alex had to admit the plan sounded like a ridiculous Hail Mary play. If you wanted to shoot someone like the general, you couldn't be out in plain sight about it. You'd need a sniper, and a sniper that hated everyone and everything.

"We get the kid to agree to it and write off the rape charges. It's not like this won't be a life sentence." The idea of letting him get away with that left a bad taste in his mouth, but he needed to reassure himself that it was justified. A murder charge for treason was a tougher pill to swallow than rape of a cadet. "Malcolm always acted out and got his daddy to clean up the messes. This one would ruin the senator's chances to move up and it would be the one thing he'd love to fuck up more than any other."

"But what about that girl? What if Harrison pulls it off and daddy gets him free, then how is that justice for her? It only matters to McGrey and to you. I can tell you without a doubt that it won't mean a damn thing to her if McGrey makes it home or not if she doesn't get the justice she deserves from the Force."

It was taking from Peter to pay Paul. The burden just shifted shoulders. While that should have been enough to end this crazy plan in his head, Alex didn't care what Cadet Ha would say. In the perfect scenario, he'd become the general after the assassination and be in a better way of protecting her. He'd have Malcolm restricted to base and extract justice for her there. In his mind, he could justify it.

"I'll ask her. If she agrees, then we do it," Alex said.

McGregor chuckled. "Fine, but I don't see how you'll convince Harrison to do it."

"Actually, I was hoping that you'd convince him. He won't trust an offer from me, but his commanding officer... well, you might be the only one that could get through to him."

"So you want me to convince this guy to die?" McGregor asked. "Wow, thanks. I thought we were friends."

Alex knew this put the man in a tight spot. The truth was that he sort of promised to get Mal out for spilling the truth about what happened between him and Heather, and then he left the guy to rot. There was zero chance that he'd even listen to a word that came out of Alex's mouth. Just like he didn't expect Cadet Ha to agree to this deal, which was why he wouldn't bother asking.

"There's no other way right now. If he says he won't do it, then that's it. The best card you'd have to play is that it would be the ultimate blow to his father. I honestly don't expect you to force him into this and the choice really is on his shoulders, not yours. If you're worried about blowback, I can protect you."

"Fuck, Tanaka! Is that all you think this is about? I have to live with knowing I had a part in it either way. It's either treason or morally twisted, and I have to try and justify that before I can agree to anything."

There was one other thing that McGregor didn't know. He didn't have solid proof, but Alex doubted any would ever really exist. The general wouldn't do anything to dirty his own hands. "He's the reason our ship crashed. He ordered for it to be tampered with and sabotaged our mission."

The man was a rock and wasn't the type to give into rumor. "What's the proof of it?"

"Brand new ship that passed all of its extensive safety tests and simulations. We should have had reserve power with the back-up engines and auxiliary power to sustain the life support systems. Diagnostics came back that our life support wasn't operational. It's fucking luck that we landed on a planet with breathable air quality. If we had stalled out in space or were marooned on a helium planet then we'd all have suffocated. No one else piloted this ship and the general signed off on the Alphecca's inspection reports. That's an awful lot of wrong things to happen to a brand new starship."

Alex could see that his point was received and understood. It was hearsay but there really was only one person that could have made it possible. The general really didn't need much as far as motive. It could have been just to get rid of Heather or maybe he feared the Harrisons' growing power and wanted Mal's death to stall that. Maybe destroying one of the new starships would be seen as a need for increased funds to pump into safety measures but – seeing as those already existed – the Force could take that all as profit. Or the general was a fucking bastard.

"I'll see what I can do," McGregor grumbled.

"Thanks." It was all he could say after realizing how stressful their meeting had been. He really needed to relax and knew how he'd like to do that.

"I'm going to make my rounds and check up on things," Alex said as he headed out the door. "Just call me on my com if you need to get ahold of me."

Alex hoped that wouldn't be the case. The only thing McGregor should be calling about would be Mal's decision. Seeing as the man was on the hesitant side that probably bought him an hour or so. If Alex had actually planned on checking up on the ship and crew, then it might be a problem. Instead, there was one specific destination in mind.

He knocked on the door and tried not to override the security code on the door. The walk over had built up anticipation and fueled his hunger. He needed sex almost as much as he needed a cigarette.

She opened the door with a sly smile on her face. She teased him by answering, "Sir?"

He had ordered her to call him Alex. He didn't know why – no, he knew why but didn't want to admit that when Heather said his name it turned him on more than anything – but it was hotter than coffee cadet calling him "commander" and playing role games.

"I want you."

She stepped out of the room and let the door close behind her. "Yea?"

"Yea, but we probably should do this inside." Alex nodded towards her room.

Anita shook her head. "I wanna do it on the bridge again."

He smirked. "Why?"

"Something about a hot guy showing me his power while he shows me exactly how much he's got." Her hand trailed over his chest and slowly down his stomach to hook in the waist of his combat pants.

"Come on." She playfully tugged him along.

Alex worried that someone might see them like this, but it was only for a second. It was nobody's damn business and it wasn't like the rest of the crew wasn't fucking around. He let her lead him to the bridge so that he could stare at her ass, which she was swaying seductively for his sake.

"Ugh, I want you now." He caught her by the waist and pushed her up against the wall outside the bridge. His lips assaulted her neck while his hands sought out a way under her clothing.

Anita giggled and tried to push his hands away. "Not yet, Alex. We're almost there. I want you to fuck me on the bridge."

He grumbled against her skin, eliciting another laugh. She wanted to do it on the bridge but he was running the risk that his dick was going to burst out of his pants. He really didn't want to move unless it was to get inside her. It seemed like she wasn't going to give him the option, and it was probably for the best to make this more of a private affair.

Alex grabbed her ass and lifted her onto him. Her legs wrapped around his waist as he carried her through the bridge doors. She got her wish – they were on the bridge – but he wasn't waiting any more. He pushed her back against the wall just inside the doors and reached between them to free himself from his pants.

"We're here now... you're mine," he growled. He reached behind her to pull down her pants enough to expose her before plunging in.

The programming was going to go so much smoother now that Cadet Ha agreed to help. Maybe two days and they could try running a launch simulation. They could be home by the end of the week!

Cadet Ha... Seeing as she wasn't a commander anymore, maybe she should just call the girl by her given name. They were basically the same rank now.

The bridge doors swooshed open and she glanced over her shoulder, smiling and expecting to see Mia. Instead, her blood froze and she stared open-mouthed at the back of the man that intruded the bridge. If she couldn't tell who he was from that mess of hair or the build of his shoulders or the fact that he wanted to have sex here, Heather would have known it was Alex by his voice.

He was going to say he loved me in the engine room.

Clearly love wasn't on Alex's mind, at least not love for her. She saw him pull out his dick and closed her eyes, wanting to hurl. This couldn't be happening. It wasn't real. But when she opened her eyes again, he was reaching between their bodies and the girl's moan was enough to know that it was over. It was just starting, but it was over.

Neither of them had noticed her yet, but they would if she tried to escape out the bridge doors. There was only one way off the bridge, and that was impossible. Slowly, trying not to look at them and trying to ignore the grunts and moans, Heather slipped out of the chair and backed around behind the navigator's console.

"Oh, Alex... oh, fuck, yes!"

She may have been hidden from sight, but there was nothing hiding her from hearing them. Heather could hear every thrust as flesh met flesh. She could hear the sound of him slapping against her and how her body was getting wet for him.

"Fucking, god, yes!" Alex grunted. "Give me that fucking pussy!"

"Mhmm, Alex," the girl moaned.

Heather closed her eyes and tried covering her ears. It seemed the harder she tried to block them out, the louder they got. His dirty mouth. Her moans. His grunts. Her screams. And then all she could hear was the sound of her blood pumping in her ears. It had stopped. Heather didn't know how long it had been and didn't care. Maybe they were gone now...

"That was awesome."

287

"I know I am."

"Round two?"

Hearing that, she wanted to hurl. There was no way she was going to be able to sit through another eternity of her boyfriend – recently ex-boyfriend who claimed he still loved her – fucking some cadet. She knew firsthand how long Alex could last in the bedroom. It had been amazing when it was her, but it was torture now that it wasn't.

"I'd love to but I got to get back. You know, stuff to do."

A chuckle.

"Later?"

Rustling of clothing.

"Yea, later."

The bridge doors swooshed open.

"Oh, hey, Commander Tanaka... Anita."

Anita? That name sounded familiar. It was on the tip of her tongue. She knew who that was.

"Oh, Cadet Ha... what brings you here?" Alex sounded nervous. Judging by how calm and casual Mia sounded, they must have fixed themselves up already.

"Commander McGrey wanted to meet on the bridge to work on programming the repair parts." There was a pause. "Have you seen her? It sounded like she was coming straight here. I thought I'd find her hard at work."

She *had* been hard at work until someone showed up hard and horny. Shit! The navigator's screen had to still be on. She hadn't worried about turning it off when she slipped around the back of the console wall to hide. If Mia walked in and looked to where she should have been, she would have seen the screen on and knew that she was here. Would Alex and... Fuck!

Coffee Cadet.

"No, we haven't. The bridge was empty when we got here."

It didn't sound like he was so confident now, but he wasn't pursuing it. Heather could feel her face heating up just imagining them seeking her out now and finding her hiding spot. They might

288

not think that she was trapped and call her a voyeur, which would be humiliating.

"Okay, well, I'm just going to wait around a bit and see if she shows up. See ya guys."

The door swooshed open and closed again. It was quiet, but Heather still strained to hear what was going on over the sound of her blood pumping in her ears. Her heart was ready to beat out of her chest.

"Commander McGrey… you here?"

The door had to mean the others had left and there was no reason to hide from Mia. Sighing, she forced herself to stand up and walk around the console. She didn't know what to say and couldn't bring herself to look at Mia.

"They suck, don't they?" Mia said, walking over. "Anita's been kissing his ass since we left and he's an asshole for jumping the first thing to look at him."

Heather had forgotten that she told the girl this morning what all happened. It was a relief to know that she wasn't being judged. She felt Mia's arms wrap around her in a hug. It felt nice, but Heather knew that she shouldn't be letting anyone close to her again. Look at where it got her.

"Um, ah, we better do that programming," Heather stammered. "Means we get home faster."

Mia took a step back, releasing her. "Alright. You can go back to the navigator's chair. I'll bring up the system on the analyst's."

CHAPTER THIRTY-SIX

Three Days Later

Heather sat on her bed, staring at the sole photograph she owned. Her grandma thought that she was dead. Alex and Lieutenant McGregor tried to reassure her that they had a plan, but she wasn't sure she'd be able to go home again. People that were reported dead are expected to stay dead. She hadn't been able to wear her com device and she'd never be able to have a cell phone again. Too many things could track her location and existence. Without them, Heather felt naked and utterly alone. Probably not as alone as her grandma was feeling.

A knock came at the door and pulled her out of her thoughts. She set the photo on top of her trunk so that she could assure that it got packed for departure. It meant that one of two people were at her door, and they both would garter polar reactions from her.

Mia had over the course of a few days become a close friend. It was almost hard to label her that way. It just seemed like having a real friend was too impossible. But the girl listened and shared her own stories. She was easy to get along with and Heather actually enjoyed her company. It was unfortunate to think that after the Alphecca docked that they'd never see each other again.

Then there was Alex.

He had tried to talk to her in the cafeteria and in the corridors. The fact that she was usually around Mia meant that he couldn't ask the one question he needed – was she there? Azvark had mentioned that his thoughts were increasingly tormented and jumbled, which was giving them all headaches. It was probably from reading her thoughts and emotions which stopped Azvark from pushing her to seek out and reconcile with Alex. So far she had managed to avoid both him and the coffee cadet. Knowing that he was sleeping around with her was just another stab in the chest and made her have a question of her own – was he fucking her the whole time?

A knock came at the door again and still Heather made no move to answer it. She was hoping that they'd call out to her. Instead, she heard the door being unlocked. Anger bubbled up inside her, but she tapped it back down. He wasn't worth it. He wasn't worth anything anymore. Heather got up and opened the door just as he unlocked it.

"Oh, Heather... you are here."

"Yes, I am." Although that shouldn't have seemed like a crime. This was her room. The same couldn't be said for him. "And why did you hack my security code? Last time I checked, there was no search warrant issued and Lieutenant McGregor would be the one to conduct those anyway."

He knew that she had him there. The proof was when he ran his hand through this hair, and the fact that he quickly changed the subject. "We're departing in twenty minutes. I know that you know you can't command or pilot the Alphecca back... but it's something we started together and I thought that maybe we should finish it together. And... I'd like it if you were on the bridge."

Heather hadn't thought of it like that but – thinking about what else he said – there was a lot of things they started together that they never finished together. While it wasn't an order, it wasn't exactly a request that she could turn down. Also, the fact that she was a dead woman meant this would be her last chance to stand on the bridge and her last chance to stare out the view screen at space.

"Okay, I'll be there." She had hoped that would be the end of it with Alex, but he didn't walk away.

"Alright, then you can walk with me. I'm heading there now."

And just like that, he tricked her into time alone where there was an opportunity for him to talk and ask that question. Unfortunately, Heather had no excuse. She stuck her hands in her pant pockets and headed down the corridor with him. She had to give him credit though – he waited almost a full minute before asking.

"Were you there?"

It was a conversation that she didn't want to have and she felt like it was one that he really didn't want to have either. Heather could say that she was there but that would leave it open for him to deny the fact of what he had been doing, even though it was more than obvious. If she played coy and got him to admit it, then there would be no denying it. That would make it real for him, finally, and maybe he could see the damage he'd done.

"What are you talking about?" Heather replied. She risked a glance over at him and saw the moment where he realized there was no getting around it. There was no other way he could say it and still get the answer he desperately needed.

"Were you on the bridge when I brought the coffee girl there? It was the day when Cadet Ha said she was meeting you to program something or other."

He was getting close to saying it and she wasn't all that sure why she needed him to clearly say it. Maybe it was more about her and justifying her pain than it was about Alex admitting it. Maybe it was that she just wanted him to hurt more.

"I did ask her to meet me there." Heather slowed to a stop. "But why does it matter, commander?"

The formal title shocked him. That much was clear on his face. "Because it matters to me."

"I'm dead and you took my com device, so you can't search the GPS history for your answer. I haven't committed a crime, I wasn't in a restricted section, and I wasn't neglecting my duties. I've done nothing wrong, so I don't need to answer your question, commander. I won't answer it either until you give me a good enough reason to." She started to walk away.

"Did you see me fucking the coffee girl or not?" Alex caught up to her and stopped to force her to stay and see this out. "I need to know, Heather. I don't want to know, but I need to."

She wasn't sure what she saw on his face – if it was guilt or regret or happiness or constipation. It didn't matter. He was going to get the same answer, no matter what.

"Yes, I saw and heard everything you two did. I was sitting right there and neither of you knew it. Or maybe she did see me and didn't care because she had you now. I'm a ghost of your past. A literal ghost. So just do what people who see ghosts do." She moved to walk around him. "Ignore them – they're ghosts."

She made it to the bridge without him speaking the rest of the way. When those doors opened up, all eyes turned to her and watched as she stepped onto the bridge. They followed her as she walked down to the navigator's station and stood beside Mia. Had people assumed that she'd take the commander's chair?

Heather caught a glimpse of the coffee cadet and watched as her face lit up when Alex walked in and took his seat. She even had a cup ready for him. It would have been innocent enough if she hadn't shot Heather a look and smirked the whole time she leaned in to hand it over, putting her cleavage on display for him.

"Here's your coffee, Alex." Her voice was saccharine sweet. She knew what she did and wasn't ashamed to hide it. If anyone else on the bridge noticed that the cadet used Alex's first name, then they ignored the breach of protocol.

"Activate main engine power. Refresh auxiliary systems and run diagnostics," he ordered to the room. A slew of people jumped and hurried on their tasks, each reporting that everything was green to go.

"Cadet Ha, set coordinates to the Dragouul home planet. We'll be making a detour there to drop them off versus scheduling a shuttle flight from HQ."

Heather watched as Mia's unsure hands started entering commands for the navigation. The more coding that was accepted by the system, the less her hands seemed to shake. The girl was skilled, but it was always her nerves that got the better of her. Heather knew that it was something a diligent commander would acknowledge and fix. She hadn't truly watched on the maiden flight and took steps to build up the cadet, but now she could.

"Great job, Mia," she said quietly. The girl heard and couldn't help but smile.

"Alright, it seems like everything is set to go. So let's get the hell out of here." Everyone in the room echoed the same feeling. "Take us up to the lower stratosphere slowly, then punch through the gravitational pull and drive this baby home."

It was all on Mia, and her fingers were flying over the keyboards to program in the coding and commands. The ship lifted gently off the ground and hovered for a second before drifting upwards. When the movement almost stalled to a stop, Mia punched in the launch sequence and initiated the thrusters to punch them through the gravitational pull and into free space.

The forces felt stronger than she could remember, but maybe it was just because Heather had been out of space for so long. The view screen played the wonderful footage of the planet's ground disappearing below them until nothing surrounded them but darkness and stars. For the first time, it felt like Heather could really breathe again. This was home. The fact that this would be her last flight was bittersweet.

"Shall I initiate hyperdrive procedures to the Dragouul planet, commander?" Mia asked.

"Do it."

Heather knew that she shouldn't – that it would hurt too much or ruin this moment – but she glanced back at Alex. He was right in that they started this mission, and their careers in the Force, together. They didn't take the same path, but they'd be ending it together. Maybe sensing her eyes on him, he spotted her and held her gaze. He offered a sad smile, but it was a smile nonetheless.

She offered one in return before directing her attention back to Mia.

Everything on the view screen went blank as they entered hyperdrive. It was clear that there was some worry about whether the ship would hold up again or not. Heather didn't even want to think about the catastrophic possibility. She knew that both her and Mia had the skill to program the systems correctly. Every second, every minute that ticked by while they were engage felt like an eternity while they waited for something to happen. After five minutes, it seemed like there was nothing.

Nothing was going to happen.

Heather decided that she had lingered long enough. There wasn't any need for her to be here anymore and, in the very least, she should go visit with Azvark and her family before they left. She knew all the kids were excited to be going home where they could eat "real" food again. It had made her laugh to hear that. She knew that feeling. Space food just wasn't the same as homemade, and a hamburger wasn't the same as glodorfian mealworms in a blood stew.

"Heather!" Alex jogged to catch up to her.

"Commander, thank you for allowing me on the bridge." Maybe it was about stroking his ego or maybe it was another attempt to talk about what happened. Either way, she hardly expected him to be ready for a thank you.

"No problem, Heather. I..." He sighed and seemed unsure why he ran after her. "I want us to stay friends. I can't have you walk completely out of my life."

Heather wasn't so sure that he had a say in that nor did he deserve to have her around. How could they really be friends after what he did to her? How could he expect her to sit around, pretend to be happy, and watch him fuck around? She knew it was going to be impossible to put aside her feelings over that. No one should be asked by someone they cared about to watch them go on and be happy without them.

"I'm not sure I can do that. It's not exactly a kind request to make." She tried to stay civil. "Besides, I do not think your new girlfriend would appreciate that."

She knew that the coffee cadet really wasn't his girlfriend. Heather doubted that he'd ever make the mistake of falling into a relationship again. It just didn't suit him. Calling the cadet his girlfriend was more to put a permanent view on the friendship he was asking for. Whether it was the coffee cadet or not, there was always going to be another woman and that woman wouldn't want her hanging around.

"One, you've known me long enough to know that's not the case. Secondly, I don't fucking care. I mean it, Heather. I need you in my life."

"If you won't accept my answer then I'll just tell you that I'll think about it." And she'd keep thinking that it was a horrible idea. She'd never be able to be his friend.

"I guess I deserve all this and just you saying that is more that I should expect." He put his hands in his pant pockets but couldn't meet her gaze anymore. "I'm really serious about you. I don't know what I can do other than say it over and over. I'm going to find a way to get you back."

It sounded like he meant as more than a friend, but she doubted Alex meant it like that. He cheated on his ex-girlfriend Maggie too and always said he was going to win her back. He never even tried to. Either way, she wasn't someone that could be won back. So at that, she walked away.

The Dragouul family was huddled up in one corner of the cafeteria. Apparently Azvark and Cryzka wanted the kids to experience one last Earth meal. He joked that it was a plot to get at least one of them to replace him in the politics of his planet. The kids weren't so convinced.

"Hey, guys. Everyone excited to be going home?" Heather smiled and took a seat next to Bilfa.

Her brain got bombarded by so many thoughts all at once that she blacked out for a second and thought her head was going to explode with the throbbing headache left in their wake. Bilfa was kind enough to reach over and touch her forehead to ease the pain.

"I'm really going to miss that when I'm back home. All the pains of getting older are going to catch up to me," she teased with the girl.

"You not old. You less old than me." Bilfa giggled.

It was Avzark that stole her mind now that everyone else went back to eating. *"I will miss you, friend. It still not too late to leave with us."*

It was an offer that was given, then re-given, then offered again. Heather knew their hearts were in the right place, but she just couldn't imagine life anywhere else. At the end of the day, they accepted the fact that she'd come for a visit to their subterranean home. Although Heather knew that she was a dead man the second she stepped off this ship. The general would either kill her on the spot or before she could hail a taxi out of there.

She didn't say no. At least he got that much. He wasn't sure he could handle it if she did. He meant what he said – he didn't want her out of his life. How she left things didn't make him feel any better though. Alex knew that she wasn't just going to wake up and forgive him. That didn't mean that he didn't wish that she would. He knew that, no matter what was waiting for them in the docking bay, once Heather left the ship that it was over. His time would definitely have ran out and there was never going to be a chance to get her back.

He did know that things needed to stop between him and Anita. As fun as she was, it wasn't serious and with her around there was no hope of mending things with Heather. At the end of the day, he had to figure out who he wanted to be with and what really was important to him. Anita was young and definitely had no problems using her looks. For all Alex knew, he was just as much a fling as she was. It was Heather that he really could see a future with, even if she couldn't. They were closer in age, had the same ambitions, and got along great – if you ignored what just happened. There was a chemistry between them that he hadn't really felt with anyone else, even if their relationship hadn't lasted very long.

He headed back to the bridge. There was no use in chasing after Heather when nothing had changed, other than she spoke to him. Besides, the ship was flying again and his place was here to command it. It would take some time to get to the Dragouulian free space. Heather probably wanted to spend this time with them before they left.

"Got you a fresh one, commander." Anita was biting her lower lip, teasing by using his title instead of his name. She had been an attempt to replace what he had with Heather, so this time he didn't correct it. It would be best if things went back to how they were. "Just how you like it... hot... wet... ready for you..."

"I'm good, thanks." He tried to walk the line between being polite and ignoring her intentions, but she wasn't going to just back down. Alex knew first hand that she took things into her own hand.

"Is this about *her*?" She hissed.

It most definitely was, but he couldn't admit that though.

"I want to thank you for the gesture, cadet, but it's not a good time for it."

She realized the double meaning and the smile slowly slipped off her face. "Are you serious right now?"

Alex didn't say anything. One, he didn't want to draw attention from the rest of the crew as to what their conversation was; and two, he was serious... mostly. It would have been a lot better to have slept with her one last time and then broke it off. Like the one-night stand it should have been.

"You're an asshole! A fucking pig!"

So much for not drawing attention to themselves. He needed to contain this and fast. "Cadet, that is not a way to speak to your commanding officer. I will give you a warning but you'd be wise not to speak to me like that again."

"Fuck. You."

She raised the coffee cup over her head and Alex knew it was going to be aimed at his groin. She was going to burn his dick right off. But then it splattered all over the floor and his combat boots. It was a shock that she hadn't gone for bodily harm. In the back of his mind, he processed this as a successful break-up. Before he could form a sentence, Anita had stormed off the bridge. He knew that he should be worried about the devastation that she might leave behind her, but he wasn't. He knew that somehow he had to keep pushing forward and not run after her. She wasn't his goal.

"Um, s-status report?" Alex wasn't sure how else to restore order on the bridge after that. All eyes were on him and it was making him anxious. He didn't like the burning sensation in his toes, but it was the lesser of two pains. "And someone hail janitorial and have them send someone up to clean this."

"Ship is currently operating at one hundred percent and utilizing forty-three percent of engine capabilities," one cadet replied.

The percent of power the ship was using seemed a little high, but then that was most likely over the fact that they were in hyperdrive. He was more used to it only pulling ten percent. It didn't seem like the rest of the crew was bothered by that and maybe it was just the lack of knowledge on his part. Heather would have known about power consumptions.

"Estimated time until arrival?" It felt like he was a pointless piece of the puzzle on the bridge, firing off questions.

"Three minutes, sir. Dragouulian free space has a warped gravitational field that I didn't account for in my calculations." It was Cadet Ha that pipped up. It didn't make sense though when Heather had been with her. She should have known to factor in the gravitational field. "There's eight light-years of space surround the planet and it's orbital bodies have a lighter density than typical free space. It shouldn't affect much other than when we disengage hyperdrive."

Well, that didn't make a lick of sense to him at all. Even though it was all fancy talk, it really didn't seem like a mistake on the cadet's part... not unless she was comparing herself to Heather. Then, yes. Not over-thinking and over-achieving meant that she made a mistake. It was irrationally correct.

Damn, his head hurt.

He needed a cigarette.

There was no way that he could pull out a cigarette on the bridge. That would be advertising his contraband and openly disregarding protocol. There were rooms closer to the bridge that he could probably hide in to grab a quick puff, but it would be hard to explain if he got caught. There was no way that he'd make it back to his room, have his smoke, and make it back within three minutes. Technically, Alex was the only one with the authority to hail the Dragouulian planet and request shuttle transport for the diplomat and his family. That meant he needed to be on the bridge.

Alex groaned and slumped in the commander's chair. He wished that Heather wasn't dead and stripped of her rank right now. It really would have been great to toss her the reigns and let her handle all the official business. Maybe it was just this mission but it felt draining and impossible to be the commander. For the first time, the job seemed too big to handle. He was sure that it was just the emotional shit that was thrown at him, but it might also be because he hated having to be the adult when there was something else he'd rather be doing.

"Disengaging hyperdrive. Bringing auxiliary boosters online. Adjusting habitational support for differential gravity," Mia reported her run-through. Her fingers were flying across the half dozen keyboards inputting code.

He could feel a difference already. It felt like he shed ten pounds in two seconds. If only his problems could drop off his as easily as his weight, then he'd be great. Guess the ray of sunshine in this mess was that he could hail the planet, arrange a shuttle, and have the cigarette between his lips in five minutes flat.

"Open communi-" The view screen sparked to life with a transmission before Alex could finish the order.

"Earth starship, you have entered Dragouulian free space. State your business here." A dark colored Dragouul with a silver band around its forehead spoke.

"We are transporting your diplomat and his family on our starship. We found them being held hostage when our starship crashed. In exchange for passage home, they offered their ship for replacement parts," Alex explained. In the back of his mind, he wondered if their ship hadn't also been sabotaged by their government.

"We were not aware he lives. This is pleasing." It seemed like the dark alien was genuinely happy. Well, as happy as Alex could tell. Having a lizard face did make it much harder to read them. "Please advise Ambassador Cryzka that shuttle will be ready in half an ulondi."

Before he could ask what an ulondi was, the communication cut. One of the crew members asked if they should re-establish communication and get clarification, but Alex dismissed the idea. Seeing as he had to advise the family, he could just ask them how long in Earth time that was. Assuming their technology on-planet was just as good as their starship tech – which meant it had to be similar to theirs on the Force – and a flight like this in a shuttle would be a few hours.

"Switch main power to auxiliary and hold position." There was no need to overuse the new engines if they were just going to be waiting out here in space. "Also, prepare the docking bay for the shuttle's arrival."

While everyone jumped to his orders, Alex slipped out of the commander's chair and headed off the bridge. He still needed that cigarette and there was no rush. The Dragouuls still needed to be informed and he could do that on his com device as he walked. Heather was with them and... he realized that he didn't have a link to her because of the whole being dead thing. The audio for the room should still work if he used the announcement system and –

if Heather was still there – she could set up the room's data monitor for communication.

"Dragouulian shuttle is estimated to arrive in one ulondi. Please be advised and prepare for arrival," he announced to the ship.

Alex punched in the code on his door and breathed a sigh of relief. He'd finally be able to get that cigarette now. He walked over to his desk and pulled the pack out of the drawer. It took the lighter a few tries before it ignited and the spark jumped happily to the cigarette. Alex watched the tiny trail of smoke drift off the white end for a moment before putting it between his lips and taking a long drag. The smoke burned his lungs and warmed him from the inside. The nicotine relaxed his brain and his nerves. Leaning back against the wall in bed, he savored the sweet taste until his com device crackled to life and shattered the vibe.

"Commander Tanaka." Heather's voice echoed off the walls. It had been so long since her voice filled this room. "You need to ask for more time. Azvark says that they won't be ready that quickly."

"Heather, it's an ulondi." He had smiled when he said her name. Not only because of that, but also because of the fact that she didn't know that an ulondi was a long period of time kind of made her adorable. Finally, there was something that she didn't know and he got to be the prince in shining armor.

"Exactly. An ulondi is only about five minutes. They need to gather their belongings, grab something to eat, and then make it down to the docking bay."

That wasn't good. "Are you sure an ulondi is only five minutes?"

"Yes, I'm sure. I asked Azvark because I had no idea what it was."

This wasn't good. It had to be getting close to five minutes since the transmission. That meant that any moment a Dragouulian shuttle would be knocking on their door and expecting to pick up the group on-board. The crew probably had enough time to prepare for the shuttle's arrival, but then there was the question of the pilot waiting around. The pilot was picking up a diplomat, so it wasn't like they could leave or really complain much if the family was tardy. At least, if his assumption was correct this time.

"Well, they hailed us about five minutes ago and ended communications before we could clarify the time situation." She probably wanted more time with her friends before they left too. "I can have the pilot wait in the docking bay but that's about all the time I can buy you."

Heather hesitated for a moment before asking something I didn't see coming. "Azvark and Cryzka want to speak with you before they go. Can you make it to the docking bay?"

Alex stared at the glowing end of his fresh cigarette. If he said yes, then he wouldn't have time to finish his smoke and he'd be itching for a second and third the moment he could get away. If he said no, then who knew what kind of problems that would stir up between their planets' alliance. Besides, it would probably seem in poor taste for the commander of the ship not to see off its guests, especially a diplomatic family.

"Yea, I'll be there." He begrudgingly sat up and tried to snub the cigarette so he could recover it later. It wasn't pretty but the end was snuffed and what had remained of his precious cigarette was stashed in his shirt pocket.

He couldn't imagine why they wanted to speak with him. Hopefully, it was nothing more than just wanting to convey their gratitude for the rescue and hospitality. Heather was with them and – if they had been cadets – they wouldn't think to single him out for a lecture on the things that happened. They probably also wouldn't weigh in on the tension between him and Heather, and the half-doomed hope for a relationship to resurface.

CHAPTER THIRTY-SEVEN

By some fucking miracle, the Alphecca was on the approach to dock. It had resumed steady communications two days ago and once it had entered Dragouulian free space the system diagnostics came back online. The technicians were able to remotely scan the starship's operations and troubleshoot the anomaly. It being in Dragouulian free space should have been enough of a hint that that damn meddling race was involved and infected the pristine starship. What pissed him off more was the fact that the whole damn crew was returning to Earth. Well, all except Heather McGrey. At least he had that as a small consolation prize. Eventually he would reform the Force into the image that he wanted. This was only a minor setback that would be dealt with.

General Ruthesford stepped out of the transport vehicle and headed towards the docks. He walked pass the portion that was partitioned off for the crew's family members that showed up to welcome them home. The media was also out in force to capture the ill-fated Alphecca's return. They were just eating it up how a tragic story turned into some fucking miracle return. Reporters asked for comments and his opinion on the ingenuity of the crew. It sounded like a load of shit to him. All fucking roaches running around.

"General, the Alphecca has entered our free space. She's signaling and requested permission to enter stratosphere."

"Permission granted." It wasn't like he could deny the request now. Too many eyes watching.

The Alphecca slowly grew from a fiery dot in the stratosphere to a full sized starship in the matter of a couple minutes. It easily passed through the flight gates and entered the docking bay. The crowds cheered as it drew up to the dock and gently came to a stop. The docking bay doors slowly descended and opened up the rear of the ship.

Per tradition, the commander would be the first one to depart. They'd stand aside and bid farewell to the crew or spew some other bullshit at the end of the mission. It took a few minutes before the rest of the crew members started to file out. Whenever one of their family members appeared, one or two parts of the crowd started cheering. Instead of rushing to their loved ones, they lined both sides of the walkway.

The general couldn't fucking understand why until Commander Tanaka descended the starship's ramp with a medical gurney. He didn't bother trying to hide the smile that took over his face. On that damn gurney was that bitch's body. That was the best fucking sight he'd seen all week. Even though the initial report stated cremation, he was going to enjoy destroying her corpse.

Commander Tanaka pushed her passed the crew and stopped at the end of the dock. He rolled his eyes, expecting some damn long-winded speech.

"The Alphecca did not have an easy maiden voyage. She suffered engine failure and crash landed on a hostile alien planet. Through sheer determination by a crew of highly talented individuals, we were able to make it home today." The commander motioned back to his crew as the applause grew. "On behalf of myself and Commander Heather McGrey, we want to commend each and every one of you, and also welcome you home."

That was a fucking strange thing to say. It definitely was the first time a corpse ever welcomed anything. It was a crazy thing to say. It would just be fuel to the fire to remove Commander Tanaka. He had planned to do it by falsify sexual harassment reports, seeing as the man liked to get around as much as he did, and discharge him that way. Now there was the crazy angle. He could get the military's psychologist to declare him unfit for duty. There was no way anyone would touch the legacy he'd create.

But then it happened.

Commander Tanaka walked around the gurney and helped that fucking bitch sit up. Then helped her off the god damn fucking gurney. What the fucking hell was happening!? That bitch was supposed to be dead! She couldn't fucking be alive! He had ordered her death!

Everything went black.

CHAPTER THIRTY-EIGHT

Two Weeks Later

"The Purple Heart has long been an honor bestowed upon those injured in the line of duty, but everyone aboard the Alphecca is deserving of that. The Celestial Medal has long been awarded to any soldier that goes far and beyond, so far that they are considered celestial bodies themselves.

"By now, I'm sure you've all heard of the atrocities General Ruthesford caused and how they've impacted our own. There is no medal nor honor that can be bestowed upon Commander Heather McGrey to accurately recognize all that she's gone through. Not only endured, but also rose above and refused to let it define her.

"She is a fierce woman with strong determination and a set of unwavering moral standards that she holds not only herself but holds others to. She was the youngest cadet ever to enter the Academy and one of the few female commanders on the Force. For the crew of the Alphecca, we would have been lost without her pilot skills and without her leadership. Heather McGrey was born to fill a huge role and there's no larger – more important – role than as General of the Earth Celestial Forces.

"I should be welcoming Heather McGrey to the stage to announce her acceptance, but that will not be the case. She has declined the position and instead had me instituted as the new general."

He paused as a wave of applause drowned him out. It was the right choice – she knew that. She wasn't going to be able to step into those shoes and make it her own. She was always going to be taken with a degree of hesitation and look of sympathy. Any strong decisions would be targeted and dismissed as others claimed the traumatic experiences clouded her judgement. Besides, Earth had never been the place for her and her dream no longer lingered here.

"So instead of announcing Heather McGrey's appointment to general, I will be announcing her overdue promotion to Lieutenant Commander for the Force fleet and granting her the personal oversight of her own starship. In this new role, she will oversee all commanders and their operations, reporting directly to me," Alex continued.

She knew that this position was a half-assed attempt to share the general position with her. They had both dreamed of achieving that rank, but Heather realized that she needed to pass on that opportunity. Alex would lead the Force and she would be there to make changes from within. Even this role felt too lofty and knew it was just wanted to keep her from disappearing. Minus the enormous amount of paperwork and media bullshit, Lieutenant Commander was just another name for a general. After all, the title began with LIE.

"Mia, I'm going to need a pilot for my ship." Heather glanced to the cadet standing beside her backstage. She had come along more as support than anything else. Since returning home, Heather had tried to help her not only adjust to the shock of civilian life but also to work through the damage she carried. "I would like you to take the position."

The cadet shook her head. "Heather, I couldn't possibly. I'm a low ranking cadet and I'm not experienced enough."

"Bullshit," Heather called her out. "I know what you are capable of because I've seen it. I know that you know you can do the job, and I understand why you're saying all this now. Mia, you're good enough to accept the position and what happened last time won't happen again. Most importantly, you won't let me down. I can help you with anything you're unfamiliar with and, besides, who would be a better mentor?"

Mia knew that she had a very valid point. "I just don't think I can."

"Accept the position."

"So, everyone give a warm welcome to Lt. Commander Heather McGrey," Alex announced from the stage.

Heather didn't budge. She wanted Mia to take this step forward, with her. Returning to space meant that she would need to wholly trust her crew, especially after the Alphecca, and there was no other pilot on her radar.

"Heather, go," Mia urged when they called for her again.

She crossed her arms. "Not until you accept."

"Heather…"

"It would appear, perhaps, that Lt. Commander McGrey is a little shy tonight." Alex had a small chuckle. Only because they had been so close for so long was Heather able to hear the slight nervousness behind it. He was probably worried how it would look as a new general, being unable to get one soldier to follow orders.

"You need to go out there," Mia tried to persuade her again.

"Not until you say "yes", Mia."

A groan from the cadet meant that Heather had broken her down, even though she knew the cadet really wanted this. "Fine, I'll do it. Now, go!"

"We ship out tomorrow at oh-nine hundred hours from Docking Bay Five." Heather smiled as she stepped onto the stage. The lights were momentarily blinding, but there was nothing that could knock her off course now.

ACKNOWLEDGEMENTS

Deep Space Ocean is based on a story written with Alexandra Nativi. For years, we took turns making posts with our characters and playing out the plot twists on a forum-based website. We had the lofty idea to dual-publish this story, but that never came to fruition. Unfortunately, the website was sold and our story disappeared. A decade later, I've decided to retell the story as my own.

I want to thank Alexandra Nativi for being my friend and writing with me when I didn't know much about space and sci-fi. And for even reading the crappy first draft!

I want to thank you for picking up this book.

I want to thank all those who've supported my books either with purchasing, reviewing, or simply telling someone. There's no words to describe what your support means.

OTHER TITLES

KATE SPARROWS

Kate Sparrows is a Sassy Sue and a cynical, hopeless romantic. She dabbles in multiple genres, ranging from science fiction to mystery and romance. She enjoys leaving readers with unexpected turns and incorporating fringe subject matters. Aside from reading and writing, she enjoys playing video games, learning languages, and trying to sleep all day. She currently resides in the United States with her Pembroke Welsh Corgi, Roo.